I0788452

TAMING THE WILD GIRL

BY

JENNIFER BRADLEY LOPEZ

Copyright © 2025 by Jennifer Bradley Lopez

Published by Book Writing Pioneer
Cover design by Book Writing Pioneer
ISBN: Printed in the United States

Table Of Contents

Dedication

This book is dedicated to all the dreamers who dare to put pen to paper. May you find the courage to tell your own stories.

To all the teens who became adults and have felt the stings of abandonment and rejection. To all the rebels, for your good and bad decisions, they all make up your journey. May you heal all parts of yourself and know that you are whole and loved, even when the world shows you otherwise. Be strong, be brave, love yourself and others fiercely.

Acknowledgement

To my family, who are my heart living outside of my body. Thank you for your support and patience. I would be nothing without you. To all the friends along my journey who became like family, those who know the chapters left unsaid. In loving memory of Carissa Faith, who left us too soon but will never be forgotten. To my younger self, I continue to strive to make you proud. And to all the young girls in the world, if I could offer you one piece of advice, it would be to live authentically and unapologetically as yourself. Be you. Your tribe will find you.

Chapter 1

"Vanessa! What're you still doing here? You're going to be late for school!" Mom's voice snapped me out of my daze as she appeared in my doorway, her hand still clutching Lily's pink lunchbox. Her tired eyes darted around the room, zeroing in on me, still half-dressed.

I avoided her gaze, pretending to rummage through my dresser. "I'm about to leave. I just need to get some socks."

Mom let out a deep sigh, the kind that usually meant she wasn't in the mood for a fight. When I glanced at her, I noticed the dark circles under her eyes seemed deeper than usual.

"Just get there as fast as you can," she said, rubbing her temple before turning away.

I grabbed the first matching pair of socks I could find and hurriedly finished getting dressed. By the time I got to the kitchen, barely a minute later, Mom was already sprawled on the living room couch, remote in hand, flipping through the TV channels like she was on autopilot.

"I'll catch a bus at the metro," I called out, pulling on my coat and slinging my bookbag over my shoulder.

The chill of the morning air hit me as soon as I stepped outside, nipping at my nose and cheeks. I shoved my hands into my pockets as I walked briskly toward the metro. The streets were quiet except for the occasional car passing by, tires crunching against the frost-covered road. A light layer of frost sparkled on the grass by the sidewalk, and my breath came out in little puffs of steam.

As soon as I walked inside the station, the usual chaotic buzz greeted me. Buses groaned and hissed as they pulled in and out, and clusters of people hurried in every direction, clutching coffee cups or backpacks. I scanned the crowd, looking for a familiar face.

It didn't take long to spot Sophia and Mia in their usual spot near the entrance, leaning against the wall with cigarettes in hand. It was nine-fifteen now, so they were either going to school late or not going at all.

"What's up?" I asked, pulling my hood tighter against the cold.

Sophia exhaled a cloud of smoke, the faint smell of tobacco hitting me as she grinned lazily. "Thinking about what we're gonna do today."

"You're not going in, then?"

Mia rolled her eyes, a smirk tugging at her lips. "Nah. School's overrated. We'll probably head to the palace."

The palace was their nickname for the rundown movie theater a few blocks away. The seats were lumpy, and the popcorn was always stale, but it only cost two bucks to watch movies all day.

"That'll be fun," I laughed. "Two-dollar movies all day sounds better than school."

"So come with us," Sophia said, flicking ash off the end of her cigarette. "You're already late. What's a little more detention?"

She wasn't wrong. Detention had become a running joke for me and my teachers. They should've figured out by now that giving me detention is pointless since I pretty much never go. If I didn't show up to regular school, what made them think I'd stay an hour after school for detention?

Still, I hesitated. "Jasmine told me yesterday she needed to talk to me today. Said it was important."

Mia snorted. "She's always so dramatic. Bet it's something dumb."

"Maybe," I said with a shrug. "But I told her I'd be there."

Sophia rolled her eyes. "Whatever. See you at Kale's after school?"

"Yeah, sure."

I watched them saunter off, blowing smoke rings as they went and checked the schedule board. The next bus to Father Kentucky was pulling in. I jogged over and managed to squeeze on just as the doors were closing.

The bus was crowded, but I didn't recognize anyone. I grabbed a seat near the back and leaned my head against the cold window, watching the city blur past. My fingers absently tugged at the tangles in my hair, smoothing it over my shoulders and pushing it back again.

The bus ride felt longer than usual, the silence around me giving too much room for my thoughts. Jasmine's words from yesterday echoed in my mind—"I need to talk to you. It's serious." I didn't know what to expect, but the fact that she'd been so intense about it made me nervous.

When the bus pulled up near Father Kentucky High School, the recess bell rang soon, so I went over to the smoking corner. It would be the easiest place for Jasmine and me to find each other.

My friends started rushing from the building to the corner as soon as the bell rang. I made small talk with them until Jasmine showed up. We made eye contact, she nodded, and I nodded back. "I have to use the bathroom," I said to the group before slipping away to follow her.

She led me to a quieter spot behind the maintenance shed, her hood over her head, movements quick and nervous. When we were alone, she leaned close, her voice low.

"I found cocaine in my basement yesterday," she said in a rush. "I think someone left it during a party."

My stomach dropped. I don't know why I did it, but I tried some," she admitted. "It was crazy, and I felt really bad after the high wore off, but now I've been craving it so badly ever since. I tucked it under the couch cushion to try and not be too tempted, but I can't force myself to just throw it away. I feel really stupid for trying it, and now I'm scared I'll keep using it and get addicted or something. I don't know what to do."

I stared at her, stunned. Weed and cigarettes were one thing, but cocaine? That was a whole other level. I took a deep breath, trying to steady my voice.

"You're not stupid, Jasmine. Honestly, I might've done the same thing. But if you're scared, we can ditch and go to your house to get rid of it?"

Her eyes widened. "You'd help me?"

"Of course."

The bus ride to her house was quiet. Jasmine fidgeted with the strings of her hoodie, her legs bouncing nervously. When we got there, the house was empty—her moms were at work, and the place was eerily quiet.

She led me to the living room and pulled the couch cushion aside, revealing a small plastic bag. My heart thumped as I stared at it.

"That's a lot," I said quietly. "Let's just flush it," I offered. "If anyone comes looking for it, just play dumb and say you never found it and that you don't want anything harder than weed in here."

She nodded, and we went to the bathroom together. She stood back and let me do it, and she looked pretty uncomfortable with the whole situation.

I emptied the bag into the toilet while Jasmine stood back, wringing her hands.

"This is the weirdest snow I've ever seen," I joked, trying to lighten the mood.

Jasmine let out a shaky laugh, and I kept going. "This must be what Santa uses to fly around the world so fast."

She giggled, the tension in her shoulders easing slightly as I flushed the toilet.

"Thanks, Vanessa. I owe you."

I shrugged. "Well, since we're already here, do you have anything rolled?"

Jasmine grinned and led me to her bedroom. She opened her jewelry storage mirror and balanced on two of the hooks was a stuffed joint. I took the lighter from her desk drawer, where it always was, and we sat on her bed together and smoked half of it.

We were both really spacey and really hungry, so we took the next bus to the metro. I told Jasmine about meeting Sophia and Mia at Kale's Pizza after school, so we went to that busy restaurant for lunch.

After we ate, we spent the rest of the day wandering around the Côte-Vertu metro station, waiting for everyone to get off school.

Once people from Father Kentucky and Lauren Square High started getting to the metro to continue their journeys home, Jasmine and I went to Kale's Pizza. The familiar smell of grease and melted cheese greeted us. We grabbed a booth and were halfway through our second slice when Sophia and Mia finally showed up.

Mia slid into the bench next to me, and Sophia sat across from us. She pulled her long black hair out of her face and looked at me.

"So, Vanessa, I went to detention today. Mr. Collins was pretty pissed that you weren't there. He said to tell you that he's adding another two hours to your detention."

I rolled my eyes. "Oh, whatever. Two more hours onto the, like, eight hundred I already have. I wonder if he'll ever realize that giving me detention is pointless."

It didn't bother me that I'd get more detention. It did bother me that Mr. Collins would call Mom and tell her that I skipped today. I doubted she'd be too tired to start a fight now. And what was I supposed to say? I went to deal with some cocaine and smoke weed? I'd have no choice but to lie about it.

I hung around Kale's Pizza until all my friends were ready to go back home. I reluctantly headed home, too. I knew what I'd be walking into.

I went into our apartment as quietly as I could, but it didn't make a difference—Mom was already in the kitchen.

"How was school today?" she asked, her voice casual but sharp.

"It was fine," I said, brushing past Mom quickly, hoping to make it to my room before she could ask any more questions. My hand was already on the doorknob when the ring of the phone cut through the silence. Great.

Mom picked up. "Hello?"

Her face shifted almost instantly—her mouth tightened, and her brows furrowed in a way that made my stomach sink. Without waiting to hear more, I slipped into my room and closed the door, leaning against it like that flimsy barrier could shield me from whatever was coming.

There was a moment of tense silence, then a quiet knock.

I pressed my cheek against the door. "What?"

"Can I come in?" Lily's small voice asked.

I opened the door, and Lily was holding out her hands in tight fists. She beamed at me. "Wanna see what I got at school today?"

"Sure," I said, half expecting her usual playground collection of rocks or maybe some shiny wrappers she'd picked up during lunch.

Lily carefully opened her fists, revealing a small pile of colorful pencil erasers shaped like animals and stars.

"I won these for being the most well-behaved in the library today!" she announced.

I couldn't help but smile. "That's awesome, Lily. I'm really proud of you."

Her grin stretched wide, the kind of unrestrained happiness that only kids seemed capable of. But the moment was short-lived. Her eyes darted past me, and her smile faltered.

I turned to see Mom standing in the hallway, her arms crossed. Lily muttered something under her breath and darted back to her room, leaving me alone to face the inevitable.

Mom stepped into my doorway, filling the space with her presence. "So," she started, her voice low but sharp, "not only did you skip detention again today, but you skipped school, too? Why, Vanessa? What is so hard about going to school?"

I sank onto my bed, keeping my eyes fixed on the floor. "I had something more important to do."

"Oh, really? What could possibly be more important than your education?"

"I'm gonna go to school tomorrow, so it doesn't matter."

Mom sighed, long and hard, and rubbed her eyes. "Look, Vanessa. I know school isn't always fun. Believe me, I get it. But can you at least understand why it's important that you go?"

She seemed annoyed but not that mad. If she were mad, she'd start her usual rant, so I decided to bite my tongue and try to keep the peace for once.

I looked down at my lap, fiddling with a loose thread on my jeans. "Yeah, I understand. I know I need to try harder."

Mom tilted her head slightly, studying me, her expression softening just a bit. "So you're going to school tomorrow, then?"

"Yeah," I said, nodding.

Her lips curved into a small smile, not triumphant, but relieved. "Okay, good."

She left my room, and I shut the door behind her and turned on my stereo. Like always, I flipped through some of my Tiger Beat and Cosmopolitan issues until dinner, wishing I could have the fancy cars and houses that these people did and feeling almost angry at them for having what I wanted.

Chapter 2

Fridays were the best days to be at school—the teachers were tired from the week and ready for the weekend, so they didn't push as hard as usual. Everyone seemed a little more relaxed, and even the air felt lighter. At recess, I made plans with Sophia and Mia to spend the weekend at Mia's house. We were going to try to convince her parents to take us to Ottawa for a little getaway. It was a long shot, but it was worth a try.

Detention was definitely not part of my weekend plans, so I snuck out of Father Kentucky before Mr. Collins could spot me and drag me back. I didn't care what he thought—I had bigger, better things to do.

As expected, Mia's parents shut down the Ottawa idea immediately. Instead, the three of us spent the days wandering around Montreal, visiting friends, and exploring new little spots we'd never noticed before. At night, once Mia's parents were asleep, we snuck out onto the roof with a couple of cigarettes Sophia had swiped from her older brother. The cold air and the stars made everything feel a little more daring, like we were invincible.

It was a great weekend, one of those that made you forget about everything else for a while. I was still riding the high of it when I walked into school on Monday morning. That was until I got called to the principal's office.

The moment I stepped inside, I saw Mr. Collins sitting there, his expression as serious as ever. He didn't say a word to me. Instead, he picked up the phone and dialed.

"Hi, Ms. Gallagher," he said when Mom answered. "We have Vanessa in the office again today. She didn't show up to detention at all last week, and she's racked up so many hours that we have no choice but to suspend her. She can't come back to class until she starts to put in her detention hours. And with suspensions, you only have three strikes. If she gets two more after this one, well, we'd have to expel her."

My stomach twisted. Suspension didn't sound so bad—I wouldn't have to wake up early or spend hours trapped in this place. But I knew Mom was going to lose it, especially since I'd told her on Thursday that I was going to "try harder." I wasn't looking forward to the fallout.

Mr. Collins told me to stay at school for the rest of the day and then not come back tomorrow. The rest of the day dragged on, my mind spinning with all the arguments Mom was probably already preparing against me. I rehearsed a few comebacks in my head, but nothing felt like it would make a dent in her anger.

After school, I stayed around the metro with Sophia and Mia until they had to head home. I walked back to my apartment slowly, dreading what was waiting for me there. By the time I got to the door, I was already bracing myself.

Oliver and Lily were in the living room, watching TV. Lily peeked over the back of the couch at me, her big eyes wide with worry. She must've picked up on Mom's mood—who wouldn't? Mom was in the kitchen, her face set in a stony glare. She didn't even wait for me to put down my bag before she started.

"I don't know what to say to you anymore, Vanessa," she began, her voice sharp. "Is it so unreasonable to expect you to face the consequences of your actions? Instead of owning up to your mistakes and going to detention, you went and got yourself suspended! What were you thinking?"

"That I don't care about being suspended or expelled?" I shot back, dropping my bookbag onto the floor with a thud. "So what if I don't graduate high school? You didn't! Dad didn't!"

Her jaw tightened. "And your dad is a loser. You shouldn't be okay with being like him. You should try to be better."

Oliver cleared his throat loudly from the living room, though his eyes stayed glued to the TV. It was his usual way of letting us know he was listening without actually getting involved.

"Okay, fine," I snapped. "Dad was a loser. Does that make you a loser too? You didn't finish school either! Or is it because you chose to have a baby with him?"

Mom's face twisted in anger. "Are you seriously comparing me to your father? I've been raising you all by myself for the past eight years. He doesn't send child support, doesn't call on your birthday—nothing! And you have the nerve to say I'm like him?"

Her voice rose with every word, the kitchen air growing thicker with tension. My gaze darted to Oliver, but he still hadn't moved, hadn't reacted to what she'd said. He didn't act like I was part of the family, so it wasn't surprising he didn't care.

"No, I'm not kidding," I said, my voice cold. "I'm sick of you comparing me to him every time I do something you don't like. For all you know, he's changed. Maybe he's going to be a great father again."

Oliver snorted, finally giving some reaction, but it *was* one of derision. Mom crossed her arms, her expression skeptical.

"Vanessa, if he's changed, don't you think he would've at least called you by now? You're old enough to know better than to hold onto that kind of hope."

I wanted to yell something back, but the words wouldn't come. She wasn't wrong, and that made it worse. All my fight drained out of me at once. "Whatever," I muttered, storming off to my room.

I slammed the door behind me and cranked up my stereo, letting the music drown out everything else. I sat in front of my mirror, pulling a brush through my hair as a way to distract myself from everything Mom said. As I stared into my own eyes, the voice in my head tried to convince me that she was wrong and that there were important reasons Dad didn't call. The voice wasn't doing a very good job, though.

Chapter 3

Waking up early on weekdays when I didn't have to go to school was surprisingly easy. I figured I might as well get started on finding something to do. The only other option was to sit around and watch daytime soaps with Mom. That wasn't going to happen, especially since she still hadn't apologized for our argument last night.

"I'm going out to find something to do," I announced, slipping on my coat.

She barely glanced up from the TV, her eyes glued to the screen. "Don't get into any more trouble because I'm not bailing you out. And whatever you do, make sure you get to school on time to start serving your detentions. Be safe."

Her voice had that detached tone she always used when she was irritated, but I wasn't going to let it bother me. Not today.

My best bet was to head to Côte-Vertu, where I could meet up with people before they went to school. Maybe someone would want to skip out with me. A few people stopped and chatted with me for a bit, but nobody stuck around long enough to make plans. It felt like a series of missed connections, and I started feeling restless.

If I didn't find someone to hang out with soon, I'd probably start wandering aimlessly through the city. That usually led to trouble. I roamed the terminal, scanning faces and trying to look like I wasn't searching for something or someone.

That's when I spotted him. A guy leaning casually against the payphone, his posture relaxed but alert. He looked about my age, with tan skin, dark hair, and striking dark brown eyes. His features were sharp yet familiar, tugging at something in my memory. Or maybe my brain was inventing excuses for why I should go talk to him. Either way, he was attractive enough to justify the risk.

I walked over, my heart thudding harder with every step. He noticed me approaching and flicked his gaze toward me before returning to idly scanning the terminal, pushing his skateboard back and forth with one foot.

"Hey," I said, trying to sound casual. "I might be crazy, but I feel like I recognize you from somewhere."

He shrugged, his eyes locking on mine for a moment longer this time. "I'm not sure. Do you go to Lauren Square?"

"No, I go to Father Kentucky," I replied, studying his face like it was a pop quiz I hadn't prepared for. Suddenly, a memory flashed—a vivid image of him chasing after a big white dog. "Wait a second... You live on Garnet Street, don't you? You had that huge white dog."

His eyes widened, and his stance straightened slightly. "Not anymore, but yeah, I grew up on Garnet. How'd you know that?"

"My photographic memory saves the day," I said with a small grin. "I've lived on the corner of Garnet my whole life. I used to be scared of your dog, actually. It barked so loudly."

The boy's face lit up with a grin. "She was a really nice dog. She just wanted to be everyone's friend." He nodded toward me. "I'm Adrian, by the way."

I smiled back, giving him my most charming look. "Vanessa. Nice to meet you."

Adrian ran a hand through his dark hair, a nervous yet confident gesture. "Most of the Father Kentucky kids have already left for school. What are you doing hanging around here?"

"I got suspended yesterday," I admitted, trying to sound nonchalant. "No school for a while."

He raised an eyebrow, a teasing smirk tugging at his lips. "Suspended? You must be a bad student."

"Says the guy who's also skipping school," I shot back.

Adrian laughed, the sound warm and easy. "Yeah, good point."

I laughed with him, feeling a spark of excitement I hadn't felt in a while. Talking to Adrian felt like flipping on a light in a dim room.

"Look," he said, his tone regretful, "I gotta go. I promised a friend I'd meet him at his place. I don't know if you'll be here again tomorrow or what, but..."

"Do you have a pen?" I interrupted, the idea forming faster than I could second-guess it.

He blinked, surprised, before fishing a pen out of his bag. I took it, held out his hand, and wrote my number on his palm, the ink looking bold against his skin. Then, I handed the pen back and held out my hand for him to do the same.

Adrian grinned as he wrote his number on my palm, his movements slow and deliberate. "All right, then," he said, tossing the pen back into his bag. "I'll see you around."

I watched as he skated away, effortlessly weaving through the crowd. My eyes stayed on him until he disappeared from sight.

Nothing else in the day could top meeting him, so I left the metro with a bounce in my step, feeling lighter than I had in weeks.

At home, Mom was right where I'd left her, immersed in her daily marathon of soap operas. The TV droned on about scandalous love triangles and shocking betrayals. Her routine never changed—*Days of Our Lives, Another World, General Hospital*, and then *Oprah*. She'd only get up to grab food or use the bathroom. I used to watch with her when I was five, so I could call *Abuelita* and tell her everything that was happening on the shows.

But now, I couldn't imagine how she did this every single day. It seemed so empty. I wondered if she was depressed. Maybe I would be, too, if I had to raise two daughters on my own without a job or much else to fill my time.

Still, I wasn't about to let those thoughts bring me down. I was having a good day. Actually, a *great* day. Determined to stay in a good mood, I decided to get dressed up and go to school later. Detention wasn't exactly thrilling, but it was a step toward something better.

I dug through the clothes strewn across my floor until I found my favorite pair of dark skinny jeans and a snug red sweater. I slipped on my black boots, the ones with just enough of a heel to make me feel confident without being impractical, and turned on my stereo. The opening chords of an upbeat pop song filled the room, and I sang along as I curled the ends of my hair with my round brush. I kept replaying my conversation with Adrian in my mind, smiling at the memory of his grin.

Going to detention reminded me why I usually skipped it. Sitting in silence while Mr. Collins glared at everyone made an hour feel like a year. But I went, and honestly, I was proud of myself for sticking it out. Besides, getting back to school was the best way to meet up with friends and keep boredom at bay.

On the bus ride home, I was practically floating. I'd decided that as soon as I got back, I was going to call Adrian. Normally, I'd wait for him to call—it felt more traditional that way. But something about the way his deep eyes looked at me, and the way he smiled when we wrote on each other's hands, made it feel like I almost *had* to. I already had him on the line. Now, I just had to pull him the rest of the way in.

I ran into my bedroom without acknowledging Mom, who was still glued to the couch. I glanced at the slightly faded ink on my hand and picked up the receiver of my old landline phone. Before I could dial Adrian's number, my little sister Lily peeked her head into my room.

"Get out!" I said before she could say anything. She stuck out her lower lip, looking hurt, but quickly closed the door and ran away.

I sighed, sitting on the edge of my bed, waiting a moment before trying to call again. Anytime I yelled at Lily, she made a beeline for Mom to complain. Sure enough, I heard heavy footsteps heading toward my bedroom.

Mom swung the door open and stood there, arms crossed, her face set in that familiar scolding expression. "What's with you, Vanessa?" she demanded. "All she wanted was to ask you to play with her, and you scream at her? Why be so mean?"

"Because she doesn't knock!" I argued. "I told her she has to knock if she wants to come into my room. How else am I supposed to have any privacy? I could've been naked, and the whole house would've seen!"

Mom rolled her eyes. "She's only *six*, Vanessa. You can't expect her to remember every rule you make for her."

I opened my mouth to argue more, but Mom held up a hand and kept going. "All I'll say is that one day, you'll regret the way you treat her. I suggest you start being nice before she ends up wanting nothing to do with you."

With that, she turned on her heel and left, slamming the door behind her. I groaned, falling back onto my bed. Mom was such a drama queen sometimes. It wasn't like I was mean to Lily all the time. Most of the time, I was pretty nice. And was it really unreasonable to want a little privacy every once in a while?

Once I calmed down, I sat up and focused on what I'd been so excited about. Finally, I dialed Adrian's number, my heart racing with nervous anticipation. The phone rang twice before a deep, warm voice picked up on the other end.

"Hello?" he said, his tone casual.

"Hi, is Adrian there?" I asked quietly, not wanting anyone in my house to hear his name.

"Yeah, that's me. Who's this?"

Thank goodness he picked up and not one of his parents. "Vanessa, from the metro. Are you busy?"

"No, no," he replied, his voice suddenly brighter. "I'm not busy at all. What's up?"

"Not much," I said, twirling the phone cord around my finger. "I wanted to make sure I called you before your number washed off my hand. What's up with you?"

Adrian chuckled. "Well, thanks for that. I was just working on my skateboard. It's got some chips, and I've been meaning to fix it up."

"That sounds cool. What kind of repairs are you doing?"

He launched into an explanation about sanding down the edges and applying grip tape. I kept asking questions—not just to keep the conversation going, but because I was genuinely interested. His voice was mesmerizing, and I hung on to every word he said.

Eventually, the conversation shifted. He told me about how he liked spending time with his friends and family, and I asked him more about what he liked to do. When he turned the question back on me, I told him about some of my favorite hobbies—reading, music, and the little sketches I liked to do in my notebooks. He seemed genuinely excited to learn about me, asking thoughtful follow-up questions. There were no awkward pauses, just a natural rhythm to our conversation, with laughter filling the gaps.

"All right," Adrian said after a while, his tone shifting slightly. "Since I kind of feel like we're already friends at this point, I have a confession to make."

My stomach flipped. "What's that?"

"I was checking you out at the metro before you came over to talk to me," he admitted, his voice laced with playful honesty. "I'm really glad you did, though, because I don't think I would've had the guts to approach you."

I felt heat rush to my cheeks, my grin so wide it made my face ache. Butterflies fluttered in my stomach, and at that moment, I knew I officially had a crush on him.

We talked for hours, the kind of conversation that made time slip by unnoticed. Eventually, Adrian had to go—his throat was getting sore from talking so much, and I could tell he didn't really want to end the call.

"I'll call you tomorrow," I said, and when we hung up, I lay on my bed, smiling at my ceiling until I fell asleep.

Chapter 4

I left detention the next day and made a beeline for the sign in front of Lauren Square High across the street, where Adrian said he'd meet me when he called me from a payphone during recess this morning. Promptly, he was there, leaning against the sign with his skateboard propped against his thigh, just like at the metro yesterday. The thought that he was waiting for me made me jitter, and butterflies floated inside my stomach, triggering an involuntary smile.

"Hey," he said, grinning at me and slightly waving his hand to garner attention, as if he already didn't have mine. He held his arms out. I was happy to hug him and wouldn't miss such a generous opportunity.

"Anything special you want to do?" he asked me.

"I don't really have any ideas. How about you?" I was blank, something that happened quite often when he was around. But it was also more because I wasn't much of a planner and knew anything he suggested would surely be more interesting than what I might have in mind.

Adrian smiled again. "I have it all planned out. Are you into bird watching?"

"Haven't really given it a go yet…"

"Well, that is one thing. And how about Esports? You into gaming? Please say yes!"

"I was about to suggest just that. I have been meaning to try them – see what all the fuss is about." My insides were floating, and there wasn't anything I would have refused him.

"Oh, that is music to my ears. You are with a veteran lady, and I know everything about everything there is to know about gaming. What would you like to start with? The arcade is close by."

"Okay then, Mr. Veteran, what would you suggest to someone who has no clue about them?"

"Well, there are popular sports games, FIFA, NBA, Rocket League. But I don't think you'd want to try them. I can bet you'd love the Pedal-to-the-Metal action or something in the fantasy realm. I can already think of some spectacular games you might dip your feet in." Adrian teemed with excitement as he explained. I didn't think he could have seemed cuter or more handsome, but here he was, glowing like a firefly.

"Woah! Woah! Easy there. And yes, I would like to start something in the Fantasy realm." I replied, feeling lucky I had chosen gaming. He had mentioned it briefly in our conversation over the phone, and I just didn't want to sound boring to him. Luck seemed like it was on my side for once.

"So it is decided. It's Battle of the Jotenhiem…" he started.

"Battle of what?" I teased.

"Oh, never mind – So it is decided. It is the arcade, then bird-watching. And yes, let's not forget the grub! The VR arcade is going to make you hungry!" Adrian exclaimed.

I had no idea how a virtual game was going to make me actually feel hungry. It wasn't going to send me on an actual quest through the mountains, but I wasn't curious; I wasn't going to argue. "I have heard there is a new burger joint just next to the arcade. Their turkey whoppers are the talk of the town these days."

"This day is getting better and better!" Adrian chirped, making me giggle.

We started walking to the arcade, and he started explaining to me about the game. It was a lot of information, and I could understand one bit. Yet, I kept asking questions to seem interested. Every now and then, he would crack a joke that would almost have me rolling, and both of us would burst into a roar that would turn heads.

I loved it when people turned to look at us when we laughed loudly. I loved taking his hand or linking my arm through his when girls' eyes lingered on him to show them he was mine. The best part was that he would respond with the same warm energies. I *loved* doing the same when guys looked at me, plus smiling at them to make them jealous, before leaning more into Adrian. It felt surreal. Every now and then, a ripple of anxiety would wash over me, making me queasy briefly. Was I looking okay? Oh please, I hope my hair *isn't* making me look like a lollipop rolled on a carpet. How do I smell? Has my perfume already gone into thin air? Frightening thoughts would nudge at my brain, and I had to fight them off.

The VR arcade went well. Too well, to be exact. He would lead me to a different game every now and then, each one more confusing than the other, but they were all fun. There was this boxing game he wanted me to play, and I almost knocked him with one of the VR controllers. We laughed about it for a few minutes. He would then funnily flinch at any sudden movement I made all our time at the arcade, teasing me and calling me Ms. Mike.

We both lost track of time – weren't keeping any in the first place. But we knew that we had to be home before dark. Adrian looked at his watch, sighed, and told me we should get going. Reluctant, I agreed.

"But not without a round of bird-watching. I have seen a rare new species I have never seen there before." Adrian announced, sounding dictatorial.

I knew I had been in detention and that being late could be a costly affair with my mother, but spending more time with Adrian seemed a worthy gamble.

"Before? You bird-watch often?" I asked as we ambled toward the whopper joint.

"Every Sunday, with my little brother and sister. My brother is a big fan of birds. Remembers quite a few of their names too. Plus, I wasn't sure I was going to enjoy it at first, but I was wrong." Adrian was getting interesting by the minute.

We quickly dashed to the whopper joint, grabbed our orders, and went straight to Hartenstein Park.. There weren't that many kids here, so Adrian and I went to the top of the slides to have some privacy and get away from the wind. It was getting towards the later part of the day, and some chill had crept up into the air.

"This is one of the most fun days I've had in a long time," he said, scooting close to me.

"I don't think I have had a better detention than this one," I replied, chuckling.

His warm smile quickly turned into a funny giggle that made him look more boyish than he was. We sat in the park, gazing at the birds. He would offer me the names of the birds, first in layperson's terms and then their scientific names. The second bit was always a laughable pronunciation of something that would make both of us burst into raucous laughter. The day had indeed been fun, but I realized it had also been exhausting. I rested my head on his shoulder, and making the move made my belly warm.

We were quiet for a while, just watching the people and birds around the park. Every time I thought about what I was doing with Adrian, I got excited all over again. I kept getting reminded of the first time I felt this thrill of falling for someone.

I'd been friends with Mia since we were five, and I met her older brother, Michael, a few times. But he rarely left his room when she had friends over until one day when I bumped into him in the hallway.

I hadn't seen him in a long time, and he looked different—he was tall and skinny, with tanned skin, dark hair, and light blue eyes. I could feel my eyes bulging out of my head. He was the most gorgeous boy I had ever seen.

My crush on him was instant. But he was thirteen, and I was only ten. And I wasn't sure how to process all that. Plus, he saw me as a little girl, no matter how mature I tried to act around him. It was like all I could ever be to him was his little sister's friend.

I, on the other hand, would spend time churning up perfect scenarios in my head of us being together. For a brief period, I almost believed he was the guy for me. He was funny, popular, tough, and perfect in my eyes. He was easy to talk to and would always have the wittiest of things to say. It even felt like the dream was coming to life the day he agreed to have a foot race with me down Poirier Street. I thought it was his way of subtly wanting to strike up a conversation.

We were neck-and-neck. I had given all I had to make sure I left an impression. I knew I wasn't going to win. He was athletic, maybe even part of one of the school teams, but I was proud of myself for being able to keep up with him. With the wind blowing my hair back, my whole body tingled with the thrill of the moment, even though it didn't change the way he looked at me.

Now, sitting with Adrian and having spent the day with him, I was feeling the same thrill. In fact, this time, it was even more exciting because Adrian liked me back. Something told me we'd be an official couple before the day was over. The anticipation only added to the excitement.

"I don't think I could've had so much fun like this with anyone else," Adrian said, breaking the long silence. "You're really special, Vanessa," he added, gulping hard, his uncharacteristic nervousness evident in his flushed cheeks.

It was a bit surprising and flattering to see him like that. He was one of the most good-looking boys in the school, and I never expected him to find me amusing. I nuzzled closer to him, and Michael's image that had been taking form due to my mind's wandering dissolved like smoke in a gust of wind.

"I feel the same about you," I smiled back, even though I wasn't sure if that was true. It felt like an understatement of the year, and I had to ensure not to make it sound like one. I loved the way Adrian was always looking at me, and I loved how we always seemed to be holding hands or touching each other. Every time he would smile or crack a joke, the butterflies in my stomach would start a dance I couldn't stop or dismiss. But I was also wrestling with another, more mind-boggling thought. I couldn't tell if it was him I really liked or the physical feelings he gave me. Sure, I could get these feelings from anyone. Right now, the adrenaline rush was definitely making me like Adrian.

"The sun is gonna start setting soon," Adrian squinted into the sky, trying to hide away his blushing cheeks and steer the conversation, which had suddenly turned a little queasy. "I'll have to head home soon before my Mom freaks out. Can I walk you home first?" he said, getting up.

I agreed, of course, and we walked to my house hand-in-hand. It wanted to go slower than we already were and tugged his hand a little. He didn't protest in any manner. "This is perfect," I told him as we ambled towards my apartment. We stopped a few meters before my apartment. I didn't want him to see that I lived in a place with paint peeling off the walls and overgrown grass.

He hugged me again, a little tighter this time, then pulled away, but only enough to look me in the eyes. "I hope it's not too soon to ask this…"

A weird medley of funny feelings wrapped around and in me. My heart throbbed and thumped, and tickling pricks went dancing inside. There was also a tinge of dread in the anticipation of what was about to come. I knew the question would come, I wanted the question to come, but now that it was here, all words escaped me as I tried to ready an answer to the question he was about to ask.

"Will you be my girlfriend?" Adrian completed his thought, putting up a brave face when he was surely as nervous inside as I was, maybe even more.

I smiled, stood on my tiptoes, mustered all the courage I had, and kissed him.

"Of course," escaped my lips, which were pressed against his lips before we kissed again, this time Adrian easing and wrapping me in his arms.

Chapter 5

My relationship with Adrian was off to a thrilling, almost cinematic start. Every night, we snuck out of our apartments like rebellious teenagers in a romance movie, meeting in the exact spot where he'd dropped me off after walking me home. There, tucked into the shadowy embrace of an alley between duplexes, we found our private haven. Time slipped away as we switched between smoking, whispering secrets into the night, and making out like our lives depended on it.

It was the kind of setting that begged for more than just stolen kisses—a secluded corner in the dark, the air thick with adrenaline and the faint scent of his cologne. But every time I tried to take things to the next level, Adrian stopped me. "It's not personal," he'd say, his voice calm but laced with restraint. "You know how attracted to you I am. I just want to take things slow so you know I'm not with you just for sex."

I told him every single time that I knew that already—that it was okay to move forward. But he always stood firm. It was frustrating and endearing all at once, like he was some modern-day knight insisting on keeping his honor intact. I guessed I shouldn't be too upset; it was rare to find someone who could be so patient and thoughtful. Still, a part of me burned with curiosity, wondering when, or if, he'd finally let his guard down.

On Monday, as school let out, Adrian met me at our usual spot on Garnet Street. His smile was that perfect blend of charm and mischief, the kind that made my stomach flutter every time. I had spent the morning with Jasmine at the metro station, where she'd casually invited me to her house that afternoon to hang out with the infamous T.W.A.

"What's T.W.A.?" Adrian asked once we'd kissed and hopped onto the sixty-four bus heading to Jasmine's neighborhood.

"'Teens with Attitude,'" I explained with a grin. "Just a group of people from around the area. We're kind of a thing now—about twenty of us, give or take."

Adrian's face lit up in amusement. "Teens with Attitude. I like it. Jasmine's parents are cool with me being there, even though they don't know me."

"Yeah, they're chill," I reassured him. "Her mom is super laid back. She let us hang out in the basement. We can blast music, plus smoke if we want to. The only actual rule is that Jasmine's only allowed to have ten friends over at a time, so there isn't too much drama."

The walk to Jasmine's house from the bus stop was short, just a few quiet minutes to breathe in the cool afternoon air. When we reached the house, we went around to the side, where I crouched down and knocked on the small basement window. Pressing my face close to the glass, I peered inside, my reflection barely visible against the warm glow of lights and smoke. Jasmine was sprawled across the couch, her red-highlighted green eyes standing out like gemstones in the hazy air. She jumped up to open the window, a smile already curling her lips.

"What's up, Vanessa?" she asked, her voice a little raspy from the blunt in her hand.

I gestured behind me. "I brought my new boyfriend, Adrian. Can we come down?"

Jasmine sized Adrian up with a quick, amused glance before shaking her head. "Sorry, not right now. I already have nine people over."

"So, kick someone out," I countered with a smirk.

She laughed. "No, that would be so mean."

I pulled the trump card from Adrian's pocket: the eighth of weed he'd brought along. I dangled it in front of the window, raising an eyebrow. "Would it really?"

Her eyes widened like I'd just handed her a golden ticket. "On second thought…hold on."

As she closed the window, Adrian gave me a look of mild disbelief. "Is this normal around here?" he asked, his tone somewhere between amusement and curiosity.

"Yeah, no big deal," I replied, shrugging like it was the most natural thing in the world. "Whoever brings the most weed gets in. That's the rule."

A few moments later, the basement door opened, and one of the newer T.W.A. members came trudging out. I pretended to study the horizon as he walked past us. The unspoken code of Jasmine's house was survival of the fittest—or, in this case, whoever had the better stash.

Once inside, the basement was both chaos and comfort at the same time. The air was dense with the smell of weed and laughter, the kind of atmosphere that made you feel untouchable, even if just for a few hours. We headed straight to Jasmine's room, a cozy enclave at the far end of the space. She was on her bed, flanked by Mia and Ryan Carter, who were lazily passing a joint between them.

"Hey, Adrian, right?" Jasmine said, smiling up at Adrian.

"Quenton," Brad didn't seem bothered by his comment, not even a little. He reached into his pocket and casually pulled out a cigar, then emptied its tobacco into Jasmine's garbage can. He broke off tiny pieces from the weed in his baggie and sprinkled them into the cigar paper.

Jasmine's glassy eyes were glued to Adrian as he worked. He licked the stuffed paper closed, lit it, and took a big hit. Then he passed the newly rolled blunt to her. She took it without hesitation, exhaling her approval. "You're welcome here anytime," she declared, her voice thick with smoke.

By the time the blunt was burned down to a stub, the room was a kaleidoscope of giggles, tingling skin, and conversations that felt like they could stretch into infinity.

There was something electrifying about being this close to him, surrounded by friends but entirely lost in each other. Jasmine did what she always did when she was stoned and went over to her floor-length mirror to dance in front of it like she was auditioning for a music video. She could stare at herself dancing for hours, so I took Adrian's hand and led him to the living room to socialize with everyone else.

Adrian sat on the futon next to a couple of T.W.A. members from Lauren Square and talked to them. Mia and I squeezed onto a chair together on the other side of the room from them and slipped our shoes off to bury our toes in the old, shabby rug. It always felt so good to do when we were high.

Adrian fit in seamlessly, his easygoing charm earning him a spot on the futon with a couple of Lauren Square kids. I watched him from across the room, admiring the way his words seemed to draw people in like moths to a flame. The way he sat—confident but not cocky—sent a thrill through me that I couldn't ignore.

I didn't.

The best thing about hanging out in Jasmine's basement was being able to smoke weed and cigarettes. The second best thing was being able to make out without anyone caring or any parents checking in.

I went over to Adrian and sat on his lap. I took his chin in my hand and turned his face toward me, then pressed my lips against his. He kissed me back but hesitated when I slipped my tongue in his mouth. He was probably unsure if it was okay to make out with people all around.

But then, one of the guys he was talking to whistled, and the other jokingly said, "Get a room." That gave Adrian more confidence, and he kissed me more passionately. He wrapped an arm around my waist and pulled me closer to him.

Making out with him in front of all my friends was a rush. It always was, but even more so now because this was with a guy from a different school, and that made it cooler. It was my escape, my adventure, my ticket to a world that felt alive in a way it hadn't before. And I knew, at that moment, I'd be bringing him around a lot more often.

Chapter 6

I'd been to detention a few times since my suspension, but apparently not enough to earn my way back into regular classes yet. The days were dragging, the hours stretching like taffy, and the isolation from my friends was starting to wear on me. Boredom was my constant companion.

Before I could wander out of the house to find something to do, my phone buzzed. It was Sophia. "What're you up to today?" she asked, her voice casual but with a hint of excitement.

"Not sure yet. Why, what's up?" I replied, grateful for the distraction.

"My mom got a call from Mr. Collins yesterday. I'm being suspended for skipping class and hanging out in the bathroom all day," she said, laughing like it was nothing more than a funny anecdote. "Oh well. I'm just gonna go hang out with my boyfriend today, so I'm calling to see if you want to come with me and meet him."

I nearly dropped my phone. "Since when do you have a boyfriend?"

"Officially? A few days ago," she said, her tone light and breezy, as if she wasn't casually dropping a bomb. "So, do you wanna come?"

"Yeah, duh," I said, already pulling myself out of bed. "Where should I meet you?"

"Hartenstein Park? That's kind of in the middle of where we all live," she suggested.

"Perfect. I'll leave right now," I said. Sophia lived closer to the park, so I knew I'd have to hustle if I didn't want to keep her waiting.

I threw on some jeans and an old T-shirt, rummaging through my closet like I was in a speed-dating round with my wardrobe. No time for hair or makeup, but it didn't really matter. It wasn't like I was trying to impress anyone—I was just tagging along to meet Sophia's mysterious boyfriend.

The weather was perfect, a slice of early spring optimism. The sky stretched above me, impossibly blue, and for the first time in what felt like forever, I didn't need a jacket. The sunlight kissed my skin as I walked to the park, and I couldn't help but smile and stretch out my arms to soak it in.

When I arrived, Sophia was already there, of course. She was perched on the edge of a bench, her **outfit** a stark contrast to my thrown-together look. It was obvious she'd put serious thought into what she was wearing—she must really like this guy.

"He lives right down this street," she said, gesturing with her chin as she fell into step beside me.

"Is he skipping school to meet you?" I asked, half-joking but also genuinely curious.

Sophia hesitated. The air between us suddenly charged with something unspoken. Finally, she leaned in close, her voice dropping to a conspiratorial whisper. "Okay, you're gonna find out when we get there anyway, but I have to tell you something."

"Spit it out," I said, bracing myself.

"He's twenty-three."

I stopped in my tracks, staring at her like she'd just told me the moon was falling out of the sky. Before I could even process it, she grabbed my arm and tugged me along, her words rushing out in a frantic attempt to keep me from bolting.

"You know my parents would kill me if they found out, so you can't tell anyone!" she pleaded, her eyes wide with panic.

"*Twenty-three*? Sophia, that's insane! He's basically twice your age!" My voice rose, disbelief and concern spilling out in equal measure.

"I know," she said, tightening her grip on my arm like she was anchoring me to her side. "But I can't help who I like. Promise me you won't tell anyone."

I sighed, torn between wanting to talk some sense into her and not wanting to ruin her excitement. "Fine, I promise. But seriously, how did you even meet this guy?"

"I went to Tassel Park after school on Friday just to smoke in peace, and he was there with his brother," she said, her voice softening as she recounted the story. "I told him I was eighteen so he'd talk to me, and once we really hit it off, I told him I was actually thirteen. He didn't care. You have to promise me you won't tell anyone!"

My stomach churned, but I forced myself to nod. "Yeah, sure, I promise," I said, even though the whole thing made me feel uneasy.

We walked up to a duplex apartment, and my stomach turned. I wasn't sure I would've come if I'd known this guy was so old. Maybe he was nice, but what kind of twenty-three-year-old dates a *thirteen*-year-old? I didn't want to upset Sophia, but that really creeped me out.

I followed her down the hall. The building's peeling paint and overgrown yard did little to calm my nerves. My discomfort only grew as we descended into a basement suite. The heavy thrum of loud music seeped through the door, vibrating in my chest as Sophia knocked.

The door swung open to reveal a blond guy with a scowl that could sour milk. "Oh, great," he said, his voice dripping with sarcasm. "The munchkin is back. What part of 'don't come back here' don't you understand?"

Sophia brushed past him like he wasn't worth the effort of a response. "This is Aaron," she said to me, rolling her eyes behind his back. "Sean's brother. He lives here, too."

Aaron glared at me as I stepped inside. I avoided his gaze, already feeling the weight of being unwelcome. The room was dark, with ratty furniture and drawn curtains that made it feel like we'd stepped into a cave. Three older-looking guys sat in the living room; none of them acknowledged Sophia or me. I was getting more and more uncomfortable here.

Then, a bedroom door creaked open, and a tall, red-headed guy walked into the room. His smile was warm and disarming like he was trying to make up for the tension radiating from everyone else. "Hey. Vanessa, right? I'm Sean. Make yourself at home."

He pulled Sophia into his arms, and she melted against him as he carried her to an empty chair. They were kissing within seconds, oblivious to the rest of us.

I didn't know what to do besides hovering awkwardly nearby, feeling out of place and increasingly aware of how young I must look in this room full of older guys. One of the guys seemed to realize there were two more people in the room suddenly and looked right at me.

"Sean, what the hell are these kindergarteners doing here? You wanna attract the cops?" He shook his head. "What the hell is wrong with you people?"

My palms were clammy, but my temper flared at the insult. I stared him down. "Don't worry about Tyler," he told me. "And don't listen to that whole kindergartener thing. He's only seventeen."

There's a big difference between seventeen and thirteen," Tyler grumbled, his voice dripping with disdain. He leaned back in his chair, crossing his arms as he glared at me like I was personally responsible for ruining his day. "You're the only one who wants these young girls here." His words felt like they were meant to cut, sharp and deliberate, and I could feel the weight of his scorn settling on me like an unwelcome shadow. "When you leave, you better not come back."

The hostility in his tone caught me off guard, but I refused to let it show. Everyone else in the room seemed unbothered by Sophia and Sean's relationship, so why was this guy making such a big deal out of it? More importantly, what did it have to do with me? I didn't even want to be here—I'd only come because Sophia invited me.

I could feel my nerves buzzing under my skin, like static electricity that wouldn't dissipate. But as much as his attitude made me uneasy, it also made me angry. If it was such a huge problem for him, he could take it up with Sean—the one who had invited us— rather than aiming his irritation at me. And if he was going to snap at me like that, I wasn't just going to stand there and take it.

"Don't worry," I said, my voice steady and sharp as I locked eyes with Tyler. "I won't come back. Next time I want to listen to someone throw a bitch fit, I'll just stay home with my six-year-old sister."

"Oh, shit," Sean laughed. Sophia looked at me with wide eyes and a big smile.

The other guys exchanged glances, their curiosity clearly piqued as they waited to see how Tyler would react. His glare softened, and a smirk crept onto his face. "Huh. You're fiery," he said, a grudging note of approval in his voice. "I guess you're all right for a kindergartener."

The comment wasn't exactly flattering, but the way he said it felt more like a challenge than an insult. A small wave of relief washed over me as the tension in the room eased. The others seemed to relax, too, and the weight of Tyler's earlier hostility lifted just enough for me to breathe easier.

Aaron had retreated to his room by then, and Tyler was still playing the tough guy, but the rest of the group started to feel more welcoming. Especially Sean—he went out of his way to include Sophia and me in the conversations, steering the topics toward things we could actually contribute to. Every now and then, I'd catch him looking at Sophia with this wide, genuine smile that seemed to light up his entire face. It was easy to see why she liked him so much.

These guys were obviously more mature than the boys we usually hung out with. They talked differently, carried themselves differently, and their jokes were sharper and smarter. It made me proud whenever I said something that got a genuine laugh out of them or when one of them nodded in agreement with something I said.

By the end of the afternoon, I started to understand why Sophia was so excited about dating someone older. In their own way, these guys were impressive—confident, worldly, and far removed from the high school drama we were used to. Still, I couldn't entirely shake the uneasiness that lingered in the back of my mind. For now, though, I decided to let it go and enjoy the moment.

Chapter 7

In the weeks after I first went to Sean's house with Sophia, she and I went over a lot. Tyler would usually say something smart about it, some snide comment or teasing remark that carried his usual sarcastic tone, but I'd shoot back right away with a sharp reply of my own, and that would be the end of it. It almost seemed like he only said anything so that we could have that back and forth.

Despite Tyler being a pain, I became more comfortable being at Sean's house every time we went. The place had an odd charm about it—the cluttered coffee table strewn with video game controllers and soda cans, the faint scent of incense that Sean was always burning, and the way the guys just seemed so relaxed, like they had no worries in the world. The guys weren't as intimidating as I'd thought at first. Sean really seemed to care about Sophia, always finding some excuse to pull her closer to him, whether it was wrapping an arm around her shoulders or tugging her hand so she was sitting right next to him. His affection for her was so genuine that it was hard not to like him, even if he could be annoyingly protective.

The guys often complimented us, going on about how much more mature we were than most thirteen-year-olds. That boosted my confidence in how I interacted with them. They didn't treat me like a little kid anymore—well, everyone except Tyler. He still cracked jokes about my age, but even he had started to acknowledge me more as part of their group. The shift made me feel bold, almost grown-up in a way I hadn't felt before.

Adrian and I weren't sneaking out to see each other every night anymore, just a couple of times a week. He was still a great boyfriend, and I was still crazy about him, but the thrill of being with him was starting to fade. It wasn't the same rush it had been before. Instead, I found myself looking forward to the times I spent with the older guys. There was an edge to being around them, a sense of stepping into a world I didn't fully understand yet but wanted to.

One Sunday morning, a soft knock on my door woke me up around ten. "Are you up?" Mom's voice called quietly through the crack in the door.

"Uh huh," I grumbled, still half-asleep.

"Oliver just left. He'll be gone all day playing cards at a friend's house. I was wondering if you and Lily wanted to help me make a nice lunch for us, and then maybe we can go do something?"

I rolled over, rubbing my eyes, and looked at her. She was leaning in the doorway, smiling at me. It wasn't her usual tired, strained smile; this one was warm and genuine, with a little spark in her eyes that made her look younger somehow.

"Uh, yeah, sure," I said, sitting up.

Her smile widened, and she nodded. "Do you mind waking up Lily?" she asked. "I'll start getting some supplies ready."

I yawned and stretched before slipping out of bed. I thought about changing into something else, but decided against it. If it were just us girls at home, I could stay in my pajamas a little longer.

Lily's door was slightly ajar, and I pushed it open gently, stepping inside. The soft sound of her breathing filled the room as she lay curled up under her blanket, her hair fanned out across the pillow. She looked so peaceful that I almost felt bad waking her.

Almost.

I lifted her blanket and fanned it up and down, letting the cool air ruffle her hair. She groaned and curled into an even tighter ball, so I decided to turn it up a notch. Leaning down, I squeezed her sides and whispered, "Wake up, wake up!"

Lily jerked awake, giggling as she rolled away from me. "Quit it, I'm awake!" she said, her voice still thick with sleep.

I laughed with her. "Mom wants us to help her cook lunch."

Her eyes lit up, instantly wide awake. "Really? What are we gonna make?"

"I'm not sure yet. Let's go find out."

The two of us headed to the kitchen, where Mom had already pulled out a bunch of pots, pans, and random ingredients. The counter was covered in jars of spices, cans of tomatoes, and a box of pasta. Lily clapped her hands excitedly and ran over to hug Mom.

"This is gonna be so fun!" she exclaimed. "What are we making?"

"Well..." Mom placed her hands on her hips, surveying the spread in front of her. "We have all the ingredients here to make spaghetti bolognese, if that sounds good to you two."

Lily and I nodded enthusiastically, and Mom gave us each a job. She took charge of cooking the meat, I was in charge of boiling the pasta, and Lily got to measure out the other ingredients, with help from both of us, if she needed it.

Standing over the stove, I stirred the pasta in the boiling water, watching the steam rise in thick clouds. "I feel like the pasta's been in for a long time," I said, frowning. "How do I know when it's done?"

Mom, who had just taken the meat off her burner, walked over and peered into the pot. "I'll show you a trick," she said, grabbing the spaghetti spoon from my hand. Carefully, she scooped out one noodle.

"Ready?" she asked, holding it up.

Lily and I nodded, leaning forward in anticipation.

With a quick flick of her wrist, Mom threw the noodle against the cabinet. It stuck with a wet slap. "If it sticks, it's done!" she announced.

Lily burst into laughter, clapping her hands. I couldn't resist grinning as I grabbed the spoon and scooped out two more noodles. "Here," I said, handing one to Lily. "One, two, three!"

We threw our noodles at the same time. Mine stuck right next to Mom's, but Lily's missed entirely, sliding down the cabinet and onto the floor. "Hold on," Mom said, already laughing. She brought the pot over to the sink and drained it into a colander. "Grab one and try again."

Lily took her time choosing the perfect noodle. She even closed one eye as she aimed before throwing it with all her might. This time, it hit a drawer and stuck.

"Yes!" she shouted, dancing around the kitchen. Mom and I cheered her on, laughing so hard that our sides ached.

"Can we do it again?" Lily asked, looking up at Mom with a hopeful grin.

Mom smiled indulgently. "We *did* make a little too much pasta, so..."

And that's how we spent the next several minutes flinging noodles around the kitchen like we were in a food fight. Each successful throw earned a round of applause, and even the misses were met with laughter. By the time we were done, the kitchen was a mess, and we were all breathless from laughing so hard.

Chapter 8

A few weeks had passed since I first went to Sean's house with Sophia about the way they carried themselves—confident, untethered—that made me crave their attention. Deep down, I was a little ashamed to admit to myself that I enjoyed the power I felt when I knew they wanted me. It was addictive, that thrill of being noticed.

At this point, my relationship with Adrian felt more like an obligation than a passion. I didn't want to let it go—not yet. But the truth was undeniable: his presence no longer lit me up the way it once had.

What *did* excite me was Thursday. Sophia and I were lounging at Sean's house, the familiar haze of weed and laughter filling the small living room, when a new group of guys arrived. Their voices filtered through the door, low and unfamiliar, sparking my curiosity. They followed Sean into his bedroom, their footsteps heavy on the worn floorboards. I couldn't get a good look at them, but I hoped they'd drift into the living room before they left. The anticipation buzzed under my skin, a quiet thrill.

Sophia noticed my gaze lingering on the hallway and leaned forward, her curly hair catching the light. "What are you doing this weekend?" she asked, her voice pulling me back to the present.

"I'm not sure yet. You?" I replied, keeping my tone casual even as my attention flicked back toward the hallway.

She started chattering about her weekend plans—something about heading to the park and maybe a party at some guy's house.

As she spoke, I caught her sideways glances, like she was trying to keep me grounded. It wasn't the first time she'd done this. Whenever guys came over to buy weed from Sean, Sophia seemed determined to distract me, her words a shield between me and the parade of strangers. I figured she was nervous I'd get too involved or, worse, judge them. But honestly? I didn't care. Sean was careful, and I wasn't naive.

I shifted from the ripped-up leather armchair to the sofa, deliberately choosing a spot where someone would have to sit beside me if they joined us. Just as I got comfortable, the door opened, and the group of guys followed Sean out into the living room. My heart gave a tiny jolt of excitement.

"Hi," I said, smiling at them.

Two of the guys barely glanced at me, their noses wrinkling as they sat as far away as possible. Another ignored me entirely and dropped into the armchair I'd just vacated, his attention on rolling a joint. Their dismissive attitude sparked a flicker of defiance in me. They probably thought we were too young to be interesting, their arrogance plain as day.

The fourth guy, though, caught my eye. He smiled—a warm, easy expression—and gestured to the space beside me. "Do you mind?" he asked.

I shook my head, trying to seem casual even as my heart skipped. He sat down, leaning forward to roll on the coffee table. His dark hair caught the light, gleaming like polished onyx, and his soft features held an understated kindness. As he focused on his task, I fluffed my hair with my fingers, letting it fall around my shoulders in a way I liked.

"I'm Vanessa," I said, my voice loud enough for everyone to hear.

The guy in the armchair raised an eyebrow, his smirk sharp. "Since when do you babysit?" he asked Sean, his tone dripping with condescension.

A wave of anger and discomfort surged through me, heating my stomach. Sean chuckled, brushing it off with a casual, "Be cool."

But the guy next to me—Leo—turned to face the armchair guy, his expression firm but kind. "Yeah," he said, "She's just trying to be nice. Chill."

I smiled at the guy next to me as the armchair guy said, "Come on, Leo. We're twenty-three, and we came here to smoke. Am I supposed to feel comfortable doing that around these kids?"

Leo shrugged, and his face was still kind as he said, "You got what you came here for. You can always just leave now."

The armchair guy shook his head and stood up. The other two rude guys did the same. One of them glanced at Sean. "Next time we call about coming over, let us know if the kids are here so we can pass," he said before the door slammed behind them.

They left the apartment, and even though my heart was beating a little fast, Sophia and Sean just laughed. "Ignore them," Sean told me. "They probably just think you two are like the other girls your age."

"Yeah," Leo said, smiling at me. He hadn't stopped smiling since he came to the living room. "If they want to be jerks before they even get to know you guys, that's their loss."

I gave Leo my best smile. "Whatever. You seem a lot cooler

than them, anyway."

Leo chuckled, his gaze lingering on mine. As we passed the joint back and forth, the conversation flowed easily. He told me about his job at an electronics store and his love for local band shows in Québec and Ontario. His voice was gentle, his words painting pictures of nights spent under dim concert lights and the thrill of finding new music.

Sean and Sophia alternated between making out and chiming in on our conversation, but I preferred it when it was just Leo and me. There was something about the way he spoke, the softness in his tone, that made me feel like I was the only person in the room.

Eventually, Leo stood, brushing his hands on his jeans. "I gotta go," he said, his gaze steady on mine. For a moment, his hand rested on mine, warm and reassuring. "It was nice meeting you, Vanessa."

"It was nice meeting you, too," I replied, fighting back a wide smile.

As soon as the door shut behind him, Sophia's grin spread across her face. "Seems like you two really hit it off," she teased.

My cheeks flushed, my body already warm and fuzzy from the high. "He was really nice. Do you know if he has a girlfriend?" I asked, my voice quieter than before.

"Woah," Sean laughed, shaking his head. "Don't tell me you're forgetting about my friend Adrian."

I flipped my hair over my shoulder, dismissing his comment. "I won't," I said, though the truth was more complicated.

Leaning back onto the sofa, I let my thoughts wander. Leo's kind smile and his soft voice lingered in my mind, lighting me up in a way that felt thrilling and dangerous. This heat in my lower belly, this anticipation, was all too familiar. It was how I felt when I was falling for Adrian. But this? This was more.

Chapter 9

On Friday morning, I woke up with a determination I couldn't shake. I decided I'd spend as much time at Sean's house as possible. The logic was simple: if I was there, I'd have the best chance of seeing Leo again. Just the thought of it made my stomach flutter, though a small voice in the back of my mind warned me against getting my hopes up.

Before heading out to meet Sophia at Hartenstein Park, Adrian called. His warm voice filled the line, telling me he'd be spending the weekend with his grandparents in Québec City. I could hear the slight disappointment in his tone, but I told him I'd miss him anyway. When we hung up, though, a pang of guilt shot through me.

What kind of girlfriend was I? Adrian was sweet, dependable, and completely into me, but my heart raced at the thought of seeing Leo. *Maybe Adrian had other girls chasing after him,* I rationalized. *He probably didn't only have eyes for me. Right?* That thought didn't make the guilt vanish entirely, but it dulled the edge enough for me to move forward with my plan.

Sophia and I headed to Sean's right after serving our detention. The weight of Friday detention was quickly replaced by a buzzing anticipation as we approached his house. We stayed there for hours, lounging on the beat-up couch and passing the time. But Leo didn't show up. Disappointment settled in my chest, and I started wondering if he was avoiding the place because of me. Maybe he had decided I really was too young to be there, too immature for his time. The thought stung.

Later that night, Mom insisted I stay home to babysit Lily while she and Oliver went to play cards at a friend's house. Lily was easy to manage, but my mind kept drifting back to Sean's living room and Leo's absence.

The rest of the weekend flew by in a blur of monotony. Jasmine had a sleepover with some T.W.A. girls on Saturday, and I tried to distract myself with anything else. But by Monday, I was back at Sean's with Sophia, hoping my luck would change. And then, it did.

Leo was there.

The sight of him sitting on the same spot on the sofa where he'd been last Thursday nearly made me stumble. His warm smile when I walked in was like sunshine piercing through the clouds. My chest tightened as I fought the urge to run straight over to him.

Tyler, sitting at the other end of the couch, noticed my reaction immediately. He rolled his eyes in exaggerated disdain. "Did anyone even invite you two, or do you just show up whenever we feel like it?"

The heat of embarrassment crawled up my neck, but I forced myself to stay calm. Snapping at Tyler was tempting, but with Leo watching, I didn't want to come off as rude. "I can just leave if that's what you guys want," I said, putting on my best look of mock sadness. I wasn't leaving, no matter what Tyler said, but I wanted to make a point.

"Yes," Tyler said flatly, at the same time that Leo interjected, "No, you don't have to leave. We're cool with you being here."

I flashed Leo a grateful smile, ignoring Tyler's second eye roll behind Leo's back. "Thank you!" I said with genuine warmth.

While Tyler and Sean immersed themselves in a hockey game

on TV, Sophia, Leo, and I passed a joint around. Tyler usually didn't like it when Sophia and I smoked here, but apparently, he didn't want to argue with Leo about it.

Leo's presence made me hyperaware of everything I did—the way I sat, the words I chose, the way I tried to sound mature without being over the top. My crush on him had grown into a full-blown infatuation, and I was determined to prove I wasn't just a kid.

The three of us got halfway through the joint when it burned out. Instead of relighting it, Leo leaned back casually and nodded at Sean. "Sean, can I get another half off you?"

"You got it," Sean replied, leading Leo to his bedroom.

The moment they disappeared, Tyler turned to me with a knowing smirk. "You want him so badly, don't you?"

Sophia didn't miss a beat, chiming in with a grin. "You've got a massive crush on him."

"Shut *up*," I hissed, darting my eyes toward the closed bedroom door. "I just think he's nice."

"You know who else is nice?" Tyler shot back. "Adrian."

The mention of Adrian felt like a bucket of cold water over my head. I glared at Tyler. "Yes, I know that. I'm not allowed to talk to another guy if I have a boyfriend. I'm *talking* to him, not hooking up with him, so chill out."

Tyler snorted in amusement but didn't press further. My heart pounded, both from irritation and a lingering sense of guilt. When Sean and Leo returned, Sean elbowed Leo and grinned at me, a gesture that made my stomach drop. Great. Sean noticed my crush, too, and told Leo about it. Seemed like everyone had trouble minding their own business.

Leo's behavior toward me didn't change as we finished off the joint. I assumed he wasn't interested in me and really was just being polite.

We spent the rest of the evening hanging out, but my hope that Leo might be interested in me faded with each passing moment. He treated me no differently than he did Sophia, and as much as I tried to hide it, my shoulders slumped with disappointment.

The next evening brought another chance. Sophia and I were at Sean's again when Leo arrived. He was dressed more casually than usual, and his easy smile lit up the room. My heart did its now-familiar leap, but I reminded myself to stay calm. He probably wasn't interested. Better not to get too excited.

"It's a really nice day out," Leo said to Sean. "You want to go up on the lookout?"

"If Sophia can come, definitely. If not, maybe later?"

Leo smiled. "Yeah, she can come." Then, he glanced at me. "Do you want to come too?"

He was probably only inviting me because I was the only other one there. Still, the invitation made my heart flutter. I couldn't deny how thrilled I was to go on a little adventure with him, even if it wasn't just the two of us. My excitement buzzed under the surface, but I forced myself to keep my tone casual.

"Yeah, sure," I said, leaning back slightly as if this was no big deal. "Sounds fun."

Sophia immediately grabbed Sean's phone and dialed someone. Her voice turned syrupy sweet. "Hey, Mom?" she said with practiced innocence. "Vanessa invited me over for the night, so I'll see you tomorrow."

When she hung up, she smirked at me, shrugging as if she'd just pulled off an elaborate heist. "Just in case we get caught up with something really fun," she added, winking.

I nodded knowingly. This wasn't our first rodeo. I took my turn, calling Mom and adopting the same tone of familiarity that Sophia had mastered. "I'm sleeping at Sophi's house tonight," I said breezily.

Mom sighed into the phone, long and weary, the kind of sigh that told me she wanted to say no but couldn't find a good enough reason. Sophia and I had been best friends for years, so sleepovers were almost a formality at this point. After a pause, she finally relented. "Okay," she said, her voice laced with resignation. "Be safe. I love you."

"Love you too," I replied, the words automatic but genuine. Hanging up, I glanced at Sophia, who was already grinning like we'd won the lottery.

The four of us headed out to Leo's Sunfire Z24. The car looked a little worn but had a charm to it like it had been through a few adventures of its own. Sophia and Sean immediately claimed the back seat, where they could cling to each other without interruption. That left me in the front seat next to Leo. I tried not to overthink it as I climbed in, my heart thudding louder than it should have.

Leo kept fidgeting as he drove, adjusting the volume on the stereo and tweaking the temperature controls. "Is the music too loud? Are you comfortable?" he asked, his voice tinged with something that felt like nervousness.

"Everything is perfect," I said with a small, reassuring smile. I couldn't help but notice how thoughtful he was, and it made my chest tighten in a way I wasn't used to. Was he nervous because of me, or was I just imagining things?

He drove us to a secluded spot at the lookout, where the world seemed to pause for a moment. The view stretched out before us, the town's lights twinkling like tiny stars against the velvet darkness. It was the kind of place where you could forget everything else, and that made it magical.

We sat against the side of Leo's car, passing a joint around slowly. The scent of the weed mingled with the cool evening air, creating an atmosphere that was both calming and electric. As the joint made its rounds, I found myself stealing glances at Leo. Every now and then, he caught me looking, and I'd quickly glance away, my cheeks heating up.

After a while, Sean and Leo wandered to the other side of the car to talk, leaving Sophia and me sitting where we were.

"So," I asked, lowering my voice conspiratorially, "if we both lied to our parents, where are we *actually* sleeping tonight?"

Sophia, always ready with an answer, got on her hands and knees, peering under the car. "Hey, Sean," she called out, her voice sing-songy, "Where are we all sleeping tonight?"

The word "we" made my heart skip a beat. Did that include Leo? My mind raced ahead, imagining the possibilities.

Sean's voice came from the other side of the car, accompanied by his trademark grin as he leaned down to look at us. "We were just talking about that. I don't know yet. Maybe we'll get a room at Motel Paul."

My nose wrinkled instinctively. Motel Paul wasn't exactly the Ritz. I'd been there once with Mom to visit some family friends who were passing through. The place reeked of mildew and bad decisions. But what choice did we have? And if Leo was going to be there, I could make it work.

"Sounds good," I said, forcing my tone to stay nonchalant.

We lingered at the lookout until the sky started to darken, and Leo decided it was safe to drive again. As we pulled into the parking lot of Motel Paul, the place looked even sketchier than I remembered. Dimly lit and lined with tired-looking cars, the motel felt like the backdrop of a bad crime movie. I fought the urge to shiver.

Leo, Sophia and I waited in the car while Sean went inside to get us a room. The seconds stretched like hours, and I found myself fiddling with the hem of my shirt. When Sean finally waved us over, Leo got out first and held the door open for everyone, his manners once again reminding me how sweet he was.

Inside, the room was even worse than I'd imagined. The furniture looked like it hadn't been replaced since the Great Depression, and a faint smell of must lingered in the air. Dust coated the surfaces, and the bedspreads were an unsettling shade of brownish-green.

"Oh, man," Sean said with a laugh as he stepped inside. "This place is a shit hole."

Sophia exhaled loudly. "Yeah, you guys really picked a winner here."

I trailed behind her, trying to keep my face neutral. But it was hard not to grimace. The thought of sleeping here made my skin crawl, but I kept my complaints to myself. I was used to going with the flow.

"Ahh, it'll be fine," Sean said, pulling Sophia into his arms. "At least we get to be alone."

Sophia giggled as they flopped onto one of the beds, leaving me and Leo to figure out the other one. I hesitated, feeling a twinge of nervousness as Leo sat at the foot of the second bed. Finally, I forced myself to sit beside him, my hands fidgeting in my lap.

Leo started rolling another joint, his movements methodical and precise. Meanwhile, Sean cranked up the volume on the TV to an almost obnoxious level.

"Why so loud?" Sophia asked, her brows furrowing.

Sean shrugged. "I don't want to hear anything the neighbors are doing."

As the room filled with smoke, the tension in my body slowly melted away. The weed dulled the edges of my anxiety, leaving behind a soft buzz of excitement. Leo's presence next to me was magnetic, but I couldn't tell if he felt the same pull. My thoughts tangled with doubt and hope, each one louder than the last.

Would he have come here if he wasn't interested in me? Or was he just playing wingman for Sean? I couldn't figure it out, and the weed just made my thoughts even more confusing.

When the joint was finished, Sean turned off the lights, leaving the TV on, though, flipping through the channels until he found one that was dark and didn't light up the room too much.

As I watched what Sean was doing, Leo went to the head of the bed, tucking himself under the sheets. My pulse quickened as I realized I'd be sharing the bed with him.

When Sophia and Sean started making out on the other bed, I took it as my cue. My heart raced, and I got hot between my legs as I crawled up to lie beside Leo.

"Thank you for inviting me along," I said softly, my voice almost a whisper.

"You're welcome," he replied, his tone warm. In the faint glow of the TV, I could see the curve of his smile. "I'm glad you came."

Taking a deep breath, I cuddled into him and rested my hand on his chest before I could think about what I was doing. But it paid off. He wrapped an arm around my back and waist, and his hand touched the skin where my shirt had come up.

My body was practically aching for him now, so I slowly moved my fingertips around his chest. He didn't move his body at all. I didn't mind making the first move, so I lifted his shirt and ran my fingertips up and down his chest and stomach.

Leo turned his face toward me, and I put mine right against his. I couldn't tell who moved in, but our lips were touching, and we gently kissed.

He pulled away almost instantly. "Are you sure you want this?"

"Yes," I said, trying to kiss him again.

"Okay," he said, "but you can ask to stop any time."

I rolled on top of him and kissed him once before saying, "I know," and then kissing him again.

Leo was moving slowly. Maybe he was tired? I decided to move faster, to make him as hot for me as I was for him. I pulled off his shirt, then mine, then kept kissing him.

That should've done it, but I couldn't feel his manhood against my legs like I always did with guys during a makeout session. I lifted my head to reevaluate the situation, and I noticed him pushing his head back into the pillow.

I pushed my head into his for a second, but then he gently wrapped his hands around my upper arms and pushed me away from him.

Before I could say anything, Leo sighed. "I'm sorry, Vanessa, but I can't do this."

My heart sank. "Why not? Did I do something wrong?"

"No, no," he said quickly. "You didn't. You're just...really young. It feels wrong."

"But I don't act my age. You know that."

Leo rubbed his eyes and stumbled over his words. "Yeah, I know, but that's not enough. I'm sorry, I just, I can't do this."

He helped me off of him, handed me my shirt, and put his own back on. He didn't look at me again before rolling over and facing away from me.

I felt like a robot as I put my shirt back on. I lay down as carefully as I could. I didn't want to jostle the mattress and disturb Leo. I wanted to pretend I wasn't even here.

Nothing like that had ever happened to me before. I'd never

been rejected, much less after already kissing a guy and being all over him. I was embarrassed, and I felt like an idiot for thinking I had a chance with him.

My stomach got cold, and my eyes stung with tears when I realized I'd cheated on Adrian just to be rejected.

Chapter 10

Leo and I didn't make eye contact the next morning. The atmosphere in the car was heavy, filled with unspoken words and awkward silences. Sean and Sophia were subdued, too. They weren't exactly the most sensitive people, but even they could tell something had gone wrong between me and Leo last night. It was like the lingering tension weighed down the air.

As Leo pulled up to my apartment, he finally spoke, his voice careful and distant. "Bye, Vanessa."

I didn't respond. My throat was too tight, and my face burned with embarrassment. Instead, I just nodded stiffly, climbed out of the car, and shut the door behind me. I couldn't bring myself to say anything more, not even a simple "thank you." The sting of rejection was still too fresh.

As I walked up to the door of my fourplex, my stomach rumbled, a sharp reminder of how little I'd eaten in the past twenty-four hours. The plan was simple: eat something quick, take a long, hot shower, and then bury myself in bed until the world felt less humiliating.

When I stepped inside, the faint smell of coffee greeted me. Mom was on the couch, her eyes fixed on the TV but not really watching. She looked up as I entered, her tired smile tinged with concern.

"I got a call from the school, Vanessa," she said, her tone a mix of relief and sternness. "You can go back tomorrow. And you better, okay?"

Her face was set like she was ready for a fight. But as she studied me, her expression softened slightly, her forehead wrinkling with concern. I guessed she could see the exhaustion and defeat etched across my face. Thankfully, she chose not to press further, returning her attention to her show.

I mumbled something about being hungry and made myself a peanut butter sandwich, eating it in record time. The familiar taste was comforting, but it did little to soothe the storm in my chest. Upstairs, I brushed my teeth with a vengeance, scrubbing away every trace of Leo from my lips. In the shower, I scrubbed my skin raw, hoping it might somehow wash away the shame clinging to me.

When I was as clean as I could possibly get, I collapsed into bed, my damp hair fanning out on the pillow. Music played softly in the background as I flipped through a stack of magazines, but none of it held my attention. My mind kept replaying the events of the night before, the rejection looping like a cruel, endless reel. Frustrated, I tossed the magazines to the floor and buried my face in my pillow, letting exhaustion drag me into an uneasy sleep.

I didn't wake up until six in the evening. Missing detention today wouldn't affect me going back to school, apparently, because Mom definitely would've woken me up if that were the case.

The knock on my bedroom door woke me sometime around six in the evening. For a moment, I lay there, disoriented and groggy, until Lily's voice came through the door.

"Sophia is on the phone for you."

"Thanks," I called back, rubbing my eyes as I reached for the receiver. "Hello?"

"Hey," Sophia's voice was chipper, a stark contrast to how I felt. "What're you up to?"

"Just woke up from a nap," I said, stifling a yawn. "What's up?"

"Want to come for a ride to the lookout again? It'll be me, Sean, and Sean's friend Marcus. He has a girlfriend and definitely won't try anything with you."

I hesitated, torn between wanting to wallow in my feelings and needing a distraction. The memory of last night rose unbidden, twisting my stomach into knots. Maybe going out would help.

"Yeah, sure," I said, trying to sound more enthusiastic than I felt. "Will Sean pick me up?"

"Uh-huh. Can you be ready in, like, twenty minutes?"

I pulled on a pair of jeans and a t-shirt, running a brush through my damp, tangled hair before giving up and tying it into a ponytail. My reflection in the mirror didn't inspire confidence, but I figured it didn't matter. This wasn't about impressing anyone.

When the red Trans Am pulled up, I opened the back door, expecting to see just Sophia and maybe Sean. Instead, Adrian was sitting there next to her.

Sophia didn't mention Adrian would be here! My heart started racing, but I forced myself to stay calm. I plastered on a smile as I climbed in and leaned over to kiss him. He kissed me back, and the simple gesture sent a wave of relief through me. At least he didn't seem mad.

The drive to the lookout was filled with idle chatter between Sean and Marcus while Sophia, Adrian, and I stayed quiet. I explained my subdued demeanor by mentioning my nap, hoping it would cover any awkwardness on my part.

When we arrived, Marcus parked the car in a familiar spot overlooking the city. The view was breathtaking, but I barely noticed it. Sophia, Sean, and Marcus wandered off, leaving Adrian and me leaning against the grill of Marcus's car. The city stretched out before us, its lights glittering like scattered jewels against the darkened sky.

Adrian shifted around next to me, and I looked at him. He was so handsome, with his brown eyes, dark hair, and tan skin. I felt even more regret standing here with him now that I had done all that with Leo.

He put his hands in his pockets and quickly glanced at me, breaking the silence. "I've missed you, Vanessa," he said quietly, his eyes focused on the horizon. "We've barely been hanging out anymore."

The sincerity in his voice cut straight through me. I rested my hand lightly on his pocket, a substitute for holding his hand. "I know," I admitted. "I'm sorry. I've been trying to get my life turned around so I could go back to school and actually be good for once."

"That's what you've been doing?" He finally looked at me, his gaze intense. "Trying to become a better person?"

I nodded, but the lump in my throat made it hard to speak. His expression hardened slightly, and he turned away, shaking his head. "Because I've been hearing some shit."

My heart sank to my toes. Oh, God, who told him? "What do you mean?"

"Aaron called me this morning," Adrian said, his tone heavy

with accusation. "He told me you spent last night in a motel with some guy."

Panic surged through me. My mind scrambled for a response. Before I could come up with some kind of lie or half-truth, Adrian said, "Like, you know what, Vanessa? Can't you even bring yourself to find the decency to tell me the truth, at least? What did I do to deserve ?"

With that, Adrian stormed off and climbed into the backseat of the car. The sound of the door slamming echoed through the otherwise still night. I stood there for a moment, trying to collect myself, my chest heaving with a mixture of anger and frustration. My blood was boiling, and a large part of me wanted to march straight to Aaron and give him a piece of my mind. But this wasn't about Aaron right now—it was about Adrian. If I had any hope of salvaging things, I had to handle this carefully.

Taking a deep breath, I followed Adrian into the car and sat down beside him. The tension in the air was palpable. He stared out the window, his jaw clenched so tightly I could see the muscles twitching. "Look," I began, my voice softer than I expected. "Aaron probably didn't tell you the full truth. Yeah, I was there, but only Sophia and Sean hooked up. We shared a bed because it was our only option, but we didn't hook up. Nothing happened."

Adrian didn't respond. He continued to glare out the window, his silence more cutting than any words he could have spoken. Desperation made me lean in closer, trying to bridge the gap between us. "Did you hear what I said?" I asked, my voice breaking slightly.

His reply came quietly, but it was laced with accusation.

"Why'd you even go at all?" He turned to face me, his dark eyes narrowing. "Hanging out with a guy and another couple is pretty suspicious, honestly."

I felt a flicker of frustration spark within me. "I was hanging out with Sophia when she was invited, and they invited me to be polite. That's all."

Adrian didn't look convinced. His brows knitted together as his gaze bore into mine. "You hang out with Sophia *all the time*. You couldn't leave her alone for one night? You just *had* to sleep next to Leo?" He spat Leo's name like it left a bitter taste in his mouth. "I feel like you're still lying to me."

His words hit me like a slap, and for once, I didn't have a quick response. My mind raced, but nothing came out. He was angry, and a part of me knew he had every right to be. Still, his accusations stung, and a different kind of anger bubbled up inside me.

I wanted to yell at him, to defend myself, to make him stop painting me as some sort of villain. Growing up, I'd watched Mom and Dad fight constantly, each refusing to let the other get the upper hand. It was messy, but at least they stood their ground. Maybe that's what I needed to do.

"You know what?" I shot back, my voice sharp. "Maybe if you weren't such a child, I wouldn't spend so much time with Sean and his friends. I like hanging out with mature people, not kids who just skate around and do nothing all the time."

Adrian's expression hardened his face into a mask of cold fury. His eyes, usually so warm, were now icy. "I'm a child? Better than a lying, cheating bitch."

The insult was a direct hit, and before I could stop myself, my fist connected with his jaw. Pain shot through my hand, sharp and immediate, but it was nothing compared to the wave of regret that crashed over me. My mind reeled. *Why did I do that?* I hadn't meant to. It was as if my body had acted on its own, bypassing any rational thought.

Adrian's eyes blazed with anger, and I instinctively backed away, scrambling out of the car as fast as I could. My heart was pounding, and I felt like I couldn't breathe. I needed to get away from him, from the suffocating tension, from the mistake I'd just made.

I ran toward the others—Sophia, Sean, and Marcus—who were standing a little ways off. "Can you take me home?" I blurted, my voice high-pitched and unsteady.

Sean raised an eyebrow, his usual smirk replaced with concern. Sophia's mouth was hanging open, and Marcus stepped forward, his face etched with worry. "Yeah, no problem," Marcus said gently. "You okay?"

"Yeah," I lied quickly, my voice trembling. "I just wanna go home."

Sophia followed me toward the car, and I grabbed her arm before she could climb in. "Will you sit between me and Adrian?" I asked, my voice barely above a whisper.

Her brows furrowed as she studied me. "What happened?" she asked, her voice cautious.

"I'll explain later," I said, shaking my head. I could feel the tears threatening to spill over, and I knew if I tried to explain now, I'd completely fall apart. "Please, just sit between us."

"Okay, yeah," she said softly, her concern evident.

The car ride back to my fourplex was dead silent. Marcus focused on the road, occasionally glancing in the rearview mirror as if debating whether to say something. Sophia sat stiffly between me and Adrian, the tension in the backseat so thick it was almost unbearable.

When we finally pulled up to my building, Marcus parked the car and turned to look at me. His gaze was kind but hesitant like he wanted to ask if I was really okay but didn't want to push. I couldn't handle another concerned look or probing question, so I quickly opened the door and climbed out without saying a word.

As the car pulled away, I stood there for a moment, staring at the taillights disappearing into the distance. The weight of everything that had just happened settled over me like a heavy blanket. My hand throbbed, my chest ached, and my mind was a whirlwind of emotions—anger, regret, and shame swirling together in an unrelenting storm.

Without another thought, I turned and walked into my building, the door clicking shut behind me. It felt like the end of something, but I wasn't sure what. All I knew was that nothing felt right anymore.

Chapter 11

Going back to school on Thursday was surprisingly nice. The comforting routine of seeing familiar faces and the mundane hum of teachers droning on was exactly what I needed. Reuniting with my friends brought a flicker of warmth back into my chaotic life, like a faint light breaking through storm clouds. Trying to focus in, my classes gave me something to anchor myself to, a temporary escape from the storm raging in my head. Even the hour of detention at the end of the day felt more like a blessing than a punishment—a quiet space to think without the constant hum of emotions threatening to overwhelm me.

But the moment I walked through my front door, the quiet stillness of home dragged me back into my thoughts. The walls of my room seemed to close in on me as I flopped onto my bed, staring blankly at the ceiling. I reached for a pile of magazines on my desk and flipped through the glossy pages, hoping for some kind of distraction.

The **images of female celebrities** I admire stared back at me, their perfect smiles and flawless poses a reminder of strength and confidence. I cranked up my favorite **artist,** whose empowering songs never failed to get me **pumped,** and I let the music flood my senses. The lyrics reminded me of who I was—resilient, bold, and unwilling to let life's curveballs keep me down. I wasn't the kind of girl who fell apart over one mistake. Sure, I screwed up, but if I was honest with myself, my relationship with Adrian had been on its last legs for weeks. It was only a matter of time before it ended, with or without my mistake. It was time to bounce back before I let this spiral any further.

Almost as if she had psychic powers, my phone buzzed with a call from Sophia. "I'm thinking about going to Tassel Park tonight. Want to come?" she asked, her voice casual, like she already knew I'd say yes.

I hesitated. Tassel Park. The name alone sent a thrill through me. I'd heard about it from the guys at Sean's house—a hangout spot for older kids, the kind of place where things happened. If I was going to remind myself of who I was, there was no better place to start.

"Who's going to be there?" I asked, trying to sound nonchalant.

"I don't know," she admitted. "I think Sean might be there, maybe Tyler too. I do know Leo is working and won't be there." She paused, then added carefully, "So, you and Adrian. Are you two done for good now?"

"Yes," I said firmly, though a pang hit my chest. I shoved it down, refusing to let it linger.

"Good," Sophia said. "Sean and I agree you're better off without him. He was too immature compared to the rest of us."

Hearing that sent a wave of relief through me, like a weight I hadn't realized I was carrying had lifted. I exhaled deeply, letting the tension melt away. "I'll meet you at Tassel," I said, feeling lighter already.

****

The air was cool and crisp that evening as I met Sophia at the park. The stars sparkled overhead, a sharp contrast to the hazy glow of streetlights nearby. Groups of teens clustered around benches and playground equipment, their laughter and chatter filling the night air.

"There's Sean," Sophia said, nodding toward the swings.

I squinted through the dim light and made out his familiar shape. "Is that Aaron with him?" I asked, my voice tinged with irritation.

Sophia glanced over. "Looks like it."

I wrinkled my nose. "I'm not going anywhere near him. He's the one who told Adrian about me and Leo."

Before Sophia could respond, a car horn blared behind us. We turned to see Tyler pulling up in a sleek car, his arm resting lazily on the open window. He nodded at us with a casual confidence that made him seem older than he was.

"You go with Sean if you want," I told Sophia, my heart picking up speed. "I'll hang out with Tyler."

Sophia gave me a look that clearly said she thought I was insane, but she didn't argue. With a shrug, she headed toward Sean, leaving me to approach Tyler on my own. His gaze followed me as I walked over, and for the first time, I noticed how his dark eyes gleamed under the streetlights, a mischievous smirk tugging at his lips.

"I heard you've been getting yourself into trouble lately," he said, his voice low and teasing. The smirk widened, and I could tell he liked the idea.

I matched his smile, determined to keep up with his game. "It's the best way to keep life interesting."

His eyes glinted. "That means you're single now, then?"

I nodded, and he leaned back in his seat, clearly pleased. "My relationship actually just ended too," he said, a hint of mock sympathy in his tone. Then he winked. "Since we're both so heartbroken, maybe we could help each other out."

I laughed, feeling a mix of amusement and intrigue. "What did you have in mind?"

Tyler tilted his head toward the passenger seat, where his friend John sat, grinning. "We're going out tomorrow night. Not sure what we're doing yet, but we're looking to get into trouble. Since you're an expert, you should come along. Bring a friend, just not Sophia. She and Sean would give us shit if they knew we were hanging out."

The thought of proving myself to a guy who had always judged me for being young was electrifying. There was something about the challenge of changing Tyler's perception of me that made my pulse race. It wasn't just about impressing him—it was about showing him that I wasn't the naive girl he might have once thought I was. And the possibility that he could start to genuinely like me when I knew he hadn't before? That was like fuel to a fire I hadn't realized was burning inside me.

I tried to play it cool, though. I smiled, careful not to seem too eager, and said, "You've got a date."

****

School the next day was pure torture. Time seemed to move slower with every passing minute, and the monotony of the classroom walls felt like they were pressing in on me. Every tick of the clock above the blackboard sent a jolt of impatience through me. By the time the afternoon rolled around, I could hardly stand it. My legs bounced under my desk, and I found myself staring at the clock as if willing the hands to move faster would make it true.

Finally, I couldn't take it anymore. Eight minutes before the dismissal bell, I asked to go to the washroom. The teacher waved me off absently, and I bolted out of the classroom, my bag already slung over my shoulder. I didn't head to the bathroom, of course—I headed straight for the bus stop. The three o'clock bus was pulling up just as I arrived, and I slipped on, feeling a small thrill of rebellion. Today wasn't about following rules; it was about getting ready for something bigger, something exciting.

****

The moment I got home, I dove into preparation. Tyler was picking me up tonight, and I wasn't about to let him see me looking anything less than my best. I cranked up the radio, letting the music fill the apartment as I set to work. The familiar beat of my favorite songs coursed through me as I curled my hair with precision, applied makeup until every detail was perfect, and tried on outfit after outfit until I found the one that made me feel unstoppable.

As I worked, the anticipation buzzed through me, an almost unbearable excitement. This wasn't just about going out—it was about stepping into a version of myself that I hadn't felt in a while. Bold, confident, free. The kind of thrill I felt reminded me of the first time I'd had sex—a dizzying mix of nervousness and exhilaration of venturing into the unknown.

I checked the clock constantly. Seven o'clock felt like a lifetime away. When six-fifty finally rolled around, I grabbed my bag and slipped out of the house. My chest tightened as I walked to the corner where I always told people to pick me up. It wasn't just about not wanting Tyler to see where I lived—it was about what it represented. No one needed to know that we didn't have a car, that money was tight, or that the fourplex I called home wasn't much to look at. Especially not Tyler.

The sound of an engine pulled me out of my thoughts. Tyler's car rolled up to the curb, his window already down, and his grin as he saw me sent a little jolt through my chest. How had I never noticed how attractive he was before? The lazy confidence in the way he leaned against the car door, the way his hair fell just right—it was impossible to ignore.

"Did you invite a friend?" he asked as I slid into the passenger seat.

"Uh-huh," I said, pointing ahead. "Turn left up here, and I'll tell you the rest of the way."

We drove in companionable silence to pick up Georgia Smith. She was the first person who had come to mind—a classmate with a reputation for being down for anything. The perfect wing girl. When she climbed into the back seat, she gave me a sly grin, clearly catching on to the energy of the night.

Tyler drove us halfway across town to a hotel that made my jaw drop. It was nothing like Motel Paul—this place was sleek, modern, and way too nice for just a group of teenagers. As we pulled into the lot, it became clear that Tyler and John had planned this whole thing ahead of time. And their intentions? Well, those were crystal clear, too.

The room they'd rented was spacious, with plush furniture and a giant hot tub taking center stage. Tyler whistled as we walked in, heading straight for a small table in the corner, where he started rolling a joint. John, meanwhile, made a beeline for the hot tub, fiddling with the controls to heat the water and turn on the jets.

"Let's get in!" Georgia exclaimed, already kicking off her shoes. Within moments, she and John had stripped down to their underwear and slipped into the bubbling water. The two of them didn't waste any time—they were kissing before they'd even fully settled in.

Tyler shook his head, laughing softly. "They're not wasting any time, huh?"

"At least they both know exactly what they want," I said with a shrug, keeping my tone light. "And that it's the same thing."

He raised an eyebrow at me, his expression teasing. "Yeah? Do you know what you want?"

His flirtatious tone sent a thrill through me, but I wasn't about to let him think he had the upper hand. "That joint you're rolling," I said, meeting his gaze with a smirk.

Tyler squinted at me, clearly caught off guard. "You're telling me you came all the way here just because you want to smoke?"

I shrugged, leaning casually against the wall. Messing with him like this was more fun than I'd expected. "Depends. Can you offer me anything more exciting?"

He stared at me for a moment, his smirk fading into something more serious. The intensity in his eyes sent a shiver down my spine. "Don't worry," he said finally, his voice low. "I have a few ideas."

He finished rolling up, so we followed the others' lead and undressed to our underwear and joined them in the hot tub. John and Georgia didn't acknowledge Tyler and me as we took our hits and just kept feeling each other up.

Tyler punched John's shoulder. "You want to smoke or not?"

They took a break from each other to take their hits, then went right back to it once they'd passed the joint back to us. It was the same for the first few rotations, but once Tyler and I started feeling it, he put an arm around my waist.

"I've never been high in a hot tub before," he said to me. I felt his warm breath against my neck, and a chill of pleasure ran through my body.

I turned my face toward him to reply, but he kissed me before I could. My whole body tingled, and I decided then and there that I didn't want to take things slowly. I climbed into his lap right away and wrapped my legs around his waist.

Nobody talked as we kept passing the joint around. We were all too preoccupied with other things. Once Tyler put out the roach, he said, "Joint's finished."

John immediately left the hot tub, taking Georgia's hand and helping her out as well. They went straight to one of the beds, slopping water everywhere.

Tyler and I got out, too, but took the time to dry off with towels. "I don't want to roll around in soaking wet sheets," Tyler said.

I went to the other bed as Tyler went to the TV stand where he'd left his wallet. He pulled out a condom, turned off the light in the room, then joined me in bed.

Unlike Leo, Tyler didn't ask all kinds of questions to try and get out of being with me. He must have been able to tell by my body language that I wanted him because before I knew it, we were undressed and touching each other everywhere.

Tyler and I finished up, and Georgia and John weren't far behind us. Once we'd all put our clothes back on, Tyler said, "Well, we only rented this room for a few hours, so we might as well get out of here now."

I felt a little upset at first as the boys rushed us all out of the hotel, but then I realized this was better. I was riding on the high of hooking up with Tyler, but if we spent the night together, there was a chance that he'd try to start an argument with me. I liked our small squabbles, but I liked him too much now to be okay with him getting upset with me.

They dropped off Georgia first. "Thanks for inviting me, Vanessa," she said with a big smile. "I had fun."

I smiled back. "Thanks for coming."

Tyler dropped me off now. "Remember," he said as I got out of the car, "keep what happened tonight between us. We don't need people judging us, right?"

"Right." I leaned in through the driver's window and kissed him hard before walking away.

When I was sure he couldn't see me anymore, I skipped a few times. This was probably the most exciting night I'd ever had, and I asked God to let me meet up with Tyler again soon.

Chapter 12

On Saturday night, Mom and Oliver were gearing up for one of their usual outings to the Williams' house. The Williams' place was practically legendary, at least among the adults. It wasn't just a home—it was a mini-party hub with a fully stocked bar that could put any restaurant to shame. Every time Mom and Oliver went over there, it was almost a guarantee they'd get so drunk they'd end up staying the night. It was their way of cutting loose, and I didn't begrudge them for it. They deserved a break, but that meant I had to hold down the fort at home.

"We'll need you to stay home to keep an eye on Lily," Mom said, giving me a look that said there was no room for argument. "You can invite a friend over if you want."

I was still riding the high from the night before, so I didn't mind staying in. Besides, Lily wasn't much trouble to watch, and this felt like the perfect excuse to invite Mia over for a sleepover. It had been ages since we'd hung out, just the two of us, and I knew Lily adored her.

By the time Mia arrived, Lily was already buzzing with excitement. We decided to make the most of it and turned the living room into our personal runway. With clothes pulled from both mine and Lily's closets, we had a full-on fashion show, complete with music blasting from my old speakers. Lily twirled around in a too-big dress, giggling wildly as Mia and I clapped and cheered like she was a star on the red carpet.

Afterward, the three of us curled up on the couch to watch a movie. Lily snuggled between us, her head resting on my shoulder until her eyelids started drooping halfway through. When I carried her to bed, her tiny arms wrapped around my neck, and for a moment, the warmth of her trust made everything else feel small and distant.

Once Lily was fast asleep, Mia and I slipped out into the little tunnel of walls between my apartment and the neighbor's to smoke. The cool night air made me shiver as I lit up, and Mia leaned against the wall next to me, her breath curling in the air like smoke from a dragon's mouth. It didn't take long for the weed to hit, and soon Mia's laughter bubbled out, loud and uncontrollable. Her giggles were infectious, and before I knew it, I was doubled over, clutching my stomach as tears of laughter rolled down my cheeks.

The two of us stumbled back inside, still laughing over nothing in particular, and collapsed into bed. The moment my head hit the pillow, I felt that familiar, contented haze settle over me. It had been a long time since I'd felt this light.

Sunday passed in a blur, and before I knew it, Monday morning was staring me down. At school, Sophia found me as soon as recess started, linking her arm through mine and steering me toward the edge of the smoking corner where we could talk in private.

"Where were you Friday night?" she asked, her voice curious but tinged with the kind of playful accusation only a best friend could pull off. "Everyone at Jasmine's house went to Hartenstein. We missed you."

I hesitated for a moment, remembering Tyler's warning to keep quiet about what had happened. But Sophia was my best friend—keeping secrets from her felt wrong, and it would've been weird not to tell her.

"You have to keep this between us," I said in a hushed voice, glancing around to make sure no one else could hear. "You especially can't tell Sean."

Sophia's eyes widened, and I had to fight the urge to grin at her expression. "Me and Georgia went to a hotel with Tyler and his friends. I hooked up with Tyler."

Her jaw dropped. "Like, all the way?"

"Yeah," I said, unable to keep the smile off my face. "It was a lot of fun, and I actually really like Tyler now, so be cool, okay?"

"Okay, yeah, no judgment here," Sophia said, though her lips curved into a strange smile. "I just never would've thought Tyler would hook up with a 'kindergartener.'"

I shrugged, grinning. "I guess there's just something special about me."

Sophia laughed, shaking her head in disbelief, and passed me a cigarette. We smoked together before heading back to join the rest of our friends.

****

The rest of the week crawled by, the monotony of school and detention stretching out each day like a rubber band about to snap. By the time the dismissal bell rang on Friday, I was desperate for something fun. I went with Sophia and Mia to Jasmine's house, where we were the first to arrive.

The moment we stepped into Jasmine's basement, the smell of weed and cigarettes filled the air. Someone passed a joint to me within minutes, and soon, the room was filled with laughter and hazy conversation. As the sun began to set, someone suggested heading to Hartenstein Park, and everyone agreed. It was the perfect spot to drink and smoke without worrying about parents or younger kids.

****

At the park, the group scattered, some sticking close to the playground equipment while others wandered into the shadows to drink and smoke in peace. I sipped my drink slowly, feeling the buzz of the alcohol settle over me. Sophia and Mia, on the other hand, got pretty drunk. The three of us decided to take a walk around the park, laughing and stumbling over nothing in particular until a car horn startled us.

The blinding glare of headlights turned off, and I blinked as my vision adjusted. It was Tyler and John. "You girls want to come for a ride?" Tyler called out the window.

"I'm good," Mia said, waving them off.

Sophia, however, let out a wild laugh and climbed into the car without a second thought. My heart leaped at the opportunity to see Tyler again. I turned to Mia. "I'm gonna go, too."

"Have fun," Mia said with a shrug, heading back to join the others.

I hurried to the car, my knees going weak. The four of us hotboxed the car as Tyler drove us to a hotel, a different one from last time. My heart was racing in excitement the whole walk to our room.

As soon as the four of us were in the room, Tyler and John sat on each bed. I took maybe half a step toward Tyler when Sophia bumped into my shoulder as she walked past me. And sat on the bed next to Tyler.

"What're you doing bringing us to a hotel?" she slurred, leaning toward Tyler.

He grinned. "I'll show you."

I could only stare, frozen, as Tyler and Sophia got under the sheets together. Right away, they started making out.

"Vanessa."

I managed to turn my head to look at John, who was patting the bed next to him. The thought of hooking up with John made me want to throw up. I went to the table in the corner and sat down, not looking at or talking to anyone.

I heard John exhale and turn on the TV, but it wasn't loud enough to cover up the sounds of Tyler and Sophia starting to have sex.

What Sophia was doing made me want to throw up, too. Not only was she hooking up with a guy I told her I liked, but she raced to get to him before I could, and she was doing this all right in front of my face. I wanted so badly to jump on the bed and beat the hell out of her, but I was so hurt that my muscles were cold and weak, and I couldn't move.

Tyler and Sophia finished up, and then the four of us left the hotel. The other three of them were talking to each other, but I stared silently out the window the whole time. When I saw we were heading to Hartenstein, I finally spoke.

"Take me home, Tyler," I said quietly.

"Uh, sure," he said.

He pulled up to my drop-off spot, and I left the car without a word. As I was going to shut the door, Sophia and I made eye contact. Her face was blank, and as badly as I wanted to attack her, I just returned the blank stare and slammed the door in her face.

I could barely see as I walked to my fourplex because of the tears rolling down my face. I couldn't believe that my best friend would do that to me. I would've never done anything like that to her, and realizing that she apparently never cared about me was one of the most painful things I'd ever felt.

Chapter 13

I didn't get out of bed the next morning. I couldn't. My body felt like lead, every movement weighed down by the ache in my chest. The blankets felt suffocating, but at the same time, I couldn't bring myself to throw them off. I stared at the ceiling, tracing invisible patterns in the cracks of the plaster, while my mind played a loop of last night over and over. I had no appetite, no energy, and absolutely no motivation to do anything. My chest felt hollow, yet somehow it still hurt. I felt sad, angry, and empty all at once because of what Sophia did to me.

The phone rang, piercing through the silence of my room, dragging me out of my haze. The sound made me wince, but I didn't move. Not long after, there was a knock at my door. Mom's voice followed, soft but concerned, "Ness, it's Sophia."

My heart sank, then twisted into something ugly and bitter. **Sophia.** Who the hell did she think she was, calling me after last night? The mere thought of her voice made me clench my jaw. I didn't want to talk to her. I didn't even want to think about her. But trying to explain any of this to Mom right now felt like too much. I was drained.

"Thanks," I said, my voice flat and barely above a whisper. Mom gave me a hesitant look before leaving the room, and I picked up my phone with trembling hands, half-wanting to throw it across the room. Instead, I put it to my ear and muttered, "What?"

"Hey," Sophia said, her voice annoyingly chipper. "What're you doing tonight? Want to go to Tassel Park again?"

My jaw literally dropped. My hand tightened around the phone as her words registered. The nerve she had to act like nothing had happened. Like she hadn't betrayed me in the most blatant, gut-wrenching way. I felt a surge of anger, hot and overwhelming, surge up from my stomach. It took me a moment to find my voice, and when I did, it was sharp, each word cutting. "Well," I said, venom dripping from every syllable, "to be honest, I'd rather get hit by a bus than ever hang out with you again, so no."

There was a pause, and I could almost picture her confused, clueless expression. "Huh? What do you mean, what did I do?"

She couldn't be serious. Was she genuinely that dense, or was she playing dumb? "Oh, nothing," I snapped, my voice rising, "besides literally pushing me aside so you could go hook up with the guy I told you I liked. What the hell is wrong with you?"

Her response came quickly, tinged with an air of indignation. "Are you kidding me? What are you being so dramatic about? Tyler isn't your boyfriend, and you could've told me to stop. If it was that big of a deal to you, you would've done something besides just sit there and let us go to bed together."

I stared at the wall, my grip on the phone so tight my knuckles turned white. The audacity in her voice, the way she twisted the situation to make it my fault—it was too much. I took a deep breath, the kind that made my chest shake, and let it out slowly. When I spoke again, my words were measured but cold. "You want to know what I'm mad about? You ignored my feelings and basically bullied me right in front of my face. I hope the sex was worth destroying eight years of friendship over." I shook my head, the weight of my emotions threatening to pull me under. "You know, you're lucky I'm a better person than you are because if I stooped to your level,

I'd probably tell Sean about what you did. Hell, I might even tell your parents about Sean."

I hung up the phone before she could reply, slamming it onto the bed. My chest heaved, a mix of anger and sadness swirling inside me like a storm. Screw her.

Before I had the chance to start crying, there was a soft knock on my door. Mom peeked in again, her face lined with worry. "I promise I couldn't hear what you were saying, and I wasn't trying to eavesdrop, but I could tell by your voice and tone that you were upset. Is everything okay?"

"Yeah," I mumbled right away, though my voice cracked at the word. Mom wasn't convinced. She hovered in the doorway, watching me with those gentle, knowing eyes of hers. I tried to keep it together, but my face crumpled as the tears started spilling over. "My friendship with Sophia is over."

Mom was by my side in an instant, wrapping me in her arms. She held me tightly, letting me sob into her shoulder. I felt her hand stroking my hair, her presence warm and comforting. She didn't say much, just murmured softly, her words a soothing hum I couldn't quite make out but appreciated all the same. Her shirt was damp with my tears and snot, but she didn't pull away. She stayed.

Several minutes later, the door creaked open again. Lily tiptoed in, her small hands clutching a folded piece of paper. Her eyes were wide with concern. "I heard you crying," she said softly, her voice a whisper. "I made you something to maybe make you feel better."

I wiped my face with the back of my hand and took the paper from her. Opening it, I saw a simple but heartfelt drawing of two stick figures hugging. One was labeled "Lily," and the other

"Vanessa." My chest ached in a different way now, something warm and bittersweet blooming in its place.

"I don't know why you're sad," Lily said, looking up at me with wide, earnest eyes, "but I'm here if you need me."

My heart melted. I pulled her close and hugged her tightly. "I do need you," I said, my voice trembling. "I need you to make a group hug with us."

Lily scrambled onto the bed, her little arms wrapping around me and Mom. I was squeezed between them, their love radiating through me like a warm blanket. Physically, it felt comforting, but emotionally, it was healing. I felt a little less alone.

When my tears finally slowed, Mom squeezed me once more and, to my surprise, started singing in a silly, exaggerated voice. "Hush, little baby, don't you cry…"

I rolled my eyes, though a faint smile tugged at my lips. "That's a baby song. That won't make me feel better."

Lily lifted her chin, her voice loud and proud. "You down with O.P.P., yeah, you know me!"

Mom gasped, her eyes wide, while I burst out laughing. "That's an *adult* song!"

The three of us dissolved into laughter, the sound filling the room and chasing away some of the lingering darkness. For the first time all morning, I felt like maybe, just maybe, I would be okay again.

Chapter 14

I kept feeling better as the day went on. The heavy fog that had settled over me in the morning began to lift, bit by bit. By mid-afternoon, I managed to get out of bed. It felt like a small victory, a glimmer of normalcy. Now, I was sitting cross-legged on the carpet in Lily's room, surrounded by her dolls, stuffed animals, and the chaotic, colorful mess that could only belong to a child's world. Lily had an imagination that could spark life into the simplest toys, and playing with her was a kind of therapy I hadn't realized I needed.

She handed me a doll, one with hair so tangled it looked like it had been struck by lightning. "This one's the bad guy," she declared, her face solemn. "She's going to try and steal all the cookies."

I nodded, pretending to be shocked. "Not the cookies! We have to stop her!"

Lily giggled and started setting up the scene, her small hands moving the dolls around with the same determination as a theater director. For a while, I let myself get lost in her world. It felt nice. Light.

Then Lily suddenly announced, "I have to pee!" and dashed out of the room, leaving the dolls mid-rescue mission. I chuckled softly and began tidying up some of the accessories strewn across the floor.

The phone rang, cutting through the quiet hum of the house. The sound sent a strange ripple through me, but I ignored it and continued playing with the dolls. A few minutes later, I heard soft footsteps. I looked up to see Mom standing in the doorway, a strange, unreadable expression on her face. Her hand rested lightly on the doorframe as if she needed the support.

"Your dad called," she said, her voice calm but tinged with something I couldn't quite place.

I froze. My heart gave a sharp, unexpected jolt, and my stomach twisted. "What?" I managed to say, though it came out more like a whisper.

Mom stepped inside, her hands fidgeting slightly. "He said he'll be flying up next month to visit you."

She tried to smile, but it didn't reach her eyes. It felt forced, like she was trying to be encouraging but didn't quite believe her own words. I didn't say anything, and after a few moments, she left the room, her presence replaced by the lingering silence.

I sat there for a moment, staring at the dolls, my body stiff and unmoving. My mind, however, was racing. **Dad. Visiting.** The words looped in my head, each repetition bringing a fresh wave of emotion. I hadn't seen him since I was five. Memories, long buried but never forgotten, began to resurface, pulling me back into the past like an undertow.

The bedroom door creaked open, breaking my trance. Lily came bounding back in, her little face glowing with excitement, completely unaware of the emotional storm brewing inside me. "Okay, where were we?" she asked, grabbing a doll and diving right back into our game.

I tried to keep playing with her, to match her enthusiasm, but my movements felt mechanical. My body was on autopilot, going through the motions, while memories of Dad consumed my thoughts. If I focused hard enough, I could bring myself back to that time so vividly, it felt like I was there again.

When I wasn't napping or having a snack, my little nose was pressed against the cool glass of the car window. The world outside whizzed by, a blur of trees, buildings, and skies that seemed endless. Mommy and I were on an adventure—a big, important adventure—and I wanted to see everything. Every sign, every car, every bird flying in the sky.

But the best part of the adventure? We were on a mission to find Daddy. Mommy had said he'd gotten lost in America, and we were going to bring him back. The idea filled my little heart with hope and excitement. Daddy was lost, but we were going to find him.

I had been so confused the day Mommy told me Daddy was moving to Miami with Abuelita and Abuelito. Miami sounded like a magical place, but it also felt so far away from our home in Montreal. I'd just come back from visiting them, and I didn't understand why everything was changing. As Mommy and I were leaving their house, Abuelita had smiled at me and said, *"Hasta mañana!"* like she always did. I had smiled back, but it had left me puzzled. I won't see her tomorrow, so why did she say that? Didn't she know it hurt my feelings?

I leaned back in my seat and took a sip of the juice we'd gotten at a gas station. My little brain was working hard, trying to make sense of things. Maybe the move had something to do with the time I heard Abuelito yelling at Daddy. I wasn't supposed to hear it—I was supposed to be napping—but I remembered the words.

"Carlos, we're sick and tired of getting you out of jams all the time. Your drinking problem is getting worse, and don't even get me started on everything else."

I hadn't understood then. How could drinking be a problem? I drank juice all the time, and nobody ever got mad at me for it. And why was Daddy eating all the jam? I liked jam too, but nobody ever yelled at me about it. The grown-up world was so confusing.

I must've fallen asleep again, because the next thing I knew, Mommy was gently shaking me awake. "We're here, sweetheart," she said, her voice soft and full of love.

I rubbed my eyes and sat up, peering out at the unfamiliar house in front of me. It didn't look like any house I'd ever seen. The doors had metal bars on them, and everything about it felt strange.

"Go ahead and ring the doorbell," Mommy encouraged, her smile reassuring.

I did—over and over because I was so excited. I wanted to do my special knock like I always used to, but the bars on the door made it impossible. "Abuelita? Abuelito?" I called out, jumping up and down, trying to see through the window. "It's me, Vanessa!"

The door finally opened, and there she was—Abuelita, her face lighting up like the sun when she saw me. "Is that really our princess?" Abuelito called from behind her, his voice warm and familiar. "All the way from Canada to see us?"

"Yeah!" I squealed, already reaching out for hugs. Abuelita knelt down and wrapped me in her arms, her kisses raining down on my cheeks. Her hugs always smelled like her perfume, a mix of flowers and something sweet, like vanilla. It made me feel safe. Abuelito joined in, scooping me up like I weighed nothing, his laughter rumbling in his chest as he held me close. I giggled as his scruffy beard tickled my cheek.

"We missed you so much, mi amor," Abuelita said, brushing my hair back from my face.

I beamed up at them. "I missed you too!" But then, as though the thought had just popped into my head, I looked around eagerly. "Where's Daddy?"

Abuelito's face changed. For just a moment, his smile faltered, and something sad flickered in his eyes. "He'll be home soon, *amor*," he said, his voice softer now.

"Let's take a tour of the house!" Abuelita chimed in quickly, her energy bright and cheerful again.

I followed them inside, and as soon as I stepped through the door, a delicious smell hit me. My mouth watered instantly. "Is that *arroz con pollo*?" I asked, my voice rising with excitement. I started jumping up and down, my little hands clasped in front of me.

"Of course," Abuelita said, her eyes twinkling. "We had to make our special girl's favorite meal! It's almost ready, but before we eat, there's something I want to show you."

She took my hand and led me down a hallway, with Abuelito and Mommy following close behind. The walls were painted in bright colors, and there were pictures of my family hanging everywhere. Finally, we stopped in front of a door. Abuelita opened it and stepped aside, gesturing for me to go in first.

I gasped.

The room was like a dream. The walls were painted a soft pink, and a white princess bed with a fluffy comforter sat in the middle. A matching pink rug covered the floor, and on the nightstand was a pink telephone—just like the ones I'd seen in movies.

"This is your room, *amor*," Abuelita said, her voice full of pride and love. "It's all yours."

My little heart swelled with joy. They hadn't forgotten me after all! I ran to Abuelita and threw my arms around her. "Thank you so much, Abuelita! It's beautiful!"

She hugged me tightly, laughing softly. "You're welcome, mi amor. Anything for our princess."

We made our way back to the kitchen, where the table was already set for dinner. The smell of the arroz con pollo was even more mouthwatering up close. After we said grace, I dug in eagerly, savoring every bite. The meal was perfect, just the way I remembered it.

Halfway through dinner, the door opened, and I heard footsteps in the living room. My heart leaped. "I'm just dropping by to grab a few things before heading back out," a voice said.

I knew that voice. I dropped my fork and bolted out of my chair. "Daddy!" I shouted, running toward the living room.

I had pictured this moment a thousand times in my head. I would run to him, and he would scoop me up in his arms, spinning me around while telling me how much he missed me. I would laugh, and he would hold me tight, and everything would feel right again.

But that's not what happened.

Before I could reach him, he pulled some money out of his pocket and placed it on the table by the couch. "Here's some money," he said casually, not even looking my way. "In case you want to go do something." Then, just as quickly as he had come in, he turned and walked out the door.

I stopped in my tracks, staring at the door as it clicked shut behind him. My hands hung limp at my sides, my heart sinking lower and lower until it felt like it had disappeared entirely. Didn't he see me? Didn't he miss me? Why didn't he hug me?

Tears pricked my eyes, but I didn't want to cry. Not yet. My throat burned as I swallowed hard, trying to push the feelings down.

Abuelita found me standing there, frozen. She knelt beside me, her warm arms wrapping around my small, trembling frame. She didn't say much. All she whispered was, "I'm so sorry, *mi amor*," over and over, her voice heavy with sadness.

I couldn't hold it in any longer. I buried my face in her shoulder and sobbed, my little body shaking with the force of it. She rocked me gently, humming a soft tune I didn't recognize, but it made me feel just a little less broken.

****

The next day was different. When I woke up, my cheeks still felt sticky from crying, but there was a quiet kind of hope stirring in my chest. I walked into the kitchen, and there he was—Daddy. He was sitting at the table, his eyes clear and his smile wide.

When he saw me, he stood up and opened his arms. "Finally, my favorite girl came to see me," he said, his voice warm and full of love.

I ran to him, and this time, he picked me up, spinning me around just like I'd imagined. I laughed so hard my sides ached.

"What do you think about going to the beach today?" he asked.

"Yay! Let's go!" I squealed, clapping my hands.

He chuckled and patted my head. "Let's have some breakfast first, okay?"

We had breakfast, and then Mommy helped me get dressed in my bathing suit, my favorite one with the red and yellow stripes.

"Hold *still,* Ness," she said with a smile.

But I couldn't hold still. I was so happy that I couldn't stop dancing.

My whole family went to the beach together. Mommy put some floaters on my arms, and then she and Daddy took me into the water. Daddy put his hands out and let me lay on them so that I could float and look up at the sky. The waves made my body wiggle. It was the most fun thing I'd ever done.

After that, Daddy let Mommy and me bury him in the sand. I used my bucket to find the best sand and poured it all over him, except for his head.

"All done!" I said, looking at the lump his body made under the sand.

"No, you aren't."

I scratched my head. What did Daddy mean? He was all covered.

"You forgot my arms!" Daddy pulled his arms from under the sand and tickled my belly. I screamed and laughed, and it was the happiest sound I'd ever heard.

We had sandwiches for lunch under an umbrella, and with my belly full, I needed a nap. I cuddled up on Daddy's lap. My last thought before I fell asleep was how great it was to know where my family was and that I'd never have to miss them again.

***

Lily's bedroom door swung open, snapping me out of my daydream.

"Supper time!" Mom said.

Chapter 15

Three days had passed since I found out Dad was coming to visit. Every morning since then, I woke up with a bubbling excitement that made it hard to sit still. I'd lie in bed for a moment longer, staring at the ceiling, letting the idea of seeing him sink in. Each time I thought about his visit, it felt like a little jolt of electricity in my chest. I wanted to scream into my pillow from excitement, but instead, I'd just smile and start my day with a little more energy than usual.

I tried to just go with the flow, but questions kept swirling in my mind like leaves in a whirlwind. Why now? Had Dad been wanting to visit for years but couldn't afford it? Was this visit something he had planned for a long time, or did something suddenly push him to come? Was he nervous that I wouldn't want to see him after all this time? The idea of calling him to tell him how excited I was crossed my mind dozens of times. I'd even picked up the phone once, but I froze. What would I even say? My mind went blank every time I imagined the conversation.

But regardless of the reasons or my nervousness, Dad was coming. That was all that mattered. The whole world felt brighter now, like someone had adjusted the saturation on my life; even ordinary things like walking to school or hearing the birds chirp outside my window seemed to hum with a kind of hidden joy.

In music class on Thursday, the day practically glowed. We had a substitute teacher—a kind-looking middle-aged woman who wore oversized glasses that kept sliding down her nose. She enthusiastically explained that we would be listening to music from the sixties and seventies to "gain an appreciation for the classics." Most of the kids groaned, slouched in their chairs, and muttered complaints about how lame it was to listen to anything other than the latest pop hits.

But not me. I perked up the moment she mentioned the sixties. Mom loved music from that era, and some of my happiest memories were of her blasting her favorite songs on our old stereo in the apartment. The scent of her jasmine perfume would mix with the faint aroma of dinner simmering on the stove, and we'd dance around the living room, singing at the top of our lungs. Those moments felt like magic—like we were the only two people in the world.

The substitute played a song by Michael Jackson, *I wanna rock with you*, and I closed my eyes, letting the melody transport me. I could almost see Mom twirling me around the living room, her laugh echoing through the air. I made a mental note to ask her if she wanted to do that today, if she was in a good mood when I got home.

But just as I was soaring high on nostalgia, the assistant principal stepped into the classroom. He carried a clipboard and a somber expression. The energy in the room shifted instantly, like someone had flipped a switch. His announcement was brief and to the point: "Father Kentucky High School will be closing after the ninety-fifth school year."

The words hit me like a brick. My classmates murmured and whispered to each other, but I just sat there, stunned. Father Kentucky had been part of my family's history for generations. Mom and all her nine siblings had gone there. I wasn't overly attached to the school, but it still felt like the end of an era.

When I got home, Mom was sitting at the kitchen table. Her fingers traced absent patterns on the wood grain as if lost in thought. Her face wore an expression that was a mix of sadness and fatigue. My stomach twisted. Had the school already called the parents?

"I guess you heard the news?" I said, dropping my bookbag by the door.

Mom's forehead wrinkled in confusion. "What news?"

Oh, great. I'd have to be the one to break it to her. "Father Kentucky is closing. After the ninety-fifth school year."

Her eyes widened. "What? Where did you hear that?"

"One of the assistant principals came to our class today to tell us. He didn't explain why, though."

She stared at the table, her sadness deepening. Her connection to Father Kentucky was much deeper than mine. This was the school where she had formed lifelong friendships, attended her first dance, and proudly graduated. I hated that I had to be the bearer of bad news.

But if she hadn't already heard, why did she look sad when I first walked in?

Her expression shifted again—this time serious, layered with emotions I couldn't quite read. "Let's...put that news to the side for now. There's something more important I need to talk to you about."

I raised an eyebrow, bracing myself. Mom sighed deeply as though she were gathering her strength. "I found some weed in your room today. And I've noticed how often you come home with red eyes and smell like it. Vanessa, you—"

"What were you doing in my room?" I snapped, cutting her off. "Can't I have any privacy?"

Mom sighed again, but this time, it was different—less exasperation, more weariness. "I grabbed some candy at the store today. I thought it would be nice to leave some on your bed as a little surprise for when you get home."

My shoulders slumped under the weight of guilt. Of course, she was trying to do something thoughtful. But I wasn't in the mood for a lecture about drugs. I wasn't going to stand around and get told how stupid I was, especially when it would be hypocritical of her.

"Weed is harmless," I said, crossing my arms. "It doesn't make you sick, or hungover, or act crazy. And it's not like I'm addicted to it or anything; it's just...innocent fun."

Mom's eyes softened with concern. "But it's still a drug, Vanessa. You're too young for all that. And smoking weed doesn't always stop there. It can lead to much more dangerous things."

I put my hands on my hips. "You mean like cocaine? You're right; using and selling cocaine is a lot worse."

Mom's jaw clenched. I knew I had hit a nerve. Years ago, I had found a wad of cash in the pocket of her fur coat, the one she only ever wore that coat when she was around Uncle Jack, and he never tried to hide his "job" of selling cocaine. Even as a kid, it wasn't hard for me to put two and two together.

"Yes, I've dealt with drugs in the past," she said, her voice steady but taut. "And I shouldn't have. That's exactly why I'm so adamant about you being careful. I know how badly it can mess you up and how hard it is to stop. I want better for you."

Her words hung in the air, heavy with unspoken pain. I shifted uncomfortably.

"Okay, fine," I said, wanting the conversation to end. "I'll cut back."

Mom's face softened slightly. "Thank you, Vanessa."

"Yeah, sure," I muttered.

When I retreated to my room, I found two chocolate bars neatly placed on my pillow. My chest tightened. She had been thinking about me when she bought them. Guilt weighed me down like a stone. I wasn't actually planning to cut back, but I'd definitely be more careful so she doesn't find out again.

Chapter 16

Every day that passed, I found myself growing more comfortable with the changes in my life. It wasn't seamless, but little by little, I felt like I was adjusting. One of the biggest changes was how little I'd been hanging out with Mia and Jasmine. They were still part of the T.W.A. group, and Sophia was around them far too often. I was doing everything I could to avoid her, which meant keeping my distance from people who used to be part of my daily life.

It wasn't easy. Sophia and I still shared so many mutual friends, and it stung to see how everyone still adored her. They didn't know the truth. That was on me—I hadn't told anyone what happened. The thought of explaining it made me anxious. I didn't want to put people in an awkward spot where they'd have to choose sides. Still, it hurt to see her laughing and joking as if she hadn't completely betrayed me. A part of me wanted to shout the truth to everyone, to rip off her mask and show them who she really was. But I kept quiet.

Instead, I started hanging out with Georgia more. She wasn't part of T.W.A., and her friend group didn't overlap much with mine. That made it easier to confide in her. I had told her everything about what Sophia had done, and her reaction was immediate and explosive. Georgia was outraged for me, pacing the room as she went on a hilarious rant about Sophia's character-or lack thereof. By the time she was done, I was laughing so hard my sides ached.

"That girl," Georgia said, planting her hands on her hips, "is the human equivalent of a paper straw in hot coffee—completely useless and falling apart in seconds."

Her humor lifted a weight I didn't realize I was carrying. My only regret was not getting to know Georgia sooner. She had already proven to be a loyal and genuine friend.

Things were going smoothly until Friday at recess. My class was right by the door closest to the smoking corner, so I usually got there first. It was my usual routine: slip outside, light a cigarette, and enjoy a moment of calm before everyone else showed up. But today, Sophia was the second person there.

"Hey," she said, her voice tentative and her eyes wide with surprise. For a moment, we just stared at each other, caught off guard by the encounter.

I broke eye contact first, pulling a cigarette from my pack and lighting it as if she hadn't said anything.

"I wish you'd stop ignoring me," she said, louder this time, her tone tinged with frustration. "One stupid guy isn't a reason to end a friendship. I can't believe you'd drop me so easily after all the times I've been by your side. It almost feels like you're choosing a guy over me, and that's really—"

"Did I ever give any indication that I want to talk to you?" I cut her off, blowing a slow stream of smoke and finally meeting her gaze.

Sophia's mouth opened slightly as if to argue, but no words came out. I didn't look at her again, but I could feel the tension radiating off her. She was fuming, but she wouldn't dare cause a scene in front of the growing crowd.

A few moments later, Georgia showed up. She hooked her arm through mine and glanced at Sophia with a grimace. "Hey, Sophia," she said casually, "if you're not doing anything tonight, I hear Kim

Archibald has a new boyfriend. Maybe you can go to a hotel with him.”

I couldn't hold back a snort of laughter, but Georgia pulled me away before I could completely lose it. Her grip was firm, and when we were a safe distance from the corner, she shook her head.

“Boys are dumb,” she said with a dramatic sigh. “How could anyone choose Sophia over you?”

I smiled, warmth blooming in my chest. “It's a mystery.”

Having Georgia by my side made everything easier. Her loyalty and humor were like a shield against Sophia's passive-aggressive attempts to win me back.

Later, when the bell rang and Georgia and I split up, Mia ran over to me in the hallway. “Hey!” she said, her face lighting up. “I feel like I haven't talked to you in forever.”

“I know,” I said, feeling a pang of guilt. I'd been avoiding Mia because of Sophia, but I missed her. “How've you been?”

“I've been fine,” Mia said brightly. “My dad's going out of town this weekend to visit family, and my mom's planning a sleepover with her best friend. You should come over! I bet they'll let us drink wine with them.”

The offer made me grin. “Am I the only person you're inviting?”

“Of course. Is that okay?”

“Yeah, that sounds awesome. I can't wait.”

I was sure Mom would say yes—she loved Mia and her mom, and they were good friends.

"So, you and Georgia," Mia said. "Since when are you two so close?"

I shrugged. "We hung out a few weeks ago, and we clicked. She's a great friend—really fun to be around."

Mia raised an eyebrow. "Good to know. There've been rumors about her being...you know, hard to get along with. I'm glad that's not true."

"Not at all," I said. "It already feels like we've been friends for years."

Mia smiled warmly. "Well, maybe we can invite her to hang out with us sometime. I'd like to get to know her."

We reached my classroom, and I gave Mia a quick hug before heading inside. I couldn't help it—I was just so happy to have such amazing friends.

As I expected, Mom was fine with me spending the weekend at Mia's house. Friday night was perfect—sipping blackberry wine while giving each other pedicures and watching chick flicks. It was lighthearted and innocent, a refreshing change from my usual Fridays.

On Saturday, Mia's mom and her friend took us to the botanical garden and on a walking tour of the city. Mia asked if Georgia could come, and I happily called her. When I met her outside, I gently reminded her not to bring up Sophia.

The five of us had a fantastic time exploring the city. We had dinner at a nice restaurant before dropping Georgia off and heading back to Mia's house for round two of our sleepover.

It was an amazing weekend—until early Sunday morning.

Mom called Mia's house, and the moment her mom handed me the phone, I knew I was in trouble.

"Get home *right now*," Mom said, her voice sharp and furious.

My stomach dropped. "What's wrong?"

"Just get here. Now."

Mom's tone was terrifying. I hurried to pack up my things, muttering a quick apology to Mia before rushing out the door. My mind raced the entire way home, trying to figure out what I'd done wrong.

Chapter 17

Mom was waiting for me at the kitchen table. The sharp glare of the overhead light cast harsh shadows on her face, making her look even angrier than she had sounded on the phone. Her hands were clasped together tightly on the table, and her lips were pressed into a thin, trembling line. The air in the kitchen felt heavy, thick with tension, and I could feel every inch of it pressing down on me. The smell of leftover coffee lingered in the air, mixing with the faint scent of dish soap from the sink.

"You have one chance," she said slowly, her words deliberate, "to come clean and get a reduced punishment." Her voice was calm, but the undertone of fury was unmistakable.

My hands were clammy, slick with nervous sweat as I shifted awkwardly from one foot to the other. I could feel my heart pounding in my chest, each thud echoing in my ears. "Mom, I honestly don't know what you're talking about. I don't know what I did. I promise I have no idea." My voice wavered despite my efforts to stay calm.

Her expression darkened further, the muscles in her jaw tightening as she took a breath through her nose. "Well, let me help you out," she said, her tone laced with bitter disbelief. "I was at the store this morning, and I met up with someone whose child is in your class." She paused for effect, letting the weight of her words sink in before continuing. "They were told that you have an STD. An STD, Vanessa, what the hell is that about?"

My stomach dropped like a stone, and for a moment, I thought I might actually throw up right there in the middle of the kitchen.

The bile rose in my throat, but I swallowed it down, though my hands began to tremble at my sides. I didn't throw up, but my eyes began to fill with hot, stinging tears that blurred my vision.

"No, I don't!" I blurted out. It was painfully clear that I was on the verge of a full-blown meltdown. "That's totally untrue. I swear, Mom, I don't. Someone must have just made that up." My chest was heaving as I tried to control my breathing, desperate to stay composed but failing miserably.

Mom's face softened—just a little. Her shoulders dropped slightly, and her eyes searched mine, looking for any sign of deceit. I never cried. It wasn't my style, and she knew that. My tears had to be convincing.

I sniffled and took a shaky breath, wiping my eyes with the sleeve of my hoodie. "You know that if it was true, I'd just argue with you about it. You know me. Please trust me."

She tilted her head, her gaze lowering to her hands, which were now drumming rhythmically on the table. The sound was steady but loud in the otherwise silent room. Seconds dragged into what felt like hours before she finally spoke again. "Why would a rumor like that exist, Vanessa? Who would want to hurt your reputation like that?"

"I have no idea," I answered quickly, too quickly. The words were out of my mouth before I had time to think them through, but as soon as they hung in the air, my heart sank. Adrian. It had to be Adrian. My stomach churned as I thought about what I had done to him and what he might do in return.

But telling Mom the full truth about Adrian wasn't an option—not now. I scrambled for something plausible, something she might believe. "The only thing I can think of," I said cautiously, "is this one guy who asked me out, but I turned him down. Maybe he did it for revenge? I don't know." I bit my lip, hoping the lie would stick.

Mom stared at me for a while, and it was hard not to break down even more. Finally, she gave me the smallest smile. "I believe you, Vanessa."

The relief that washed over me was immediate and overwhelming. I exhaled so hard that my chest seemed to deflate, and my shoulders slumped as the tension drained from my body. I thought that having her on my side would make me feel better, and in some ways, it did, but the relief was short-lived. Before I knew it, the tears came back, harder this time.

I buried my face in my hands, the sobs wracking my chest as I let go of everything I'd been holding in. The sound of the kitchen chair scraping against the floor barely registered, but then I felt her arms around me, warm and firm and steady. She pulled me into a hug. It felt too good, too safe, and I clung to her like a lifeline as I cried into her shoulder.

****

On my way to school on Monday, my whole body was a furnace, burning with anger. The tears were gone now, replaced by a seething, simmering rage that bubbled just beneath the surface. I wasn't sad anymore. I was pissed.

No matter what it took, I was going to find out who had started this rumor about me. My fists clenched involuntarily as I walked, my nails digging into the soft flesh of my palms. I could almost feel the tension radiating off me like heat waves, my anger building with every step I took toward school. I wanted to scream, to throw something, to hit someone—anyone who had been part of this.

But everything changed the second I stepped through the school doors. The halls felt darker somehow like the walls were closing in around me. Every glance in my direction felt like a dagger, and the whispers weren't whispers at all—they were razor blades slicing through my skin. I could feel their eyes on me, boring into me, dissecting me. I wanted to scream at them, to tell them they were wrong, but my throat closed up, the words sticking there like cement.

I tried to keep my head high, to act like it didn't bother me, but the weight of their judgment crushed me. No matter how much I told myself it was a lie, it still made me feel disgusting. How was it possible for something completely untrue to make me feel so dirty? My skin crawled with every sideways glance, every half-hidden smirk.

By the time the recess bell rang, the fire inside me had burned out completely, leaving nothing but ash and exhaustion in its place. My feet felt heavy as I pushed my way through the crowded hallway, my only thought being to get away from all of it. I made a beeline for the bathroom, shoving past people who gave me curious or annoyed looks.

Inside the stall, I locked the door behind me and leaned my forehead against it, the cold metal soothing against my burning skin. My chest heaved, and then, finally, the tears came again. Hot, uncontrollable sobs that shook my entire body. I covered my mouth to muffle the sound, but it didn't matter. I was alone now, and for the first time all day, I didn't care if I broke down.

Chapter 18

I'd had some bad days at school in my life, but nothing like yesterday and today. People looking at me like I was diseased, the snickers and murmured jokes that weren't even subtle—none of it was anything I had ever experienced before. I was used to being liked or, at the very least, tolerated. This? This felt like I had been dropped into some awful alternate reality where everything I knew about my world was turned upside down.

Even my friends were hesitant to be around me, their smiles uneasy and their hands twitching nervously like they didn't want to get too close. I couldn't blame them, I guess. Rumors were like smoke, and no one wanted to get caught in the suffocating haze. It felt like they thought being near me might make people assume they had STDs, too. The only people who stuck by me were Mia and Georgia, my lifelines in this storm.

Mia was like a detective on a mission. She overheard something in the halls. She was relentless and determined to trace the rumor back to its source. Georgia, on the other hand, was my shield. She stayed by my side, literally glued to me as much as she could be, like a bodyguard with a vengeance. If anyone so much as whispered within earshot, she'd whip around with a glare that could freeze a volcano. She even threatened to fight a guy in the cafeteria when he made a snide comment loud enough for me to hear. She was the definition of ride-or-die, and I was constantly thanking God in my head for having such amazing friends.

But even with their support, the ache in my chest didn't go away. As much as I loved and appreciated them, they couldn't make me feel completely better. I'd always thought I didn't care what people thought about me, that I was above that kind of insecurity, but apparently, I was wrong. Their whispers crawled under my skin. Their stares seared into me like brands. I didn't know what to do about any of it.

After school, I went straight home. I didn't want to linger in the halls or around the campus a second longer than I had to. I needed the safety of my room, where no one could look at me like I was some kind of disgusting creature. The house was quiet when I got in, the kind of quiet that made me feel even lonelier than I already did. I hadn't even set my bag down when there was a loud, urgent knock on the front door.

It was Mia, wide-eyed and breathless. Her hair was a little messy, like she had sprinted all the way here, and her face was flushed with a mix of exertion and nerves. Before I could even open my mouth to invite her inside, she blurted out one word: "Sophia."

I blinked, confused. "What?"

Mia stepped past me into the house as if she couldn't wait another second. She was panting slightly, her words tumbling out between breaths. "Sophia started the rumor about you."

Her words hit me like a punch to the gut. My brain couldn't process them at first; it was like she was speaking in a language I didn't understand. I just stood there, frozen, staring at her with my mouth slightly open. Without waiting for me to respond, she grabbed my hand and led me to my own bedroom. Once we were inside, she shut the door firmly behind us, her expression grim.

"She told everyone at Hartenstein Park last Friday," Mia said, her voice quick and low. "I could tell Jasmine knew something. She avoided eye contact every time I brought it up. So I figured it had to be someone in T.W.A., and Jasmine didn't know whose side to take. But finally, I told her how hurt you were, and she cracked."

My chest felt tight as Mia continued, her words like daggers. "Sophia told everyone you'd been sleeping around. She said that's why you hadn't been hanging out with T.W.A. lately and why you and Georgia are such good friends now."

Anger bubbled up inside me, hot and sharp, rising so quickly that I felt like I might scream. I clenched my fists, my nails digging into my palms to keep myself grounded. It must have been clear on my face because Mia leaned back slightly, her eyes wide with concern.

"What's going on, Vanessa?" she asked softly. "Did something happen between you two? There has to be a reason she'd do that."

Mia was the last person I wanted to tell about this. She was my best friend, but she was also Sophia's cousin. It would put her in such an impossible position. But after everything she'd done for me—standing by me, digging for the truth—I couldn't lie to her anymore. She deserved the truth.

I took a deep breath, my voice shaking as I spoke. "I told her I had a big crush on a guy," I admitted, the words tasting bitter in my mouth. "And a few days later, she hooked up with him. I mean, it went all the way. They had sex while I was in the same room."

Mia's jaw dropped. Her face was a mix of shock and disbelief, and for a moment, she looked like she didn't know how to respond. I kept going, unable to stop now that I'd started. "Georgia was the only person I told. We were a little snippy with her last week because, honestly, she damn well deserved it. But I guess that wasn't enough for her. Sleeping with my crush wasn't enough—she had to ruin my reputation too."

Mia stared at me, her expression softening into something like sympathy. "I think I hate her, Mia," I said, my voice breaking slightly.

She reached out and took my hand, her grip warm and steady. "I don't blame you," she said quietly. "I think you have every right to."

I nodded, a lump forming in my throat. "Thank you. I think I need some time to think about this."

Mia gave me a hug before she left. I watched her walk down the street from the kitchen window, then went straight to my phone.

Sean answered on the second ring, his tone bright and casual, like he hadn't been part of the mess that turned my life upside down. "Hello?"

"Hey, it's Vanessa. Is Sophia there?" I kept my voice as calm as possible, almost sweet, masking the fury boiling just beneath the surface.

"She's in the bathroom," he said, clearly amused by something. I could practically hear the smirk in his voice. "We haven't seen you around in a while. From what I hear, you've been...*busy*. You know, you should be more careful, Vanessa. People don't really wanna date people who have STDs."

My grip on the phone tightened so much I thought it might crack, but I forced a smile onto my face, even though he couldn't see it. "Well, then that's really unfortunate for you, Sean. I probably passed my diseases on to Tyler when we hooked up, and he would've passed them on to Sophia when they had unprotected sex a couple of weeks ago. I'm sure whatever I have, you have it by now, too."

There was a stunned silence on the other end of the line. For a second, I thought the call had dropped, but then he spoke again, his voice quieter and laced with anger. "Did you say she...and Tyler?" He was grinding his teeth; I could hear the frustration bubbling up in his words.

"Oh, yeah," I said, feigning casual indifference. "She jumped into his bed like she'd been dying for a chance with him. In fact, if he's there right now, you might want to keep an eye on them at all times. I'm sure they're screwing around and laughing at you every time you're not around."

Sean inhaled sharply, and I imagined the veins in his neck bulging with the effort it took to keep his composure. "Well, that's good to know," he muttered, his voice low with barely contained rage.

I heard Sophia's voice in the background, distant but unmistakable. If she was out of the bathroom, it was showtime. "Glad I could help!" I chirped before hanging up.

I set the phone down, my heart racing. For a moment, I let myself picture the chaos unfolding on the other end of the line— Sean confronting Sophia, accusations flying, maybe even a tearful confession. It brought a sense of satisfaction that I hadn't felt in days. But I wasn't done yet. There was one more call to make.

I picked up the phone again, dialing the next number with deliberate precision. Sophia's dad answered on the second ring, his voice warm and cheerful. "It's great to hear from you, Vanessa!

How have you been?"

I sighed, letting a hint of sadness seep into my tone. "Not great, honestly. Sophia and I have been growing apart. I've been trying to support her, but she's...well, she's been making some really bad choices, and I'm so worried about her. I just had to call you."

"What's going on?" he asked, his tone shifting immediately to concern. "What's Sophia doing?"

I sighed again, louder this time, for effect. "Try not to be too mad at her, but...she has a boyfriend. They've been dating for a few months, and they've been, you know, having sex. I don't even think she's using protection." I paused, letting the weight of my words sink in. "She skips school to go to his house, and he's always there because he's twenty-three, and he makes money by selling drugs to people who go over to his house."

There was a long silence on the other end of the line, and when Sophia's dad spoke again, his voice was tight with barely controlled anger. "Where is this guy? What's his name?"

I gave him all the details, listing Sean's full name, his address, and the names of the people who lived with him. Every word dripped with sincerity, and I made sure to sound as heartbroken as I could. "I just thought you should know," I finished. "I'm really worried about her."

When we hung up, I leaned back against the kitchen counter and laughed out loud, the sound echoing in the quiet house. I could already picture the fallout from this. Sophia's dad was not the kind of man to let something like this slide. That would probably be the last time Sophia messed with me.

****

The next few days were some of the happiest I'd had in weeks. The storm clouds that had hung over my life seemed to lift, and for the first time since the rumor started, I felt like I could breathe again. My revenge scheme against Sophia had worked perfectly. Every time I saw her at school, her face was puffy and red like she'd been crying, her usual confident strut replaced with hurried, embarrassed steps. People whispered about her now, not me, and it felt good. I knew it wasn't the healthiest way to handle things, but after everything she'd done, I didn't feel bad.

Still, even with my small victory, the sadness lingered. Losing a friend, no matter how awful they turned out to be, left a hole that was hard to fill. I hoped this feeling wouldn't last forever.

When the weekend came around, I found myself sitting by the phone, staring at it like it held all the answers to my problems. I picked it up and put it back in the receiver six times without dialing. I wanted to call Dad, to ask him about his trip up here, to talk about anything, really. But every time I worked up the nerve, the words stuck in my throat. I wasn't sure how I would even face him in person if I couldn't muster the courage to talk to him on the phone.

****

On Sunday, the phone rang. My heart leaped into my throat. Maybe it was Dad calling me because it was Father's Day! I snatched up the receiver, barely letting it ring twice. "Hello?"

"Hola, mi amor."

My heart raced at the sound of her voice. "Abuelita! Hi!"

"It's so good to hear your voice, *mi amor*. How are you?"

"I'm really good. I've been wanting to call, but...anyway, I'm so happy you called. I wish you and Abuelito could come up when Dad comes because I—"

"Vanessa." Abuelita's tone shifted, soft but heavy, and it stopped me mid-sentence. She sounded off, and my heart started pounding again, but this time, it wasn't with excitement. "Yeah?" I asked hesitantly.

"I'm so sorry to tell you this, but your dad..." She sighed, her voice thick with emotion. "He's in jail. Not so unusual for him, I know, but because of the hearings and things that he'll have coming up, he just won't be able to visit you. I'm sorry, Vanessa," she said again, her voice breaking slightly.

My head buzzed, the words not fully registering. "Okay," I said, my voice flat. "Thanks for calling me."

"I wish things could be different," Abuelita said, and I could tell she was trying not to cry. "*Te amo*, Vanessa."

"I love you too," I said softly before hanging up.

I stared at the phone in my hand, my mind blank. This was all so unsurprising that I felt stupid for being disappointed. Embarrassed, even for actually believing, for one fleeting moment, that things could be different this time.

And just like that, the weight of everything came crashing back down on me.

Chapter 19

Mom came into my room, towel-drying her hair. The damp strands clung to her face, and she looked exhausted but still managed that tired smile she always wore for me. "Who was that on the phone?" she asked casually.

Her face dropped immediately when she saw mine. I didn't have to say much. The slump of my shoulders, the dull ache in my eyes—it was all there for her to read. I just shrugged, but my voice came out uneven when I replied, "Abuelita. She said Dad's in jail and won't be coming to visit."

Her breath caught, just for a second. Mom lifted her chin and raised her eyebrows, the way she always did when she wanted to say something cutting about Dad but thought better of it. She stood there for a moment, visibly collecting herself. Her fingers tightened around the towel. Then, she exhaled slowly, took a couple of deep breaths, and said, "I'm sorry, Vanessa," with a kind of practiced gentleness that I knew wasn't easy for her. She left my room quietly, shutting the door with a softness that felt like an apology in itself.

I stared at the closed door, my mind buzzing. Why did Mom always apologize when Dad messed up? It wasn't her fault. It was all him—every mess, every broken promise, every absence. She had nothing to do with this.

It was unbelievable but completely believable at the same time. How could he not manage to keep himself out of trouble for just one month? Just one month so he could come see me. Was that really so much to ask? The worst part—the part that hurt even more than the disappointment—was that I wouldn't be surprised if he got arrested on purpose, just so he didn't have to visit me.

I rubbed my eyes, feeling the weight of frustration press down on me. For a second, I thought about getting out of the house, heading into the city to distract myself. But I stopped just as quickly as the thought came. The city would be full of fathers and daughters today, smiling families celebrating Father's Day. I could almost see it: dads carrying their kids on their shoulders, sitting with them at restaurants, laughing over ice cream. The image made my stomach churn.

My face burned with frustration and anger. I hated hearing my friends talk about their dads like they were heroes. I hated shows like *Full House*, where the Tanner girls had not one, but three father figures—three! Meanwhile, I couldn't even have one. It wasn't fair. I hated the jealousy that twisted in my chest when I saw people with everything I wanted, knowing that the reason I didn't have it was all because of Dad.

I leaned back on my bed, staring up at the ceiling as my thoughts spiraled. The plaster above me looked cracked in the corner, almost like it was splitting apart, and it reminded me of how I felt inside. "I wish I knew what You saw in him when You made him a father," I said to God, my voice quiet but heavy. "Because to me, it doesn't seem like he was ever meant to be one."

It was true. Dad seemed destined *not* to be a dad. Ever since he was my age, he'd loved drinking, getting high, and picking fights with anyone who gave him the wrong look. When he left Cuba for Canada with Abuelita and Abuelito, he didn't leave those bad habits behind. And when I came along, he didn't bother to slow down for me.

There were pictures of us together from when I was small—probably buried somewhere deep in a box in a forgotten closet. I hadn't looked at them in years, but the images were still clear in my mind. Back then, I thought I looked so happy. Maybe I was.

But memories fade, and so much time had passed since I'd last seen him. The good memories were hazy now, like a dream slipping out of reach. The bad memories, though—they stayed sharp. They lived in the corners of my mind, creeping out in nightmares or striking suddenly, leaving me feeling sick. The worst memory was always the last time I saw him—and why it was the last time.

My eyes stung with tears. I wiped at them angrily, ashamed of how much it hurt. I don't think I had ever said out loud how much I wanted to have a dad. Even if I wanted to tell someone, I wouldn't know how. It was like a secret I carried inside me, too painful to share. How could I admit that I wanted someone in my life who made it so clear that he didn't want me in his?

PART 2
3 Years Later

Chapter 20

"Hey! What's up?" Mia's voice came through the phone, bright and full of energy. I could already tell she had something exciting to share.

I lay back on my bed, already smiling at her enthusiasm. "Nothing at all. What's up with you?"

"Michael and his roommates are finally fully moved into their new apartment," she said, the words spilling out in a rush. "They're having a housewarming party tonight. You in?"

I rolled my eyes, even though she couldn't see me. "Yeah, duh. What time?"

"I had a feeling you'd say that." She laughed. "It starts at nine."

I glanced at my clock. It was already three in the afternoon. Time to start planning. Tucking the phone between my ear and shoulder, I began rifling through my closet for something to wear. "What are you wearing?" I asked Mia. Knowing her, it would be something bold—especially with her major crush on Bruno, one of Michael's roommates.

"That black backless dress with a slit on the hem," she said, and I could hear the grin in her voice.

I grinned back, even though she couldn't see it. "You'll look so hot. I need to make sure you don't outshine me too much."

She scoffed. "Like I could ever outshine you." Then, without skipping a beat, she added, "I'm thinking I'll meet you at your place around nine, and we can walk to his place together?"

"Sounds good," I said. We hung up, and I immediately got to work, straightening my hair and applying my makeup with the kind of precision that only came when you really wanted to impress someone.

By the time Mia arrived, the city was dark, the streets glowing softly under the orange haze of streetlights. When she stepped into the light, I took one look at her and smiled. "If Bruno isn't already into you, he will be soon."

She laughed and hooked her arm through mine. "I hope so. I finally tried that eyeliner trick Georgia taught me. She was right—it's a game-changer."

"Ugh," I groaned playfully. "I miss her. I mean, I'm glad her dad found such a good job in Toronto, but—"

"I know," Mia said, her voice wistful. "We'll visit her this summer. We have to."

From the outside, Michael's apartment looked decent, cleaner and more put together than most student apartments. The building had the faint smell of fresh paint, like the landlord was trying to make it seem more appealing than it actually was. Mia knocked on the door, and we waited for what felt like forever before Cedric, Michael's cousin and one of his roommates, opened it.

Cedric grinned as soon as he saw Mia, leaning in to kiss her cheeks the way they always did because of their French grandparents. I stayed back, already bracing myself. That grin of his always meant trouble for me. Sure enough, his gaze shifted to me, his smirk widening like he'd just thought of the perfect way to mess with me.

"Hey, Vanessa," he said, his voice dripping with mockery.

"How come your boobs look smaller than the last time I saw you? Do you stuff your bra or something?"

The words hit me like an annoying itch I couldn't scratch. But I'd been dealing with Cedric for long enough to know how to handle him. Without missing a beat, I replied, "Yep. You know, you should try it. Maybe if you stuffed the front of your underwear, people would stop mistaking you for a girl."

Mia tried to hide her laugh by walking away quickly, but Cedric and I both heard it. His smirk vanished, replaced by a glare. "Keep talking, and I'll kick you out," he said, his tone sharper now.

"Sure you will," I shot back, brushing past him to step into the apartment.

The place was packed. Music pumped from speakers in the corner, and the air was thick with the scent of alcohol and something else I couldn't quite place—probably weed. People were scattered everywhere, lounging on furniture that looked like it had been salvaged from thrift stores, talking loudly over the music. It was exactly the kind of party I'd been expecting.

Mia had already found Bruno. She was leaning toward him, her laughter louder and more exaggerated than usual. I smiled to myself. She was playing the game perfectly. But then my stomach twisted. Michael. If Bruno was busy with Mia, I needed to keep Michael distracted so he wouldn't notice. He was the kind of big brother who wouldn't be thrilled about his sister hooking up with his roommate, and I wasn't about to let him ruin Mia's chance with Bruno.

I started weaving through the crowd, scanning for Michael. But he was too popular for his own good. Every time I caught sight of him, he was surrounded by people, laughing, talking, and generally being the life of the party. I sighed, realizing I wasn't going to get him alone tonight.

Fine. If I couldn't get Michael's attention, I'd do what I always did: make the best of a bad situation. I grabbed a drink from someone's outstretched hand and joined a small group of people, chatting and laughing as if I wasn't completely preoccupied. One drink turned into two, then three, and before I knew it, I was drifting from group to group, taking whatever was offered to me. The apartment seemed to blur around me, the music growing louder and fuzzier in my ears. I was laughing at jokes I didn't really understand, smiling at people I didn't really know. Somewhere in the haze, I lost track of time—and Michael.

When I finally decided to crash, I could barely keep my eyes open. My body felt heavy and disconnected, like my limbs didn't belong to me. I collapsed onto the floor in the living room, not even bothering to find a couch. The last thing I remembered was the way the world spun when I closed my eyes.

****

The sun was fully up when I woke, its bright light streaming through the curtainless window and hitting me square in the face. I groaned, shielding my eyes as I sat up. My head throbbed, and my mouth was dry as sandpaper. Blinking, I looked around. I was on the floor, surrounded by empty cups and passed-out partygoers. The couch beside me was empty. I must have been too drunk to even climb onto it.

I stood slowly, my legs wobbly beneath me. My stomach churned, a nauseating reminder of how much I'd had to drink. I needed water, but more than that, I needed to find Mia. Carefully, I tiptoed through the apartment, stepping over sleeping bodies and trying not to wake anyone.

Bruno's bedroom door was cracked open, and I peeked inside. Mia was there, curled up next to Bruno, her arm draped over his chest. I couldn't help but smile. She'd done it. Good for her.

But my smile faded as something cold settled in my stomach. Michael. If I wasn't in his bed, did that mean someone else was? The thought sent a wave of nausea through me that had nothing to do with the alcohol.

I made my way to Michael's room, my heart pounding harder with every step. His door was closed, and I hesitated before opening it just enough to peek inside. Relief washed over me when I saw him alone, sprawled out on his bed. But the relief was short-lived. I still couldn't remember what had happened last night. Had he hooked up with someone? Could that someone have been me? The thought made my stomach flip. If it was me, why wouldn't he have asked me to stay in his bed?

I stood in the doorway, staring at him as he slept. His chest rose and fell evenly, his face peaceful in a way I rarely saw when he was awake. For a moment, I let myself imagine that he'd been waiting for me last night, that he'd chosen me. But the truth was, I didn't know what had happened, and not knowing was almost worse than any answer.

Michael stirred in his sleep, exhaling loudly, and I jumped back, hiding behind the wall. My heart raced as I pressed myself against the cool surface, trying to calm down.

"Vanessa?" a voice whispered behind me.

I spun around, startled. It was Mia. She looked groggy but

happy, her makeup smudged and her hair a mess. "What are you doing?" she asked, her voice soft so she wouldn't wake anyone.

I hesitated, my cheeks burning. "Just trying to remember what happened last night," I admitted.

Mia gave me a knowing look, like she'd been waiting for me to say that. "Well," she said slowly, a small smile creeping onto her face, "I hooked up with Bruno."

I started to smile, but before I could say anything, she added, "Twice."

We shared a quiet high-five, grinning at each other like conspirators. "Congratulations," I whispered.

Her smile faded slightly when I asked, "What about me? I don't remember anything after a certain point."

Mia sighed, her shoulders slumping. "He hooked up with some other girl. I didn't find out until they were already finished, so I couldn't stop them. I'm sorry."

The words hit me like a punch to the gut. My stomach twisted painfully. "Who was it?" I asked, my voice barely above a whisper.

"I don't know her name," Mia admitted. "But I think they might have a class together."

So that was it. Some other girl, probably nineteen like him. I wasn't good enough when Michael and I hooked up years ago, and apparently, I wasn't good enough now.

"I'm ready to go home," I said, trying to keep my voice steady. But inside, I felt like I was falling apart.

Mia nodded, her expression softening. "Okay," she said quietly.

She reached out to squeeze my hand, but I pulled away, pretending to adjust my bag. I couldn't let her see how much it hurt. Not now.

We left the apartment in silence, the bright morning sun harsh and unforgiving. But the worst part wasn't the light. It was knowing that no matter how much I wanted Michael, he'd never want me back.

Chapter 21

I didn't do much the next week. Summer break had just started, and a lot of my friends wanted to hang out, but I was still so bummed and embarrassed about what had happened at Michael's party that I didn't really want to go out and do anything with them. Every time I even thought about stepping outside, I could feel the ghost of my own humiliation creeping over my skin, reminding me of every awkward moment, every misstep, every sideways glance I imagined people giving me.

Luckily, I didn't have to come up with any excuses. Lily would be switching schools next year to an upper elementary school, and she was so excited about it that all she wanted to do was go shopping for new clothes and school supplies. Her energy was endless, bouncing from store to store, holding up shirts to her small frame, turning every notebook over in her hands like it held the secrets to the universe. It was the kind of excitement only kids had—the kind that could make something as mundane as pencils and backpacks feel like treasures.

Oliver was more than happy to hand me money to take her shopping if it meant he didn't have to be involved. He hated crowded places and even more than that, he hated making choices about things he didn't care about. As long as Lily was happy, that was enough for him.

So, I'd been out and about with Lily almost every day that week. The days blurred together in a haze of clothing racks, checkout lines, and Lily's bright chatter about all the things she was looking forward to. The excitement in her voice made it hard to feel too sorry for myself, even if the sting of my own problems still lingered beneath the surface.

But school shopping felt weird, considering I wouldn't be going back myself. Father Kentucky had officially shut down, and since I legally didn't have to return to school, I wasn't going to. The decision had felt bold, almost freeing, but now, in the quiet moments between Lily's laughter and the clatter of hangers, doubt crept in. Was I making the right choice? Would I regret it later? It was impossible to know. But in that moment, standing under the fluorescent lights of another department store, it felt right.

Then Friday came, and with it, a restless itch under my skin. I was tired of wallowing. I wanted to do something. I wasn't sure what yet, but I knew I couldn't spend another night in my own head.

I decided to go to the metro, hoping I might run into someone I knew.

The air in the underground station was thick with the familiar mix of sweat, metal, and the faint sting of tobacco smoke. I went straight to the tucked-away corner where I always smoked because if any of my friends had the same idea, they'd end up here sooner or later. The moment I leaned against the grimy wall and lit my cigarette, I felt a sense of familiarity settle over me—something close to comfort, even if it was laced with solitude.

Then, suddenly, someone bumped into me.

I turned, a sharp inhale caught in my throat. The girl in front of me looked just as startled as I felt, her eyes wide in surprise. And mine? They had to be just as wide but for a different reason.

She was breathtaking.

Jet black hair cascaded down to her waist like something out of a shampoo commercial, catching the dim station light in a way that made it almost shimmer. Her deep brown eyes glinted with curiosity, her features sharp yet soft in the same breath. I felt an odd kind of heat creep up my neck, something between awe and intimidation.

"Mind if I smoke here with you?" she asked, offering me a smile that showed off a perfect row of white teeth.

I snapped out of my daze and smiled back. "Not at all. I'm Vanessa."

"Sandy." She held out a cigarette to me, and I instinctively leaned in, using mine to light hers. Our fingers brushed for half a second—barely anything—but my skin tingled anyway.

"What're you doing here alone on a Friday night?" she asked, exhaling a slow stream of smoke into the air.

"Waiting for fun to find me," I said. "Or trouble. Whichever comes first."

Sandy liked that answer. I could tell by the way her lips curled up, the way her eyes sparkled.

She was nineteen, she told me. Her family had moved here from Morocco when she was a baby. She worked as a makeup artist at a local mall. She had a voice like melted chocolate—smooth, rich, and somehow comforting. She was so effortlessly cool, and I felt drawn to her instantly like she was magnetic.

And the best part? She seemed to feel the same way about me.

We sat there talking, laughing, trading stories and secrets like we'd known each other for years instead of minutes. The cigarettes burned down between our fingers, replaced by fresh ones. The night stretched on, but neither of us seemed to notice.

Then, as she lit her next cigarette, Sandy grinned. "So, I'm going out clubbing with a friend tomorrow. Three is more fun than two—you should come with us."

She rattled off the address to her apartment, telling me to meet them there.

I had a really good feeling about this.

So, of course, I agreed.

****

The next night, at exactly eleven, I walked to Sandy's apartment.

It was only a few blocks from mine, close enough that the night air felt like an old friend instead of something unfamiliar. The city buzzed around me: the hum of traffic, distant laughter, the occasional honk of a horn.

When Sandy opened the door, I was struck all over again by how pretty she was. The overhead light in her apartment bathed her in a warm glow, making her seem even more unreal than before.

"Hey!" she greeted, flashing me a wide smile before leading me inside.

The place was small but cozy, the kind of apartment that smelled like perfume and warm fabric softener. The walls were lined with string lights, casting a golden hue over the space.

She led me to the bathroom, where another girl was perched on the counter, doing her makeup.

"This is Sarah," Sandy introduced.

Sarah had long, blonde hair and the kind of bone structure you saw on magazine covers. She was just as stunning as Sandy, and suddenly, I felt like an outsider in my own body—too young, too plain, too… not them.

But I forced myself to play it cool. "Hey. I'm Vanessa."

"Nice to meet you," Sarah said, not pausing as she carefully dragged a mascara wand through her lashes.

Sandy grinned at me and reached for a bottle of mousse, scrunching it through her thick hair. "We're going to Sofa's After Hours Club. Ever been?"

I had heard of Sofa's After Hours, of course. Everyone had. But I'd never gone, mostly because of my age. Every now and then, I could slip into local pubs without getting carded, but Sofa's After Hours Club was on another level.

"No," I admitted. "But I'd love to go. It's just that I'm only sixteen."

Sarah barely blinked. "That doesn't matter. As long as you look old enough, you'll get in."

Sandy took my hand and led me to her closet. "You have the look—you just need to dress the part."

She pulled out a black mini skirt, a red spaghetti strap top, and a pair of black heels, handing them to me.

The clothes looked more like they'd fit Lily than me, but I wasn't about to back out now.

And once I put them on?

I couldn't stop checking myself out in the mirror.

Sandy definitely knew what she was doing.

Sarah curled my hair while Sandy worked on my makeup, and as we got ready, I felt something shift inside me. The nervousness faded, replaced by excitement. After striking some poses in the mirror together—Sandy adjusting her sleek black dress, Sarah pouting at her reflection, and me trying to match their effortless confidence—we called a cab to take us downtown to Sofa's After Hours Club. The night air was thick with the scent of car exhaust and lingering summer heat as we stepped onto the sidewalk outside the club. The neon glow from the entrance sign flickered against the brick wall, casting a hazy, dreamlike light over the queue of hopeful partygoers waiting by the roped-off entrance.

The bass inside the underground club was so powerful that we could feel it vibrating through the pavement beneath our feet. The heavy, rhythmic thump pounded against my chest, syncing with my own heartbeat. I stole a glance at Sandy and Sarah—Sandy adjusting the strap of her dress, Sarah checking her lipstick in the reflection of her phone screen. They both looked completely at ease like they belonged here. I wanted to feel that way, too.

Sarah leaned in, her breath warm against my ear. "A bouncer is gonna come to check us out and see if we're good to go inside," she whispered. "One of the smartest things to do is get to know the bouncers because that way, you'll always get in."

As if on cue, the heavy metal door swung open, and a burly bouncer with a shaved head stepped outside. His black T-shirt clung to his broad chest, and his muscular arms were crossed as he scanned the crowd. His gaze landed on Sandy first, then Sarah, then me. His expression barely shifted, but without a word, he lifted the velvet rope and gestured us inside.

Sarah beamed, throwing her arms around him in a quick but affectionate hug before pulling back and winking at me. "Told you," she murmured under her breath as we stepped past the line of envious onlookers.

The three of us linked hands, gripping each other tightly as we descended the steep, dimly lit staircase. The deeper we went, the stronger the bass became until it felt like it was pulsing through my bones. I could feel the excitement twisting in my stomach, my anticipation building with every step. My nerves flickered, but the sheer thrill of the unknown completely overshadowed them. I just knew this was going to be a good night.

At the bottom of the stairs, we stepped into the hip-hop room. The air was thick and warm, tinged with sweat and the faint scent of something sweet and smoky. Black leather couches lined the walls, filled with people in sleek outfits, sipping neon-colored drinks or lost in conversation. On the floor, bodies moved in sync with the deep bass of an old-school East Coast hip-hop track, their motions fluid and hypnotic.

I started bobbing my head immediately, unable to resist the infectious energy of the room. The beat settled into my bloodstream, matching the rhythm of my pulse. Sandy led us to an open spot on one of the couches, sliding in effortlessly, her movements graceful and unbothered. Sarah followed, draping one leg over the other as she swayed slightly to the music.

Then, Sandy reached into her bra and pulled out a tiny plastic bag. Inside were three small, blue pills.

She tipped the bag, letting one pill drop into Sarah's open palm, then another into mine, before taking the last one for herself.

Sarah didn't hesitate—she popped hers onto her tongue and swallowed dry, barely even blinking. Sandy did the same, her lips curling into a knowing smile. Their ease made it seem like the most natural thing in the world.

I hesitated for half a second, but the moment felt too perfect to resist. If they weren't worried, why should I be? Without overthinking it, I tossed mine back and swallowed.

For a while, we just sat there, soaking in the music and the atmosphere, letting time stretch and fold over itself. People came and went, conversations drifting in and out like waves. Laughter rang out over the bass-heavy track, mixing with the clinking of glasses and the shuffle of feet on the dance floor.

Then, it hit.

One moment, I felt good. The next, I felt amazing.

A rush of warmth spread through me like liquid light filling my veins. My fingertips tingled, my chest expanded with an overwhelming sense of euphoria, and my heartbeat, oh God, my heartbeat, was alive. Every sound, every color, every movement around me was suddenly sharper, clearer, more beautiful. I needed to move. I needed to dance.

"Let's go!" Sandy shouted over the music, her eyes glittering like fireflies.

We sprang from the couch and ran straight to the dance floor, laughing as we shoved past groups of people. The music swallowed us whole. My arms lifted, my body swayed—I didn't even know how I was dancing, but I didn't care. I couldn't care. It all felt too good. My skin was electric, and my breath came in gasps, but I didn't want to stop. I never wanted to stop.

For a second, a flicker of paranoia crept in—Was it obvious I was on something? Was I acting weird?

I glanced around, but the moment my eyes landed on the crowd, I knew. Everyone was feeling the same thing. Their bodies moved just like mine, faces lifted toward the flashing lights with the same blissed-out expressions. We were all in this together, all part of the same heartbeat.

The song ended, but the energy between us didn't. Sandy grabbed my hand, Sarah grabbed the other one, and we squeezed our fingers together as we headed toward the stairs. My legs felt like they were floating as we climbed, my heart hammering in sync with the fading bass. With every step, the music shifted—hip hop melting into deep, pulsing techno.

We entered a new room, where the walls seemed to pulse with color, shifting from deep purples to fiery reds and electric blues. A haze of weed smoke hung heavy in the air, curling above the crowd like ghostly tendrils. The DJ was perched above the dance floor, his hands flying over the mixer, sending wave after wave of hypnotic house beats crashing over us.

The energy in this room was even wilder. The crowd moved harder, bodies pressed together, their movements more frantic, more desperate—like they were fighting to keep this feeling alive. The bass was deeper, the beats sharper.

We threw ourselves into the chaos, merging with the tide of bodies. Strangers became friends in an instant, hands reaching out, laughter spilling from unfamiliar lips, sweat-slicked skin brushing against my own. Time lost all meaning. There were no hours, no minutes—just this moment, stretching into forever.

I felt so lucky.

To have them.

To be here.

And I never wanted it to end.

Chapter 22

The next weekend, I went back to Sofa's After Hours Club with Sandy and Sarah. And the weekend after that. The week itself became nothing more than an interruption—five dull, dragging days that stood in the way of my next electrifying weekend. The moment Friday night rolled around, my heart quickened, and my body practically vibrated with anticipation. I had finally found where I fit in.

One particular Friday night, Sofa's After Hours hosted an all-white event. The place transformed into a glowing, dreamlike sea of ivory, platinum, and cream. The strobes reflected off the sea of white outfits, making everyone look like celestial beings lost in a rhythmic trance. It was a statement, a feeling, a collective experience. It was impossible to tell where one person ended, and the next began, an embodiment of the unity we felt on that dance floor. Sandy, Sarah, and I surrendered ourselves completely, letting the music dictate our every move. We twirled, we laughed, we lost ourselves in the hypnotic beats, in the heat of so many bodies moving in perfect synchrony.

Time blurred.

Before we knew it, we were dancing under a haze of euphoria from one in the morning until ten, until the harsh overhead lights flickered on, making everyone groan in protest. The illusion shattered, but the remnants of the night still clung to us—our skin damp with sweat, our voices hoarse from screaming lyrics, our legs barely holding us up.

Sandy and Sarah, still high off the night, invited me back to their apartment, but I could feel the magic fading from my body. The pill had worn off, and exhaustion hit me like a freight train. My limbs felt heavy. My head floated somewhere between lucidity and delirium.

"I can't," I murmured, rubbing my temples. "I need sleep. I need, like, a week of sleep."

They groaned but didn't push it. "Fine, but we're kidnapping you next time," Sarah declared before giving me a dramatic hug goodbye. Sandy just smirked. "Get some rest. You'll need it for next weekend."

I nodded absentmindedly, already half in a daze, as I stumbled toward home.

****

When I reached my fourplex, I hesitated at the door. A cold realization settled in my stomach. Mom. She'd be up. And she'd be pissed.

I glanced at my reflection in the window next to the door and winced. My makeup was a smudged disaster, with black streaks under my eyes and glitter still clinging to my cheeks. My once sleek ponytail had turned into a tangled mess, and my white outfit, once pristine, was now a canvas of spilled drinks and sweat stains. There was no way I could pass for someone who had just had an innocent sleepover at a friend's house.

Steeling myself, I turned the knob and stepped inside as quietly as possible. The dim glow from the kitchen confirmed my fears— she was waiting.

Her arms were crossed, her expression a perfect mix of worry and anger. She didn't even wait for me to speak.

"Where the hell have you been?" Her voice was sharp, but underneath, I caught something else. Not just frustration—fear.

I swallowed and forced a casual shrug. "Just at a friend's house. We lost track of time and ended up never going to sleep." My voice was even practiced. "So, I'm going to go take a nap."

She studied me, her sharp eyes scanning every detail, but whether she believed me or just didn't have the energy to argue, she let me go. I took the victory without hesitation, retreating to my room before she could change her mind.

I shut my door and yanked the curtains closed, drowning my room in comforting darkness. With shaky fingers, I peeled off my clothes, too tired to care where they landed. The second my body hit the bed, I was out, slipping into the kind of sleep that felt like sinking into another world.

When I woke up, it felt like I'd been hit by a truck. My throat was painfully dry, my body sore in places I didn't even realize could ache. I groaned, rolling over to squint at my alarm clock.

1:00 AM.

My eyes widened. I had slept for fourteen hours.

The apartment was eerily quiet. I moved carefully, wincing as I sat up, my muscles protesting the motion. Hunger gnawed at my stomach, so I tiptoed to the kitchen, filling a glass with water and gulping it down like I'd just crossed a desert. Then another. And another.

Once my throat didn't feel like sandpaper, I raided the kitchen for anything edible. Potato chips, cookies, stale crackers—anything

I could shove into my mouth without effort. I ate, standing up, leaning against the counter, chewing mechanically while my mind drifted, still lost somewhere between the hazy memories of Sofa's After Hours and the reality of my kitchen.

Once I was no longer on the verge of starvation, I debated staying up. But there was nothing to do. I sighed and crawled back to bed.

Amazingly, I slept another nine hours.

When I finally woke up, it was broad daylight. I wandered into the kitchen, feeling somewhat human again. Mom and Oliver were already at the table, finishing breakfast.

The moment Oliver saw me, he leaned back in his chair, raising an eyebrow. "What do you even do these days besides go out with your friends and sleep?" His tone was sharp, laced with disapproval.

I tensed, recognizing the trap. No answer would satisfy him.

I simply stared at him, refusing to take the bait.

He didn't wait for an answer. "Since you decided you're not going back to school, you're getting a job. If you're gonna party all the time, fine—but I'm not paying for it."

Just like that, he was done. He tossed his dirty dishes into the sink with a loud clatter and strode out the door without another word.

Mom and I both watched him leave, the tension lingering even after his footsteps disappeared.

I turned to her, wary. "You're really going to make me get a job?"

She shrugged, an odd expression on her face. "I actually got a job myself. Bartender at the airport. Four days a week."

That caught me off guard. I frowned. "What's going on? Why do we both need jobs all of a sudden?"

For a split second, something dark flickered across her face. It was there and gone so fast that I almost convinced myself I imagined it. Then she smiled, but it didn't quite reach her eyes.

"It'll be nice to have some extra income," she said vaguely. Then, too casually, she added, "And besides, there are a lot of good opportunities in Alberta. Having some savings in case we move wouldn't be a bad idea."

She stood, stretching as if the conversation was over. "Anyway, I'm going to lie down for a bit." And with that, she disappeared into her room, leaving me standing there, confusion curling in my stomach.

Alberta?

We'd never talked about moving. Oliver's job was here, and I couldn't see him wanting to leave. None of it made sense.

I thought about knocking on her door, demanding an explanation—but then I remembered Oliver's words.

I had to get a job.

A deep, sinking dread settled in my chest.

I sighed, resigned. I guessed I'd have to start looking.

Chapter 23

I spent the week scouring newspaper listings, scanning every job posting I could find, and pounding the pavement in Ville Saint-Laurent. The summer air was thick with heat, and every store or restaurant I stepped into offered a brief respite of cool air conditioning before I was back out under the relentless sun. My feet ached from walking, and my fingers were smudged with ink from flipping through newspapers, circling potential jobs in ballpoint pen. Some places barely glanced at my résumé before shaking their heads. Others took it with half-hearted smiles, making promises I knew they wouldn't keep.

By Thursday, my persistence paid off. I landed a hostess job at Italienne du Saint-Laurent, a bustling Italian restaurant with red-and-white checkered tablecloths and the intoxicating smell of garlic and baked bread constantly lingering in the air. The manager, a woman named Carla with sharp eyes and a no-nonsense attitude, looked me up and down before handing me a schedule. "Twenty hours a week," she said. "Weekdays only."

I made sure to emphasize that I was only available during the week. There was no way I was letting work interfere with my weekends—those were sacred. Weekends were for adventure, for late nights and neon lights.

By the time Friday afternoon rolled around, I was sprawled out on my bed, flipping idly through a magazine, when my phone rang. Expecting Sandy or Sarah, I answered lazily, only to freeze slightly when I heard Mia's voice.

"How've you been?" she asked, her tone careful, almost

hesitant.

I sat up, running a hand through my hair. "I've been good. How about you?"

"Good, too." She sighed, the sound crackling over the line. "Look, I know things have been awkward since Michael's party, but I miss you. Can we do something tonight? Go out to The Dome, maybe?"

Her words hit me like a rush of nostalgia. The Dome—crowded, loud, the kind of place where you could lose yourself in flashing lights and swirling bodies. I hadn't realized just how much I missed Mia until that moment. There had been an unspoken tension since Michael's party, and though neither of us had explicitly addressed it, I could feel it lingering like a ghost between us. But right now, all that mattered was that she wanted to reconnect.

"That sounds perfect," I said, already feeling the familiar buzz of excitement stir inside me. "Meet me at my place around ten?"

Mia agreed, and when she showed up, I was struck by just how much I had missed her. Her presence was electric, her laughter infectious. We spent the entire cab ride catching up, our voices overlapping, stories spilling out as we filled in the blanks of each other's summer.

When we arrived at The Dome, the line was already snaking around the block, a steady thrum of anticipation in the air. The neon glow from the club's sign cast flickering shades of pink and blue over the crowd. We found ourselves standing behind two guys who claimed to be twenty-one, tall, confident, just drunk enough to be entertaining.

The moment I heard "twenty-one," I switched into charm mode.

I tilted my head just slightly, let out a perfectly timed laugh, and tucked a strand of hair behind my ear in a way I knew drew attention. Years of experience had taught me that guys loved that—small, deliberate movements that made them feel like they had my undivided attention.

Mia picked up on my game instantly, falling into rhythm with me effortlessly. It was like we had never missed a beat. We played along, sharing coy smiles, letting them talk, feigning interest just enough to keep them engaged. And just like that, we were inside, bypassing the line with a simple flirtatious exchange.

At the bar, the air was thick with the scent of alcohol and sweat, bodies pressed together in a sea of movement. I leaned over the counter, just enough to make my intentions clear, and waved at the bartender.

"A round of shots over here!" I called out, my voice cutting through the music.

I turned my attention back to one of the guys, flashing a wink. It was almost too easy. His wallet was out in an instant, and moments later, we were throwing back vodka shots, the burn of the alcohol igniting a familiar warmth in my chest.

Mia and I transitioned seamlessly from shots to mixed drinks, the colors swirling like liquid candy in our glasses. By the time we made it to the dance floor, Mia had her arm wrapped around my waist, her breath warm against my ear as she yelled over the music.

"I love going on adventures with you," she said, her voice filled with that unmistakable rush of the night. "It's a guaranteed good time."

And she was right. The night blurred into a hazy dream of

music, movement, and laughter. Once we'd had our fill of liquor, we executed the delicate art of slipping away from the guys. They barely noticed—we were ghosts by the time they turned back around. Free from any obligations, Mia and I danced with whoever we pleased, spinning from one conversation to the next, soaking in the energy of the night.

By the time the club began to wind down, we were starving. The neon lights of the pizza place across the street were calling us. The moment we stepped inside, the scent of melted cheese and crispy dough washed over us like a comforting embrace.

Mia's face lit up as she spotted familiar faces. "Tony, Noah! Hey!"

She grabbed my hand, leading me toward a booth where two guys sat.

"This is Noah," she said, nodding toward a handsome Middle Eastern guy with a scruffy face, his dark eyes flicking up to meet mine with easy confidence. Then she gestured to the guy across from him. "And this is Tony."

Tony. My eyes locked onto him, and suddenly, everything else faded. He was tall and lean, with blonde hair that fell effortlessly over his forehead and piercing blue eyes that seemed to see straight through me.

Mia's voice barely registered as she said, "This is my best friend, Vanessa."

I smiled, trying not to think about whether I looked too sweaty or disheveled from the night. "Hey," I said, keeping my voice casual, though my heart had already started to race.

Tony's gaze didn't waver. Instead, he scooted over in the booth, tilting his head slightly in invitation. It was subtle, but something about the way he did it—without breaking eye contact—sent a thrill down my spine.

I slid in beside him, my pulse hammering as I felt the warmth of his presence so close to me. He gave me a slow, knowing smile, one side of his lips quirking higher than the other.

And just like that, I was hooked.

Chapter 24

When Tony flashed that smile, Mia, Noah, and everyone else disappeared. The chatter in the restaurant, the clinking of silverware against plates, even the faint hum of music playing in the background—it all faded away. As far as I was concerned, Tony and I were the only people here.

It was magnetic, the way we connected. Not just a casual chemistry or the fleeting spark of attraction I'd felt before, but something that gripped me deep in my bones. The warmth in my chest spread to my fingertips, an unshakable certainty settling into my gut. It was bizarre—scary, even—but instead of running from it, I wanted to lean in, to wrap myself in whatever this was.

We got along so easily that even I was surprised. I was no stranger to hitting it off with people, but this was different. It wasn't just that Tony made me laugh or that our conversation flowed effortlessly—it was the way he seemed to *see* me, the way he responded with the perfect mix of wit and sincerity. Like we were speaking a language only we knew.

Once the four of us finished eating, Noah leaned back in his chair, stretching lazily before saying, "You two can spend the night at our place if you want."

"That'd be great," I said, barely able to wait until he finished talking. My voice might have been a little too eager, but I didn't care. Mia and I made eye contact, and she grinned, a knowing glint in her eyes.

The rain had started to pick up outside, fat droplets hitting the pavement in rhythmic patterns. It made the idea of staying in feel even cozier, like we were tucking ourselves away from the world.

Back at their apartment, Mia and Noah went straight to his room, disappearing with barely a glance back. Tony and I, however, took our time. His room was smaller than I expected, walls lined with posters of bands I actually liked—something I mentally noted with amusement. His bed was slightly unmade, a single lamp casting a warm glow over the space, making it feel intimate.

I got butterflies when we sat on his bed together, close enough that our legs brushed. The air between us was thick with unspoken tension, charged but comfortable. I could feel my pulse quicken, anticipation curling around me like a soft, invisible thread. If he didn't make a move, I definitely would.

"Are you tired?" Tony asked, lying on his side, his head propped up by his hand. His expression was relaxed, but there was something playful in his eyes.

I shrugged, trying to play off how fast my heart was racing. "I'm not, either."

A slow grin spread across his lips. "In that case, can you tell me more about those clubs you go to? It sounds like a lot of fun."

I exhaled, relieved that we were extending the moment instead of cutting it short. "They're amazing. Everyone's full of energy, but there's this peace in the air. You feel like you can have as much fun as you want with nothing to worry about. I'd love to take you some time."

Tony raised an eyebrow, his grin deepening. "Vanessa, are you asking me on a date?"

I fluffed my hair dramatically, giving him a teasing look. "That depends. Are you interested?"

He smiled his lopsided smile, and it made my stomach flip. "Yeah, I am."

The conversation unfolded effortlessly from there, stretching out like a comfortable, well-worn thread between us. We took turns making each other laugh, our humor bouncing back and forth in a rhythm that felt like second nature. But beyond the jokes, there was something deeper—an unspoken understanding, a mirroring of emotions that neither of us had to force.

As the night stretched on and exhaustion seeped into our limbs, our conversation shifted. We shared things neither of us had planned to say, secrets that should have felt too raw for someone I'd just met. But with Tony, there was no fear, no hesitation. It felt right.

Eventually, we were too worn down to keep talking, even though we both wanted to. The room was hushed now; the only sound was the distant patter of rain against the window. He pulled the blankets over us, and without thinking, we curled into each other. His warmth pressed against my side, his breath soft and steady against my shoulder. I fell asleep wondering if I'd ever felt this comfortable with another person before.

Booming thunder shook me awake a few hours later, rattling the windows. The storm had grown fierce, sheets of rain pounding against the glass. Tony stirred beside me, his brow furrowing slightly before he rolled over, unconsciously seeking out warmth. I smiled to myself, watching the way his hair fell messily across his forehead before carefully slipping out of bed.

My stomach grumbled. Would it be weird to raid his fridge?

Maybe not if I made him something, too.

I tiptoed into the kitchen, only to freeze when I saw Mia already there, standing in front of the open fridge, wearing Noah's oversized t-shirt. She had a piece of bread stuffed in her mouth, her eyes widening when she spotted me.

I had to laugh. "Busted."

She sighed, pulling the bread out of her mouth with a dramatic eye roll. "I was hungry, okay?"

"So am I." I pulled a carton of eggs from the fridge, shaking it slightly before setting it on the counter. "If you find a pan, I'll start scrambling some eggs for everyone."

Mia rummaged through the cabinets while I cracked eggs into a bowl. As I whisked them, I cast her a sideways glance. "How was your night?"

She didn't look at me as she found a frying pan, but her lips quirked. "It was fine."

I raised an eyebrow. "Oh, come on."

She sighed, relenting. "We hooked up. It wasn't the first time. I guess we're sort of friends with benefits. Anyway, I know you only asked so you could tell me about your night, so go ahead."

I looked at her, and she was smirking at me. I smiled back, feeling a little giddy. "It was amazing, honestly. I've never gotten so close to someone so quickly. He's like the guy version of me, almost, and I don't know. It was just a really special night."

I pinched my lips together, trying to contain myself, but when Mia let out a tiny squeal, so did I.

"How exciting!" she said. "Did you two hook up?"

"No. That's the crazy part. We got so carried away talking to each other that we just never got around to it."

Mia shook her head slowly, her eyes wide. "Oh, Vanessa. It's official. You're in love."

"Shut up," I whispered. There was movement in Tony's bedroom.

She pressed her hand over her mouth to cover her laughter as Tony came out of his room, rubbing his eyes sleepily. "Are you stealing my food?" he asked me.

"Well, I was going to share some with you, but not after that attitude."

Tony laughed and wrapped his arms around my waist from behind. "Thank you, Vanessa."

I nuzzled into him just as Noah walked in, taking one look at us before turning to Mia. "Disgusting," he said.

She nodded solemnly. "Absolutely nauseating."

The storm continued to rage while the four of us ate breakfast. "I know I'm not leaving the apartment today," Noah said, peering out the window. "You two can hang out here with us if you want."

That was an easy choice for me. Mia stayed, too, and we spent the rest of the day lounging around Tony's and Noah's apartment, smoking and watching movies. It was cozy, the kind of morning you didn't want to end.

Later that night, Tony and I shut the door to his bedroom, and this time, there was no waiting. Clothes were stripped away, skin pressed to skin, and for the first time in my life, it wasn't just about the physical. Tony was unlike any of the experiences I'd had before. It wasn't quick, or impersonal, or focused on getting pleasure and being done with it. Tony and I whispered and made eye contact and focused on being together and making each other happy. He was kind and caring, and I wouldn't be able to stop myself from falling for him if I tried.

When we woke up together the next morning, dread settled in my stomach. I had to go home before Mom reported me missing.

Mia said the same, so she got dressed, waiting in the living room while I lingered in Tony's arms.

"I don't wanna leave," I murmured against his chest.

"I don't want you to, either." He kissed the top of my head. "I'll miss you too much."

Noah scoffed from the doorway. "You're not going off to war. You can see each other again in a few hours if you want to."

Tony threw a pillow at him. "Mind your business."

Then Tony turned to me, eyes serious. "This might be fast, but it feels right. Will you be my girlfriend?"

I threw my arms around his neck and pulled myself into his lap. "Of course," I grinned, kissing him all over his face.

His lips found mine. We kissed deeply, and my body filled with happiness like I'd never felt before.

Chapter 25

Everyone who knew about Tony and me told us basically the same thing:

"This honeymoon stage you're in won't last. You'll soon get tired of hanging around each other all the time."

For the first few months of our relationship, that worried me. I never wanted the feeling of floating on clouds and glowing with happiness to end. I loved the way my heart raced when he texted me, the warmth that spread through me when he reached for my hand, the way his laugh could turn my worst days into something bearable.

Once Tony and I made it to our one-year dating anniversary, and that joy didn't fade, I officially decided that everyone who told me that was just jealous.

Even after seeing each other nearly every day for a year, I still got butterflies when I saw him. It wasn't an exaggeration—every single time his name popped up on my phone, I felt the same excited thrill I did when we first started dating. I melted every time he called me beautiful and told me he loved me. He said it in a way that made me believe him completely, like it was an absolute truth that couldn't be questioned.

Our relationship was so genuine and loving that it had only taken me a month to realize this was the first time I was ever actually in love. Before Tony, I thought I had been in love once or twice, but that feeling paled in comparison to what we had.

The more that time went on, the more assured I felt in my decision to not go back to school. I'd upgraded from a hostess to a waitress, and I worked enough hours and was likable enough to the customers that I made decent money. There were nights when I came home exhausted, my feet aching from long shifts, but I liked my job. I liked the people I worked with, the steady rhythm of busy dinner rushes, the satisfaction of walking out at the end of the night with tips in my pocket.

I had a good job, a great relationship, and incredible friends. For once, it felt like life was going my way. That was until I turned eighteen.

Oliver's birthday present to me was kicking me out of the apartment.

"It's for your own good," he said, his arms crossed, leaning against the doorframe like he expected me to throw a fit. His expression, however, made it clear that this wasn't about me. It was about him.

"You're an adult now, so you need to start acting like one."

It took all my willpower not to roll my eyes at him. He knew good and well how independent I was, so I figured this was more of a power play than anything else.

I turned on my heel without a word and went to my bedroom, slamming the door behind me hard enough to rattle the frame.

I sat on my bed, knees pulled up to my chest, waiting. Mom would come in soon and tell me that she'd talked Oliver into letting me stay. That I didn't need to pack up my entire life in a matter of days.

Minutes passed. My fingers tapped anxiously against my knee. Any second now.

But when Mom did finally come to my room, the sad look in her eyes made it clear that I was wrong.

My stomach dropped.

"So do I get to stay here until I find a new place to live, or do I need to have my things cleared out before the end of the day?" I asked her sarcastically, my voice sharper than I intended.

"You have a week," Mom said quietly.

My eyes widened. "Wait, so you're going along with this? You're letting him kick me out with barely any warning?"

She wouldn't make eye contact with me.

I searched her face, desperate for some sign of hesitation, some glimpse of regret that would tell me she wanted to fight for me but just didn't know how. Instead, she looked at the floor, twisting her hands together.

"You and Tony are really serious now, so maybe you can stay with him for a while?" she said. "Or Mia, I bet she'd let you stay with her until something else comes up."

I could only stare at her as she refused to meet my eyes.

As angry as I was, I didn't want to argue because I was even more hurt.

"You can go," I told her, my voice low.

Mom nodded, then did as she was told. She shut the door behind her, but Lily caught it before it could close. She came to sit next to me on my bed. Her eyes were glazed over, like she might cry.

"I wish you didn't have to leave."

Lily's voice was quiet, like what she was saying was a big secret. My stomach was uneasy—something felt off, but I couldn't put my finger on it.

"Me too," I told her, exhaling shakily. "Hopefully, I'm at least allowed back here to visit you every once in a while."

She nodded and rubbed her eyes with the sleeve of her hoodie. I scooted up against her, and she rested her head on my shoulder. I gave her a tight hug, and she held onto me even more tightly.

It made my heart ache.

"I have to make some calls to find a place to stay," I told her after a while. "Go find something to do that makes you happy."

Lily nodded again, then gave me another quick hug while whispering, "I'm gonna miss you, Ness," before leaving and shutting my door behind her.

My stomach went hot with anger at Oliver for doing something that hurt Lily like that. I'd have to prioritize spitting on his toothbrush before I left.

I called Tony and explained the situation.

"You can stay with Noah and me," he said right away, his voice steady and sure. "We've been talking about moving in together anyway, so it'll be perfect."

Despite everything, I smiled.

"What would I do without you, Tony?"

"You'd be better off than I'd be without you," he said, his voice warm. "I can be there in a couple of hours to pick you up and help you move your stuff out?"

I agreed, then hung up and started packing.

By the time Tony and Noah showed up two hours later, all my belongings were in suitcases and trash bags.

I stopped by Lily's room to tell her goodbye.

Mom and Oliver were in the living room.

Oliver watched from the couch as I lugged my stuff from my bedroom, and Mom came into the kitchen and offered to help me.

"Nope," I told her, avoiding eye contact. "I'm an independent adult. It would be ridiculous for you to help an independent adult with a few bags, wouldn't it?"

Mom didn't say anything else, but she stayed in the kitchen as I moved all my stuff in there.

Tony and Noah were waiting outside for me to let them know I was ready, then came in to help with my stuff. With the three of us working together, we were able to bring everything down in just one trip.

I looked at my fourplex as Noah drove away.

I was half expecting to see Mom come outside to see me off and trying not to admit to myself that I was hoping she would.

Noah turned the corner. My fourplex disappeared from sight.

Mom never came outside.

Chapter 26

With all the time I spent at Tony's and Noah's apartment, it was already pretty much a second home. The scent of Noah's cologne mixed with the faint smell of old takeout containers in the trash, the scattered video game controllers on the coffee table, the couch that had more blankets than necessary—it was all familiar to me. I knew exactly which cabinet the snacks were kept in, which of the three remote controls actually worked, and the little spot in the hallway where the carpet was loose and always tried to trip me.

I would be overjoyed to be moving in with them if only it was happening under better circumstances.

That first night, as the reality of my situation settled in, I sat on Tony's bed, feeling like a guest in a place I'd practically lived in for months. My suitcase sat in the corner, looking out of place even though I'd stayed over so many times before.

Tony sat beside me, close enough that his warmth pressed against my arm. His expression was careful, serious, but there was something reassuring in the way he reached for my hands.

"Look, Ness," he said, squeezing my fingers. "I know this day has been crazy and difficult. I'm going to tell you something that I think will make you feel better."

I exhaled, trying to shake the weight sitting heavy on my chest. "I could use some good news."

"You know that Noah and Natalie have been serious for a while," he started, watching my reaction. "Well, just like you and I have been talking about moving in together, so have they. And since

I have a long commute to work every day and Noah doesn't… we thought it might be a good idea if he and Natalie kept this place, and we got our own apartment together."

My heart dropped.

"Wait, he's not kicking you out, is he? Is everything okay?"

Tony shook his head quickly, pulling me closer. "No, no, everything's fine. We're still friends. It's just that I love you, and he loves Natalie, and we want to live with our girlfriends. The only reason I'd be the one to leave is because of my commute."

I let out a long breath, relieved that this wasn't some secret drama between him and Noah.

I had a few thousand dollars saved up from waitressing, and Tony made decent money as a forklift driver. We could afford it. Barely!

And, we had been talking about moving in together for a while now. It was something we both wanted, something that already felt inevitable.

"Okay," I told him, nodding. "Let's do it."

Tony's face lit up with the kind of smile that made me weak in the knees. The kind of smile that reminded me, no matter what else happened, that I was exactly where I was meant to be.

He wrapped his arms around me, holding me so tightly it almost made up for the mess I'd left behind.

"This is gonna be great," he said, his voice full of certainty.

I rested my head on his shoulder, letting myself believe it. It sucked that Oliver was such a jerk, but maybe this was just God's timing. I was leaving a situation that had been forced on me, stepping into one that was chosen. I was stepping into something better.

And I would be okay.

The very next day, Tony and I went apartment hunting.

We started our search as close to his job as possible since, between the two of us, he worked earlier hours and would benefit more from a shorter commute.

The first apartment we toured was gorgeous—hardwood floors, a balcony overlooking a park, modern appliances—but way too expensive. The leasing agent barely finished telling us the price before Tony and I exchanged a look that said absolutely not.

The second apartment was affordable, but it looked like it hadn't been updated since the 80s. The carpets were stained, the cabinets hung slightly off their hinges, and I was pretty sure there was something living in the wall.

But the third one… The third one was just right.

It was a fixer-upper, sure, but not bad at all. The rent was within our budget, it was in a decent neighborhood, and—most importantly—it was ours if we wanted it.

"I think it's great," Tony said, spinning in a slow circle to take it all in.

I traced my fingers along the chipped paint in the kitchen, imagining what it would look like with a fresh coat. "It just needs a woman's touch."

Considering the location, rent, and the fact that it was fully furnished, Tony and I couldn't have found much better.

So we signed the lease that day.

By noon the next day, we were moved into our new apartment.

Looking around at the apartment with all our stuff in it made it go from an acceptable place to home.

"It's *perfect*," I kept saying to Tony as we set up the living room.

Most people probably would've gotten annoyed hearing me say that over and over, but not Tony. Every time, he just hugged me and said, "It's ours."

Every few days, we'd tackle something new—replacing the beat-up coffee table with a nice one, scrubbing all the grime out of the tiles in the bathroom, repainting the kitchen walls. We poured time and money into the place, but it was worth it.

For the first time in my life, I was truly happy with where I lived.

And living with Tony? It only made our relationship stronger.

Every night, we'd watch TV together before bed, but we rarely paid attention to what was on. Instead, we talked. About everything! We talked about our goals for this year, the next five years, and the rest of our lives.

We dreamed of the same future—a house of our own, a car for each of us, and a couple of kids. We planned out everything down to the smallest details, knowing that no matter how long it took, we'd get there.

Together, we could do anything.

Months passed of Tony and me living in our fairytale.

Then, one day in July, someone pounded on our door.

It was our landlord.

"Hey, look," he said, rubbing the back of his neck. "Somethin' came up, somethin' I can't really get into with you, but I have to give up all my property. The courts are givin' me two weeks, so you got less than that to move out. I'm sorry I couldn't give more warnin', but I didn't have the warnin' myself."

Tony and I stood frozen.

I barely processed the door shutting behind him, barely heard his footsteps retreating down the hall.

Everything we'd put into this apartment, the love we had for this place. All for nothing.

"We'll figure something out," Tony said, his voice steady but slow, like he was trying to make himself believe it.

What neither of us could bear to mention was how we'd blown most of our savings, making this place ours.

We barely had enough money to afford that run-down apartment we toured months ago, let alone anything better. It was hard to keep our heads up, hard not to feel like our dreams were crashing down around us.

Tony called his mom for advice, and she didn't hesitate. She offered to let us move in with her for as long as we needed to until we found our own place. Her apartment was big, and she had an extra bedroom and bathroom for us to use. So, we called up some friends to help us move.

I'd met Lydia dozens of times, and we got along really well, so it wouldn't be bad living with her. It was just hard to lose almost everything Tony and I had worked so hard to build. It was hard to start from scratch.

Chapter 27

Uneventful months flew by, each day blending into the next in a quiet monotony. Tony and I worked as many hours as we could, desperate to build up our savings again. The exhaustion was constant, our limbs sore from long shifts, but we pushed through. Every paycheck felt like a small step toward reclaiming our independence.

Lydia, ever generous, reassured us time and again that we were welcome to stay with her for as long as we needed. We were grateful beyond words, but no matter how comfortable she made us feel, it wasn't the same as having a place of our own. We craved the feeling of locking a door that belonged to us, of cooking meals in a kitchen where every plate, every spoon, was ours.

Lydia understood. She always did. One evening, as we sipped tea at her kitchen table, she looked at me with knowing eyes and said, "There's just something about having a place to call your own. It's a special kind of joy. I'm happy to have the two of you here, but I'll be happier when you can go off on your own again."

Her words weren't said with any trace of resentment, only warmth and encouragement. I knew she meant it—she was rooting for us.

Despite the setbacks, despite the ache of losing our apartment, Tony and I remained steadfast. If anything, our relationship deepened through it all. When the weight of it became too much, when we sat on Lydia's couch at night feeling the emptiness of what we had lost, we reminded ourselves: possessions could be replaced, homes could be rebuilt, but what we had in each other—that was unshakable. As long as we had each other, we would be okay.

And for a while, that was enough.

Then, on a freezing day in January, life threw another curveball at me.

The phone rang sharply through Lydia's quiet house, jolting me out of my daze. I had been curled up on the couch, absentmindedly watching snow drift past the window, lost in thought. Since I was the only one home, I picked up the receiver.

"Hello?"

A familiar voice sighed in relief on the other end. "Vanessa." A pause. Then, hurriedly, "Thank goodness. Are you busy? Can you come out to the bus station?"

There was something off in my mother's voice—an urgency, a tension. My stomach twisted.

"Uh, sure. Give me fifteen minutes?"

I hung up, barely giving myself time to process before scrambling to get dressed. I threw on my thickest sweater, wrapped my scarf tightly around my neck, and shoved my feet into my boots. The moment I stepped outside, the bitter cold bit at my skin, the wind howling through the streets. Snow crunched beneath my feet as I walked, my breath coming out in puffs of white.

When I arrived, I spotted Mom and Lily immediately. They stood near the bus station, their arms wrapped around themselves, their cheeks pink from the cold. Around them were suitcases—far too many for a short trip. My pulse quickened.

"What's going on?" I asked, my breath uneven.

Mom wasted no time. "We're moving to Alberta. We'll be staying with Aunt Nora in Stettler."

I blinked, sure I had misheard. The words hung in the icy air, too heavy, too sudden.

"You're... moving to Alberta... today? Right now?"

Mom nodded. "Yes. Oliver doesn't know, so we have to be out quickly before he can figure out where we're going. But I didn't want to buy our tickets until I asked you if you wanted to come with us."

The world around me seemed to still. The sound of traffic, of distant conversations, of wind rustling through the streets—it all faded away.

I could only stare at Mom, my mouth slightly open, as she kept talking, her voice quieter now, tinged with guilt. "Ness, I'm so sorry about him kicking you out of the apartment. I didn't try to stop him because I thought I would've had enough money saved up just a few weeks later to take the three of us to Alberta. But I kept telling myself I needed more money, when really I was just losing courage, and..."

She exhaled sharply, shaking her head. "Anyway, Lily finally snapped and told me it was time to go. Thank God for her. So we're leaving today, and we'd love for you to come with us."

Everything inside me felt frozen. I had barely caught up with the idea of them leaving, and now I had to decide whether to go with them. To leave Tony behind? To pack up my life in the span of a few minutes?

"Can I have some time to think about it?" I asked, my voice

barely above a whisper.

Mom gave me an apologetic look. "Yes, but it can't be too long, Ness. I'm sorry." I nodded numbly and turned away, staring at the snow-covered pavement as if it held answers. The wind burned my cheeks, but the cold in my chest was worse. This wasn't just a decision about moving—it was a choice between my past and my present.

My mother and sister were about to move across the country with only ten minutes' warning. And somehow, I was expected to choose between staying with Tony or going with them. How was that fair?

I turned back to face them, ready to argue, but the words died in my throat. I saw the exhaustion in Mom's face, the dark bags under her eyes, the deep worry lines that had become permanent over the years. I saw the tension in Lily's posture, the way she clenched her hands into fists as if bracing for something.

They didn't have the luxury of giving me more notice. This wasn't just an impulsive move—it was an escape.

As much as it hurt, as much as I wanted to scream about the unfairness of it all, their safety had to come first.

My voice cracked as I finally answered. "I can't go. I can't leave Tony."

Lily stared at the ground. Mom gave me a small, sad smile. "I understand, Ness. The fact that you're so happy here is all I need to be happy. Just know that the invitation will always stand, and we'd always love to have you with us again."

She opened her arms, and I stepped into them, hugging her

tightly, memorizing the feel of her warmth.

In a hushed voice, she whispered, "If Oliver ever gets in touch with you, pretend you don't know where we are. Please. No matter how much he asks."

I held her closer. "Don't worry. I won't tell him anything."

Mom squeezed me tighter. "I'm gonna miss you, Ness. I love you."

My throat ached, my eyes burned. Hold it in, I told myself. Wait until they're gone to cry.

"I love you too, Mom. Good luck."

I turned to Lily next. Her eyes were already wet. "I wish you could come with us."

"I'll try to visit you soon," I promised. "And you can call me anytime."

Together, we walked toward the bus station. I stood with them as they bought their tickets, my heart sinking with every second that passed. The bus was already boarding. Too soon. Too fast.

Another round of hurried goodbyes, another round of I love yous, and then they were stepping onto the bus.

I watched as Mom and Lily found their seats. Mom glanced back one last time, her face lined with sorrow, and then the doors shut. The engine rumbled, the bus pulled away, and I was left standing there, feeling the crushing weight of being left behind.

For as long as I could remember, my mother's face had been creased with worry, her spirit worn down by life. Somewhere along the way, she had lost herself. If this was her best chance at finding happiness again, I hoped it worked.

But as I watched the bus disappear down the road, my vision blurred. I wiped my face, but it was useless.

I couldn't stop crying.

Chapter 28

My heart felt hollow when I stepped back into Lydia's apartment. The moment I closed the door behind me, a heavy silence settled over me, pressing against my chest like an unseen weight. I'd been too busy these past months to spend much time with Mom and Lily, but just knowing they were there, knowing I could call them, visit them, be part of their world whenever I wanted—had been enough to get me through.

I didn't have that anymore.

The apartment felt different without their presence as if it had absorbed my loneliness and was now reflecting it back at me in every shadowy corner, in the stillness of the air. If they were across the country, what would get me through now?

That thought hit me hard, irrational and sharp, twisting inside me before I could stop it. It was ridiculous, and I knew it. I had great friends, an amazing boyfriend, and his mother, who treated me like I was her own daughter. I wasn't alone. And even if—God forbid—I ever lost everyone, I would never lose God. He would always help me find my way. That was the truth, the solid ground beneath all this uncertainty.

I took a deep breath and forced myself to move. I went to the kitchen, the most comforting space I could think of, and started pulling out ingredients to make dinner for Tony, Lydia, and myself. I needed to keep busy, to find a rhythm in something familiar. As I chopped vegetables, the repetitive motion soothed me. I told myself I would stay optimistic. I would be happy for Mom and Lily, for the fresh start they deserved, and I would be grateful that I had a support system here, outside my family, to keep me grounded.

That was all a good mindset, in theory, but it didn't quite work out that way.

Even though I knew deep down that Mom and Lily didn't move to Alberta to leave me, especially since they had invited me to go along, there was a voice in the back of my mind that whispered otherwise. A cruel, insidious voice that planted doubts like weeds.

You weren't enough to make them stay.

They didn't need you like you needed them.

I would catch my reflection in the mirror sometimes and see not the woman I had grown into but the little girl I used to be—eyes wide with questions, wondering why her daddy had left. Wondering if she had done something wrong. If she had been better, would he have stayed?

Little Vanessa got left behind again, the voice would taunt. What did she do this time?

The feeling of abandonment sank its claws into me, wrapping itself around my heart like ivy. I felt it when I waited on mothers with their children at work, watching the easy, natural way they laughed together. I felt it when I saw Tony and Lydia together. I felt it worst at night, lying awake long after the apartment had gone silent, staring at the ceiling and feeling like a stranger in my own life.

This wasn't good for me.

This wasn't sustainable.

Something had to change, and I was the only one who could do it.

A month after Mom and Lily left, I stayed up for Tony to get home from work. The apartment was dimly lit by the soft glow of the lamp beside me, casting long, warm shadows across the room. I curled up on the couch, heart pounding a little as I waited.

Tony walked in, looking exhausted but alert, his sharp eyes immediately flicking to me. "Everything okay?" he asked, concern creasing his forehead as he shrugged off his jacket. Usually, I was already asleep by the time he made it home from his late shifts, so seeing me awake must have thrown him off.

I smiled, feeling a bubble of excitement rise in my chest. "Everything's great." I reached for his hands, feeling the familiar warmth of them wrap around mine. "I've been working on something for the past week. I haven't told you in case it didn't work out, but it did." I took a steadying breath. "I quit my job. Tomorrow, I'm starting a paid apprenticeship at a salon in Charles of Westmount."

For a split second, Tony just blinked at me as if making sure he'd heard right. Then, his tired eyes lit up, pure joy breaking through the exhaustion. "What? Vanessa, are you serious? That's incredible!"

We hugged tightly, his arms wrapping around me with a strength that steadied me in ways I hadn't realized I needed.

"Tell me all about it," he said, his voice warm and eager.

I grinned, heart swelling. "Well, since Charles of Westmount is a rich area, the salon is really high-end. They don't just let anyone apprentice there, but I nailed the interview, and they were impressed with how I styled my own hair. I don't know. I guess I just got lucky."

Tony pulled back slightly, his hands resting on my arms as he gave me a serious look. "Lucky?" He shook his head. "This wasn't luck, Ness. You earned this because you have the skills for it."

A warmth spread through me at his words, the kind that made my throat tighten a little. I smiled up at him, and he hugged me again, holding me close. "I'm so proud of you, Ness. I think this will help you feel like yourself again."

I closed my eyes against his shoulder, breathing in the familiar scent of him—cologne and something uniquely Tony. He was right. This was the start of something new. Something that would change me.

I could be successful.

I could move up in life without my family around.

And maybe, just maybe, I would be okay.

****

I showed up ten minutes early for my first shift the next morning, nerves fluttering in my stomach. The salon was sleek and modern, with marble countertops, enormous mirrors, and a hushed elegance that made it feel like a completely different world from the places I was used to.

My boss, a no-nonsense woman named Celeste, introduced me to Emma, the stylist who would be training me. Emma was tall and poised, her blonde hair in a perfect, smooth bun, her makeup flawless.

Without much of a greeting, she led me straight to the sinks.

"All our apprentices start by washing hair," she said briskly. "Everyone thinks it's such an easy job, but it isn't, and it's important that you learn to do it exactly right. I'll show you how we do it here with three clients. I always tell the apprentices that if you can't pick it up after watching three times, you're probably not cut out to work here."

I bristled a little at her tone but kept my face neutral. I got that she thought she was the fanciest woman in the world for working here, but that didn't mean she had the right to talk to me like I was stupid. She didn't know me. She didn't know what I was capable of.

But I wasn't about to let my pride get in the way of this opportunity.

So I swallowed my irritation, nodded, and listened carefully to everything she said.

When it was finally my turn to wash a client's hair, I focused all my energy on getting it right. My hands moved with care, massaging their scalp just the way I'd been shown.

The client let out a pleased sigh. "Oh, wow. That feels amazing."

I smiled. We chatted as I worked, and by the time I was finished, she was practically glowing.

Even Emma, who had seemed unimpressed with me all morning, gave a small nod. "If you can do that well with everything," she said, "I think you'll be pretty successful here."

Something inside me steadied.

Maybe—just maybe—I had finally found my place.

Chapter 29

Every day at the salon felt like an unspoken test—an opportunity to prove myself, again and again, to both Emma and my boss. I thrived in the challenge, relishing the moments when I could showcase my skills, whether it was blending the perfect shade of caramel highlights or styling a client's hair into a flawless updo. The rhythmic snipping of scissors, the hum of blow dryers, and the faint scent of hairspray and conditioner surrounded me like a comforting cocoon.

A month into my apprenticeship, my boss finally acknowledged my hard work with a promotion, albeit a small one. I was now a stylist's assistant—one step above an apprentice, but still a long way from where I wanted to be. The pay raise was modest—fifty cents more per hour—but the title itself felt like a small victory. It meant I could interact more with clients, take on extra responsibilities, and start carving out my own place in the salon.

At work, I was flourishing. I felt useful. I felt needed. But the moment I stepped out of the salon's doors and back into my reality, the weight of everything pressed down on me again.

At home, when the world quieted, and there was no hair to style, no clients to chat with, and no coworkers to impress, it became harder. The initial thrill of landing the job had dulled, and it was no longer enough to keep me from acknowledging the empty space left behind by my mother and sister's departure. The loneliness crept in like a slow-moving tide, filling every crevice of my mind.

I found myself retreating to the bathroom on my breaks, locking the door, and letting the tears come. I pressed my forehead against the cool mirror, hoping it would somehow ground me. My reflection was a stranger—hollow eyes, lips pressed together tightly to keep from sobbing too loudly. I could hold it together in front of others, but here, alone in the cramped space of the restroom, I let the weight of everything crash down on me.

One evening, after an especially grueling day, I decided I needed to do something—anything—to pull myself out of the dark cloud that followed me. I ran a hot bath, hoping the warmth would soak into my bones and loosen the tightness in my chest. The steam curled around me as I sank into the water, closing my eyes and letting out a shaky breath.

Then I heard it.

Laughter.

Muffled voices floated in from the kitchen—Tony and Lydia. Their laughter rang clear and carefree, the kind of laughter that belonged to people who felt at home with each other, who fit together like pieces of a puzzle. I couldn't make out the words, but it didn't matter. The sound alone was enough to remind me of what I already knew.

I was on the outside. Again.

My chest ached in that deep, gnawing way that wasn't quite sadness and wasn't quite anger—but some terrible mixture of both. I squeezed my eyes shut, pressing my wet hands against my face as if that could somehow stop the feeling from consuming me.

The bathwater had turned lukewarm by the time I finally pulled myself out of it. I pulled the plug, watching the water swirl down the drain, and it felt like it was taking the last of my energy with it. Every movement—toweling off, dressing, stepping out of the bathroom—felt like lifting weights.

Tony was in the living room when I walked out. He glanced up from the TV, his face instantly shifting from casual to concerned.

"Mom went out to get some takeout for us," he said, but his voice had changed—softer, more careful. His eyes scanned my face, and in that split second, he saw it.

"Ness, what's wrong?"

I tried to swallow the lump in my throat, but it was no use. I walked over and sat on the other end of the couch, my body tense, hands clenched in my lap. And then, as if something inside me snapped, I broke down.

Tears came fast and hard, the kind that made my shoulders shake. I couldn't even breathe properly. It wasn't graceful, quiet crying—it was raw, unfiltered, the kind I had been holding back for weeks.

Tony didn't hesitate. His arms wrapped around me instantly, pulling me into his chest like he could shield me from whatever pain I was feeling.

"What's going on?" he asked gently. "What happened?"

I tried to explain, but the words tangled in my throat.

"I just—" I took a shuddering breath. "When Mom and Lily were still here, I always felt like I was on the outside of their little family. But at least they were there. They were my constants when everything else was falling apart. Now they're gone, and even though I don't need my mom, I still really do. I feel like I got left behind. Again." I wiped my face uselessly. "I love you so much, Tony. I'm grateful for you, for Lydia, for my friends. But—"

I trailed off. How could I explain the unshakable emptiness, the way loneliness gnawed at my insides like a hunger that wouldn't go away?

Tony's grip on me tightened, his voice low but firm. "I get it. At least a little. When my dad walked out, it was horrible, but… I know what you've been through is harder."

His fingers brushed my hair out of my damp face, tucking it gently behind my ear. "What if we start spending more time together? Because honestly? I'm getting sick of my job. The hours suck, the pay sucks, and I've been thinking about looking for something else. Maybe something with better hours, so I have more time to be here with you."

I sniffled, curling into him. The idea of having more time together, of not feeling so alone in the house, was more comforting than I could put into words.

"That would be great," I mumbled. "I hope you can find something."

But even as I sat there, wrapped in Tony's warmth, the ache inside me didn't fully go away. I hoped this would fix it. I had to hope. Because if it didn't, I wasn't sure what else would.

Monday came too soon.

Dragging myself out of bed felt impossible. My body was heavy, my mind foggy with exhaustion. The idea of going to work, of smiling, of acting like everything was fine—it was unbearable.

But I had no choice.

The day at the salon blurred together—washing hair, sweeping trimmings, mixing colors, running around in a monotonous cycle. It felt endless. Like I was stuck in a loop, I couldn't escape.

I barely noticed when I stopped mid-task, staring at Emma's station as a realization struck me.

I was turning into Mom.

The thought sent a sharp jolt through me. I couldn't let myself sink into that kind of emptiness. I had to do something.

Instead of crying in the bathroom during my break, I flipped through the phone book at the front desk. My heart pounded as I found a therapist's office near the salon. I dialed the number, fingers trembling, and was told they had a cancellation that afternoon.

Maybe, just maybe, this was a sign.

Sitting in the therapist's office, my hands twisted in my lap. The room was cozy, filled with warm lighting and shelves of books. The man sitting across from me had kind eyes.

"So, Vanessa, what's going on?"

I opened my mouth, but instead of words, sobs spilled out.

For minutes, I settled down enough to explain to him that I thought I might be depressed. I told him about Mom and Lily leaving, how I worried that I wasn't worth staying with, and how I was afraid I was going down the same sad path that Mom did.

When I finally stopped, he listened patiently before telling me my mind was playing tricks on me into thinking that there was something wrong with me. He said I would adjust and that he would prescribe antidepressants to help.

And just like that, the session was over.

I left feeling hollow, hoping the pills would help. Because if they didn't… I wasn't sure what else I had left to try.

Chapter 30

As the weeks passed, things slowly began to feel less suffocating. The antidepressants weren't some magical fix — they didn't erase the grief or the hollow ache I carried everywhere — but they did something important: they kept me moving. They helped me focus at work, allowing me to push through the endless grind without breaking down every few hours. That made a huge difference. Even if the sadness lingered like an unwelcome shadow, at least I could manage the day-to-day better.

Beyond work, the antidepressants nudged me to start reconnecting with people. I'd become a recluse, barely leaving the house unless it was for work or to spend time with Tony. I'd convinced myself that isolating was safer, but deep down, I knew I was cutting off the people who cared about me most. It wasn't fair to them, and honestly, it wasn't good for me either.

So, I started reaching out.

Mia and I began spending more time together again, slipping back into a rhythm that felt comforting and familiar. We weren't exactly the same as before — life had added layers to both of us — but there was still that effortless connection. Mia had been thriving; she was in a serious relationship now and working part-time at a clothing store in the mall while finishing her college degree. Every time we talked about her life, I couldn't help but feel a surge of pride. She'd worked so hard to get where she was, and seeing her happy warmed something in my chest. She deserved this success, and I told her so every chance I got.

Sandy's life was changing, too, and she called today with big news. When she told me she was pregnant, her voice buzzed with excitement. I invited her over immediately — I needed to see her, hug her and celebrate in person.

****

The doorbell rang that afternoon, and when I opened the door, Sandy's face practically glowed. Her smile was wide, her eyes bright and warm. I pulled her into a tight hug before she even had a chance to say hello.

"You're pregnant!" I squealed as I released her. "Oh my God, Sandy!"

She laughed, following me into the kitchen. "I know! Can you believe it?"

I put a steaming cup of tea in front of her as we settled at the table. Sandy wrapped her hands around the mug, letting the warmth seep into her fingers.

"Tony's at work, I guess?" she asked, taking a cautious sip.

"Yeah," I said with a sigh. "He wasn't supposed to be working today, but his boss called early this morning and had him come in for a double."

Sandy shook her head, her brows furrowing. "That sucks. He's always stuck at the mercy of that guy. Has he thought about finding something else?"

"He's looking," I said with a shrug. "He's being picky, though — wants something with flexible hours and decent pay. I know it's hard for him, but we're both hopeful he'll find something great."

Sandy shifted in her seat, her fingers tracing the rim of her mug.

"Well," she said slowly, "that's actually one of the things I wanted to talk to you about."

My eyes narrowed slightly. "Oh?"

"Marco has a job he could use some help with," she said. "When I mentioned Tony, Marco said he'd like to meet him."

My eyebrows shot up. "Really?" I hadn't expected that. I didn't know much about Marco's work — just that it kept him busy and apparently paid well enough for Sandy to quit her job. "I'll tell him when he gets home. Thanks, Sandy."

"No problem." Sandy smiled, her eyes crinkling at the corners. "Marco's trying to delegate some of his responsibilities so he'll have more free time when the baby comes."

The mention of her baby reignited my excitement, and I let out a little squeal. "A baby! I can't get over it. I'm so excited for you!"

Sandy's grin widened. "Me too. I've dreamt about being a mom since I was a little girl. I'm already getting carried away buying toys and converting our spare room into a nursery."

"Are you going to find out the gender before you give birth?" I asked.

"Hopefully, yeah," she said, eyes twinkling. "I want to know what kind of clothes to buy. Every time I go to the store and see those tiny baby dresses, I lose my mind."

I gasped, covering my mouth with both hands. "Does that mean you're hoping for a girl?"

Sandy's expression softened. "Don't be silly. I'll be happy no matter what — so long as they're healthy."

I held her gaze knowingly until she finally cracked. "But having a girl would be amazing!" she added, her face lighting up.

We both squealed like teenagers, and I jumped up to wrap her in another hug.

"You're going to be such a good mom," I said, my voice thick with emotion. "I can't wait to spoil your baby."

"And I can't wait to have you around her," Sandy said, her smile softening. "Or him." She reached for my hand, squeezing it gently. "I know they're gonna love their Aunt Vanessa."

****

Tony was home when I got back from the salon that afternoon. I found him sitting on the couch, his legs stretched out and crossed at the ankles. He looked relaxed — more relaxed than I'd seen him in weeks.

"Hey," I greeted, leaning down to kiss him. "How'd the meeting with Marco go?"

"Great," Tony said, grinning. "He offered me the job, and I accepted it."

I blinked, surprised at how fast everything had moved. "Wow! That's awesome. I'm proud of you." My smile was genuine, but curiosity lingered. "What's the job?"

Tony's grin faltered slightly. "I'll be able to work whenever I want," he said carefully. "I can even cut back on hours and still make way more than I've been making. It's just what we needed, Ness. We'll have so much more time together."

Something about the way he was tiptoeing around my question

made my smile stiffen. "That's really great," I said slowly. "But… what's the job?"

Tony's expression shifted — guilt flickered behind his eyes. "I want you to hear me out," he said. "Everything I've mentioned so far sounds good, right?"

"Yes, but—"

He reached for my hands, squeezing them tightly. "Do you trust me to be safe? Do you understand that I'm doing this for us?"

I felt my pulse quicken. My hands went slack in his grip. "Tony…" I pulled away. "Would you just tell me? What, are you selling drugs or something?"

His shoulders slumped, and he broke eye contact.

My stomach twisted. "You're going to sell drugs?" My voice trembled.

"It'll be okay, Vanessa," Tony insisted, his tone alarmingly casual. "Really. I know how to stay under the radar and be safe about it. And I'm doing it for us. I'm not worried about it, and if you trust me, then you shouldn't be, either."

His words felt like a punch to the chest. He was excited — more excited than I'd seen him in months — but my mind couldn't shake the reality of what he was saying. This wasn't just a risk; this was dangerous reckless.

But then Tony looked at me, and I saw something else in his face — desperation. He wasn't doing this to be reckless; he believed this was the answer. That scared me even more.

I forced a breath out and tried to smile. My voice was thin and shaky. "Okay," I said. "I support you."

I wasn't sure if I was lying or just trying to convince myself.

Chapter 31

It might not have been very smart to tell Tony I supported his selling drugs before I was able to think through every aspect of it. The words had left my mouth too quickly, spurred by the relief I'd felt when I saw the excitement in his eyes — a rare kind of excitement I hadn't seen in far too long. The smile he'd worn that day had been so genuine, so much like the Tony I'd fallen in love with, that I couldn't bring myself to question the source of it.

But now, looking back, I realized how reckless it had been. Not only could my rushed approval have given Tony the wrong idea about my feelings — that I was fully behind this dangerous, illegal choice — but it also could have made him believe I was willing to stand by him no matter what happened. What if something went wrong? What if, by my careless words, I'd encouraged him to keep pushing further into a world he couldn't easily escape?

A month went by with Tony being a runner, and despite my quiet worries, everything that had come out of it so far was positive — or at least that's how it seemed. We had more time together, something I'd desperately wanted. He was making more money, and there was a light in his eyes that I hadn't seen in months.

The job made him happy. Really happy. And that mattered to me.

Even though I wasn't allowed to go on runs with him, Tony always told me about his day afterward. He'd speak with a strange mix of excitement and confidence like he was doing something dangerous but skillfully pulling it off — like he was proud of himself.

I didn't like what he was doing, but I liked what it was doing to him. I liked that his energy had returned and that he was sleeping better and laughing more. And I couldn't deny that the extra time we spent together had strengthened our relationship.

But none of that erased the knot that kept tightening inside me — a persistent unease that seemed to grow heavier every time I thought about his job. I wanted Tony to have a safer job...and legal. Something that didn't leave me anxiously checking my phone every time he stepped out the door.

There was something else about his work that unsettled me, too — something I couldn't quite name until Tony had been at it for a few weeks.

I realized what it was one afternoon while I was standing in line at the grocery store. As I handed over a few bills to the cashier, it hit me: this money had come from other people's suffering.

People who were battling addictions. People who were scraping together what little they had just to hand it over to Tony.

I found myself unable to make eye contact with the cashier as she counted out my change. I mumbled a quiet "thank you" and hurried out of the store.

From that moment on, I couldn't ignore it.

Every time I pulled out my wallet or bought something for the house, I felt a dull ache in my chest — an ache that whispered: *this isn't right*. I started feeling ashamed, like I didn't deserve to enjoy the comfort that Tony's money provided.

Still, Tony was doing this partially because he loved me. He wanted to give us a better life, and I knew that. So I pushed my guilt down and threw myself into working at the salon and helping Sandy with preparing for her baby to keep from thinking about Tony's customers.

I was straightening up the products in the salon's lobby one afternoon when Emma walked by me, her heels clicking sharply against the floor. She stopped near the window, her eyes narrowing.

"Ugh," Emma muttered, pointing outside. "I hate when the druggies come around. They scare away customers. At least it doesn't happen often, huh?"

I followed her gaze. A man stood in the parking lot, his shoulders slumped and his clothes wrinkled and stained. His face was worn, his eyes darting nervously as he tried to speak to people who hurried past him without a glance.

I felt a pang in my chest. He didn't look dangerous — just lost.

"Yeah," I said quietly. I knew better than to say what I was really thinking. If I told her how I truly felt, I'd probably get fired.

My shift ended ten minutes later, and the man had moved closer to the parking lot of the fast-food place next door.

Without really thinking, I went inside the restaurant, bought two full meals, and walked over to him.

"They got my order wrong," I lied, offering him the bags. "They gave me the messed-up orders for free. I don't like chicken sandwiches, so I figured I'd see if you wanted them."

The man's face softened, his eyes flicking between the bags and my face like he couldn't believe it was real.

"Oh, thank you, miss," he said, his voice rough and dry. "Yeah,

I'll take them. Thank you."

I smiled. "You're welcome. God bless."

"You too, miss. Thank you."

I got on the bus feeling warm inside, like I'd done something—even something small—to push back against the guilt that had been weighing me down.

But by the time I stepped off at my stop, that warmth had faded to a cold, empty ache.

The image of the man's grateful face stuck with me — and all I could think was, What if he was one of Tony's customers?

I spent the walk from the bus stop to Lydia's house blinking away tears.

****

The next day, I found out I'd have Thursday off. When I let Tony know, he said he'd take the day off, too, so we could go to the mall together.

"What stores do you want to go to?" Tony asked as he pulled into the mall's parking lot.

"I want to get some nicer outfits for work," I said. "I figure we can stop by a few different clothing stores?"

"Perfect," Tony said, flashing me a smile.

But instead of pulling into one of the front parking spots, Tony checked his mirrors, then casually drove around to the back of the mall.

"Why are you parking here?" I asked, my stomach tightening.

He shrugged. "I'm gonna meet up with a new customer real quick. It'll be done in three minutes."

The air seemed to vanish from the car. My pulse thudded in my ears.

"I thought I wasn't allowed to be on your runs with you?" I asked, trying to keep my voice calm.

"I know, I'm sorry," Tony said. "But like I said, it'll be over before you know it, and we'll go shopping. I'll buy you something extra for doing this with me, okay?"

I didn't feel like I had a choice, but I nodded. My eyes kept darting to the mirrors, half-hoping I'd spot the person before they showed up.

A car pulled up a few parking spots away.

My fingers clenched against my thighs.

The guy stepped out, walking toward Tony's window. Tony looked calm — way too calm. He reached into his back pocket and pulled out a baggie of white powder.

Before I could even process what was happening, the guy whipped out a gun.

My door was yanked open, and another man — another gun — was suddenly pointed at me.

"Hands on the dashboard, both of you."

My breath caught in my throat. My chest tightened, and my body trembled so badly I could barely lift my hands.

"You are under arrest for drug trafficking. Do you understand?"

I felt like the world was spinning too fast — like I was being yanked underwater with no way to breathe.

Tony and I nodded stiffly and mechanically, like puppets on strings. The undercover cop's voice seemed distant, yet each word cut through the air like a knife.

"You have the right to remain silent…"

His voice was steady, emotionless — like he'd done this a hundred times before. My mind barely grasped the words, but my body understood the danger. I was trembling so violently that I felt like I'd shake myself apart. My fingers gripped the dashboard tightly as if anchoring myself to the car could somehow keep me from falling apart. I was terrified the officer would think my shaking was a sign I was resisting, that I was hiding something — as if fear alone might make me guilty.

I glanced at Tony out of the corner of my eye. His face had gone pale, his usual confidence stripped away. His fingers were white-knuckled against the steering wheel. For the first time since he'd started dealing, Tony didn't look like he had everything under control.

One of the cops stepped forward, yanked the car door open, and grabbed Tony by the arm. His voice was rough and authoritative. "Out. Now."

Another cop moved to my side. "Step out of the vehicle."

I stumbled as I obeyed, my legs weak beneath me. Cold metal clamped around my wrists, biting into my skin. I winced, my breathing fast and shallow. The officer roughly adjusted the cuffs, jerking my arms back in a way that sent a dull ache through my shoulders.

Out of the corner of my eye, I saw another cop open the glove compartment. My stomach twisted into a knot as he reached inside and began pulling out one small baggie after another — tiny plastic pouches filled with white powder. There were so many.

I felt dizzy, like I might faint. How had I not known those were in there? I hadn't seen Tony put them in the car. Had they been there all along? Hidden away during the morning drives to grab coffee or the late-night fast-food runs where we'd laughed about what movie to watch?

I wanted to scream that I didn't know, that I wasn't a part of this, but my voice wouldn't come. My throat felt like it was full of sand.

I tried to zone out as the cops shoved Tony and me into separate cars, but my mind kept racing. The car door slammed beside me, and the sound seemed to echo inside my skull.

I stared out the window, watching the world blur past. We were being arrested — there was no changing that. It was happening whether I thought about it or not, so why even try to process it? What was the point?

Once we got to the jail, I didn't see Tony again. I got my fingerprints and mugshot taken. Then, the cops took me to an empty holding cell. After what felt like an eternity, one came back to get me.

"You get a phone call," he said, leading me to the telephone.

I didn't know who else I could call but Mom. Thankfully, she answered after just one ring. "Hello?"

"Mom?" My voice was shaky, and I knew that I was going to

cry, so there was no use trying to hold it in. "Mom, I...got arrested. Tony was going to sell some cocaine, but the guy was an undercover cop, and we got arrested. I didn't know he had drugs on him, and I don't know what to do now, and I'm so scared, Mom."

Mom sighed. "Oh, Vanessa." Her voice sounded as rough as mine. "Honey, I'm sorry, but I'm not sure what I can do from over here. The best I can do is call some old friends of mine from the area and see if they can help you. But there's the issue of paying bail, so...I don't know, Vanessa. I'll do whatever I can for you, but I can't make any promises."

She told me to stay strong and that she loved me, then we hung up. I was more or less a zombie as the officer brought me back to my cell.

After more time passed, one of the guys who'd arrested me came to get me from my cell. He brought me to an interrogation room, just like on TV.

My whole body was shaking, and I was silently crying. "Okay, Vanessa," the officer said. He smiled kindly at me. "We know you weren't the one selling the drugs. It's not fair that you're getting in trouble for this when you didn't do anything wrong. We wanna help you get out of here, and the best way we can do that is if you help us."

I nodded weakly, and he said, "We need to know where Tony is getting the drugs he's selling. Who his boss is, basically. Can you tell us who that is?"

I could. I could tell the cop it was Marco and hoped he would keep his word and let me out.

But that would result in Marco getting arrested, and Sandy and their unborn baby needed him. The last thing I wanted was to be in jail, but if I had to choose between myself and Sandy...

"I don't know who he's getting it from. Really. He usually doesn't involve me in this at all."

The officer's friendly, calm demeanor instantly darkened. "That's all I've got, then." He gestured for me to stand up, and he cuffed me again before leading me back to my cell.

And that was where I stayed for the rest of the night. I cried until I couldn't cry anymore, and then I curled up into a ball on my lumpy bed and begged God to help me.

Chapter 32

I woke up the next morning in a daze, my mind floating in a fog so thick I couldn't grasp a single coherent thought. That was fine by me—it was easier to stay like that than to snap out of it and face reality. Reality meant I was in jail. Reality meant cold cement walls, the dull ache in my back from sleeping on a stiff mattress, and the gnawing fear that no one was going to bail me out.

I had no sense of time—only the echo of footsteps signaling the guards' constant patrols. It felt like morning, but that didn't mean much. I stared at the ceiling, counting cracks in the paint until a sudden clank of metal startled me. The cell door slid open, and a cop barked my name.

"Gallagher! On your feet."

I staggered to my feet, my legs weak from stress and exhaustion. The handcuffs clicked tightly around my wrists again, and before I knew it, I was shuffled through the cold hallways and shoved into a courtroom.

The judge barely looked at me. His eyes flicked over the papers in front of him like I was just one more name in an endless list of criminals. My public defender stood beside me, a tired-looking man in an ill-fitting suit. He murmured something about pleading not guilty. Drug trafficking. My bail was set at a thousand dollars.

I barely heard any of it. The words blurred in my ears like a distant conversation on the other side of a wall. Before I could make sense of it, I was ushered back into the maze of corridors. The cop walking beside me didn't even bother with small talk; he just grunted when we stopped at my cell door.

"You'll stay here for now," he said in a flat voice. "If your bail isn't paid by five this evening, you'll be transferred to a provincial facility."

Transferred. My stomach lurched. I knew what that meant—a bigger, harsher place with tougher inmates. The kind of place where you don't just keep your head down and hope for the best.

My cell wasn't empty anymore. Two women sat on one of the bunks, their faces tired yet sharp. Their clothes clung tightly to their bodies, their makeup smeared but still defiant. Prostitutes, I guessed. They stared me down, cold and appraising, as I shuffled in and collapsed onto my bunk. One of them muttered something to the other, and they both let out dry laughs before turning back to their conversation.

I lay still, pulling my knees to my chest and trying to make myself small. I barely moved for hours, afraid to interrupt whatever unspoken rhythm the two women shared. The shame weighed heavier than the dull ache in my muscles. My eyes stung as I thought about where I was supposed to be—at the salon, styling hair for wealthy women who barely noticed me. Instead, I was in here. A cell. Sharing a room with strangers who didn't care if I existed.

How did it come to this?

The afternoon stretched on forever. The silence between us was punctuated by bursts of loud conversation from other cells, laughter that felt too cruel for comfort. The two women kept talking in low voices, their laughter dry and bitter, like they'd heard every joke the world could throw at them and stopped expecting anything good.

At 4:50 p.m., I heard the clatter of boots and the harsh clanking of the gate unlocking. My chest tightened when I realized what was happening. The van had arrived.

I swallowed hard, fighting back nausea. Mom couldn't find anyone to pay the bail. The bile rose in my throat as I stood, heart pounding, and lined up with the others. My feet felt heavy, as though each step dragged me closer to some grim fate I couldn't escape.

"Vanessa Gallagher?" a voice barked suddenly.

I turned, blinking in disbelief. A cop stood by the door, flipping through a clipboard.

"Your bail was posted. Come with me."

My breath caught. Relief rushed through me so fast that my legs nearly gave out. The handcuffs clamped around my wrists once more, but this time, it didn't feel like a sentence—it felt like a lifeline.

Outside the gate, Tony and Lydia stood waiting. Tony grinned wide as soon as he saw me, stepping forward to gather me in his arms. His hug was tight, his kiss warm against my temple.

"I'm so happy to see you," he whispered.

"Me too," I murmured back, though my voice shook. I wanted to feel relief—joy, even—but all I felt was cold. My skin still smelled like stale air and steel. I was free, but I couldn't shake the feeling that something was still very wrong.

On the ride home, I stared blankly out the window. Streetlights flickered by, casting shadows that danced across the glass. My thoughts twisted restlessly in my head, and I knew I had to say something.

"You bailed us out, then?" I finally managed to ask Lydia.

"I did," she answered softly.

I exhaled, the breath shaky and uneven. "Thank you. So much. That was so scary."

"You're welcome," she said, her voice warm but strained. "I'm just glad you two are safe and coming home."

I turned my gaze toward Tony, watching his reflection in the glass. He hadn't spoken since we got in the car. He stared out the window, face tense and unreadable. I wondered what he was thinking. Was he scared? Guilty? Angry? I couldn't tell.

When we got home, I called Mom right away. The moment I heard her voice, tears I hadn't realized I was holding back finally spilled over. She was worried sick, of course, but she was relieved I was home. That night, I barely had the energy to drag myself to bed. My limbs felt like lead as I pulled the blankets up to my chin.

Tony came in not long after. He sat beside me on the bed, his fingers twisting anxiously in his lap.

"I'm gonna take the full charge," he said quietly.

I blinked up at him, unsure if I'd heard him right. "What?"

"I'm gonna make sure the cops know it was all me," he said. "That you didn't even know there were drugs in the car. I'm gonna make sure you get off completely free."

I stared at him, my mind spinning. "Tony…" I started, but I couldn't finish the sentence. There was nothing I could say that would make this easier.

I was grateful for what he was willing to do, but that didn't erase the storm still raging inside me. Lydia had paid my bail—we owed her. The lawyer's fees were coming. And then, on Saturday, the salon called.

I was fired.

Not because of my work—no, they told me I was talented. "But you know," the manager had added awkwardly, "clients… they talk." And just like that, everything I'd worked for came crashing down.

I lay on the couch that night, staring at the ceiling and wondering how I had ended up here. I'd tried so hard—so hard—to be something. To build a life that felt stable and safe. And yet, with one cruel twist of fate, I was right back where I started.

Lower than before.

And I had no idea how I was going to crawl out of it.

Chapter 33

On Sunday night, Mia called to invite me to go shopping with her tomorrow.

My stomach turned at the sound of her voice. I hadn't talked to her since last week, before Tony and I got arrested. The weight of everything that had happened since then seemed to gather at the back of my throat. I darted my eyes around the room, making sure Tony and Lydia weren't nearby, and then pressed my phone tighter to my ear.

"I...can't," I stammered. My voice wobbled, and I hated that it did. "Um, Tony and I got into some legal trouble on Thursday, and I got fired because of it. So I can't afford to do that right now."

"Oh, Ness," Mia said softly. Her voice was so full of concern that I felt my chest tighten. I hadn't realized I'd started crying until I felt a tear slide down my cheek. My breath hitched as she added, "I don't have work tomorrow, so I can help you look for a new job, if you want."

"That would be great, yeah. Thanks, Mia," I whispered, swiping at my eyes.

"Of course," she said. There was a pause, one heavy with unspoken questions. "Do you want to tell me about what happened?"

I swallowed hard. The thought of talking about it while Tony or Lydia might overhear made my skin crawl. "Tomorrow," I said quickly. "When we're out together?"

"Sure thing. I'll see you in the morning, Vanessa."

I asked Mia to come as early as she could so we'd have as much time as possible to job hunt. She agreed, and we hung up just seconds before Tony came into the apartment.

"Where've you been?" I asked as he leaned down to kiss me. His lips tasted faintly like cigarettes.

"With Marco," Tony muttered. He glanced down at his shoes when my eyes widened. "Just talking."

"About?"

He sighed heavily, dragging a hand through his hair. "Whether I'd stay as his runner."

The air in the room seemed to thicken. I stared at him, waiting for him to continue, and when he finally spoke, his words were rushed.

"And I...told him I would."

"Tony..."

"I learned a lot from what happened," he cut in, his voice pleading. "We talked about ways for me to do better. I won't get caught again, Ness, and I'll make enough to help us pay off everything. I promise you that none of that will happen again."

His words tumbled out like he was desperate for me to believe them, like if he just spoke fast enough, he could outrun my disappointment.

I felt a storm of emotions twisting inside me — anger, sadness, fear — but mostly, I felt hollow. It was like something inside me had caved in, leaving nothing but a cold, empty space.

I couldn't find the strength to argue or even meet his gaze. All

I could do was weakly nod.

****

Mia picked me up at eight the next morning. The cold morning air stung my face as I climbed into her car, but the warmth of her smile soothed me.

"I got you breakfast," she said, handing me a bag from the drive-thru.

"You didn't have to do that," I protested, even as my stomach growled.

"I wanted to," Mia said firmly. "Don't fight me on this one."

The buttery smell of the breakfast sandwich hit me as I opened the bag, and I realized just how little I'd eaten since everything happened.

"Thanks," I mumbled.

Mia drove us to the nearest restaurant, a little Thai place tucked between a laundromat and a pharmacy. I tried to smooth my hair in the car window's reflection before going inside, but it didn't matter. They weren't hiring. Neither were the next several restaurants, markets, and convenience stores.

Hours passed as we walked through Ville Saint-Laurent, crossing block after block in search of "Help Wanted" signs. I felt like a balloon losing air, deflating with every rejection.

By early afternoon, my legs were heavy, and I felt like I was dragging my body forward with each step.

"There's always tomorrow," Mia said brightly as we walked back to her car. She gave me an encouraging smile, and I tried to return it, but it faltered before it reached my eyes.

I appreciated her so much, but I didn't think she really understood. The anxiety gnawed at my ribs, twisting and churning inside me. The longer I stayed unemployed, the further we sank into the debt Tony's decisions were pulling us into.

When we arrived at Mia's apartment, I noticed someone leaning against her front door. My stomach did a flip when I realized it was Michael.

He straightened up when he saw us. He looked so casual — hands in his pockets, that easy smile on his face — yet my heart lurched like I'd been caught doing something wrong.

"Hey," Michael greeted with a nod. Then he turned to Mia. "I've been in the mood for Mexican food all day. You two want to grab some with me?"

Mia beamed. "Sounds great."

I shook my head automatically. "I don't really have the money to spend on restaurants right now, but thanks anyway."

"Then I'll cover you," Michael said without hesitation. "No big deal."

His casual generosity made my chest tighten. Michael and I had known each other for years. He was my best friend's brother. This was totally normal... right?

"Okay, sure," I said, smiling. "Thank you."

The three of us piled into Michael's car. He drove us to a Mexican restaurant a few neighborhoods away. The place was warm and bustling, filled with the scent of spiced meat and freshly grilled tortillas.

The meal was nice — easy conversation, laughter, and for a little while, I forgot about everything else. But on the way home, reality crept back in.

As we drove through one of the rougher parts of Montreal, we stopped at a red light. On the corner, a woman stood waiting to cross the street. Her skin was creased and dull, her hair matted. She clutched her jacket tightly around her thin frame.

Her eyes flicked to our car, making sure we were stopped before she crossed. For a moment, our eyes met — hers sunken and hopeless.

I held my breath as she shuffled across the street. I couldn't stop myself from thinking about her — the life she must have had before, what she might have been like when she was younger.

That woman didn't deserve to be destroyed by drugs. She didn't deserve to be dependent on something that was killing her. Did Tony and I deserve to put food on our table with money that we got from doing this to people?

"Man," Michael murmured. His eyes followed her until she disappeared down the street. "I feel for people like her. I can't imagine how rough it must be to live like that."

I watched Michael's face in profile — the compassion in his expression, the quiet sincerity in his voice. My heart pounded against my ribs.

I'd fallen in love with Tony for real, but the crush I'd had on Michael never fully faded. And now... now I wasn't sure how to feel.

****

Michael pulled up in front of Mia's apartment.

As Mia got out, I hesitated.

"Do you mind bringing me to my place?" I asked.

"Yeah, no problem," Michael said easily.

"Thanks for today," I told Mia. "It really meant a lot."

"I was happy to do it," she said, giving me a warm smile. "Let me know if you want to meet up again tomorrow?"

I nodded, and she shut the door and disappeared inside.

When Michael started driving again, I hesitated. My heart raced as I said, "Are you going back to your place after this?"

"Yeah," he said. "Why?"

My fingers twisted together in my lap. "Mind if I go with you?"

I regretted it the second the words left my mouth.

Michael's gaze flicked to me in the rearview mirror. His brow furrowed slightly, but after a moment, he said, "Yeah, okay."

We didn't talk much on the way to his apartment, and the closer we got, the more my hands began to shake. This was wrong, and I was feeling almost as nervous now as I was the day Tony and I got arrested.

When Michael parked in front of his apartment, he turned around to look at me. And he smiled — warm and genuine, the kind of smile that felt safe.

Michael had an associate's degree and worked as a mechanic at a successful auto shop. He was doing well for himself, and he was normal. No drugs, no criminal records.

For a moment, I let myself imagine what it would be like — a normal life with someone steady like Michael. No drugs, no arrests.

Just peace. Even if only for a little while.

Chapter 34

After constant searching for the past week — endless applications, half-hearted interviews, and mind-numbing online job boards — I finally found a job. It wasn't glamorous, and it certainly wasn't ideal, but I got hired as a telemarketer with the first company I came across that was hiring and didn't require a background check. The relief that washed over me felt almost overwhelming. It wasn't much, but it was something I desperately needed.

My new boss, a wiry man named Greg with thinning hair and tired eyes, told me to come in on Monday morning for my first day of training. The office itself was bleak — rows of identical cubicles with faded carpeting and flickering fluorescent lights. A faint, stale odor lingered in the air, a mix of coffee, paper, and something else I couldn't quite place.

"It's not rocket science," Greg had said, giving me a crooked smile on my first day. "Just read the script, don't argue with the customers, and keep your calls short. Easy enough, right?" He patted me on the back, his hand lingering awkwardly, then turned and walked away.

The job was boring, sure, but at least it was easy. Greg spent one day training me, walking me through the script and occasionally correcting my tone when I didn't sound "enthusiastic enough." By day two, I was on my own, headset snug on my head and a screen flashing name after name in front of me. Most people hung up before I even finished my greeting, and the few who didn't were either too polite or too confused to slam the phone down immediately. I made almost no sales, but apparently, that was normal.

I felt numb as the week crawled by, each shift bleeding into the next. I could do this — I could keep showing up, keep repeating that same monotone script, and keep pretending this was all temporary. It had to be temporary. The exhaustion from last week's job hunt, combined with this week's grind, hit me hard. By the time Friday evening rolled around, I felt hollow, like my body had been wrung out and left to dry.

I decided to spend the weekend recovering — sleeping in late, binge-watching mindless TV shows, and drowning myself in comfort food. It was the only plan that seemed remotely comforting.

Tony, my boyfriend, had different plans. He told me he was going out with some friends on Saturday night.

"Don't wait up," he said casually, grabbing his jacket from the hook by the door.

"Don't worry," I called after him with a sleepy smile. "I don't think I could stay awake if I tried." He laughed before disappearing out the door.

I didn't even remember falling asleep. One moment, I was wrapped in blankets, the TV murmuring in the background, and the next —

Click.

The bedroom light snapped on, harsh and blinding. My eyes struggled to adjust as I squinted against the glare. Tony stood in the doorway, swaying slightly. His face was red, his hair disheveled, and the unmistakable scent of alcohol filled the room.

"Vanessa!" he barked, his voice slurred yet sharp. "Wake up."

It took me only a second to realize he was drunk. It took me another second to realize he was angry. Groggy and confused, I blinked up at him. "What's... what's going on?" My voice was thick with sleep. "Are you okay?"

"I heard what you did," Tony spat, his words fumbling yet heavy with accusation. "You screwed around with someone else? You cheated on me?"

I bolted upright in bed, my pulse roaring in my ears. Fear bloomed in my chest, cold and tight. I shifted slightly, subtly positioning myself so I could defend myself if things escalated.

"What are you talking about?" I asked, forcing my voice to stay calm.

"You cheated on me?" Tony's voice cracked. "With Michael? The guy who's just your best friend's brother? The one you swore I had nothing to worry about?"

His words came faster, tumbling out in a chaotic mess. His hands clenched and unclenched at his sides, and I felt my breath quicken.

"I didn't—" I started, but my throat closed up. My mind raced, scrambling for the right words.

Tears blurred my vision as I shook my head, feeling helpless. "Tony, no, I — it's not what you think."

Tony staggered forward a step, then paused. He took a deep breath, then another, as if trying to steady himself.

"Look," he said, softer this time. "Just... just tell me the truth. We can fix this. I just need to know."

Something inside me snapped. Before I could even think, words tumbled out of my mouth.

"I just got so afraid of the drug dealing," I blurted, my voice shaking. "I saw these people — people who were addicted, who were suffering — and I got so scared for them that something inside me broke. I couldn't stop thinking about how dangerous it was, and Michael... Michael said he felt bad for them, too. We started talking about it, and I don't know... I wasn't thinking. I didn't mean it, Tony. I love you. I love you so much." My voice broke into sobs. "I never wanted to betray you. I'm so sorry."

Tony stood frozen for a long moment. His face was impossible to read. Finally, he muttered, "We'll talk tomorrow... when I'm sober and I can think straight."

He turned and walked out of the room. Moments later, I heard the apartment door slam shut. I collapsed back onto the bed, shaking violently. I curled up into a ball, my face buried in the pillow as sobs wracked my body. The air felt too thin, like I couldn't breathe properly. My heart pounded so hard it hurt.

As soon as I woke up the next morning, I could sense that Tony wasn't home. The air inside the apartment felt eerily still as if his absence had drained the warmth from the space. The silence felt loud — the kind that presses down on you, suffocating and heavy. I lay there for a moment, eyes open and staring at the ceiling, trying to will myself to move. My chest still felt hollow and cold, like a dull ache that had settled in overnight and refused to leave.

But no matter how broken I felt, I needed money. That simple, crushing fact overrode everything else. I couldn't afford to lie in bed and wallow — rent didn't care about my heartbreak. So, forcing myself to move, I dragged my body out of bed. My limbs felt like lead, sluggish and uncooperative. The air was cold against my skin as I stumbled through my morning routine — brushing my teeth, getting dressed, and scraping my hair into a messy ponytail. Each motion felt mechanical, like I was just going through the motions to convince myself I was still functioning.

The thought of facing people, forcing a smile, pretending to be fine, twisted my stomach. The idea of holding myself together all day felt impossible. My throat tightened, and for a brief moment, I considered calling in sick. But no — I couldn't. Not now. I needed this job. I had to keep moving, keep pushing forward, even if I felt like I was splintering apart.

By the time I got to work, I was already exhausted. My heart pounded erratically, and sweat gathered at the back of my neck despite the cool morning air. The office felt stifling — the constant hum of ringing phones, the sharp click of keyboards, the muted conversations happening in every direction. The sounds seemed too sharp, too loud, grating against my nerves.

I spent my whole shift sweating and barely aware of where I was. My fingers shook on the keyboard, my headset slipping awkwardly every time I moved. Words blurred together on my screen, and I struggled to keep track of my calls. Half the time, I forgot what I was supposed to be saying, my voice cracking mid-sentence. I must have apologized to five different customers for my mistakes, my face burning each time.

But no matter how hard I tried to focus, my mind kept drifting — spiraling into anxious thoughts about Tony. The memory of his face the night before haunted me — his glassy, angry eyes, the way his voice shook with both hurt and rage. The way he'd left without a word. Would he even want to see me again? Was he out there right now, deciding he was better off without me? The thought made my stomach twist painfully.

I managed to sneak out of my shift a few minutes early — I couldn't take it anymore. My nerves were stretched too thin, and every minute at that desk felt like walking a tightrope over jagged glass. The moment I stepped outside, I practically ran to the bus stop, my breath coming fast and shallow.

The bus ride home was agonizing. Every bump in the road jolted my body, but it barely registered — my mind was drowning in dread. I stared out the window, barely seeing the blur of passing cars and streetlights. All I could picture was Tony — standing in the apartment, waiting for me. Or worse — gone.

When I finally reached our building, I stood outside the door for several seconds, unable to move. My hand trembled as I unlocked the door, and when I finally pushed it open, my heart sank straight to the floor.

The living room was cold and still, like a museum exhibit of my life. Everything I owned was packed neatly in suitcases — clothes folded carefully, books stacked with precision, even my toiletries tucked into zippered bags. There was no sign of chaos, no evidence of anger — just quiet finality. The neatness made it worse, somehow — like Tony had been calm and deliberate while deciding to erase me from his life.

Neither Tony nor Lydia was anywhere to be found.

I got the message.

My breath caught in my throat, and I felt like I was being crushed from the inside out. My legs buckled, and I stumbled to the side of the couch, lowering myself to the floor like a marionette with cut strings. My hands clutched my shirt tightly, nails digging into the fabric as I tried to force myself to breathe. The air seemed too thin, too sharp, like I couldn't get enough of it.

After what felt like hours—or maybe just minutes—I dragged myself to the phone and dialed Mia's number. My fingers trembled so badly that I had to re-enter her number twice before I got it right.

When she answered, I barely recognized my own voice.

"Tony and I are over," I said flatly. "Can you come pick me up?"

There was a pause — a heavy silence that seemed to stretch on forever. Then, in a low, steady voice, Mia said, "I'll be there in ten minutes."

We hung up, and I turned back to my suitcases. For a long time, I just stared at them, unable to move. Each suitcase felt like a tombstone — a grim monument to the life I had just lost. My hands shook as I knelt beside them, and I stayed there for several minutes, head bowed until the shaking finally subsided enough for me to stand.

I dragged my suitcases to the curb with slow, clumsy steps. The air outside felt colder now, the evening breeze biting against my face. My fingers were numb by the time I went back inside to lock the apartment door. The key felt small and cold in my palm as I knelt and slid it beneath the doormat.

I lingered a moment longer, staring at the door — the door that had once led to my home, to my life with Tony. My throat ached, and I turned away before the tears could start again.

Mia's car pulled up soon after. She didn't say a word as she stepped out and began loading my bags into her trunk. I could barely lift the last suitcase — my arms felt like they'd been drained of strength — but Mia took it from me without a word. We still hadn't made eye contact when we finally slid into the car.

It wasn't until we reached her apartment complex that she turned to face me. Her face was soft, eyes heavy with sadness. "You can stay here with Elijah and me for as long as you need," she said quietly. "You can have the second bedroom."

I opened my mouth to thank her, but the words stuck in my throat. My face crumpled, and suddenly, the tears came — hot, relentless, and impossible to stop. I squeezed my eyes shut, pressing my fist against my mouth to muffle the sobs.

Mia leaned over the center console and wrapped her arms around me. Her warmth and steady presence broke something inside me, and I clung to her like a child, burying my face in her shoulder. She didn't say anything — just held me tightly, like she understood there were no words that could fix what had happened.

And I cried — for Tony, for myself, for the life I had ruined and the love I had lost.

Chapter 35

I couldn't take my antidepressants anymore. I couldn't afford them on my new salary.

Not like there would be a point. The depression that weighed me down now felt like something no pill could touch. This sadness — deep, relentless, and suffocating — felt immune to medication. The chances of finding happiness at this point seemed bleak without Tony in my life.

I couldn't eat. Even when my stomach twisted in hunger, I felt no desire to fill it. Food had become flavorless, textureless — just a reminder of the empty space inside me. I couldn't sleep either. Nights stretched on endlessly, a cruel limbo where my mind wandered in circles — memories of Tony flooding in, unrelenting and raw. I'd stare at the ceiling for hours, hearing nothing but my own shallow breathing and the distant hum of cars outside.

I went through every day as an empty shell of a person, numb and hollow. I wasn't sure how I hadn't been fired yet. My calls at work were robotic; my voice monotonous as I rattled off whatever script I was supposed to say. I rarely hit my targets, and my supervisor barely seemed to notice me anymore. Not like I'd care much even if I were fired. The darkness that gripped me was relentless, and my future felt like something I no longer had to plan for.

I never talked to anyone at work. I'd arrive, clock in, make calls, eat lunch alone, make more calls, and then clock out. The routine became a dull rhythm — a mechanical motion I followed without thought. My coworkers never tried to talk to me, but I didn't blame them. I wasn't exactly radiating "come chat with me" energy.

But one day, on my lunch break, someone sat beside me.

Veronica.

I barely knew anything about her. I'd overheard bits and pieces — something about her dating our thirty-year-old boss and that she'd just turned eighteen. That was about all I'd managed to pick up. She didn't seem like the type of person who'd want to talk to someone like me — someone whose energy barely registered above zero.

But she smiled, bright and warm, like she didn't notice the cloud hanging over me.

"Hi!" she said cheerfully. "I don't know if you know me, but I'm Veronica. We started working here around the same time?"

I nodded, feeling awkward but willing to play along. "Yeah, I remember."

"You look young," she said, tilting her head curiously. "How old are you?"

"I'm nineteen."

Veronica's smile widened. "Oh, cool! You're the only person here who's around my age." Her fingers drummed lightly on the table. "I hope this doesn't sound rude since we're just meeting, but I was wondering if you could help me with something?"

I raised an eyebrow slightly, unsure what she could possibly need from me. "What is it?"

"I'm trying to move out of my parent's place as soon as I can," she explained, her voice bubbling with excitement. "But living on my own sounds boring, so I'm trying to find someone to move in with. Do you know anyone who's looking for a roommate?"

I hesitated. As much as I loved Mia and appreciated her hospitality, living with her and Elijah was hard. They were in love and happy — their warmth and affection seemed to pour into every corner of the apartment. It wasn't their fault, but being constantly reminded of the relationship I'd lost with Tony made it almost unbearable. I wanted to be happy for them, and I was — but it felt like an impossible task when every glance between them reminded me of what I no longer had.

Veronica seemed nice. And honestly, I had nothing to lose.

"I am, actually," I said.

Her eyes lit up with excitement. "Really? That's great! Do you already have your own place?"

"No," I admitted. "But I'd like to leave where I am as soon as I can."

Without warning, Veronica reached across the table and grabbed my hands. Her fingers were warm, and her touch, spontaneous and full of energy, caught me off guard. Even in my current state, something about her enthusiasm broke through the fog.

"My parents said that as long as I keep a job," she told me eagerly, "they'll pay the deposit for an apartment, plus the rent for the first several months. So we could both save up for a while before we have to worry about rent and stuff."

How could I pass up an offer like that? It felt like a small lifeline — a chance to pull myself away from the stagnant, suffocating space I'd been living in.

"That sounds great," I said, a flicker of hope barely noticeable in my voice. "Okay. Let's do it."

Veronica let out a little squeal of joy, bouncing slightly in her seat. "Yay! I already found an apartment I really like. Want to come look at it with me after work today?"

For the first time since I lost Tony, I smiled. It wasn't big, and it wasn't bright — but it was real.

"Sure," I said.

Chapter 36

The apartment Veronica had found was nestled in a charming part of Ville Saint-Laurent, a lively yet peaceful neighborhood that seemed to hum with life no matter the hour. Rows of modest brick buildings lined the streets, some crowned with rooftop gardens, others glowing warmly with string lights draped across their balconies. Cafés spilled soft jazz onto the sidewalks, and the faint scent of freshly baked bread seemed to follow us wherever we walked.

We toured the apartment after work on Monday. The place wasn't enormous, but it had a cozy charm — wooden floors that creaked under our steps, sunlight spilling through the living room windows like golden syrup, and a little kitchen that smelled faintly of fresh paint. It felt like a fresh start, a clean slate.

"I love it," I said, and Veronica's smile stretched wide.

"Me too," she agreed.

We signed the lease right then and there, our laughter echoing in the empty apartment as we celebrated. By Friday of the same week, we were both fully moved in, collapsing onto our couch that night with exhausted grins. It was a relief to be away from the suffocating air of the loving couple I'd been staying with before. Being nineteen, out on my own, and with a friend like Veronica, felt liberating in a way I hadn't expected. But despite the excitement, the weight of my recent breakup still sat heavily on my chest. The heartache was raw, sharp enough to cut through even the brightest moments.

Still, I felt hopeful. Living with Veronica seemed like the kind of change I needed — she was kind and caring, and during the week we spent moving in, we bonded quickly. By the time Friday came, she felt more like a sister than just a roommate.

On Monday, I arrived at work with a determination I hadn't felt since the breakup. For the first time since my breakup, I actively tried to be present, to listen to conversations, to pay attention to my surroundings rather than letting my thoughts spiral into heartache.

Veronica and I had shared lunch every day last week, but today, she was nowhere to be found. I waited at our usual spot in the breakroom, absently picking at my sandwich, hoping she'd turn up. The longer I sat alone, the more unsettled I felt.

I ate by myself. Then, out of nowhere, yelling erupted from our boss's office. His deep, booming voice was unmistakable, but what shocked me most was Veronica's voice rising to match his. I strained my ears, trying to piece together what was being said. The argument built like a storm — loud and fierce — before it ended just as abruptly.

The door slammed, and Veronica stormed out. Her face was flushed red, her eyes glassy and wet with unshed tears. She marched straight toward me.

"I'm sorry, Vanessa," she said, her voice trembling. "We got into a fight... and he fired me. And because you live with me, and he's a malicious asshole, he's firing you too." Her voice cracked. "He's too much of a coward to tell you himself. I'm so sorry."

I sat still for a moment, stunned. Slowly, I packed up my lunch, mechanically folding the wrapper over my half-eaten sandwich. I knew I should be panicked—angry even—but somehow, all I felt was numb.

"Well," I said, forcing a small, tired smile. "What's one more kick when you're already down?"

Veronica gave a weak laugh through her tears. "We'll figure something out," I told her, and together, we walked out.

Veronica and I decided to walk back to our apartment. The air was crisp, carrying a faint chill that clung to our jackets. The sun had begun its descent, casting a soft orange glow across the rooftops. The city seemed to be winding down, yet for us, things felt anything but calm.

The sidewalks stretched endlessly ahead, the distant sound of car horns blending with muffled conversations spilling from passing pedestrians. Each step felt heavier than the last. Our silence was punctuated only by the occasional scrape of Veronica's boots against the pavement. Neither of us spoke for a long while. We didn't need to — the weight of our situation clung to the air like fog.

"What are we gonna do?" I finally asked, my voice small and tight with anxiety. The words felt like they had been stuck in my throat all afternoon. "What kind of job can I get without a high school diploma… and without having to get a background check?" My voice cracked slightly, the helplessness I'd been fighting creeping through.

Veronica exhaled, her breath curling in the air. "Well," she said after a moment's pause, "I have a friend who dances. She makes, like, five hundred dollars a night."

I blinked in surprise. "Five hundred dollars?" I repeated, almost laughing. "Could you imagine making that kind of money?" The idea felt so distant, almost impossible. But reality quickly snapped back, and I added cautiously, "But when you say she dances… is she…?"

"She's a stripper," Veronica confirmed, her tone casual, almost dismissive.

I let out a breath, shaking my head. "I bet it isn't even that hard to do."

"Yeah," Veronica agreed quietly. "Probably not."

We were quiet the rest of the way home. The city lights flickered on one by one as the sky dimmed to navy blue. I kept my eyes on the storefront windows we passed, scanning for signs that read Now Hiring or Help Wanted, but all I found were empty displays and darkened doors. The telemarketing job had felt like a stroke of luck when I first got it, and now that luck felt like it had completely run dry.

****

The next day was a blur of frustration. I sat on the floor in our living room. Newspapers spread out in front of me. My fingers were stained with ink from circling ad after ad, but each one seemed more hopeless than the last. Receptionist. Delivery driver. Sales associate — all positions that required qualifications I didn't have. The more I searched, the tighter the knot in my stomach became.

Veronica was gone all day — hopefully, she'd had better luck than I did. By evening, my nerves had morphed into restlessness. I couldn't sit still. I paced the apartment, checked the fridge for food we couldn't afford to replace, and then returned to the couch to stare at the same lifeless headlines I'd already read twice.

By the time Veronica finally walked through the door, it was nearly one in the morning. I jumped up, relieved to see her, but the moment she sat down on the couch, I froze.

She dumped a fat stack of bills onto the cushion between us — a chaotic pile of twenties, tens, and fives. The sight of it felt surreal, like seeing treasure spill out of a chest in some pirate movie.

My jaw dropped. "What in the world? You found a job already?"

"I went to my friend's club," she said with a grin, running her fingers through the stack of bills. "And danced."

"You… danced?" I repeated slowly like I was still trying to piece it together.

"Yep," she said brightly. "And it was even easier than I thought it would be." Her smile was warm and genuine, like she was still riding the high of her successful night.

I could only stare. "How much did you make?" My voice felt dry.

"Four hundred," she said proudly, her fingers fanning the cash as if to show it off. "From just a couple of hours of being at the club."

Four hundred dollars. In my mind, that wasn't just a lot of money — that was life-changing. Rent. Groceries. Bills. All those stressors that had been tightening around my throat suddenly felt… manageable.

Don't fool yourself, my inner voice warned. You'd do just about anything for four hundred dollars.

I swallowed hard. "How was it?" I asked, my eyes still glued to the money.

"A little scary at first," Veronica admitted, her smile faltering slightly. "Since it was my first time and all. But once I got the hang of it, it was actually kind of fun. I'm not even nervous to go back."

I shifted my gaze to her face now. "Again?" I asked. "So you're officially working there?"

Veronica nodded enthusiastically. "Uh-huh. There's a lot of girls, so I don't even have to go in every night. I can just work whenever I want. And I'll probably keep making more and more once I get better at it." Her eyes lit up. "I'll have so much freedom."

Then she reached across the pile of cash and took my hands in hers. Her fingers were warm, and the way she looked at me made me feel safe, like she wasn't just offering advice; she was offering help.

"You've told me before how much you love dancing, right?" she said softly. "I bet you'd be amazing at this. You should come try."

My breath hitched. There was a world of difference between dancing at a party with girlfriends and dancing on a stage, naked in front of strangers. "I don't know..." I murmured. "It sounds kind of scary. Maybe I can just… go to the club tomorrow and watch you? See what it's like, and then I'll decide."

Veronica smiled, her fingers squeezing mine reassuringly. "I already know you can do it. You're gorgeous and charming, and if you're a good dancer too? They'll love you." She gave my hand another squeeze. "But yeah, come along. You'll see."

****

The next night, Veronica and I walked into the club together. The air was thick with the scent of liquor and cigarette smoke, but it wasn't the sleazy dive I'd imagined. The lights were dim but warm and inviting. The music pulsed steadily, making the floor vibrate beneath my feet. The men, rough around the edges but calm, sat scattered in booths or gathered quietly around the stage.

I stood nervously off to the side while Veronica disappeared backstage. I watched the dancers closely, studying their movements, their confident smiles, the way they swayed and strutted. Nothing they did seemed impossible.

Then Veronica appeared, and her energy was magnetic. The moment she stepped onstage, the room seemed to brighten. She moved with ease, spinning gracefully around the pole and took off her clothes. Dollar bills fluttered through the air like confetti, and by the end of her second song, the stage was littered with cash. Another thing that really surprised me was how polite the crowd was. Sure, men were whistling and saying dirty things here and there, but nobody was creepy or aggressive.

Dancing in front of relatively nice people for hundreds of dollars a night? I could do that.

I hung around the club to get used to the environment until Veronica's shift ended, and she found me in the crowd. "So?" she asked eagerly as we walked out into the cool night air. "What do you think? Do you want to try?"

I hesitated for only a second before grinning. "How soon can I start?"

Veronica's face lit up. "I had a feeling you'd say that," she laughed. "I already talked to my manager. She'll be ready for you tomorrow night."

That was a quick turnaround. But I knew I could do it, so I would.

Before I knew it, I was backstage at the club the next night. While music pulsed through the speakers, I ran through the club manager's rules in my head—I'd dance to two songs in a row, taking off my top by the end of the first and everything else by the end of the second. I'd do this at least twice a night, plus any individual dances that patrons would request with me, and I'd be golden.

The song ended, and the dancer walked off the stage. The DJ announced, "Help me welcome the lovely Ariel to the stage. This is her first night here, so make sure you let her know how happy we all are to have her."

The audience applauded my stage name. My heart raced, so I took a deep breath before walking onto the stage as sexily as I could.

Whistles accompanied the clapping, plus a few shouts of how beautiful I was. Oh yeah, I could definitely do this.

The song started just as I got to the pole. I moved my body to the rhythm of the song but mentally zoned out and imagined myself as the ballerina I used to want to be as a young girl. A ballerina who got naked on stage, but a ballerina all the same.

Once the second song ended, I snapped back to reality and looked around me. The crowd was excited, the manager was nodding in approval, and Veronica was smiling and giving me a thumbs up. And on the stage was a ton of money.

I smiled and blew kisses to the crowd while I gathered up the bills. Thank God for Veronica encouraging me to take this opportunity. With money like this, I'd finally be on my way to getting back on my feet.

Chapter 37

As weeks went by, and the weight of the past became more bearable, life slipped into a steady rhythm, and a sense of calm took its place. I no longer felt those flutter of nerves that once clung to me like a second skin when I first started out. My nights transformed into a steady beat; with each swap of bold red on my lips, each sway of my hips, each deliberate, playful glance, the nerves ebbed away, replaced by something akin to empowerment. I realized there was nothing all that crazy about stripping. It was just a job, like any other job I've had before, just with more freedom and a whole lot more money. I got to do my hair, put on makeup, and dress up in cute outfits, even if it was to take them off immediately. I loved looking sexy and making money from it.

As months went by, I became addicted to the lifestyle I had from dancing that I wished I'd started as soon as I turned eighteen – the fast-paced nights, the constant attention and the spell of glamour, everything grew so compelling that I no longer recognized the girl I had become. Now, I was someone else. Strong, confident and maybe even a little jaded. The money? It came fast and easy. I didn't have to scrape for bills and I made more money in a single night than I did in my entire last job.

While the spotlight had its own thrill and being on stage was fun, it was backstage that became my favorite part of the job. While we got ready and donned different personas, we turned from ordinary women to feisty dancers. Whenever we spent those quiet moments together, sharing words of encouragement and smiles, it gave me a sense of camaraderie. There was no judgment –just women supporting each other because they knew what it took to come there.

The real magic happened when we stepped on the floor. It was thrilling to give men private dances and talk to them like they were the only men in the building. Without fail, they'd melt under my touch and from my words. I loved the way their eyes glazed over, captivated by me. And the way they hung on every word I said –it was intoxicating. I felt powerful then, and I relished the control I had over them. Constantly being told I was sexy and beautiful certainly didn't hurt my confidence, either.

I did get the occasional "What's a girl like you doing in a place like this?" and initially, once my depression became more manageable and I wasn't living in such a daze anymore, I'd really consider that. In those quiet moments when my mind goes numb, and the music becomes just background noise. The loneliness would gnaw at me, and I'd question myself. Was I actually meant to be a stripper? Or was I just pretending to fit in? I'd stare at the mirror often –that thick makeup, that bold red, the glitter in my hair; unable to recognize myself, I'd ask myself: "Who was I? Did I belong here?"

But as time went on and I gained more confidence in myself, thanks to my skills and all the positive attention, I started to think that maybe I was meant to be here. My body moved with ease, every move flawless, like a muscle memory. My confidence was high with each performance –my rhythm, uniquely mine, felt as natural as breathing. Each dance, each piece of attention was a dollar earned. It got to the point where I made hundreds of dollars each night and had enough in my bank account that I really only needed to work once a week. I worked a lot more than that, though, because I liked to think of it like a reminder of the control I had over the room.

One chilly October night, I trudged up the steps to the apartment Veronica and I shared, my body weary and my heart heavy. The autumn air clung to me, seeping into my bones even as I reached the warmth of our apartment. The familiar scent of faint vanilla candles lingered in the air, a small comfort in an otherwise exhausting day. I tossed my bag on the couch, kicked off my shoes, and was about to collapse when I noticed the blinking red light on our answering machine.

I froze.

That little blinking light had become a source of anxiety for me over the past few months. Every time it flashed, I expected bad news — a lawyer, the police, some reminder of the legal mess I was tangled in. With shaky fingers, I pressed the button and waited.

"Vanessa," Lydia's voice crackled through the speaker, warm yet urgent. "It's Lydia. I'm just calling to let you know that Tony pleaded guilty to the trafficking charge and told the police you weren't involved. The charges against you have been dropped."

That was it. No more words, no explanation — just that simple truth. My knees buckled, and I sank to the floor, barely registering the sharp pain as I landed. My breath hitched, and tears spilled down my face faster than I could control them. I buried my face in my hands, sobbing as the weight of the news hit me.

Tony had done it. Even after everything — after I betrayed him — he still protected me. He could have let me take the fall, could have blamed me to lessen his own punishment, but he hadn't. Even now, he was still... him. The kind of man who would take the bullet to spare someone he loved.

And I had cheated on him.

My heart twisted painfully. Memories of Tony — his warm smile, the way his fingers used to trace circles on my back when I couldn't sleep, how he'd light up whenever I laughed — flooded my mind. I gasped for air as the ache in my chest deepened. No matter how hard I tried, I couldn't stop loving him. I wasn't sure I ever would. I couldn't wait for the day when my heart wouldn't twist like this every time I thought of him — the day I wouldn't desperately want him back.

It felt so far away.

When I finally managed to pull myself together, my face blotchy and my head pounding from crying, I knew I couldn't stay in the apartment. I needed air — or maybe just something to dull the sharpness inside me.

I grabbed my jacket and made my way to Revolutions, the bar a couple of blocks from The Strip Club. The neon sign above the entrance flickered like a tired heartbeat, and the faint thud of bass-heavy music pulsed from inside. I pushed through the doors, the familiar scent of stale beer and cologne washing over me.

The place was dimly lit, filled with clusters of people chatting and laughing. I headed straight for the corner of the bar, where I usually sat alone. The bartenders knew me well enough by now — no need for small talk. They knew what I liked and quietly kept my glass full.

I sipped my first drink slowly, letting the burn of alcohol settle in my stomach. By the time I was on my third, the buzzing warmth in my head was starting to take the edge off my thoughts. I was barely aware of the guy who sidled up beside me until his voice cut through the murmur of the crowd.

"What's a beautiful girl like you doing drinking all alone?"

I clenched my jaw to keep from rolling my eyes. Seriously? That line?

"I'm trying to drown my sorrows from a bad breakup," I said, hoping my blunt honesty would make him lose interest.

Instead, he grinned, flashing me a crooked smile that reeked of forced charm. He leaned closer, and I recoiled at the sharp stench of alcohol on his breath.

"I'm sorry to hear that," he said, his words slurred slightly. "Anything I can do to help?"

"I doubt it."

That should've ended it, but instead, he seemed to take it as a challenge. He leaned in again, his grin widening. "So what do you do for work, gorgeous?"

I let out a sigh and set my drink down deliberately. "I'm a stripper."

His grin faltered. He leaned back as if I'd just told him I had the plague. His face twisted with disgust, and as he staggered away, I heard him mutter, "Trash."

I'd heard that word before. Most of the time, it bounced right off me. Sometimes, I even shot back with a snide remark about how I probably made more money than they did. But tonight, with Tony's sacrifice weighing so heavily on my heart, the insult hit differently. I stared down at my half-empty glass, my reflection swimming in the amber liquid.

"I know," I whispered.

Months blurred by, a string of forgettable nights and hazy mornings. I found comfort in routine — waking up around noon, wasting the day in coffee shops or window shopping, then heading to the club to work. Afterward, I'd swing by Revolutions for a couple of drinks before dragging myself home. It wasn't a great life, but it wasn't unbearable either. For now, I could live with that.

One night in March, Sarah showed up at the club, grinning as she caught the tail end of my performance. Afterward, she suggested we hit Revolutions together. I agreed — having company sounded better than another night of drinking alone.

We found a table at one end of the bar, the dim glow of the neon lights giving everything a hazy tint. The music thumped low in the background, a steady pulse beneath our conversation. We were halfway through our first drink when a group of four guys filed into the bar, grabbing the table nearest to us.

They were around our age — dark-haired and boisterous. My gaze kept drifting toward one of them, a guy with tousled curls that spilled onto his forehead. He had a sharp, square jawline and broad shoulders that stretched the seams of his shirt. There was something magnetic about him — maybe his relaxed smile, maybe the way he held his drink like he owned the room. I couldn't look away.

Eventually, he caught me staring. When our eyes met, I gave him my best smile and casually flicked my hair over my shoulder. His grin widened, and he raised his drink in a lazy salute. I lifted mine in return.

Sarah noticed. "Looks like someone's interested," she teased, nudging me.

Moments later, we waved the guys over, and they eagerly

dragged their stools to our table. A curly-haired guy — Roger, he later told me — claimed the seat beside me. Up close, he smelled like aftershave and whiskey — sharp but not unpleasant.

He glanced at my empty glass. "That was almost full when I first noticed you," he said with a smirk. "You must like to party."

I smirked back and fluffed my hair. "You have no idea."

"Give me an idea then," he challenged, eyes gleaming.

I pushed my empty glass toward him. "I'll need another drink for that to happen."

He chuckled and crossed his arms. "Bold. I like that. What's your name?"

"Vanessa. And you?"

"Roger," he said, grabbing my empty glass. Without hesitation, he wove through the crowded bar, effortlessly flagging down the bartender. Something about that simple confidence — the ease with which he moved, like he knew exactly how the world worked — had me hooked.

I watched him from across the room, already wondering what would happen next.

Chapter 38

Sarah and I went home with Roger and his friend Jesse that night. Roger and Jesse shared an apartment, a cluttered, perpetually smoky two-bedroom that smelled like stale beer and laundry that had been left in the washer too long. The couch cushions were worn thin, and the coffee table was a chaotic mess of ashtrays, half-empty bottles, and crushed cans.

I went to Roger's room with him while Sarah went off with Jesse. Roger's room wasn't much better, clothes piled in corners, an unmade bed, and a faint scent of cologne battling the stale smoke lingering in the air.

Roger and I were drunk, too drunk to bother with conversation beyond surface-level facts about ourselves, bits and pieces shared between increasingly heated moments. Between kisses, I learned he was twenty-five, worked at the local oil refinery, and that his grandparents had moved to Québec from Israel. In return, I told him I was a stripper and about to turn twenty. That was about as much talking as we did the whole night.

Still, even in our foggy, alcohol-fueled state, I sensed something about him — a sharp edge. The reckless way he spoke, the aggressive way he pulled me closer, the carelessness in his movements, he was trouble. But nothing I couldn't handle. Honestly, I kind of liked it. There was something thrilling about his roughness, something that felt dangerous in a way I couldn't explain but kept craving. Maybe I was drawn to it because I couldn't stop thinking about Tony, and no matter how hard I tried, Roger couldn't match up. At least this way, I felt like I was still playing the game.

Roger had enough fun with me that night that he started inviting me over a lot. He and Jesse seemed to have an endless rotation of people passing through their apartment, mostly to drink, smoke, and party. There were always girls hanging around, most of whom knew exactly what they were getting into.

Sarah only went over that first night. She wasn't interested in Jesse after learning she was just one of many casual hookups, which was fair. I found out pretty quickly I wasn't special to Roger either; I was just one in a long string of girls. Surprisingly, that didn't bother me. In a weird way, it almost felt like it leveled the playing field like it justified my constant comparisons to Tony. Roger could never win in those comparisons, but I was still hopeful that if things with Roger somehow grew serious, maybe that would help dull the ache Tony left behind.

Roger and I mostly hung out at his apartment or at Revolutions, the dive bar where he liked to drink. But one Thursday, Jesse's mom was visiting, and Roger wasn't interested in playing the good host. Instead, I invited him over to my place.

When we arrived, Veronica and Sandy were already home, sprawled out on the couch, watching some reality show rerun. Roger barely muttered a hello before heading out to the patio with me. We sat on the creaky metal chairs, chain-smoking and passing a bottle of beer back and forth while he waited for Jesse's mom to leave.

We didn't talk much — just brief comments about random things. I mentioned how my landlord still hadn't fixed our leaky kitchen faucet, and he went on a rant about Jesse never cleaning up after himself. I knew he was stalling, dragging out the time just to avoid his apartment.

When I went back inside and Roger had left, Veronica and Sandy exchanged a look — one of those unmistakable "we need to talk" looks.

"Please tell me you're not going to see him again," Veronica said, her voice low but firm.

I frowned. "What do you mean?"

"Girl," Sandy jumped in, her eyes wide with disbelief. "He's a complete ass. He talks to you like you're an idiot."

My mouth fell open. "He was only in here for two minutes."

"Yeah," Veronica said, "and that was long enough to see what kind of person he is."

Veronica leaned closer, lowering her voice like she was afraid Roger might still be lurking outside. "Seriously. I can't imagine how he talks to you when it's just the two of you if that's how he acts in front of us."

"Yeah," Sandy added. "There's no reason for you to be with someone like that, Vanessa. You can do so much better."

I shook my head and turned away from them. They didn't understand. Roger and I could both be sarcastic, and sure, we argued sometimes, a lot, actually. Over dumb things, like who forgot to put the cap back on the juice carton or whose cigarette butts ended up on the patio floor instead of in the ashtray.

I knew what they meant, though. Roger had a sharp tongue and a mean streak when he was pissed. But I wasn't innocent, either. I started just as many fights as he did, and I had my own temper that flared up after long nights at work. Maybe we both needed to work on toning down how fiery we could be.

"We're not even dating, really," I told them. "We just both like partying and stuff. I'm not worried about it, so you shouldn't be, either."

Veronica and Sandy exchanged another look, one that said they'd expected that answer.

****

The following Friday night, Sandy called Veronica and me, asking if we wanted to go clubbing with her and Sarah. The four of us hadn't had a girls' night in forever, so we jumped at the chance.

"Sarah had a rough week at work," Sandy added with a smile in her voice. "So she wants to go all-out tonight."

We all knew what that meant. I put on a tight miniskirt, a tank top, and my favorite black stilettos. Veronica dressed to match the vibe—short skirt, glittery heels, hair wild and perfect.

Veronica and I drove to Sandy's apartment that evening, buzzing with excitement. The cool air outside did little to calm the warmth growing inside me, that familiar feeling of anticipation before a good night out. The night promised freedom — dancing, drinking, and the sweet escape from whatever had been weighing us down.

When we arrived, Sandy was still getting ready, so I spent some time playing with her sweet baby girl, who was nestled in her playpen. She had Sandy's big brown eyes, full of curiosity and mischief. She giggled and cooed whenever I made funny faces, her tiny fingers grabbing at my bracelets. I held her chubby little hand and smiled. There was something grounding about her; her innocence, her softness. In a life filled with chaos, moments like that felt like a breath of fresh air.

"She loves you," Sandy said from her bedroom doorway, curling her hair with a hot iron.

"She's perfect," I replied, wiggling the baby's tiny toes. For a second, I wondered what it would be like to have a life that simple — one where nothing mattered except giggles and reaching for shiny objects.

Soon enough, Sarah arrived, and we pulled ourselves away from Sandy's daughter to focus on the night ahead. The four of us squeezed into a cab, Sandy sitting shotgun while Veronica, Sarah, and I crammed in the back. Our energy was infectious — our laughter filled the car, and our excitement buzzed louder than the pop music blaring from the speakers.

"I'm so ready for this," Sarah grinned, already swaying to the beat. "I need this night."

"Girl, we all do," Sandy chimed in from the front.

"Sarah had a rough week at work," Sandy explained, turning to us with a knowing smile. "So she wants to go all-out tonight."

We knew what that meant. Sarah didn't do things halfway. When she wanted to party, she really partied. Tonight would be one of those nights — the kind you don't forget, even if you can't remember all the details the next morning.

We chose our club wisely — a place downtown that was always packed. The music was so loud we could feel the bass vibrate through the floor as we stepped inside. Colored lights spun and flashed above us, bathing the crowd in pulses of blue and red. Bodies pressed together on the dance floor, and the air was warm and heavy with sweat and perfume.

We dove right in.

The four of us danced together in a tight circle, laughing and moving like we had nowhere else in the world to be. Sometimes strangers would join in — guys sliding up beside us with hopeful smiles, their hands hovering a little too close to our hips — but none of us cared. We were in our own world, letting the music guide us. Between songs, we stumbled to the bar for shots, tossing them back like water before running back to the dance floor.

When the heat became too much, we stumbled outside to cool down, breathless and glowing. Our makeup was smudged, our hair messy, but we didn't care. Tonight was about cutting loose — about feeling wild and untouchable.

I didn't want the night to end, but when it finally did, I was drunk. The comforting buzz had fully settled in, making my limbs loose and my thoughts floaty.

In that state, my body had learned to expect Roger. The routine had become familiar — drinking, dancing, and ending the night in his bed. My mind, dulled by alcohol, practically demanded it.

When our taxi stopped at a red light, I leaned forward and tapped the driver on the shoulder.

"Turn left here, actually," I said, my voice louder than I intended. "I'll guide you, I promise."

Veronica, Sandy, and Sarah were too busy singing along to the radio, swaying and giggling in the backseat, to notice my directions. Even if they had noticed, I was too drunk to care.

The cab jerked to a stop in front of Roger's apartment complex.

I clumsily fumbled for my purse, tossed some cash at the driver, and muttered a quick "Bye!" before climbing out.

It wasn't until I was standing at Roger's front door, swaying slightly on my heels, that I realized how late it was. The clock on my phone read 2:03 a.m.

"Uh oh," I whispered, biting my lip. If everyone inside was asleep, I'd be stuck out here. Still, I knocked.

To my relief, Jesse answered almost immediately. He looked half-asleep, his hair sticking up in random directions, but he stepped aside to let me in without a word.

A girl was sitting on the couch, curled up with a blanket around her shoulders. She blinked at me, her brow furrowed.

"I'm just here to see Roger," I told her, smiling a little too brightly. "You're so pretty, by the way."

The girl's confusion softened into a smile, and Jesse chuckled dryly.

"He's been in bed for a while," Jesse said, "but go ahead and try."

I stumbled into Roger's room. He was lying in bed, curled up on his side, snoring softly. The room smelled faintly of stale smoke and his body wash — something clean and sharp.

I crawled onto the bed and slid on top of him, poking at his shoulders until he stirred. He shifted beneath me, groaning as his eyes cracked open.

"What're you doing here?" he muttered sleepily, his voice rough and scratchy.

"I got dropped off here on the way home from the club," I said, curling into him. "I wanted to see you."

Roger's arms circled my waist, but instead of pulling me closer, he pushed me back just enough to get a look at me. His eyes narrowed, and I saw something flicker behind them — something sharp and cold.

"You went out to a club wearing that?"

I blinked at him, confused. "What, you don't think I look good?"

Roger sat up, and I tumbled off him, landing on the bed beside him.

He gestured roughly to my clothes. "Your ass and tits are hanging out of your clothes, and you wanna know if I think you look good? I think you look like trash."

I stared at him, the words stinging worse than they should have. "I'm a stripper, but you're mad at me for wearing a miniskirt?" I scoffed, half-laughing. "Are you stupid?"

"I'm stupid?" Roger shoved the blanket aside and stood up, towering over me. "You can't see the difference between stripping for your job and dressing like a slut for attention, but I'm stupid?"

I scrambled to my knees on the bed, standing up so I'd be taller than him. My blood boiled — I could feel it pounding in my ears. "Yeah," I spat, putting my face inches from his. "You're stupid."

Roger's jaw flexed, his teeth grinding. Without warning, his hand shot out and grabbed my arm, his fingers digging into my skin hard enough to hurt.

"Get off my bed, you fucking—"

Before he could finish, I slapped him, hard and fast, my palm cracking against his face. It wasn't planned; it just happened. Rage shot through me, raw and electric.

Roger's eyes blazed. He didn't let go of my arm like I hoped he would. Instead, his grip tightened, painfully so, and his face twisted with rage.

I felt the air shift. Something sharp, something dark, loomed between us. I knew, deep down, that things were about to get a lot worse.

And I wasn't sure I was ready for it.

Chapter 39

The ache in my head and the pains in my body hit me the moment I woke up the next morning. A dull throb pulsed through my skull, and every limb felt like it had been wrung out and left to dry. I groaned when I sat up, the sound escaping my lips before I could catch it. I must've taken a bad fall last night. Alcohol and high heels didn't always mix well.

I stretched my arms and legs out in front of me, trying to shake off the stiffness, but my stomach dropped when I saw that I was covered in bruises. Purple, blue, and red splotches bloomed across my thighs and forearms like I'd been in a car crash, not just a night out. My breath caught in my throat.

A door behind me opened, making me jump and whip my head around so fast it sent another sharp pang through my neck. My heart was already racing by the time I saw her. It was a girl I vaguely recognized, one of Jesse's friends, maybe? Her expression was a mix of concern and wariness like she wasn't sure how I'd respond.

"You okay?" she asked me.

I looked around and saw that I was in an unfamiliar room, though there was something eerily familiar about it. The layout matched Roger's place almost exactly—same cracked ceiling, same battered coffee table, but it wasn't his. Jesse's, maybe?

"What happened last night?" I asked her, my voice raspy and dry like I'd swallowed sandpaper.

The girl pursed her lips, shifting her weight from one foot to the other. "Jesse and I heard a commotion coming from Roger's room last night, so we went in and saw him yanking you around by your arms and throwing you against the walls."

Her words sliced through me like a blade.

"I was able to pull you to Jesse's room while he calmed Roger down. I left you in the room to get you a glass of water, and you were passed out on the floor when I came back. I just left you there 'cause I figured sleeping was the best thing for you."

My chest went cold. It was like the air had suddenly been sucked out of the room. "Thank you," I told her, my voice barely above a whisper. "For getting me out of there."

She nodded, looking genuinely concerned for me. I used the foot of the bed to pull myself to my feet, but a wave of dizziness hit me. I paused, took a breath, then bent over and pulled my heels off, wincing as I touched a bruise on my ankle. Only then did I try again to stand, wobbling slightly as I took a step toward the door.

Then I hesitated. "Is he out there?" I asked the girl quietly, like speaking too loudly might summon him.

"No," she said. "He left about an hour ago. I'm not sure where he went or when he'll be back, though."

No time to waste, then. I nodded quickly, thanked the girl again, really meaning it this time, then left Roger's apartment with my heels dangling from my hand. My bare feet slapped against the cold pavement.

The nearest bus stop was pretty close, thankfully. Still, the short walk felt like a thousand miles. I was still in only my tiny tank top and skirt, clothes that suddenly felt like paper against my bruised skin. And I was very aware of all the people passing by and staring at my bruise-covered body, eyes that lingered too long, expressions that flickered between pity and judgment. I did my best to avoid eye contact with everyone. I kept my gaze low, pretending not to see the whispers or the tilted heads.

Finally, my bus came. I climbed aboard and made my way to the least crowded section, where I sank into a seat, wrapped my arms around myself to hide my body as much as possible, and stared out the window until the glass turned blurry. Until the world beyond faded into shapes and colors. Until I could slip into a daydream and get away from the present for a while.

***

After the most fun weekend of my life, Abuelita and Abuelito went to work on Monday morning. They would be gone for a lot of the day, but when Mommy woke me up this morning, she told me that she was gonna take me to the mall because there was a train that drove around it just for kids to ride. Plus, she said I'd even get a new princess dress!

Mommy made breakfast for us—scrambled eggs and warm toast with butter that melted right into the bread. She let me sprinkle cinnamon on mine, which made it taste like dessert. Then, she helped me put on the princess dress that was my favorite right now: a pale pink one with tiny sparkles and puffy sleeves. The whole time, Daddy hid in his room. I didn't even get to tell him good morning before Mommy took me to the mall.

Mommy and I rode the bus to the mall, and we got there just in time for me to get on the train! It was painted like a real steam engine, with a smiley face on the front and little bells that jingled whenever we passed a store. Mommy walked on the side of the train as it drove me all around the mall, past the candy shops and toy stores. I waved at everyone we passed.

Once the train ride was over, Mommy took me into a clothes store to look for the new princess dress. I tried on a couple, but the one that looked the best when I twirled like a ballerina was a blue, puffy, sparkly, Minnie Mouse dress. It had little polka dots and a bow on the chest, just like Minnie's. It was the most perfect dress I'd ever seen, and I couldn't wait to show it to Daddy.

When we left the store, Mommy looked at her watch, and her big smile disappeared. "We have to go," she told me.

She grabbed my hand and made me run with her all the way to the bus stop. It was fun, but it made my legs tired. I giggled at first, pretending we were being chased by pirates, but soon I started to huff. Good thing we were sitting on the bus now because I could rest them a little.

But then, once we got off the bus, we raced all the way back to Abuelita and Abuelito's house. "I think I need to slow down, Mommy," I told her once, but she must not have heard me because she didn't slow down.

Mommy swung open the front door, and Daddy was waiting for us in the living room. I opened my mouth to let him know about my amazing dress, but I didn't when I saw his face. He was looking at us in a really scary way.

"I told you to be home in under two hours," Daddy said quietly, "did I not?"

Mommy pulled my hand, she was holding a little one so that I was behind her. "I'm sorry, Carlos. I lost track of time while she tried on clothes and—"

"You didn't come here to gallivant around town," Daddy said. He was loud this time. "What are you doing, meeting other men while my daughter is with you?"

"Come on, of course not. You can see we have bags from the mall!"

Daddy started walking toward Mommy and me. Mommy picked me up and ran to my bedroom faster than I'd ever seen her move before. She tried to close the door behind us, but Daddy blocked her with his arms.

Now that we were all in my room, Mommy tossed me on my bed. I bounced once before settling. She turned away from me, and I looked right at Daddy's face as he punched Mommy in the cheek.

One time, I accidentally punched my cheek while I tried to open a really tight bottle of juice. That hurt. Daddy was way stronger than me, and he punched way harder, so I knew Mommy had to be hurting really bad.

Daddy hit Mommy again, then again. I kept trying to scream at him to stop, but my voice wouldn't come out. It stayed stuck inside my body and made me shake. I tucked my legs up under my dress and curled into a ball because I just didn't know what else to do.

Mommy was trying to block Daddy's hands with her arms, but he was going so fast that she couldn't stop him. She kept yelling, "Please, Carlos, not in front of her," but he didn't seem to be listening to her.

Daddy pushed Mommy into the wall with his big hand around her neck. There was blood coming out of her nose and mouth.

"You never listen," he said to her. "You better start. Because you won't be so lucky next time." He took his hand off of her and walked out of my room.

Mommy fell to the ground, then crawled to the door really fast to close and lock it. She sat against the door for a while. She looked dizzy, like after we'd spun around the living room in circles really fast. I stared at her and waited for her to tell me what was gonna happen next.

She finally got up and came over to me. It looked like it was hard for her to walk in a straight line. She sat next to me on the bed and asked, "Are you okay?"

That was such a crazy question for Mommy to ask me because she was the one who got hit and had blood on her face. I nodded my head, even though I wasn't sure. My body was okay, I thought, but my heart wasn't.

Mommy hugged me now, and she was crying really hard. "I'm sorry, Vanessa," she kept telling me.

That was weird, too. Daddy was the mean one. *He* was the one who should be sorry. I didn't tell that to Mommy, though, because I was scared it would make her stop hugging me.

I patted her back like she always did to me when I cried. I rested my face on her shoulder, and I saw that there was blood on my white bed sheets.

***

The bus jolted to a stop, and I jolted back to reality. The sound of the brakes hissing, the shudder in the seat, it all yanked me out of the memory like a slap to the face. I wrapped myself in a hug, but it did nothing to stop how badly my body was shaking.

When Mom had stopped crying, she used my pink telephone to call the police. They came and waited for about an hour before Dad came home and arrested him when he did.

It had been fifteen years since I was a child watching Dad beat up Mom. It had been fifteen years since I'd seen Dad at all because when Mom and I flew back up to Montreal, she filed for divorce and a restraining order.

I remembered how hard it was for Mom to get out of that relationship and how terrifying it all was. And here I was, in the exact same situation.

I was angry with Roger until the bruises faded. He'd apologized several times, and I finally apologized for hitting him first.

We weren't officially boyfriend and girlfriend, but we felt entitled to each other in a way that did nothing but cause more fights. We'd say terrible things and shove each other, then have great sex, get drunk, and forget all about it. It was how we made up, and it worked well enough that we never bothered changing our behavior to avoid the fights in the first place.

Putting aside the occasional temper flares, our relationship was great. We had a lot of fun together, enough that I figured this was just how relationships were.

Chapter 40

Canada's first hot spell of the year came at the end of May, and Mom decided that it was a good time to take a week from work and fly down to Montreal to visit me.

We hadn't seen each other in over a year, and it had been quite a year for both of us. From what she and Lily told me over the phone, Mom was doing great. She loved her job as a secretary at the pediatrician's office, and she was happy to be making new friends. She wasn't dating at all, and she loved that, too. She said it gave her clarity and peace, a chance to focus on herself and the little things— walking to work with her coffee, trying out new recipes, and sitting in the quiet stillness of her little condo with an old book on her lap. She sounded lighter on the phone like she'd shed something heavy without realizing it.

The past year wasn't so great for me. Mom knew about the arrest and my breakup with Tony, but I never told her about my depression and the issues with Roger. I didn't plan on it, either. No point in worrying her when she was across the country and unable to do much for me. It wasn't like she could show up and fix everything the way she used to when I scraped my knee or cried after a nightmare. Things had gotten complicated, murky even, and I didn't want to watch her eyes dim with helplessness.

When we spotted each other at the airport, Mom dropped her bags and ran to me as I ran toward her. The moment we collided, I felt the familiar warmth of her arms wrap tightly around me, and suddenly, I was eight years old again, hugging her waist after the first day of school. We hugged each other for several minutes, rocking back and forth without saying a word, letting the crowd blur around us. Even then, I didn't want to let go.

"This is so nice," she told me, looking around my car as I pulled away from the airport. She reached out to trace a finger across the dashboard, smiling with a kind of maternal pride that made my chest ache. "When did you get it?"

"Just a couple of weeks ago," I told her. "Veronica and I share it, so it's pretty affordable."

Mom smiled, her eyes warm and full of that steady light that never seemed to dim, no matter how many miles stretched between us. "That's wonderful, Ness. I'm so proud of you."

I took Mom to my apartment to drop off her stuff before going out to dinner. Veronica was cooking dinner for herself when we arrived, but she stopped what she was doing when she saw Mom. The kitchen was filled with the scent of garlic and simmering tomatoes, and the hum of soft jazz played from her phone speaker.

"It's so nice to meet you!" Veronica said, giving Mom a hug, a wooden spoon still in one hand.

Mom laughed, surprised and clearly charmed. "It's great to meet you, sweetheart. I'm so happy Vanessa has you in her life."

I watched, smiling, as Mom and Veronica got to know each other. They were having such a time that they seemed to forget I was in the room.

I loudly cleared my throat to get their attention. "I'm glad you two are becoming best friends, but we'll miss our reservation if we don't leave soon. We'll all be hereafter to talk as much as we want."

Mom held up her hands in surrender, laughing. "You're right, you're right. Let's go."

I'd made a reservation at Mom's favorite Japanese hibachi restaurant. It was the same place we went the last time she visited— where she giggled like a child when the chef made the onion volcano, and we both cried laughing when he flipped a shrimp into Veronica's glass of wine. The place hadn't changed. The same koi pond gurgled out front; the same bamboo wind chimes clinked in the breeze.

The waiter came by to get our drink order as soon as we sat down.

"A glass of red wine for me," Mom told him. She smiled at me. "And you?"

"Just water, thanks."

The waiter left, and Mom raised an eyebrow at me. "It's not like you to turn down alcohol." Her voice was teasing, but her expression was a little more serious, her eyes narrowing just slightly in concern. "Everything okay?"

I nodded, but my heart was racing. This was all going according to plan, but I was incredibly nervous. My hands were damp, and I could feel my stomach fluttering like it might take flight. "Yeah. Everything's great, actually. I found out a few days ago that I'm pregnant."

Mom's jaw went slack. She stared at me for a while, eyes wide with disbelief, before she was able to sputter out, "Do you know who the father is?"

"His name is Roger. I've been dating him for the past couple of months. We were never serious, but since we learned about the baby, we're becoming more serious."

"Are—" Mom shook her head, clearly trying to make sense of this. Her mouth opened, then closed again. "Did you plan this? And what plans are you making now? What are you going to do?"

I smiled, hoping it would reassure Mom, but she was staring down at the table now, her wine untouched, the color drained from her face. "Well, I'm going to keep dancing until I can't anymore to save up as much as possible. Roger has a steady job at a refinery. We didn't plan for this to happen, but we're both really excited and ready to take it on."

Mom stared at the table for a while longer. When she finally looked up at me, a chill ran through my body. I'd never seen her eyes look so haunted before. It was like she was staring into the future, trying to see what kind of life I was walking into.

"Is he a good guy?" she asked me in a low voice.

She didn't have to explain what that meant. Anything but an enthusiastic "yes" would devastate her, so I did my best to give her what she needed. I smiled widely. "He's amazing, Mom. He's such a good guy. And I know he'll be a great father."

Mom nodded, looking only a little relieved. Her eyes were still shadowed, like there was something behind them she wasn't ready to say out loud.

The rest of our meal was pretty tense, and we didn't talk all that much. We mostly picked at our food and watched the chef put on his show, clapping politely, but neither of us was really present, not on the drive back to my apartment either. The silence in the car was thick, filled with things we weren't saying. I kept both hands on the wheel and tried to breathe evenly.

But when I parked, Mom surprised me by resting her hand on mine.

When she had my attention, she took my hand in hers and squeezed it. Her skin was warm and soft like always. And for the first time since I mentioned my pregnancy, Mom smiled.

"You're going to be a great mother," she told me.

I told Mom that Roger worked long, crazy hours at the refinery as an excuse not to introduce them. I assumed he would be smart enough to behave in front of her, but I didn't want her to get any bad feelings from him. I couldn't risk her catching a glimpse of the truth—his moods, his quiet coldness, the way his voice could go sharp without warning.

The rest of Mom's visit went wonderfully. We went to our favorite spots in the city—the little bakery tucked between two alleyways, the antique store that always smelled like lavender and old books, and the fountain at the park where we used to sit and toss coins into the water. We cooked dinner together, made a mess in the kitchen, and talked for hours, curled up on the couch with mugs of tea like we used to. One night, when Veronica was out dancing, we even blasted *Fleetwood Mac* in my apartment and danced around together, laughing until we collapsed onto the floor, breathless and happy. I hadn't felt that kind of joy in a long, long time.

Back at the airport on Friday, Mom hugged me tightly and said, "I wish I could stay here to help you enter motherhood, but Lily will kill me if I make her stay with Aunt Nora any longer and deal with her constant off-key singing."

Mom and I laughed together. "I'll be okay," I told her. "I have a bunch of girlfriends here if I need help."

We said our last goodbyes and I love yous, then Mom was off to her flight. As I watched her disappear from my sight, the lie I told her came bubbling up inside me until I started to cry. The truth was that I'd actually never needed her so badly.

Chapter 41

One thing I hadn't lied to Mom about was that Roger was excited about my pregnancy. His face had lit up in a way I hadn't seen before when I told him—eyes wide, stunned silence at first, then this low laugh that bubbled out of him like pride. For a brief second, I thought maybe things would be okay. Maybe, just maybe, this would shift him into something softer, something resembling love.

As time went on, though, I began to see that it was just because it gave him another reason to feel like he had some kind of hold over me. His words started to change, sharpen, and curl like smoke around my thoughts. He'd say things like, *"You need to think about what's best for the baby,"* or *"Don't forget you're carrying my child."* It wasn't love. It was leverage. He could tell me what to do because I was carrying his child.

He was either too stupid to realize or too evil to care that throwing me around wasn't good for his child. That every time he raised his voice, the baby heard it. That every time he grabbed me, something inside me cracked, emotionally and physically. It was like he picked a fight anytime we saw each other, just so he'd have an excuse to hurt me, but how could I leave him? I couldn't raise a child on my own. Not without money. Not without a safe place. Not without someone to hold my hand when labor came and everything split open.

Less than a week after Mom went home to Alberta, I went over to Roger's apartment. I hadn't wanted to. Everything in my body said *no*—my stomach, my skin, even the muscles in my legs tensed as I approached his building like they wanted to turn and run. But I'd started getting terrible morning sickness, and with Veronica spending the day with her parents, I needed someone around since I could hardly move without throwing up. My body felt like it was no longer mine—it was a vehicle of constant nausea, cramping, fatigue, and dizziness that left me hunched over the toilet more often than not.

I was sitting on the couch when Roger stormed over to me. His footsteps were heavy, stomping with that familiar rhythm I'd learned to dread.

"Do you know how disgusting it is to put your bare feet on our coffee table? You realize people put their food there, right?"

I squinted at him, barely able to keep my head upright, the sickness rolling in waves through my body. "How dirty do you think my feet are? I'll clean the coffee table once I'm up if it's that important to you."

"No. You're going to get off your ass and clean it now."

Roger had me so angry that I couldn't look at him. I stood up and headed for his bedroom while saying, "I don't give a damn how dirty the coffee table is. You want it clean, *you* move your lazy ass and do it yourself."

"You're gonna walk away from me?" he shouted.

I heard his footsteps coming after me, each one louder, closer, like thunder rolling in from a blackened sky. So I ran the last few steps to his room and tried to shut the door on him. My breath was shaky, vision narrowing. He caught up to me, though, and used his body to stop the door from closing.

Roger grabbed me from behind, wrapping his hand around the back of my neck. The grip was cruel—tight enough to make my vision blur for a moment. He threw me into the wall and put his mouth against my ear, his breath hot and furious.

"You don't walk away from me," he screamed, punctuating his words by slamming my head into the wall.

"You don't disrespect me in my own apartment." Again, he slammed my head into the wall.

My head throbbed in pain, and I was dizzy. The room pulsed in and out of focus like a slow, flickering lightbulb. He slammed me into the wall one more time, saying, "I'm going to buy a pack of smokes, and if that coffee table isn't scrubbed clean by the time I'm back, I promise you, there will be hell to pay."

Roger threw me against his bed, then left. The door slammed shut behind him with a finality that made my body shudder.

I stayed completely still, kneeling on the ground with my upper body against the foot of the bed, until I heard him drive away. The silence that followed was so loud it felt like it might crush me.

When I finally lifted my aching head, I saw that there was a bloodstain on the white bed sheets, just like on that bed in Miami fifteen years ago.

But this time, I was the one bleeding.

My disoriented mind conjured up the image of a little girl sitting on the bed. She had my face and Roger's black curls. She was so small and helpless as she cowered under a puffy dress and watched her father beat up her mother.

The image wouldn't leave me. I could see her tiny legs dangling off the side of the bed, trembling, her eyes wide and terrified. She didn't cry. She was too used to it. Her little fists were clenched, nails biting into her palms because she knew that if she made a sound, he might turn on her, too.

I managed to stand up and make it to the bathroom before vomiting. My knees buckled in front of the toilet, and I heaved, body wracked until there was nothing left but dry sobs.

What a nightmare it would be for Mom to know that her terrified daughter, who watched from the bed, was now the one getting abused.

What a nightmare it would be for the baby in my belly to be forever connected to a violent and unpredictable man like Roger.

Bringing this baby into the world would cause pain for Mom, me, and the baby. I couldn't let that happen. We all deserved better.

I knew what I had to do.

Chapter 42

I carefully lowered myself into Mia's car. Every movement felt deliberate and heavy, like my body was moving through water. Mia watched me from the driver's seat, her hands clutched tightly around the steering wheel. Her face was sadder and more apprehensive than I'd ever seen. I looked down at my lap, avoiding her eyes, afraid that if I met them, I might fall apart before we'd even left. I could feel the heat of her glance lingering on me, but she didn't push. Instead, she gently shifted the car into gear and started to drive.

As soon as I made an appointment to get an abortion last week, I called Mia and asked her to take me. She agreed, of course, because she was an amazing friend. The kind of friend who didn't ask questions, just showed up, who brought snacks when I hadn't eaten, who held my hand even when I didn't ask her to. Mia had always been that person for me.

Mia parked in front of the clinic. The building was small and unassuming, tucked behind a row of hedges, with a pale blue door and windows that refused to let in any stares from the outside world. She'd picked me up at my apartment early so that we'd arrive early, and now I knew why. The few minutes of stillness in the car before going in felt like their own kind of grace.

She took my hand, told me I was doing the right thing, and held me while I cried. She didn't try to talk over my sobs, didn't rush me or fill the silence with platitudes. She just held me. My tears soaked through her sleeve, and she didn't flinch. She just breathed with me; slow, deep breaths like we used to do when we were kids, hiding under blankets during thunderstorms.

Mia took me back to my apartment when it was all over. The ride home was quiet, filled only with the muffled sound of the tires rolling over the road and my occasional sniffling. I was hollowed out, both physically and emotionally, floating somewhere outside of myself.

"You stay here," she told me softly. "We'll take care of everything."

I nodded, unable to say anything. There was a lump in my throat the size of a fist. She left the car and walked up to my building without needing to be asked.

A few minutes later, she came back with one of my suitcases. Behind her were Veronica, Sandy, and Sarah, all carrying out my things and packing them into Mia's car for me. I didn't even know they were coming. My eyes filled again, not from sadness this time, but from the way they'd shown up. No fanfare, no questions. Just love and action.

Once everything I owned was in Mia's trunk, Veronica, Sandy, and Sarah took turns hugging me and saying their goodbyes. Their arms wrapped around me like home—tight, shaking, reluctant to let go. We all cried together because none of us knew when we'd see each other again. There was a heaviness in the air, like something sacred was ending. Each goodbye felt like a small breaking.

Mia drove me to her apartment, where I'd be spending the night. She tried to replicate our old sleepovers to make me happy. She lit candles, put on our favorite nostalgic rom-com, and pulled out the same bag of gummy worms we used to devour in seventh grade. We put on face masks and wrapped ourselves in soft blankets, laughing at dumb memories and pretending, just for a little while, that we were still those girls who danced in pajamas and whispered secrets after midnight.

It was nice to reminisce on times when my life was better, but nothing fully distracted us from the elephant in the room—our lives had changed since then, and they were about to change again. The innocence of those sleepovers had been replaced with the bruised wisdom of experience. We could act like our carefree middle school selves as much as we wanted to, but we'd never be like that again.

Mia took me to the Greyhound bus station this morning with all my things in tow. The sun had barely risen, and there was a pale gold haze over the city, casting long shadows across the pavement. We didn't talk much on the ride—there was too much to say and no good way to say it.

I clung to her while I bought my ticket to Alberta, my fingers laced tightly with hers like a last tether to the life I was leaving behind.

We hugged each other and cried together. "I'll be back as soon as I can," I told her through my tears.

She sniffed. "You do whatever you need to be healthy and happy. Even if that means never coming back."

Mia's voice broke on the last words, and she took a shaky breath. "I'll miss you, though," she whispered.

I told Mia just how much I'd miss her, too. There were a few people in my life whom I loved as much as Mia and who loved me equally. Despite all the sadness I'd felt over the past year, I couldn't believe how lucky I was to have had someone like her in my life for so long. Someone who didn't leave. Someone who knew how to carry the weight with me.

Thank You, God! I thought as I watched her disappear when my bus pulled away, *for putting Mia in my life*.

The bus reached the outskirts of Montreal. I pressed my forehead to the cool window and watched the streets unfold outside. I frequented this part of the city, so I took in as much of the scenery as I could—familiar cafés, old street art peeling off brick walls, the curve of the river, the same graffiti-tagged overpass I used to walk under every day.

This city had always been my home, and I used to think it always would be. It had watched me grow up, fall in love, and fall apart. But as I looked at all the familiar places, it didn't feel like home anymore. The warmth was gone. The roots I thought I had here had been pulled up, slow and brutal.

I didn't have a home anymore.

All I could do now was hope that I'd find a new, better home in Alberta.

Part 3
Taming the Wild Girl

Chapter 43

I stared at the sign welcoming me to Stettler, trying to grasp that this was my new home.

It was strange to be surrounded by brown rocks and open air instead of tall buildings and city streets. The red, dusty earth stretched endlessly in every direction, and the wind carried a dry, whispering breath that seemed to come from ancient bones buried beneath the surface. It felt like I had stepped into another time entirely, like I'd wandered onto the set of some slow, quiet Western.

It was interesting, to say the least, to see dinosaur statues everywhere. They were scattered around town like oversized mascots of a forgotten theme park—cheerfully painted tyrannosaurs and grinning triceratops that peeked out from street corners and public parks. I even passed a velociraptor posed dramatically outside a pizza place, and I couldn't help but laugh.

Still, the town was small and quiet, which I probably needed. There was a kind of hush here, a stillness that I hadn't known I was craving. No honking taxis, no neon signs blinking at 3 a.m., no shouting couples spilling out of bars. Just birdsong, the rustle of wind against dry grass, and the occasional bark of a dog behind a white picket fence.

I took a cab from the Stettler bus station to Mom's house. The cab smelled faintly of cinnamon gum and old leather, and the driver kept glancing at me in the mirror, probably wondering what someone like me was doing here with two duffel bags and shadows under her eyes.

When she opened the door and saw me, her jaw dropped. "What are you doing here?" she asked, hugging me tightly.

"I wanted to see if the offer still stood for me to live with you."

Mom broke the hug to look at me, her eyes scanning my face like she was trying to read the entire story of what had happened to me just by looking. "Of course, Ness. But why...?"

Lily appeared behind Mom, her eyes going wide as she recognized me. She looked older, taller, maybe, with her hair in a messy ponytail and a smear of paint on her cheek. I said, "Maybe you guys can help me get my stuff inside, then we can all sit down and talk?"

They agreed, and a few minutes later, all my bags were in the extra bedroom, and Mom, Lily, and I were stuffed onto the couch together. The cushions were overstuffed and smelled like lavender and laundry detergent. Lily pulled a blanket over her knees even though it wasn't cold.

"I took the bus here from Montreal," I started. I had to grin. "I called Lily to get your address when I knew you'd be at work. I knew that if you knew I was coming, you'd be worried the whole time."

Mom squinted playfully at Lily, narrowing her eyes like she was staging an interrogation, but when they saw how my face had changed, they became more serious.

"I didn't tell her why I was coming, though. I figured it would be easier to tell you both everything in person, when you could see that I was okay. So..."

I told them every detail about what brought me here, how Tony and I broke up, which led me to become a dancer, which led me to meet Roger, which led to abuse, a pregnancy I had to abort, and the decision to leave Montreal.

The words spilled out like a dam breaking. I cried from the moment I talked about my relationship with Tony ending. It wasn't just the grief of that loss—it was the grief of everything that had followed. The way I kept convincing myself I was okay when I clearly wasn't.

Mom started to cry when she heard that I'd lied about Roger treating me well. Her hands trembled as she reached out to squeeze mine. Her lips were pressed so tightly together that they turned white. She looked like she wanted to go back in time and fight for me.

Lily started to cry when I said that the only way I could think to protect my baby was by not having it. Her sobs were quiet but raw, and she leaned her head into my shoulder, her arms winding around me like she was trying to hold all the broken pieces together.

They hugged me between them, a human sandwich of warmth and trembling forgiveness, and despite the pain I still felt over all of it, I finally, at least, felt safe. Safe in a way I hadn't felt in years.

"You can stay here as long as you want to," Mom said, wiping her eyes with the sleeve of her cardigan. "I'm so happy you were able to get out safely, and I'm so sorry about...everything else."

Lily rested her head on my shoulder. "I'm sorry, too. I can't offer you a house, but I can sing to you, if you think that would help."

I laughed and hugged her tightly. "No, I don't think it would."

Mom and Lily laughed with me. The laughter was watery and choked but real, like the sound of light cracking through storm clouds.

Being here with them again, I began to feel the first semblance of peace in my life since they moved away. There was a tension in my chest that had been building up for a year and a half, and finally, it started to go away.

****

I spent the weekend and the whole next week mentally and physically healing, resting, and getting used to living with my family again. I slept in until noon. I took long baths. I sat on the back porch and let the prairie wind comb through my hair. I helped Lily with a school project. Mom made tea every night. The house became a cocoon where nothing could touch me.

On Monday, I started venturing out into Stettler to look for a job. The thought of interacting with strangers again made my stomach clench, but I knew I couldn't hide forever. I needed something to focus on, something that reminded me I was still capable.

I decided to start by checking restaurants and bars for serving positions. My record was once again clean, which was a plus, but I wasn't sure how people would react to my past of dancing. It was always this unspoken risk, like if someone found out, they'd look at me differently.

Since I didn't think anyone would bother to call my old bosses in Montreal, I just told everyone that I spent the whole time working as a waitress. It wasn't a total lie. I *had* served drinks, just... in fishnets and heels under pulsing strobe lights.

I applied at a few places every day. The rejection was tough; some managers barely looked at my resume before sliding it aside, but I kept at it. On Wednesday, I applied to be a waitress and bartender at Montana Bar & Lounge, a bar and lounge in the center of town. The place had this laid-back, wood-paneled vibe and smelled faintly of beer and citrus cleaner.

Luckily for me, someone quit hours before I showed up, so I got the job on the spot.

Getting a job so quickly made the tension in my chest continue to fade. It was like a small flicker of confidence reigniting inside me.

It faded even more when I went into my first shift the next day. Serving was something I was good at, and bartending came naturally to me. I liked the rhythm of it; the clink of glasses, the soft hum of music, the flow of casual conversation. The shift flew by, and my manager kept complimenting how quickly I caught on.

Having such an easy job meant I'd be able to work a ton of hours, which meant I'd be able to keep saving up money. I wasn't sure what I'd need it for yet because I had no idea what the future held for me. But I did know that I would do everything in my power to make sure it would be better than my past.

Chapter 44

Time passed quickly out here. I moved to Stettler in July, and in the blink of an eye, it was already October. The summer had slipped through my fingers like sand in the palm of my hand; hot, golden, and gone too fast. The days were long, but they blurred together like brushstrokes on a lazy painting. Every morning, I woke up to skies so wide it made me feel like I could fall into them. There was something healing in the stillness of the place, even if that stillness sometimes bordered on loneliness.

By the standards I held as a teenager, life was boring now: I would go to work, then go straight home. The only exception was that I'd go out to The Carbin Club on some weekends with Annie and Hannah, girls I worked with at Montana Bar & Lounge, and quickly became friends with. It didn't take long for us to fall into an easy rhythm, laughing at inside jokes, gossiping over shared shifts, and sharing a kind of camaraderie that came from slinging drinks and cleaning sticky counters under neon lights.

The Carbon Club was the only "night club" in Stettler, and it served to show just how different life was here than in Montreal. The first night I went, I dressed up in a miniskirt and heels. My usual nightclub attire. The kind of outfit that turned heads on Saint-Laurent or Crescent Street. Annie and Hannah picked me up wearing sweatpants and sneakers, which was much more common at The Carbon Club. I remember blinking at them in disbelief as I climbed into Annie's dusty old Jeep, feeling like I had shown up for a costume party no one else got the memo about.

Even with a few culture shocks, I soon realized that this really was a good place for me. The calm, slow pace of the town was great for all the emotional healing I had to do, and despite everything I'd gone through the past few years, I was happy. I spent more time journaling. I took long walks by the Red Deer River, letting the prairie winds mess up my hair. I started sleeping through the night again.

The night before Thanksgiving, Annie invited Hannah and me to join her at The Carbon Club. "I just want to have one glass of wine," she told me over the phone. "Kind of like a mini Thanksgiving celebration for us."

I was happy to go, and so was Hannah. The three of us had grown close, effortlessly close, like we'd known each other far longer than just a few months. That night, we curled our hair with lazy waves, threw on whatever was clean, and piled into Annie's Jeep. The heat turned up too high, and the radio crackled with static as it fought to keep the station.

Once the three of us finished our glass of wine, Hannah said what we had all been thinking the moment Annie invited us. "We all know there's no way we're stopping at just one glass." With that, she signaled for the bartender to bring three more.

We didn't stop after our second glass, either. We were having too much fun singing along to the songs being played and laughing at nothing. The kind of laughter that bubbles up for no reason other than the warmth in your chest and the safety of being surrounded by your people. We yelled out lyrics we didn't fully remember, shouted compliments across the table, and took blurry selfies that would make us laugh the next morning.

Once I finished glass number four, I had to use the bathroom.

The hallway smelled faintly of industrial cleaner and cheap perfume. On my way back to the bar afterward, I noticed three guys sitting at a table across the room.

One of those guys had blond hair, blue eyes, fair skin, and was very attractive. All the alcohol in my system brought out my boldness, so I walked right over to them and sat in the empty chair at their table.

It must have been obvious how hard I was eyeing this guy because his friends smirked at each other and went over to the pool table. The attractive guy watched them go, then leaned toward me.

"Can I help you?" he asked with a grin that made it clear he wanted me to say yes.

I couldn't disappoint him, so I said, "Yes. You can tell me your name since you're the best-looking guy in this place."

His grin widened. "That's quite a conversation starter. I'm Ryan. And you're?"

"Vanessa."

"Nice to meet you, Vanessa. I've never seen you before, which is weird since this town is small enough that I usually recognize everyone in here."

I pushed my hair off my shoulder. "I just moved here a few months ago from Montreal."

Ryan widened his eyes. "You left Montreal for here? What's that all about?"

"Just needed a change of scenery, is all. Plus, my mom and sister were here, and I missed them. Have you lived here your whole life?"

He nodded. "Twenty-three years. I'll move away someday, I'm sure. Go to Vancouver, maybe."

I had a lot to say about Vancouver. At least, I acted like I did. I needed a reason to keep this conversation going because I didn't want to stop talking to Ryan anytime soon.

And it worked. Ryan and I got so lost in conversation that I had no concept of where Annie and Hannah were or how much time was passing. His voice was low and easy, like warm honey. He laughed in a way that made me feel seen, not just heard. It wasn't until I heard them laughing at one point that I noticed they'd joined Ryan and his friends at the pool table.

"They seem to be having fun," I said when Ryan noticed me looking over at them.

"I bet they wouldn't notice if we snuck outside to get some fresh air."

I looked back at Ryan, and there was a flirtatious smile on his face. I knew what that meant, and I was certainly down for it.

He and I left The Carbon Club and turned the corner to go to the alley beside the building. The air did feel really nice, and I was about to comment on it when Ryan put his hand under my chin and kissed me until I forgot what I was going to say.

We kissed each other in the alley for who knew how long, only stopping every now and then to catch our breaths. The night air was crisp against my cheeks, contrasting with the heat between us. His hands were warm against my waist; his breath was tinged with wine and something sweet I couldn't place. I could've stayed there with

Ryan all night, but eventually, his friends came outside and found us.

"Bar's closing," one of them slurred to Ryan.

I went back inside and found Annie and Hannah slouched over at the bar. "You guys okay?" I asked them.

They smiled at me. "Yeah, tonight was great," Annie said. "I'm just so tired now."

Hannah nodded in agreement. Annie had driven us here in her car, but she was clearly too drunk to drive us home. I'd been so busy talking to Ryan and kissing him that I stopped drinking hours ago.

"I can drive you both home," I said, helping them balance as they hopped off the barstools.

"Can I sleep at your house tonight?" Annie asked me. "So you don't have to drive to my place and then walk home?"

"Yeah, that'll be perfect."

Ryan ran into 'The Carbon Club.' He said, "I have to take them home," pointing his thumb over his shoulder, "but I had to come and get your number first."

The bartender overheard and stopped cleaning to pass me a pen and napkin while winking at Ryan. I made sure to write my number neatly, then handed him the napkin. "You better call me."

He smiled, making my heart skip a beat. "I definitely will," he said.

Chapter 45

I managed to get a few hours of sleep before Mom, Lily, and I went to Aunt Nora's house for Thanksgiving lunch. The food was great, and everybody was happy, but I couldn't get my mind off Ryan. The warm, comforting smells of roast turkey and mashed potatoes filled the air, but even the best stuffing in the world couldn't distract me. My thoughts kept drifting to him; his smile, the way his eyes had lit up when we talked, the feeling of his hand gently guiding mine. It was like he'd already carved a space in my heart, and I wasn't sure what to do with it.

The last thing I intended to do here in Stettler was get involved with a guy, at least not for a long time. I'd moved here to escape the mess I'd left behind, to focus on myself and the pieces of my life that still needed mending. But there was something about Ryan that drew me to him. Something about the easy way we got to know each other, and how our thoughts seemed to be in sync constantly. He was the perfect balance of funny, thoughtful, and incredibly easy to talk to. Each conversation felt like stepping into a warm hug, like he'd been waiting just as long as I had to meet someone who understood.

He stayed on my mind all week, but he never called me like he said he would. The wait, the uncertainty, had me tossing and turning in my bed, replaying everything over and over again in my head. It was a feeling I hadn't missed—the gnawing insecurity of wondering if I'd said something wrong or if I was just another fleeting moment in his life. I'd pretty much given up hope when, finally, on Friday, he called.

"I was starting to think I'd never hear from you again," I told him, my voice carrying a mix of relief and playful accusation.

Ryan sighed into the phone. "I wanted to call you the minute I woke up on Monday, but my friends convinced me not to. Said I'd look too desperate. Sorry to keep you waiting."

I pressed the phone against my ear, relieved that he couldn't see my smiling and blushing. "Better late than never."

"Well, in that case...as much as I liked kissing you in that alley, I'd rather take you out on a proper date if that's okay with you."

"I'd love to," I said right away, feeling my heart skip. It was like I had just been waiting for him to take that next step.

"Perfect. Does tonight work? I can pick you up at around seven?"

I gave Ryan my address, then told him, "I'm going to start getting ready now."

Once we hung up, I went to my bedroom, the anticipation swirling inside me like a hundred butterflies. I paused in front of my closet, staring at the rows of clothes. What was I supposed to wear? I had no idea where he was taking me, but I wanted to feel like myself; confident, comfortable, and not trying too hard. The safest bet would be something that wasn't too revealing but also not too prudish. I decided on a cute skirt and top, something that made me feel feminine but casual. My gut told me to choose flats over heels this time, so I followed my instincts.

At exactly seven, Ryan rang the doorbell. When I opened the door for him, he looked me up and down in a way that made me confident I'd chosen the right outfit. His eyes softened with admiration, making me blush, and I felt that familiar flutter in my chest.

"I figured we could go to the restaurant where I work as a waiter?" he said as he opened the car door for me. "I hope that doesn't sound dumb, but the food is really good there. And you're dressed perfectly for it."

"No, that sounds great. Let's go," I said, my excitement building as I slid into his car. The night felt full of possibilities.

The restaurant had a nice atmosphere—dim lighting, soft jazz playing in the background, and a kind of quiet elegance that felt perfect for a first date. "So, you're a waiter here?" I asked Ryan as I scanned the menu. "You must be pretty good to make some of the things they have here."

Ryan smiled widely, clearly proud. "Thank you. Yeah, I'm not bad."

"Did you go to culinary school?" I asked, intrigued by his passion.

A light flashed in his eyes. "No, this is just a side gig. I'm passionate about music. Been playing guitar my whole life. I've been spending the past couple of years saving up to go to the Canada Music Academy in Toronto. It's a six-month course, but I'd want to quit working while I go through it so I can give all my energy and focus to learning as much as possible."

"That's such a cool goal to have. And it's obvious you've thought about it a lot. What exactly are you wanting to do in the future?"

We paused our conversation to give the waiter our orders. As the waiter walked away, Ryan asked, "What about you? What are your big dreams?"

"I'm not sure," I admitted. "I'm hoping that I've finally reached a point in my life where I can start trying different things. I don't want to make a lifelong decision until I've explored all my options, you know?"

I leaned back in my chair, imagining myself at thirty and wondering what I wanted my life to look like by then. "I want a career that makes me happy, but I also want to start a family. I think I'd like one or two kids. That's been the one dream of mine that hasn't changed since I was a little girl."

Ryan proceeded to tell me that he, too, wanted kids one day. At least two, because having grown up the youngest of three siblings, he thought it was really important for children to have a brother or sister to grow up with.

The more we talked about what we wanted for our futures and some of the things we'd done in our past, the clearer it became just how much we had in common. Similar dreams, similar stories from when we were teenagers, and identical senses of humor. We both ended up taking over an hour to eat our one plate of food because we couldn't stop talking to each other, our conversation flowing like a familiar song.

When Ryan drove me home, I felt a twinge of sadness in my heart. I didn't want our date to end. I wanted to stay with him all night. Not to do anything sexual, but just to keep talking and laughing with him. The night had been perfect in a way I couldn't fully explain.

He walked me to my door and smiled. "I'm not afraid of looking desperate anymore, so call you tomorrow?"

I kissed him. "You better," I said against his lips, making him chuckle before kissing me again.

From the time Ryan drove away until the time I finished showering and went to bed, I sang to myself, a soft melody that played in my heart. Maybe it wasn't the best choice to start dating again so soon, but I could feel in my heart, my soul, my fingers and my toes that this was going to lead somewhere great.

Chapter 46

"Hey, beautiful. What are you up to?"

My heart sped up. Four months had passed since Ryan and I had gone on our first date, and this was how he started all of the dozens of phone calls we'd had since then. His voice was always smooth, like it carried the warmth of the sun, and it still made me smile like the first time we spoke. We became boyfriend and girlfriend three months ago, but his compliments still made me melt every time. It was like a little spark each time, even after all this time.

"I just finished up some chores, and now I'm going to look for something more fun to do. Do you have anything in mind?"

"Well," Ryan said, his voice laced with affection, "it's the perfect weather to lay around in front of a fire and watch some movies. I can pick you up if you're interested."

"I'll be ready." I could already picture the cozy evening ahead, just the two of us, wrapped up in blankets and the kind of quiet companionship that made everything feel right.

Ryan showed up at my house not long after, a grin plastered across his face. He always looked so at ease, like he was truly happy to see me, like I was the best part of his day. He took me to his place, where his parents were both at work, so it was just the two of us. We went down to the basement, where the best TV was, a room that felt like our own little sanctuary from the world.

We picked a movie from his family's collection, lit up the fireplace, and cuddled up next to each other on the couch. The warmth of the fire mixed with the chill in the air made it feel like we were in our own little world, and for the first time in a while, I felt like I could fully relax. Halfway into the movie, he laughed.

"What?" I asked, glancing up at him.

"You keep trying to scoot closer to me, even though we're already wrapped together like a pretzel."

"Fine." I untangled myself from him and pushed myself against the far edge of the couch. "I'll just be over here then. Cold and alone."

Ryan groaned dramatically. "Okay, drama queen." He jumped across the couch, practically landing on top of me.

"Hey, watch what you're…"

He cut me off by grabbing me, laying me on the couch, and hugging me tightly. "You wanna get close to me? How's this for close?"

I started laughing uncontrollably. "You're crushing me!"

"You asked for this," he said, squeezing me tighter, making me squirm with laughter.

I managed to get one arm free enough that I could tickle Ryan's side. He jerked his body away from me, laughing. "That's cheating!"

I pushed myself up on my elbows to go after him again and ended up shoving the remote deep into the crack between the couch cushions. "Time out," I said. "I lost the remote."

Ryan and I grinned at each other, slightly out of breath, as I blindly dug my hand around between the cushions. My fingers bumped into the remote, and I grabbed it and pulled it out. But it wasn't the remote. It was a tiny, clear glass pipe. "What...?"

I looked at Ryan. The flush had disappeared from his cheeks, leaving him pale. He darted his eyes to mine for an instant before looking at the ground.

"What's wrong?" I asked him, getting worried. "What is this?"

He was quiet for so long that I wasn't sure he'd heard me. I was about to ask again when he quietly said, "A cocaine pipe."

My heart sank. I had no idea what to say. He still didn't look at me, but he explained, "I didn't know it was there. I haven't used it in a year. I went to rehab, and I'm totally clean now, but..."

Ryan was obviously ashamed, and I wanted to comfort him, but I needed to think things through first. It took me a second to even process that he used to do cocaine. I never would have guessed. He seemed so normal, so steady, so… real. It was hard to reconcile with the idea of him ever being involved in something like that.

He was telling the truth about being clean now. I could see it in his eyes, in the way he talked, in the way he was right here with me, showing me the person he had worked so hard to become.

My feelings for Ryan were strong enough already that I was fully convinced I was in love with him. I hated the thought of him feeling bad about himself, especially when he probably worked really hard to get clean. And I was the last person to judge him for doing it in the first place, considering all the bad choices I'd made in my life.

"I believe you," I told him, my voice steady and sure. He finally looked at me, and I smiled. "I can tell that you're clean now, and I really appreciate you being honest with me. This won't change the way I feel about you. I promise."

Chapter 47

Ryan fully expected me to leave him when I stumbled upon his former habit. When I didn't, he showered me with even more affection than he had before. He would look at me with those warm, grateful eyes and tell me, over and over, how much he appreciated that I loved him despite his rough past. He confessed how afraid he had been that I'd run away, that I'd see him as damaged, as too much to handle. But I reassured him each time, telling him that as long as he stayed the person I fell in love with—the kind, funny, thoughtful man he was at his core, nothing would change between us. He made me feel like I was his saving grace, but in truth, we were saving each other.

We were on cloud nine for the next several days, basking in a sense of contentment that felt like it could last forever. Ryan had planned to take me out on Saturday night to the fanciest restaurant in Stettler, and I couldn't wait to get all dressed up, enjoy a night of fancy food, and just be with him. But I woke up on Saturday morning feeling unlike myself. My stomach churned, and I barely made it to the bathroom before the first wave of nausea hit. It was like someone had flipped a switch in my body, and I was suddenly at war with it.

I threw up twice more before the afternoon. By that time, all the heaving had left my lower back aching, and I could hardly sit up without feeling like the world was spinning. It wasn't just the nausea, it was a deep exhaustion that I couldn't shake, and all I could do was lay in bed, motionless, trying to calm my body enough to keep both the nausea and the pain under control. The sheets were twisted around my legs, but I didn't have the energy to adjust them.

It was the kind of exhaustion where your body aches just from existing, and all you want is not to feel anything at all.

I kept assuring Mom that I was fine, though I could feel my words slipping away as I said them. The truth was, I wasn't fine at all. The queasiness wasn't letting up, and the pain in my back was growing. But I didn't want to worry her. I didn't want her to get involved in what felt like a personal struggle that was probably nothing. But as evening drew closer and I hadn't been able to eat anything all day, Mom started to grill me.

"Do you think you might've eaten something bad yesterday?" she asked, her voice filled with concern. "Do you have any other symptoms? You didn't take anything dangerous, did you?"

"No," I told her, my voice weaker than I intended, "everything I ate was fine, and I didn't take anything. My back hurts, too."

Mom stared at me, her brow furrowing in the way it always did when she was trying to figure out what was wrong, what she was missing. She didn't say anything, but I could see the wheels turning in her mind. I was wondering too, because I was starting to feel lightheaded, dizzy from all the vomiting and not eating. I needed answers, but nothing seemed to fit.

Finally, her eyes widened, and I saw her go through the same mental checklist of possibilities that had been circling in my head. "Ness. There isn't a chance you could be pregnant, is there?"

The words hit me like a punch to the stomach. My stomach rolled, and without thinking, I slowly moved my hand to my belly, almost as if I were trying to comfort it. "…yeah. There's a chance."

Mom didn't say anything. She just stared at me for a second, her face unreadable. Then, she turned and left the room without another word. I heard her car start outside, and I knew she was going somewhere, but I wasn't sure where. My head was swimming, my heart was pounding in my chest, and my stomach was still unsettled, as if my body itself were holding its breath.

Twenty minutes later, she came back. She didn't say anything at first, but I noticed the bag of electrolyte drinks in her hand and the small white box she was holding, the one that sent a jolt of panic through me just by looking at it.

"I have to go get Lily from her friend's house," she said quietly, her tone slow, like she was giving me space to breathe. "You go ahead and take that test, and whatever the results are, we'll work it out when I'm home, okay?"

I nodded, unable to speak, the nervousness welling up inside me, choking me almost. Once I heard the sound of her car pulling away, I walked to the bathroom and shut the door behind me. I stared at the test for a long time, the weight of the moment pressing on me.

Every minute that passed felt like an eternity, my heart racing faster and faster, my hands shaking. The test sat there in front of me like a cruel game of fate, and when the results finally came through, my heart seemed to stop altogether.

Positive.

I didn't have time to process what this meant, didn't have time to let the reality sink in, because suddenly, the doorbell rang. Ryan. He was here to pick me up for our date, completely unaware that everything had just shifted in my world. I had completely forgotten to call him and cancel.

I tossed the test in the garbage with a shaking hand and went to open the door. Ryan raised an eyebrow in confusion when he saw me still in my pajamas. "I'm not early, am I?"

"No," I said, my voice unsteady. "Come in."

I led him to the couch, too tired to fight the wave of emotions crashing over me. We sat next to each other, and I finally said, "I'm sorry. I should've called you. I've been throwing up all day."

His expression hardened, concern flooding his features. "What's going on? Are you okay?"

"I'm fine. I'm…" I tried to steady my voice, tried to keep my face and tone neutral, but I knew it was a losing battle. I had no idea how he was going to react. "…I'm just pregnant."

There was a flash of surprise on Ryan's face, but it quickly morphed into something else, something that could only be described as joy. His mouth fell open, his eyes wide with disbelief. "You're pregnant? Are you serious?"

Before I could answer, he was already wrapping his arms around me, lifting me off the couch in a tight hug. "Oh my God, Vanessa, this is amazing. We're having a *baby*."

He pulled back just enough to look me in the eyes, his hands framing my face gently. His voice cracked with emotion. "We're going to be *parents*. Oh my God. You're going to be the best mother, and I'm going to do everything I can to take care of you two."

Tears blurred my vision as I processed his words, his overwhelming happiness, and the way his hands cupped my face so tenderly. I put my own hand on my belly, feeling an odd mix of awe and uncertainty. And then, because it felt right, I kissed him. "We're going to be *parents*," I whispered.

We hugged again, laughing a little as we tried to absorb

everything. But then, the reality of it all hit me, and I said, "This won't be easy. We'll have to work hard to make sure we can provide this baby with everything it needs. It'll be tiring, and stressful, and…"

"And we'll be fine," Ryan interrupted, his tone firm and full of confidence. He took my face in his hands again, looking into my eyes like I was the most important person in the world. "I love you, Vanessa, and you love me. This will be so worth it, no matter how hard things might be at first."

He was right. We'd make it work. We always had. We were starting a family, and I was ready to face whatever came next with him by my side.

Our parents weren't as excited about the news. Over the next few days, their reactions were laced with concern, doubts, and questions. They focused on all the practical issues—how we lived at home, how we'd only known each other for a few months, how neither of us had particularly high-paying jobs. They weren't happy we hadn't been more careful. But still, we stayed optimistic, and slowly, they began to see how serious we were about doing the best we could. They even offered their help, though reluctantly.

Once our parents started to come around, we began sharing the news with other people. Lily was ecstatic, almost jumping up and down with joy when she found out she was going to be an aunt. Ryan's sisters were thrilled as well, and even though things were a bit shaky, we couldn't help but feel the warmth of the love and support that started to build around us. There wasn't much left to be unhappy about.

The only real bump in the road came a week later when I had to quit my job. The morning sickness had become so intense that I couldn't keep up with anything. I hated the thought of losing the extra income, but my manager was understanding, assuring me that whenever I was able to come back, there would be a spot for me.

Then, just a few weeks later, came great news: Ryan's middle sister, Bella, called him. She and her husband, Jacob, had just signed a lease for a rental home. There was an upstairs unit and a downstairs unit, both of which were spacious enough for a couple to live in. They'd decided to live upstairs and rent out the downstairs unit, and they wanted to offer it to us before they put it up for rent.

Ryan came over to tell me all this, and he looked at me with those hopeful eyes. "What do you think? Should we say yes?"

"That'll be perfect for us!" I said, my excitement bubbling over. "Can we call them right now and say yes?"

And just like that, we did. It was settled. Bella and Jacob would be moving in just three days, and Ryan and I would follow right behind them.

"I told you we'd be fine," Ryan said, his arms wrapping around me in a tight, comforting hug. "Everything is going to work out, and you and I are gonna have a happy little family."

Chapter 48

Our apartment was great. It was in a good location in town, and it was pretty new, so everything was in near-perfect condition. The light poured through the big windows, and the cozy layout gave it a warm, inviting feel. The furniture was minimal but functional, and every little corner had the promise of becoming a place to make memories. Ryan and I spent our first couple of days in the apartment chattering constantly about how amazing it was to finally be living together and starting the next step of our journey as a family. We talked about how it felt like we were building something real, a life we could call our own. The excitement in the air was palpable, like we could conquer the world together, with this apartment being our first true home as a couple. We laughed over the smallest things, like trying to figure out where to place the couch or what color to paint the nursery, but every moment felt special, like we were in this new chapter together.

It wasn't long before we realized that our new reality wasn't quite what we'd expected it to be. The bills began to pile up quicker than we thought, and with the addition of baby supplies, we started to feel the pressure. Our money situation had been fine when we lived at home, with no rent, no groceries to buy, and no responsibilities beyond showing up for work and school. But suddenly, it felt like we were carrying the weight of the world on our shoulders. We were stretched thin, constantly having to prioritize what was more important—keeping the lights on or buying diapers.

Ryan started working longer hours to compensate. At first, it didn't seem like a big deal. He was always the type to put in extra hours when needed. But soon, I could see how tired he was. I felt awful that all I was doing was laying around at home while he was working so hard. My nausea was persistently bad, and my body ached more often than not. The exhaustion and discomfort were almost constant. I wanted to help, but I could hardly get out of bed some days. He often told me he was okay, but he became a little less convincing each time. There were days when I'd see him slump into a chair after a shift, his eyes distant, his shoulders sagging as though he'd been carrying a weight much heavier than the one on his back.

We both tried to stay optimistic, but the strain was beginning to show. Ryan was stressed and exhausted from working all the time, and my pregnancy hormones were a disaster, making my mood swings worse than ever. We both knew it, but neither of us knew how to fix it. For the first time since we'd met, Ryan and I started to argue. It was over petty things, like not closing the cereal box properly or leaving shoes in the wrong place. Little things that didn't matter but felt so much bigger when you're both running on empty. We'd apologize and forgive each other quickly, but the arguments were taking a toll on our relationship regardless. I hated the tension that hung in the air, the cracks in what had always been so easy and natural between us.

I coped by having Annie and Hannah over to drink tea and plan things for the baby. We would sit together, laughing about the silly things we'd read in parenting books or talking about all the things we still needed to buy. The conversation was comforting, a small distraction from the stress. Ryan coped by going out with friends after work. At first, I thought that was completely fair. He was working hard, and everyone needs an outlet. But then it started happening more often—Ryan going out later and later, staying out longer than I thought was necessary, to the point where he was spending more time out with his friends than he did at home.

I began to feel a pang of unease, but I told myself it was just the pregnancy hormones. I told myself that he deserved his time with his friends, that he was stressed and needed to unwind. But then, things began to change. It came to be that when he was home, he was... off. He'd stay up hours after I went to bed, staring at the wall or pacing around, looking like he was carrying something heavy in his mind. He was anxious all the time, always fidgeting, and I never saw him eat. It was as if the energy had been sucked out of him. He'd tell me he was fine, but I could tell he wasn't. I asked him if he was doing okay one day, trying to mask my concern with a casual tone, and he insisted he was just stressed from work. He'd never given me a reason to think he'd lie, so I accepted that his job was just hard on him right now. I wanted to trust him, to believe that this was just a phase, but there was a knot in my stomach I couldn't untangle.

One Tuesday, when Annie was off work, she came over to help me build the crib Ryan and I had bought. Our conversation floated from one topic to another until I mentioned Ryan's recent behavior. I didn't mean to bring it up, but it had been eating at me. I needed to talk to someone to get another perspective.

Annie stopped what she was doing and looked at me hard. "Does he still hang out with Perry, that guy he was with that night at The Carbon Club?" she asked, her voice quiet but pointed.

"Yeah, he's one of the guys Ryan meets up with a lot after work. Why?" I replied, not thinking much of it at first.

She looked at me sadly, her eyes filled with concern. "Perry and

I went out a few times after that night. He was acting exactly how Ryan is now, and I learned it was because he was on cocaine. Cocaine. I'm not saying that's what Ryan's doing, but if they're hanging out, there's a possibility."

My heart dropped into my stomach. My mind raced, my pulse quickening as I tried to stay neutral. I didn't want to give away the fear that was slowly creeping up on me. "I'll just have to talk to him and see what's going on," I said, though my voice felt tight.

We changed the subject, but I could hardly focus. All I could think about was the possibility that Ryan had started using again. The fear gnawed at me, a constant weight in my chest.

Once Annie left, I called Ryan's restaurant and asked his manager to let Ryan know I needed him to come straight home when his shift was over. Thankfully, he did.

He walked right up to me, his eyes wide with concern. "Are you okay?" he asked, gesturing to me and my stomach. "My manager said you sounded freaked out when you called."

I took his hand and led him to the couch, feeling the weight of the moment pressing down on me. I wasn't sure how this conversation would go, but I felt that, somehow, we'd stay calmer if we were sitting down.

"You love me, Ryan," I started, my voice soft but serious. "And you want to be a good boyfriend and a good father, right?"

"Of course, Vanessa. You know that." His voice was steady, but I could see the flicker of worry in his eyes.

"Then I need you to tell me the truth," I said, trying to keep the tremble out of my voice. I had to know.

Ryan's face changed in an instant. He knew that I knew. His shoulders dropped, and he nodded, saying nothing.

"Have you been using cocaine again?" I asked, each word heavier than the last.

He looked at the ground and sighed, his breath shaky. His chest deflated as though the weight of the world had just settled onto him. "I'm sorry, Vanessa." His voice was so small, so full of regret, that I felt my heart break just a little.

I waited. When I didn't reply immediately, he continued, trying to explain himself. "The stress of being the sole provider and becoming a father has been wearing me down. I'm still excited to be a father, I swear, but it's just a lot."

"It'll always be a lot, Ryan," I said gently. "Being a parent is constant hard work. Do you expect to do cocaine until our child moves out?" I shook my head, the frustration rising in me. "If we're going to be parents, we need to find better ways to deal with stress."

Ryan rubbed his eyes, the weariness etched on his face. "I know, I know. I just haven't figured it out yet. It used to be that cocaine was all I had when I was going through the worst times of my life. It's hard to move past that."

"The worst times of your life?" I repeated the words, heavy in my mind. "They must have been pretty bad to lead to cocaine. Can you tell me what was going on?"

His eyes grew wide, the fear almost palpable. "No. That's not a good idea, I don't—I don't think I can do that."

Ryan was clearly ashamed at first, but now, there was something deeper in his eyes—distress, confusion, and maybe...

fear? It was like he was afraid to face something he'd buried too deep.

"Ryan," I said gently, moving closer. I rested my hand on his, and he flinched before lacing our fingers together as if needing the connection but not fully trusting it. "If we're going to be good parents, we need to deal with any issues we have as a couple and as individuals. Whatever bad things we've been through or done, we need to lay them out in the open so we can start to work through them together."

I could tell he was about to protest, so I said quickly, "If we're not putting in an equal amount of effort to better ourselves for our baby, I'm not sure how this relationship will work out, to be honest."

Ryan's eyes filled with tears, and he blinked them away before quietly saying, "Okay. I'll do it. Can you start?"

Whatever it was that Ryan had gone through to make him turn to cocaine was obviously traumatizing for him. The fact that he was willing to talk about it with me flooded my heart with sympathy and love for him. I hugged him tightly, whispering, "Of course."

We sat facing each other on opposite ends of the couch. "This won't be easy for either of us," I said softly, my heart heavy with the weight of everything we were about to face. "Let's agree that no matter what comes out, there won't be any judgment here. After all, we're doing this for our baby more than anything."

Ryan nodded, his face drawn but determined. I swallowed hard. "Great. But if there's anything that's a dealbreaker for one of us, well...we'll cross that bridge when we get to it?"

He nodded again, but the fear returned to his face. He must have thought I meant his actions would be a dealbreaker for me when, really, it was the opposite.

"Okay." I exhaled slowly, steeling myself. "Here goes."

I decided it would be easiest to go in chronological order. I told Ryan how Dad left me, how he abused Mom, and how I spent most of my childhood with a depressed mother and a distant stepfather. I told him how this led to me hooking up with older guys, cheating on past boyfriends, and becoming a stripper. By the time I told him about how Roger abused me and how I had to abort my baby and run away to Alberta to stay safe, I was crying.

"So that's my life," I told him through sniffles. "I made a lot of choices I'm ashamed of, and I'll never make again."

For the first time since I started telling my story, Ryan spoke. "I'm sorry you went through all that."

I looked at him just in time to see him move in to hug me. He held me tightly, saying, "I'm sorry people have treated you so terribly. I won't ever do that to you, Vanessa. I promise."

"Thank you." We kissed, and I said, "Your turn."

Ryan nodded, his face pale. "I didn't go through as much as you. Just one thing, really..."

He took a deep breath. "When I was ten, my parents went out of town for a week. I don't remember why. But I couldn't go because of school, so my sisters and I stayed with my dad's brother for a week.

"Bella and Christina shared a room, and I had my own. Everything was fine until the last night we were there. I was just falling asleep when my uncle came into my room."

It was a struggle not to be sick, as Ryan told me about the terrible things his uncle did to him. Like me, he cried when he told his story. "I didn't know what to do. I just froze and lay there. I knew I should've tried to fight back, but I couldn't.

"He told me not to tell anyone, and I was so scared that I didn't. It destroyed me more as time went on, and I couldn't ask for help. Smoking weed and drinking made things worse. It wasn't until I tried cocaine with some guys from my high school that something finally took the pain away for a while. I didn't care how bad it was for me because I was so desperate to get rid of that pain."

Ryan buried his face in his hands, sobbing quietly. I moved over to him, wrapping my arms around him and holding him tight. "Thank you for telling me all that," I whispered. "I know how much courage that must've taken."

We sat there for a long time, just holding each other. "I'm going to help you through that trauma," I told him. "I'm going to help you get off cocaine and get you healthy."

Ryan smiled weakly. "And I'm going to help you heal from the abuse you went through. We can do this."

I smiled back, a warmth spreading through me. "We can definitely do this."

Chapter 49

Ryan stopped using cocaine the day we had our discussion. It was a huge step for him, and it felt like a weight had been lifted from our lives, but the road to recovery wasn't without its struggles. Dealing with withdrawal symptoms for the first few days was rough for him. He could barely sleep, tossing and turning in bed, his body wracked with the kind of fatigue that only comes from going through a physical and emotional detox. He had no energy, his body felt heavy and drained all the time, and he wasn't able to feel any kind of happiness; everything just felt like a blur of exhaustion and frustration. There were days when his face was pale, and he couldn't hide how much it hurt. But despite all of it, he pushed through.

He apologized for his withdrawal, putting more stress on me, but I promised him that I didn't mind at all. "The stress will pass, Ryan," I told him gently, holding his hand. "And if it means you getting healthier, it's worth it." I meant every word. We were in this together, and I knew the pain wouldn't last forever. We would get through this, just like we'd gotten through everything else.

Instead of using drugs or starting arguments as we had in the past, Ryan and I worked on communicating our issues in a healthy way. At first, it was uncomfortable to admit when we were struggling. The silence that would hang between us sometimes felt thick with unspoken things, but we made sure to always remind each other of our love, which made talking things out easier as time went on. Every little gesture—like a reassuring touch or a whispered word of encouragement—helped to bring us closer. We were learning how to support each other, how to listen, and how to be there, even when the answers weren't easy.

Our constant stress was fading away, which was improving other aspects of our lives. As I entered my last trimester, the constant sickness I'd had since getting pregnant disappeared. It was like I could finally breathe again. I woke up feeling like a different person—less weighed down, more alive. Ryan, too, was beginning to feel better. He got a job at a nicer restaurant, which meant better paychecks and less worry about our financial situation. Things were really looking up for our little family. I felt like we were finally on the right track, and I had a growing sense of excitement about what the future held for us.

Our baby was being a bit stubborn, though. My due date had come and gone, leaving me six days late. I had been ready to meet our little one for weeks now, but the baby was still active inside my belly, kicking and moving around, reminding me that the little person inside of me was doing just fine. I wasn't incredibly worried, but my OBGYN wanted me to go in for an ultrasound to make sure everything was okay. I appreciated how cautious he was, even though I could feel that everything was going to be fine.

"Baby's looking good," Doctor Leonard said, studying my new ultrasound. His eyes scanned the screen, and he gave me a reassuring smile. "Just not ready to come out!"

I let out a small chuckle. "What happens now?" I asked, trying to keep things light despite the anticipation building inside of me.

He shrugged, his expression warm and understanding. "We'll set you up with an appointment two days from now. If your water doesn't break before then, come in, and we'll induce you. No big deal."

Doctor Leonard squinted at the ultrasound, his eyes narrowing with concentration. "Weren't the legs in the way for your first ultrasound?"

"Yeah," I said, smiling a little. "We still don't know the gender."

He smiled back at me, clearly enjoying the moment. "Well, the legs aren't in the way anymore. Do you want to know?"

Ryan and I looked at each other, both of us smiling. My heart sped up, a mix of excitement and nervousness bubbling up. Ryan smiled widely and nodded. "Please."

Doctor Leonard turned the ultrasound toward us, pointing at it as he spoke. "One leg, two legs...nothing in between. A girl."

I let out a squeal of joy, my hands flying to my face in disbelief. Ryan laughed, his voice full of happiness, and he immediately hugged me. I would've loved a boy, of course, but I couldn't help but feel a little relieved that it was a girl. There was something so special about having a little girl, and the thought of it made my heart swell.

"Congratulations," Doctor Leonard smiled at us. "See you both, and your daughter, soon!"

Ryan and I were filled with joy at the news of our girl, and so were our families. When we shared the news, his oldest sister, Christina, brought us tiny dresses and cute little hairbows, and Lily bought the prettiest little charm bracelet for our daughter. The excitement in the air was contagious, and it felt like everyone shared in our happiness.

My water never broke, so eight days after my due date, Ryan drove me to the hospital to be induced. It felt surreal to be at the hospital, ready to finally meet our baby. Mom, Lily, and Ryan's parents all met us there, all of us buzzing with nervous energy and excitement. It was the moment we'd been waiting for, and it felt like time had slowed down.

"Ready?" Doctor Leonard asked as I was wheeled to my delivery room, with Ryan and Mom following right behind us.

"Yeah. Nervous, too," I said, my voice wavering slightly, but I was determined to stay calm.

He put his hand on my shoulder, his voice comforting. "Understandable. But don't worry, we'll take great care of you."

Ryan pulled a chair over to one side of my bed for Mom, then one on the other side for himself. He held my hand through all the contractions, squeezing it with a strength that grounded me. He took it like a champ when I squeezed him with all my strength; he never let go, even when I could see the pain in his eyes from how tightly I gripped him. Mom brushed my hair from my sweaty face and held a damp cloth to my forehead while encouraging me through every wave of pain. The room was filled with love and support, and it gave me the strength to keep pushing.

At eleven-thirty, I gave one final push. A minute later, Doctor Leonard was holding my baby in his arms.

Ryan's eyes were glued to the nurses as they tended to our daughter, his expression a mixture of awe and disbelief. Mom kissed my cheek, her voice full of pride. "You did it, Ness."

Doctor Leonard looked me over and called out to the nurses, "How's she doing?"

"Great," one of the nurses said as she turned around, my

bundled-up newborn in her arms. She beamed at me and brought my daughter over, her tiny body wrapped in a soft blanket.

"Congratulations, Mom and Dad," Doctor Leonard said with a smile as the nurse placed my baby in my arms. Her face was squishy, red, and wrinkled, but to me, she was the most perfect thing I had ever seen.

Tears streamed down my face as I looked at her, overwhelmed with love. I could hear Mom and Ryan sniffling beside me, their emotions spilling over, and I could see how deeply they were moved by the moment. My team, my family, was all smiles, their happiness radiating around us.

"Have a name in mind yet?" the nurse asked, her voice full of warmth.

Ryan and I looked at each other, our hearts in sync. We smiled and nodded. "Jenny," I told the nurse, my voice soft but filled with certainty.

Jenny squirmed in my arms, and once she got my attention, she looked up at me with the most beautiful blue eyes.

"Hi," I whispered to her, my voice full of wonder. "I'm your mommy. I wish I could hold you forever, but I think someone else really wants a turn."

I carefully angled my upper body toward Ryan and held my arms out just a little. His eyes were wide as he slowly took Jenny from my arms, his heart clearly bursting with love.

He stood up and walked her around the room, talking to her under his breath, his voice gentle and soothing. Mom took my hand, her smile full of warmth.

"I think you picked a good one, Ness," she whispered, nodding toward Ryan as he paced around with our daughter in his arms.

It was clear in Ryan's eyes how much he already adored Jenny. I could see it in every small gesture, every tender look he gave her. And with everything he did over the past few months to prepare to be a great father to her, I knew Mom was right.

Doctor Leonard had Jenny and me stay in the hospital overnight. While he assured me everything was fine, he explained that they wanted to monitor us both a little longer to make sure there weren't any hidden issues from the delayed birth. It was a precaution, but it didn't make the separation any easier.

Once Lily and Ryan's parents had a chance to meet Jenny, the nurse took her to a special room to be monitored. It was painful to be separated from her, even though I knew in my gut that she was fine. I just wanted to be near her.

Ryan and Mom both insisted on staying with me, but I insisted harder that they both go home. "All we'll be doing is sleeping," I told them, trying to ease their concern. "You two should go home to get as much sleep as you can before Jenny makes that impossible."

They finally agreed, kissing me goodbye and leaving reluctantly. My nurse told me I should take my own advice and go to sleep until it was time for me to check out tomorrow.

"Can I see Jenny first?" I asked her, my voice small with longing. "Just to tell her goodnight?"

She smiled warmly and helped me from my bed. "Of course."

My nurse brought me to Jenny's room, and when she was sure I could walk on my own, she let me go over to her bed by myself.

Jenny was fast asleep, her little chest rising and falling gently with each breath. Her face was so soft and peaceful. For the hundredth time since I gave birth, I silently thanked God for giving her to me. I was so overwhelmed by the miracle of her existence.

I was a different woman now, without a doubt. I had to be. I was a mother. And I was going to be the mother she deserved.

"You're my biggest blessing," I whispered to Jenny, my voice full of promise. "I'll never take that for granted. I'll do everything I can to give you the life I never had. I promise."

Chapter 50

By noon the next day, the doctors were confident that Jenny and I were completely fine. They wished me luck and, after a few last-minute checks and paperwork, released me. The sterile hospital room felt empty and too quiet as I gathered our things. I was eager to leave, but the thought of going home, of facing the challenges of motherhood without the safety net of the hospital staff, made me feel both relieved and anxious. As I left the building, the weight of what had just happened still lingered in my chest, but I felt like I could handle it—at least, that's what I kept telling myself.

Ryan's parents drove me home, where Mom had made up a bed for herself on the living room couch and was already busy cooking something in the kitchen. The familiar scent of home-cooked food filled the air, and my heart swelled with a mix of gratitude and exhaustion. I was glad when she'd told me she was taking the week off from work to help me with Jenny, but actually seeing her here was a huge relief. It was one thing to hear it from her, another thing entirely to have her here, putting in the effort to make my life just a little bit easier.

"When did you get here?" I asked her, settling myself onto our armchair with Jenny, carefully cradling her tiny body close to mine. The baby's warmth made me feel so protective, so in love.

"Around ten," she said. Her eyes were tired but warm, and she offered me a reassuring smile. "Ryan was leaving the street as I was turning in."

I nodded. I was still bummed that Ryan couldn't take any time off to help with Jenny and bond with her. He was upset about it, too, but his job was too new to be taking time off, and we needed the money. That guilt weighed heavily on him. He was doing his best, but his best wasn't enough for everything that needed to be done.

Thank God for Mom. She told me from the start that as long as she was here, she would be handling the hard stuff, waking up in the middle of the night to feed the baby, the diaper changes, and the crying spells that seemed to last forever. My priority was to heal from the birth, snuggle with Jenny, and sleep as much as possible. I even found the time to mail some Polaroids of Jenny down to Dad, Abuelita, and Abuelito in Florida. It had taken longer than I expected, but the pictures made me feel connected to them, especially since they weren't here with us, and I could sense that they needed to see Jenny, to see how she was growing, even without their physical presence.

I would always be grateful for how Mom helped me, and while I hated for her to leave and go back to work, I felt ready to tackle motherhood on my own. I knew I had to, but I didn't feel completely confident yet. I wasn't sure if I ever would.

My confidence faltered quickly. I had to change Jenny, then coo her to sleep, then try to prepare her bottles and eat my own lunch without waking her, then feed her when she woke up crying, then get her to stop crying long enough for me to go to the bathroom, which was still painful and hard to do, but I had to do it quickly because she was crying again, and I had to figure out why she was crying and make sure she was okay. All within an hour. The hours blurred together with the weight of the same never-ending tasks. I couldn't escape the feeling of being trapped, but I knew I had no choice but to push forward. If every day was going to be this overwhelming, I wasn't sure how I was going to make it.

Ryan couldn't do much. He had to go to bed early in order to wake up early for work. He could only do baths and night feedings on the weekends, and his diapering and evening feedings on weekdays were limited. Bella and Jacob both worked all day, so they weren't available to poke in and help me, either. I felt isolated. The weight of the silence in the house was suffocating, with only the occasional crying of Jenny and the hum of the dishwasher or microwave to break it.

It wasn't long before I became lonelier than I'd ever been. And since I was doing ninety percent of the baby and housework by myself and couldn't stop myself from becoming resentful of Ryan, I couldn't avoid the growing bitterness that simmered inside me. I knew he felt bad that he couldn't help with Jenny more, so I was also incredibly guilty for resenting him. I tried to tell myself that he was doing his best, but the lack of support was making it hard to hold onto that rational thinking.

Especially since his life wasn't exactly sunshine and rainbows right now, he had a lot of responsibility at his job, and while it was great that he was doing so well at work, it also took a lot out of him. There were nights when he would come home, looking so drained, and I would feel a wave of sympathy for him, but it would quickly dissolve into frustration as I was left with the same mountain of tasks, and he would retreat into his own exhaustion, leaving me to shoulder the weight.

It was impossible for Ryan and me to help each other when we were both exhausted all the time. The healthy communication skills we'd worked so hard to build began to crumble. He couldn't take his stress out at work, and I certainly couldn't take mine out on Jenny, so we ended up slipping back into our old ways. Petty arguments became a daily thing until they eventually escalated into daily fights. Annoyances over outside circumstances became anger targeted directly at each other. We'd do things specifically to hurt the other. He would call me fat and ugly, and I'd throw empty baby bottles at him, the slap of plastic against the walls echoing through the house. Jenny was a heavy sleeper, which was at least something to be thankful for, but Bella and Jacob were starting to get annoyed by it. The sound of our fighting seemed to reverberate through the walls and into the air, suffocating and unbearable.

When things started to get noticeably bad, I feared that Ryan would start using cocaine again. I saw the signs—the way he seemed to zone out sometimes, the dullness in his eyes, the way his hand would tremble when he held a bottle or a glass—but he never did, as far as I could tell. What he did pick up, though, was drinking. A beer every day when he got home from work. Just one. It mellowed him out enough that we didn't fight nearly as much. But the distance between us grew like a wall was slowly rising, brick by brick. It wasn't just the stress; it was the emotional disconnection, and I didn't know how to bring us back.

I honestly wasn't sure which was better. All I knew was that this was far from how I had pictured our family life to be, especially so soon. The dreams I had in my mind about raising a family together felt distant, like they belonged to someone else.

****

Over a month after I mailed them pictures of Jenny, Abuelita and Abuelito called me. They said she was beautiful and that they were proud of me. Hearing their voices was like a balm to my weary heart, but there was an undertone to their words that made me uneasy.

I asked them if Dad had seen the pictures. They refused to answer and tried to change the subject to other things. It was so strange, so awkward, and I could feel my pulse quicken, anxiety curling in my stomach. As excited as I had been that they called me, I told them I had to go and ended the call early, my mind swirling with unanswered questions.

Maybe he saw the pictures and didn't care, and now they feel like they can't tell me that to keep my feelings from getting hurt? The thought stuck with me like a splinter under my skin. I wanted so badly to tell them how frustrating it was that they always acted so mysteriously when it came to Dad, but I didn't. What would it change? Nothing. All I could do was check on Jenny. She was still fast asleep. This was my best chance to catch up on dishes, or laundry, or shower for the first time in days.

Instead, I leaned against her crib and cried. The tears came unbidden, and I let them fall freely. There was no one else around to see, no judgment, just the quiet rhythm of my sobs as I grieved for the things I couldn't change and the family I'd hoped for, which felt so far out of reach.

Chapter 51

At the end of January, Ryan came home and said, "I have news."

I raised my eyebrow, feeling a sense of unease mixed with hope. "Good or bad?"

"Good," he said with a hesitant smile, but there was something in his tone that still made me wary. "I got a promotion. I'll be a chef some days, and work as a manager on others. I'll be making two dollars more an hour."

I stopped stirring the soup I had simmering on the stove, my hands frozen in mid-motion. The warmth of the kitchen, the soothing scent of the broth, and the sound of the bubbling soup all seemed to fade for a moment as I processed his words. "That's great! That'll help a lot." A genuine smile pulled at my lips, but as I saw Ryan's tired expression, I knew this wasn't all good news.

Ryan shrugged, looking less than thrilled. "Yeah, the money will be good, but managing a kitchen is stressful. I'm gonna come home even more tired."

I felt my stomach twist slightly, but I nodded. "I'm sorry about that, but it sounds like you're implying that this means you won't be able to help with Jenny as much." The words left my mouth before I could stop them. It had been an unspoken fear of mine that his promotion, while a financial boost, would push him further away from us.

He clenched his jaw, his face hardening slightly. "Do you have any idea how hard it is to be on your feet, rushing around all day?

It'll only be worse for me now."

I felt a flare of frustration rise in my chest. "Do you ever see me stop moving except to sleep? And that's only before I have to wake up every hour to tend to Jenny. How is it fair that you get to finish with work at the end of the day, but I'm on call twenty-four hours a day?" The anger in my voice was raw and honest, born from days of exhaustion, resentment, and the weight of my responsibilities.

Ryan walked to the fridge and pulled out a beer with a resigned sigh. "I'm not doing this with you right now, Vanessa. I'm tired."

"So am I, and yet I'm here making dinner for you while you sit and work on your drinking habit. How is it fair?" I barely recognized my own voice—sharp, biting, full of resentment. I didn't even care anymore if I hurt him with my words. They spilled out, unfiltered.

That struck a nerve. Ryan's eyes darkened, and he took a step closer to me, his voice rising in anger. He started to scream, his words cutting deep. "You don't know anything. My mom stayed at home with me and my sisters and never complained like you do. You should be thankful that all you have to do every day is change diapers and throw food in a pot." The words felt like daggers, each one landing with a sharp sting.

The sound of the spoon hitting the floor was drowned out by the chaos that followed. Without thinking, I threw it at him, and the soup splashed across the kitchen. The hot liquid splattered everywhere, making a mess of everything. He yelled even louder. The tension in the room reached a boiling point, and we were firing on all cylinders now. Our tempers completely unraveled.

Then, there was a loud knock on our door. It was like the universe had decided to add one more layer of stress to an already unbearable situation. Somehow, that sound managed to wake Jenny, and her cries pierced through the air, cutting through the tension in the room like a knife. Ryan shot me a look of pure frustration before walking to the door, and I rushed to Jenny's side, scooping her up into my arms, desperately trying to comfort her.

I rocked her gently, whispering soft reassurances as I sang to her in a quiet, almost trembling voice. In the background, I could hear Ryan arguing with whoever was at the door, but the words were muffled, too distant for me to make out.

It wasn't long before Ryan stormed back into the room, his face twisted in anger. "Pack your shit," he told me, his voice cold and detached.

"Excuse me?" My voice trembled, not entirely sure if I had heard him correctly.

"That was Bella. She and Jacob decided that they're sick of hearing us fight all the time, so we have to find a new place to live." His words felt like a punch to my stomach. I couldn't process what was happening fast enough. I didn't know what to say. I just watched, stunned, as Ryan started to pull his clothes from the closet and dresser, his movements sharp and mechanical.

"They want us out tonight?" I asked, my voice barely a whisper, but it carried a weight of disbelief.

"Yeah." His response was blunt, like it had all been decided without any thought for what it would do to me, to us.

I held Jenny closer to me, feeling her tiny body press against mine as my mind spun in confusion. "Well, I guess Jenny and I will stay with my mom until we find a new place," I said, the words coming out in a rush. I felt detached, like I was floating above it all, watching my own life unravel.

Ryan looked at me with an expression that was almost sad, almost regretful. But there was something in his eyes that made it clear he had made his decision. "I'll stay with my parents," he said, the words heavy with finality.

I rocked Jenny slowly, trying to steady myself. I watched Ryan as he packed his things, and then he took her from me so I could gather mine. Bella and Jacob had told him that we could take a few days to move out our furniture, but as long as we were gone, we had to leave that night.

We loaded what we could into Ryan's car. I barely registered the drive, my thoughts a blur. When he dropped me off at Mom's house, I felt numb, like I was walking through a dream I couldn't wake from.

"I'll let you know when I find a new place for us," he said, his voice quieter now. He kissed Jenny softly and then hesitated for a moment before kissing me on the cheek. It was a strange, fleeting moment of tenderness amidst everything that had just happened. And then, without another word, he got back into the car and drove off.

When Mom asked what happened, I told her that the landlords raised the rent too high for us, so we were going to get a more affordable place. I felt bad for lying, but telling her the truth, with all the emotions and anger that came with it, would be more than I could handle right now. I wasn't ready to share all of it.

She helped me set up a sleeping mat for Jenny, and I went straight to bed, my body aching, my mind racing. Despite losing our apartment, despite everything that had just happened, I slept more peacefully than I had in weeks. It was like the weight of everything had finally been lifted, even if just for a moment.

****

Ryan stopped by two days later to let me know he had found us an apartment. It was apparently a nice one-bedroom flat that he could afford with his promotion, though I could hear the hesitation in his voice.

Christina borrowed her husband's truck while he was at work and helped us move our furniture from our old place into the new one. The apartment was about the same size, and it was close to Mom's house. It was convenient, at least, but I couldn't bring myself to feel excited about it.

It was nice to have the apartment problem solved, but I couldn't say I was excited about living with Ryan again. The tension between us was palpable, hanging thick in the air, even as we tried to be civil to each other. But his drinking had picked up, and I noticed the subtle changes; he went from one bottle of beer a night to three. I suspected he was even drinking before he left work. I wasn't sure how to approach the subject, but I knew I couldn't keep ignoring it.

I was tired of fighting. Even though Jenny slept through it all, I knew it wasn't good for her to be around this. The constant tension, the drinking, the arguments, it wasn't the environment I wanted to raise my daughter in.

The only idea I had was to try and be more supportive of him with his job, to make things easier for him in some way, though it meant I'd have to swallow my pride and deal with the extra exhaustion it would bring me. But if it could help Jenny, if it could help us, then I had to try.

Chapter 52

As it turned out, I was far too physically and mentally exhausted at the end of the day to be very in tune with Ryan's needs. I had been running on empty for days, just trying to keep everything together for the sake of Jenny and our home. But somehow, I managed to bite my tongue whenever he ticked me off. It wasn't ideal, but it was better than letting the frustration boil over. I kept telling myself it was better to let things slide than to erupt every time something irritated me. It was better than nothing. I just had to keep my focus on what mattered most: our daughter, Jenny, and keeping her world as stable and loving as possible.

A couple of weeks later, I called Ryan at work, trying to stay calm despite the mounting stress. "Hey, babe," I said, my voice thick with exhaustion, "could you pick up a few things on your way home? We're down to one pack of diapers, and we're running low on formula, too. Could you grab some?"

He was quiet for a beat before agreeing. "Okay, no problem," he said, the sound of papers shuffling in the background as he was likely wrapping up something at work.

I didn't think too much about it until he came home. He walked in with a pack of diapers, two cans of formula... and two twelve-packs of beer. My stomach dropped as I stared at him, unable to believe what I was seeing. The pack of diapers and the formula were good, but the beer? The cold, hard reality of it hit me like a ton of bricks.

I stood there, staring at him, dumbstruck.

"What?" he asked, clearly noticing the shock written across my face.

"Jenny is going to go through these diapers so quickly," I said, trying to keep my voice even. "Why didn't you grab a few more?"

He looked at me like I had lost my mind. "Because baby stuff isn't cheap? I can't just buy a ton of it at a time."

"But you can buy beer," I snapped, not able to hold back anymore. "You're right. That's more important than our baby having diapers."

Ryan raised an eyebrow and held up his arms in a defensive gesture. "She's not gonna run out of diapers, Vanessa. I'll get more when we need more. Jesus, you'll find any reason to start a fight with me."

I shook my head, trying to keep my voice steady despite the flood of anger that was threatening to overtake me. "I don't ever want to fight with you," I said, the words coming out quieter, almost pleading. "I just don't understand how you can claim the things Jenny needs to live are too expensive, but you feel comfortable buying alcohol."

Without another word, he turned around, grabbed a beer from the pack, and started walking outside. "I'll get more diapers before she runs out. I'm going for a walk."

I stood frozen, staring at the closed door for what felt like forever, the weight of everything crashing down on me. His irresponsibility, his indifference, it all felt like a burden I couldn't carry anymore. But then, something in me shifted. I wouldn't let Ryan's reckless behavior hurt me, and more importantly, I wouldn't let it hurt our daughter. Not again.

I searched through our list of phone numbers, my mind racing as I scrolled. Finally, I found Christina's number and dialed it, my fingers trembling slightly as the phone rang. When she picked up, I did my best to sound cheery, despite the heavy emotions hanging over me. "Hey, Christina! So, Ryan and I were talking, and we think it might be best for the family if I go back to work part-time. I know you adore Jenny, and you're so good with her, so I was wondering if you'd mind watching her sometimes while I'm working."

Christina's voice came through bright and warm, a ray of sunshine in the gloom. "I would love that! Seriously, I'll take her anytime!"

She loved children, but she and her husband didn't have any of their own. She was one of the kindest, most genuine people I knew, and she adored Jenny. Since she was a housewife, it seemed like the perfect fit. "Thanks so much, Christina," I said, relief flooding through me.

"I'm happy to do it! Any idea what kind of job you're going to get?"

"Not yet. My old manager said I was welcome back there, but I'm not sure if I'd be able to get the same schedule every week. I want to keep some kind of routine for Jenny, you know?"

"No doubt," she replied sympathetically. "You know, one of the stylists at the hair salon I go to just retired, and they're looking to replace her. If you'd like to go back to hairstyling again, that might be a good opportunity. I know all the stylists work on the same days, at the same times, every week."

A huge smile spread across my face as I listened. Thank you, God, for letting me call Christina. This was exactly what I needed.

"That sounds amazing. If you don't mind watching Jenny, I'll go over and apply tomorrow."

Christina agreed without hesitation, and I felt a spark of hope reignite in me.

The next morning, Christina came over to sit with Jenny while I went to the salon. I had to borrow Christina's car because mine was out of commission, but I didn't mind at all. The youngest stylists at the salon were in their thirties, while most of the others seemed to be in their forties or fifties. I was a little worried that they might think I was too young to be considered, but when I met Marianne, the manager, I felt instantly at ease. Marianne was one of the nicest, most down-to-earth people I'd ever met, and when I told her about my experience, she seemed genuinely impressed.

She set up a mannequin with a long wig, told me the kind of style she wanted, and handed me a pair of scissors. I focused, cutting with precision and care. When I finished, Marianne ran her fingers through the wig, examining the work. "What a beautiful job!" she exclaimed. "Our last stylist worked from ten to four on Mondays, Tuesdays, and Wednesdays. Would that schedule work for you?"

I could barely contain my excitement. "That's perfect. I'll see you on Monday."

Ryan was surprised when I told him I went out and got a job. I explained that Christina was so thrilled to babysit for Jenny that she refused to accept any payment, and the salon paid surprisingly well. When he realized he wouldn't be the only one bringing in money anymore, I saw the weight lift off his shoulders. He looked lighter somehow, less burdened.

I reassured him that I wasn't worried about sticking with this job for the long term. Everyone I worked with—stylists and customers alike—was so kind. The environment was warm, and it felt like I had found my place. I was recharged every day I came home from work, and that made all the difference. I could be present for Jenny and for Ryan. We were becoming a stronger family with each passing day.

As for Ryan, now that he wasn't the sole breadwinner, his mood improved. He started enjoying his job again, and more surprisingly, his drinking decreased. It was only a few drinks a week now, and his presence in Jenny's life grew stronger. It was clear he loved spending time with her. The change in him proved just how good a father he really was.

With everything falling into place, things between Ryan and me were better than ever. And so, when June came around, he proposed. I didn't even hesitate. It was the easiest "yes" I've ever said.

Chapter 53

The money Ryan made from his job was enough to pay for pretty much all of our essentials. We managed to cover rent, utilities, groceries, and even some of the things Jenny needed—diapers, clothes, toys—without feeling strapped for cash. It wasn't glamorous, but it worked. We were able to put most of the money I earned directly into savings; half into my account for emergencies, and half into his to fund his future in the music academy. The feeling of financial stability, even in its modest form, was a small victory in a world that often felt out of control.

In early October, Ryan started talking more seriously about music school. He had been dreaming about it for years, and now, with a little more money in the bank and a bit more confidence, he felt that we had enough saved up for him to go to the Institute of Music and Arts. It was a huge step, one he had been working toward since before Jenny was born. He sent in an application, and we held our breaths, waiting for their answer. I could feel his nervousness every time he checked the mailbox, his hand hovering over the door as if it might be the key to a future that had always felt just out of reach.

A few days before Jenny's first birthday, Ryan got his reply from the Institute. When I got home from work that day, he was pacing, clearly nervous but also hopeful. He handed me the letter, and I could tell by the way his hands were shaking that it was either going to be good news or devastating.

"They accepted me," he said, his voice a mixture of pride and doubt. His smile was wide, but his eyes, those eyes, told a different story. I could see the unease creeping in.

I was thrilled, of course, this was the break he had been waiting for, but when I looked at him, I saw something darker in his expression.

"What's wrong?" I asked, my excitement suddenly stifled by the worry in his tone.

He sank onto the couch and let out a long, slow breath. "It's so much more expensive than I thought it was," he said quietly, his voice barely above a whisper. "We're thousands of dollars short."

My heart sank, and I felt a lump form in my throat. I sat beside him, taking his hand into mine. "Oh, Ryan. I'm so sorry," I said, my voice soft but full of emotion. I wanted to fix it, to make everything better, but I knew I couldn't.

We spent over an hour brainstorming, trying to figure out any possibility that we could make it work, maybe we could cut back on living expenses, maybe I could pick up more hours at my job, maybe we could find some kind of scholarship or loan. Every idea came up short. As the conversation stretched on, I could feel his discouragement grow. He was becoming increasingly agitated, like the weight of it all was pressing down on him.

"It's just not meant to be for me," he finally said, his voice barely audible. His shoulders slumped, and he walked toward our bedroom.

I watched him go, feeling helpless and completely powerless to make things right. He crawled into bed without another word. His body curled into itself, retreating further into his own disappointment.

Ryan's self-confidence suffered a lot in the following days. He became quieter and more withdrawn, and I could see how hard it was for him to even get out of bed in the morning. I tried to reassure him, told him that we would find a way to make it work, that we'd save more, and that he could go next year instead. But nothing I said seemed to make him feel better. It only seemed to deepen his sense of failure.

To distract him from the weight of it all, I suggested we start planning our wedding. He agreed to help, but his efforts were half-hearted. I could tell that, like everything else, the wedding was just another thing on his list of things he felt he wasn't doing well enough. And though I understood his frustration, it didn't stop the pain of seeing him so defeated.

After a while, I started to recognize in him the depression I had felt when Mom and Lily moved to Alberta. The same kind of hopelessness, the same kind of heavy sadness. It was the kind of sadness that wasn't easy to snap out of, that didn't just disappear with time. "I know it'll take some time to stop being upset about the school," I told him one night, "but seeing someone might help you at least deal with it better. Seeing a therapist helped me when I was a teenager."

That wasn't completely true, though. My therapist had been less than helpful, but I knew that just because my experience wasn't great didn't mean Ryan wouldn't find someone who could really help him through this. He didn't seem thrilled about it, but he agreed to at least try.

The next day, Ryan came home and told me he'd managed to schedule weekly appointments with a therapist, with his first one being tomorrow. I felt a spark of hope. "I'm so proud of you for taking the initiative to do this," I said, pulling him into a tight hug. "I have a good feeling about it."

I never asked Ryan what he talked about in therapy, though I was incredibly curious. After all, his mood seemed to improve almost immediately after his first session. It was like a weight had been lifted off his shoulders. But as much as I was happy to see him getting better, there was something else that began to worry me. His drinking started to pick up again.

At first, it was subtle—a second drink now and then when he usually had just one. But then it became more frequent, and soon he was drinking every day. It was worrying, but I convinced myself that his therapist would be aware of it and would help him work through it. I didn't want to make things harder for him by confronting him about it, so I kept my concerns to myself.

But a few weeks later, things took a darker turn. He was eating less, his energy seemed depleted, and he looked tired all the time. That could've been from the increased drinking, but it also mirrored the signs of something else, a pattern that I had seen before when he had been using cocaine.

Now that I had that possibility on my radar, I couldn't just ignore it. I needed to talk to him to make sure he knew I cared. But I had to do it carefully so that he wouldn't feel attacked.

"How have your therapy sessions been going?" I asked him one Wednesday evening when he came home from work.

"Fine," he said, but there was an edge to his voice that made it clear he wasn't being entirely truthful.

I tried to keep my tone calm, to keep my questions nonchalant. "Anything special you're working on with your therapist?"

"Nothing special," he replied curtly.

He turned away from me and opened a beer, his back to me. I couldn't let him shut me out without saying something. My heart raced, but I pressed on. "What's your therapist's name?"

He froze, his hand still holding the beer bottle. "What?"

"Your therapist's name? One of my coworkers wants to get an appointment, and I figured I'd recommend your therapist to her since they're helping you so much."

For a moment, he didn't say anything. He just stared at me, his mouth opening and closing like he was trying to find the right words. But no words came.

I swallowed hard, my voice trembling as I asked, "You haven't been seeing a therapist, have you?"

He clenched his jaw, a flash of anger in his eyes. "Do you know how expensive it is to see a therapist?" His voice was rising now, sharp and defensive. "If I'm upset because I can't afford to go to school, I can't afford to see a therapist about it."

The words hit me like a punch to the gut. I felt a wave of nausea, a knot tightening in my chest. After everything we had been through, everything that had been going right, how could this be happening? My emotions boiled over, and tears spilled down my face. I didn't know what to say, so I just stayed silent, unable to even breathe through the pain.

Ryan's eyes flicked to my face, and the sight of my tears seemed to irritate him even more. "I think I'll spend the night at my parents' place," he muttered, storming off to our bedroom to grab his things.

I stayed at the table, frozen, my hands clenched into fists, too stunned to say anything. From the living room, Jenny's little voice bubbled up, her soft, sweet babble was a stark contrast to the tension in the air. I got up to play with her, trying to force a smile and pretend everything was fine, but I could feel the weight of everything pressing down on me.

I sat with Jenny in my arms, trying to distract myself from the mess unfolding around me. She cooed as I made faces at her, but no amount of her innocent joy could stop the storm brewing inside me. Ryan's words rang in my ears, and the anger I felt was slowly turning into something else, something darker. It was a painful mix of sadness, betrayal, and fear for what was happening to us.

The evening stretched on in silence after Ryan left, and soon, the house felt too quiet. It wasn't just the absence of him that bothered me; it was the void he left in our lives, the gulf between us that seemed to grow with each passing day. My heart was heavy, and I knew that no matter how hard I tried to hold on, something was breaking.

Around 2 AM, I was jolted awake by loud banging sounds from the kitchen. My mind raced as I squinted at the bright numbers on the clock beside me. Two in the morning. My heart started to pound in my chest as I listened carefully, hearing the fridge door open and close.

I crept out of bed, heart pounding, and as I stepped into the living room, I saw Ryan stumbling around, his movements sluggish and uncoordinated. He had that vacant, distant look in his eyes; the same look I had seen so many times before when the alcohol had taken over.

"Ryan?" I whispered, my voice trembling with a mix of fear and exhaustion.

He looked at me, his expression unfocused, before he collapsed into a kitchen chair with a heavy sigh. His breath smelled of alcohol, and his movements were slow as if he was struggling to stay upright.

"You didn't go to your parents' house, did you?" I asked, the hurt bleeding through my words. "You went to a bar with your friends."

He just stared at me for a long moment as if my words didn't fully register. Then he slurred, "I don't wanna hear you bitching at me anymore," and took another swig from the bottle in his hand.

My heart sank. I shook my head, trying to make sense of the chaos swirling around us. "Why do you lie to me, Ryan?" I asked, my voice thick with emotion. "If you told me the truth about what's going on, I would be on your side. I'm your fiancée, and I want to support you. But if you keep lying to me, how can I be there for you?"

His face twisted into something ugly, something I didn't recognize. His anger flared up suddenly, a violent storm in his eyes. "Support me?" he spat, his voice full of venom. "You don't do shit for me. All you did was push out a baby, but you had to get a stupid job because you couldn't even handle being a mother. If it wasn't for me and everything I do, you would have nothing."

The words hit me like a slap to the face. I knew he was drunk and that this wasn't really him talking, but it didn't matter. The hurt still cut deep. My whole body trembled with the force of it. I had taken so much from him, I had sacrificed, and yet here he was, tearing me down.

I couldn't keep it in anymore. "All right, fine, then," I said through gritted teeth, my anger bubbling over. "I'll go. I'll take our daughter, and you know what'll happen next? You'll have no one. You'll become nothing but a crackhead living on the streets."

As soon as the words left my mouth, I saw the rage in his eyes deepen, and before I could react, he lunged at me.

The next moments felt like they happened in slow motion. I didn't have time to move out of the way before Ryan grabbed my upper arm with one hand, the grip so tight it hurt. With his other hand, he slapped me across the face. The force of it spun me back, and I lost my balance, stumbling backward. My mind went blank for a split second, and then, with the momentum of the hit, I instinctively punched him in the mouth.

We grappled with each other, crashing into the table and chairs, knocking them over with a deafening noise. The fight was messy and chaotic as if everything we had been holding back was spilling out in one explosive moment.

Our noise was loud enough that it woke Jenny, and I heard her crying from the bedroom. The sound of her sobs was enough to jolt me back to reality. My heart twisted in my chest.

I broke free from Ryan's grip and dashed to the other side of the room, putting the kitchen table between us. My hands were up, trying to signal peace to stop this madness.

"The baby is scared," I said, my breath coming in short, desperate gasps. "We need to stop, for her sake."

Ryan was leaning against one of the chairs, grabbing it for support, his breathing ragged. He didn't seem to hear me, or maybe he didn't care. His anger didn't abate, and before I knew it, he lunged at me again.

This time, the alcohol had clouded his movements so much that he misjudged the distance, charging straight into a chair and knocking himself off balance. That was the moment I needed. I sprinted to the bedroom, slamming the door behind me and locking it.

Jenny was still crying in her crib. I rushed to her, picking her up and holding her close, trying to comfort her as best I could. I whispered softly to her, rocking her back and forth, hoping that my calmness would soothe her fear. Ryan's pounding on the bedroom door was deafening, but I held my breath, hoping he would give up and that he would leave us alone.

The longest two minutes of my life passed, filled with the sound of Ryan yelling at me from the other side. He called me names and screamed accusations, but slowly, his voice began to fade. Finally, there was silence. I listened for a moment longer, making sure he wasn't still outside the door.

"Ryan?" I whispered, but there was no response.

I slowly stood, careful not to wake Jenny, and left the closet where I had been hiding. I could hear him snoring from the living room, a heavy, intoxicated sleep that made me realize just how deeply he had fallen into his addiction.

I moved quietly through the apartment, gathering anything I could; clothes, toiletries, Jenny's favorite toys and stuffed everything into the largest suitcase I could find. My hands were shaking, my heart racing, but I couldn't stay here. I couldn't let Jenny grow up in this chaos.

When I was sure we had everything we needed, I bundled Jenny in her warmest clothes and made my way to the bathroom. I stared out the window, my mind spinning with what had just happened, with everything that was falling apart. But I couldn't waste any more time thinking.

I saw the headlights of the taxi pull up outside, and I made my way out the door as quickly as I could. I hesitated for just a second, a final, lingering look at the apartment that had once been a home. Then, I turned and slipped back inside.

I walked over to where Ryan was passed out on the couch. His face was slack with sleep. With trembling fingers, I removed my engagement ring and placed it gently on the coffee table in front of him. My chest felt tight as I looked at him one last time.

Then, I walked out. I gathered Jenny and our things, and I closed the door softly behind me, knowing there was no turning back.

I gave the taxi driver Mom's address and sank into the backseat, feeling the weight of everything—the years of love and pain, of hope and disappointment—crushing down on me. And yet, somehow, I knew it was the right decision.

I had to protect Jenny. I had to protect myself.

And I had to keep moving forward.

Chapter 54

I used my key to Mom's house to let myself in when the taxi dropped me off a little before three in the morning. The driver gave me a look through the rearview mirror—somewhere between tired curiosity and concern—as I fumbled for the right key on the chain. Jenny was heavy in my arms, her tiny body completely limp, her breath soft against my neck. The night air clung to us like wet cotton, humid and thick, and I whispered a quiet "thank you" to the driver before nudging the door closed behind me with my foot.

The hallway smelled like lavender and old wood polish, a scent so achingly familiar it made my throat catch. My eyes adjusted slowly in the dark. Nothing had changed. The same family photo collage on the wall, slightly crooked. Lily's ballet shoes were left by the stairs, her glittery backpack hanging on the coat hook beneath Mom's oversized sun hat. I moved quietly, padding across the floor on socked feet, cradling Jenny tighter.

In a perfect world, Jenny wouldn't cry until after Mom and Lily left in the morning, and we could hide in my old bedroom without them ever knowing we were there. I didn't want to answer questions, not yet, maybe not ever. I had no excuse for why we would've snuck in in the middle of the night since I wasn't sure yet how I'd handle things with Ryan.

He'd been upset since the whole music academy issue, but he'd tried to keep the extent of his distress to himself. Holding it in, pretending. Smiling at dinner, silent in bed. He didn't lash out until I confronted him. Being ashamed and blackout drunk were two believable excuses for why he'd acted the way he had. But believable didn't mean forgivable.

So it was me, then. I thought I was supporting him, but I was really just making him feel like he couldn't be honest with me about his struggles. I'd confused encouragement with pressure and concern with control. And then, once he hit a low point, I pushed him until he attacked me. The memory of it made my skin crawl. I had to take my sweet, innocent daughter out of her home, all because I couldn't properly care for my fiancé when he needed me. That thought landed like a stone in my stomach, heavy and sharp.

Jenny was cuddled up against me now, her breath warm and rhythmic against my chest, and I checked to make sure she was still sound asleep before crying myself to sleep, quiet tears soaking into the pillow, my hand still protectively curved over her small back.

I woke up the next morning when Mom and Lily were moving around. Their voices floated faintly down the hallway—Mom reminding Lily about her jacket, Lily complaining about cereal again, the clink of mugs and the closing of the back door. I stayed still except to gently rub Jenny's back in hopes that it would keep her from waking up.

She ended up sleeping through Mom and Lily leaving the house, long past her usual wake-up time. Sunlight streamed through the crack in the curtains, painting soft gold stripes across the carpet. I decided I wouldn't wake her up so she could catch up on sleep. Her little fists were curled near her face, her dark lashes brushing against her cheeks, her mouth slightly open in complete trust. I brushed her hair off her forehead, my heart twisting.

I lay awake beside her, wondering what I'd do about Ryan. Wondering if it was possible to rewind, to start again without dragging the pain with us. Could I trust him? Should I? Was it better to let go or fight for the life we'd tried to build?

I was deep in those questions when there was a knock on the front door. My heart skipped. I froze, listening. It was firm but not loud, almost hesitant. I got out of bed carefully to not disturb Jenny and tiptoed to the living room, every floorboard creaking louder than I remembered.

I peeked through the peephole and saw Ryan hugging his coat around him and crying. His shoulders were hunched like the cold had already defeated him. His eyes were red-rimmed, his lips trembling even as he seemed to try to pull himself together.

I ran back to my bedroom, panic and confusion tangling in my chest, and reached above the doorframe to make sure the key was still up there. It was slightly dusty from disuse. I locked Jenny in the room, just in case and returned the key to the door frame before opening the door for Ryan.

We stared at each other, the silence dragging out between us. His shallow breaths puffed white in the early morning chill. I said nothing, my face unreadable, arms wrapped around myself like armor. Finally, he opened his fist to show he was clutching my engagement ring. It was smeared with something—maybe sweat, maybe tears—but he held it out like it meant everything.

"What happened?" he asked. "Why'd you leave?"

"Is that a serious question?"

Ryan shook his head quickly. "Yes, I, I don't remember last night, Vanessa. The last thing I remember is being at the bar with my friends. I don't even remember going home."

I crossed my arms in front of my chest, my fingers digging into my sides. "Well, let's see. Basically, you told me I was a terrible mother who was nothing without you, and when I snapped back at you, you grabbed me and slapped me across the face. You have that busted lip because I hit you back to defend myself, and when I asked you to stop because Jenny was crying and scared, you tried to attack me again. I was able to lock myself and Jenny in the bedroom until you gave up on screaming at me and passed out on the couch."

Ryan's eyes widened, and his face went pale. He swayed like the words had physically struck him. "I hit you?" he whispered.

I nodded, unable to say it again. His hand came up and covered his face, his fingers trembling. "Oh my God," he said, crying harder.

He reached out to me, then jerked his hands back like he was scared to hurt me again. "Vanessa. I'm so *sorry*. I don't understand how I could've got to the point where I would do that to you. Jenny, is she okay?"

"Yeah, she's fine. She's sleeping."

Ryan nodded, then looked at me with haunted eyes. "I love you so much, Vanessa. I understand if you don't believe me anymore, but it's true. I hurt you by drinking and using cocaine, and the drugs made me attack you. That's not who I am, and I promise you I won't ever do that again if you give me another chance. I'll never drink or use cocaine again, I swear. I'll go to therapy for real this time, I'll go to rehab, I don't care. I'll do whatever I need to to show you how much I want this to work."

He seemed so desperate that I had to believe he was genuine. I wish I could be totally unbiased about this, but I was desperate, too. Desperate to give Jenny the family I never had. Desperate not to feel like I was alone in everything.

"Okay," I told Ryan. "I'll give you another chance. But…" I said before he could get too excited, "I have rules."

He held out his hands. "Anything. Just say the word."

I paused for a second to make sure he grasped how serious I was. "No more alcohol. I mean *none*. You take so much as one sip of beer, and we're done. I don't care how much you beg and cry. That is not a life I will have for our daughter."

Ryan nodded. "No more alcohol. I promise."

"That means you need to figure out another way to cope when you're stressed or feeling down," I told him. "All the fighting we used to do is over. We're going to handle things like adults, and you're going to find a way to take care of yourself first before I commit to trying to take care of you again. Therapy is a good place to start looking, but I don't care what you do, so long as it's healthy and doesn't hurt anyone."

"I'll call into work today and start looking for a therapist. I won't stop looking until I find one."

I was quiet for a few seconds just to make sure everything I said had sunk in. "Help me bring our things to the car," I told him.

Ryan exhaled and held his arms open to me. I stepped into them cautiously. He hugged me, and he squeezed me tightly like he was afraid I'd slip through his arms. "I love you, Vanessa," he said. "I won't let you down again. I promise. I'll be the man you and Jenny deserve."

"Good," I said. I took the engagement ring back from him and slipped it on my finger. It felt heavier than I remembered. He smiled widely at me, and I smiled back, though mine was smaller, tinged with exhaustion.

Jenny woke up when we buckled her into the car. She blinked in the sunlight, still half-asleep, her voice croaky as she mumbled a question I didn't quite catch. Ryan spent the ride back to our apartment talking to her, soft and sweet, telling her about how they'd make pancakes together again soon. I kept quiet and made a few final decisions.

I wouldn't tell anyone about our blowout. Ryan had convinced me it wouldn't happen again, and it would be hard to build our relationship back up if people were worried about us being together.

I also decided to keep careful track of my income. It seemed wise to know how much money I had to my name, in the event that things went wrong again and I needed a clean break.

Ryan helped me unload everything from the car, then grabbed the phone book. "I'm going to head out," he told me, gesturing to the book. "Start looking around Stettler for therapists or out of town if there aren't any here. Would you mind pouring out the rest of the beer once I leave?"

I happily agreed. He kissed Jenny and me goodbye, then drove off.

First things first, I put Jenny in her high chair and gave her some breakfast that she could eat all by herself. Tiny banana slices, dry cereal, and little cubes of cheese. She hummed as she ate, feet swinging under the tray. Once she was settled, I took the beer from the fridge and poured every bit of it down the sink before burying the empty bottles deep in the garbage. It was even more satisfying than I thought it would be.

I started gathering supplies to make myself breakfast when I noticed our answering machine flashing. I pressed the button to play the message before going back to what I was doing.

The gruff voice of a man came from the machine. *Hey, Vanessa.*

I froze. I knew that voice, but... maybe I didn't. I could have sworn it was familiar, but I couldn't place it. I waited several seconds before the machine spoke again. *It's Dad.*

I stared at the machine, dumbfounded. There was no way.

I, uh, heard about your daughter. That's great. I know it's been a while, but, uh, I thought I'd call, in case you wanted to tell me about her. I'm living with your grandparents again, and I know you have their number, so, uh, call back if you want. Talk to you soon, maybe.

The message ended. I didn't realize how long I'd stood there, frozen, until Jenny giggled and pointed at me. "Mommy."

I walked over to her and pushed her hair out of her face. She smiled up at me. "Mommy," she said again.

"Hi, beautiful." A smile grew on my face. "I think your grandpa wants to get to know you."

Chapter 55

Breakfast could wait. The familiar, comforting smells of sizzling bacon and warm coffee drifted through the house, but I couldn't think about any of that now. My fingers hovered above the phone, still trembling slightly from the shock of hearing my dad's voice on the answering machine. The sound of him saying my name—*Vanessa*—had sent a ripple through me as if the years of silence and distance between us had suddenly collapsed in on themselves. Now that I'd finally snapped out of my surprise, I called Abuelita and Abuelito, praying to God that Dad was still around.

The phone picked up after only a couple of rings. "Hello?" Abuelita's voice came through, soft and warm, yet a little surprised. She probably wasn't used to hearing from me either.

"Hi, Abuelita. It's Vanessa. I missed a call from Dad, and he said I could call you guys to get in touch with him?"

I could hear her sigh gently into the phone, the kind of sigh that comes from a place of knowing and compassion. "Yes, *mi amor*. He's outside. I'll go get him for you."

My heart raced as I heard the shuffle of her feet moving away from the receiver. I couldn't wrap my head around the fact that I was about to talk to my father for the first time since I was five. There was a nervous buzz in my stomach, and I squeezed the phone tighter, wondering what I would even say to him. Should I talk to him like my dad, the man I'd once known, or should I speak to him like an adult who was meeting him for the first time in years? Maybe, since he called me, I'd let him lead the conversation. I had been wishing for this moment for seventeen years, and now that it was happening,

I felt terrified and unprepared, like an actor thrown on stage without a script.

There was a brief noise on the other end of the line, the shuffle of a door opening, then a second of silence. And then, my dad's voice.

"Vanessa?"

My heart leaped so hard I thought it might escape my chest. "Hey, Dad."

There was a pause, a shift in the air, and then I heard him clear his throat, his voice suddenly uncertain. "It's, uh, good to talk to you. You been doing good?"

At least Dad sounded as uncomfortable as I was. It almost made me laugh, a small, nervous laugh, but I kept it in check. The fact that we were both fumbling through this made it feel just a little bit easier. "Yeah, I've been good. Motherhood suits me, I think."

He chuckled softly, the sound thick with emotion, and I realized how much I had missed it. "I saw the pictures you sent of your daughter. Jenny, huh? That's a nice name. She's a beautiful baby."

Hearing Dad say that filled me with a rush of emotion that I wasn't prepared for. I felt tears prickling behind my eyes, but I blinked them back, trying to maintain my composure. The conversation was awkward, but each word we exchanged felt like a small, precious step forward. The fact that it was even happening, after so many years, had me overflowing with joy. For once, there was a bridge between us, however fragile it may have been.

When I sensed the call would end soon, I summoned all the courage I could muster and said, "I'm really glad you called.

I'd...like to keep in touch if you can. I can update you on Jenny, and, you know..."

There was a long pause. I held my breath. It felt like this moment was hanging in the air, like it could fall apart with just one wrong move. But finally, Dad spoke again.

"Yeah, yeah. That sounds great."

I exhaled slowly, my chest tight with relief. I'd been half-expecting him to come up with an excuse then and there as to why staying in touch wouldn't work. I wasn't exactly convinced that he would keep in touch, and in a way, that was good. It would protect me from being too disappointed if I didn't hear from him again. But in that moment, hearing him say he wanted to stay in touch despite everything gave me a tiny flicker of hope.

I was pleasantly surprised when, two weeks after talking to Dad, I got a letter in the mail from him. The envelope was a little worn, the edges bent, but the handwriting on it was unmistakable. The simple, familiar scrawl of his name made my heart race again. In the letter, he told me that it would be easier for him if we mostly sent each other letters, as he was very busy and it would be hard for him to find the time to make phone calls.

I didn't mind at all if our relationship took place through letters. For me, this was already more of a relationship than I'd had with him for most of my life. It was a starting point, and I was willing to take whatever I could get. The letter also mentioned that he hoped to visit sometime, but he was uncertain about when. His life was unpredictable, but he wanted to stay involved.

In the letter I wrote back to him, I gave him my new address. It felt strange to share such a personal detail, but it felt necessary. Ryan had found us a two-bedroom, two-bathroom apartment for the same price we were paying now for our smaller one. It was built in the fifties, which was why it was cheaper, but it was in great condition. It was two stories, with the bedrooms and a bathroom on the second floor, and the living room, kitchen, and other bathroom on the main level. It was small, cozy, and had just enough space for Jenny to run around in, which was perfect.

Ryan had also started seeing a therapist. He found her the day he went out searching, but her fees were too much for us. So, he went to his parents and admitted that he was struggling with his addiction again and trying to get help. I could hear the vulnerability in his voice when he told me. It took everything in him to be that open.

Apparently, they had to send him to rehab against his will once before, so they were thrilled that he was seeking help on his own this time. They were excited enough that they offered to pay for his sessions. I was grateful, but at the same time, it was hard to let go of the resentment I'd built up over the years. Still, I made it a point to tell Ryan just how proud I was of him for being man enough to admit his problem to his parents and ask for help.

He made it a point to have his therapist sign a paper for him at every appointment as a way to prove to me that he was actually going. He didn't have to do that, though. His attendance was obvious in how much he was improving. With practice, he gained the ability to look on the bright side whenever something didn't work out for him. His therapist also recommended that he keep a journal to get out all his negative thoughts so they wouldn't overwhelm him anymore. He wrote in his journal every day, a small act of accountability that made a big difference.

Ryan, doing well meant that I was doing well, too. I was thriving at my job, and I felt more confident as a mother than I had since Jenny was born. I was also having a blast spending all my free time planning our wedding.

Ryan didn't really care about all the little decorative details, but he helped me with whatever I needed him to. Most of my help came from Christina, Annie, and Hannah since their schedules were the most flexible. Mom, Lily, and Ryan's mom were happy to help me whenever they had the time. It was a group effort, and I was grateful for the support.

The most fun part of all was going dress shopping. I asked Mom, Lily, and Ryan's mom to go shopping with me, and Ryan's mom offered to drive us all to Calgary, so we had lots of stores to choose from. We spent the day laughing, sipping iced lattes, and browsing through boutique after boutique, but I found the perfect dress at the first shop we went to. It was so perfect, in fact, that it made Mom cry when she saw me in it. Her hands trembled as she wiped away the tears, and I couldn't help but smile at her reaction.

Of course, I invited Dad, Abuelita, and Abuelito to the wedding. I mailed them an invitation in February, as soon as the date was set, and I got a reply three weeks before the wedding. Dad said they wouldn't be able to go because they couldn't afford to fly out to Alberta.

If that was just an excuse, it was at least a reasonable one. It didn't make me any less sad about it, though. I would've liked for him to be there, but at least he'd tried to reach out. That was something.

The day I told Ryan they weren't coming, he wrinkled his

forehead. "Who are you going to ask to walk you down the aisle?"

I went blank. I had never really thought about it before. "I... don't know. I never thought about it until now."

There were hardly any men in my life, much less one who would be fit to walk me down the aisle. Honestly, the closest person I had who fit the bill was Mom.

I stopped by her house the next day to ask her, almost jokingly, in case she thought it was weird. But she didn't. Her face lit up when I asked, and she hugged me tightly, squeezing me as if she never wanted to let go.

"Oh, Ness. I'd be honored to," she said, wiping a tear from her eye. Everything about my wedding was emotional for her, and it was hard not to get caught up in that energy.

That was it, then. Everything was booked and paid for. In less than a month, I will be a married woman. And despite all the chaos and heartache leading up to this moment, I felt a strange sense of calm. Things were falling into place, slowly, cautiously, but they were falling into place.

Chapter 56

Ryan and I were married on a warm evening in July. The sun had started to dip behind the trees, casting a golden hue over the church, making everything look like it belonged in a dream. The gentle summer breeze whispered through the open windows, the scent of fresh-cut grass mingling with the floral arrangements that decorated the pews. All the members of his large family filled the church, the sound of their laughter and chatter filling the air, while the comparatively small number of guests on my side seemed so much quieter. Mia, Sandy, Sarah, and Veronica had flown out from Québec to stand as my bridesmaids, along with Annie and Hannah. Jenny was our flower girl. Lily escorted her up the aisle and had to keep reminding her to toss the flowers because all she wanted to do was wave at the guests, soaking up all the attention on her.

I watched this from the back of the church, hiding behind a tall post so nobody would see me. The air was heavy with anticipation, and I could feel my heart racing in my chest. The guests smiled and waved back at Jenny, and I couldn't help but giggle softly over how cute she was. Her bright eyes twinkled, her little hands clutching the basket of petals, oblivious to anything but the smiles that surrounded her. She was radiant, so innocent and pure, and at that moment, it felt like the whole world was watching her.

When she made it up to the front, Lily pointed out Ryan, and Jenny shouted, "Daddy!" over the soft piano music that had been playing in the background for the entire ceremony.

Ryan's face lit up, his eyes softening at the sound of her voice. He picked her up, and I could see the love in his gaze, even from where I stood. Once Lily was in her place, the priest motioned for everyone to rise for me.

Jenny pressed her cheek against Ryan's as he turned around to face the aisle. He looked at me with a love in his eyes I'd only seen once before; when he first laid eyes on Jenny, the same expression of awe and joy. The memory of that moment flashed in my mind, and I felt the weight of it all, how far we'd come, how much we'd fought for this. Tears streamed down my face as I clung to Mom's arm, walking down the aisle toward him. I was trembling with excitement, but my heart felt so full it could burst. I wasn't just walking down the aisle to Ryan, I was walking toward a future, a life that I never thought I would have.

When Jenny noticed me, she waved at me, too. "Hi, Mommy!" she called out, her voice high and filled with that special joy only a child could express.

I laughed, a few tears slipping down my cheek. "Hi, baby."

I could see the whole church smiling at us. I could feel the love that surrounded me, and I realized that this day was just as much about Jenny as it was about me. Everyone always said that a wedding was the bride's day, but I felt like this was even more for Jenny, who was getting a unified family, a family that had fought to be together. It was the least she deserved, and I was so blessed to be able to share this special day with her, to be able to look at her and see hope for the future in her eyes. She was the one who made everything real for me.

Our wedding day was magical. One of the most special days of my life. The ceremony was perfect, the reception full of laughter and dancing, the food delicious, and the decorations beautiful. But the newlywed bliss was short-lived.

As the days passed, I realized that while we had shared an unforgettable day, reality was starting to settle in. I did not doubt that Ryan was happy to be married to me. He told me how glad he was to be my husband, often, sometimes with his arms wrapped around me in the quiet moments after Jenny had gone to bed. But now that it was all said and done, our financial situation was starting to sink in.

The wedding, as perfect as it was, had taken a lot out of us. Even with Mom and Ryan's mom helping to pay for the wedding, Ryan and I still had to use some of our own money. The loss we took wouldn't keep us from paying bills or buying groceries, but it did take away from the savings we had been building up for Ryan to go to the music academy. The dream we had for his future seemed just as far away as it had been before we'd gotten married.

In early September, Ryan began to mention, more and more frequently, that it had been nearly a year since he'd applied for the Institute of Music and Arts, and we weren't any closer to being able to afford it. The hope that we'd had when he first applied seemed to fade with each passing month. It was as if the weight of our financial struggles was pushing everything else further out of reach. It seemed as though nothing I said to try and encourage him helped, and it was then that he went back on his promise to me to never drink again.

It started slowly, like it always did. At first, there was just the faint smell of alcohol on his breath when he came home from work. I wasn't sure if he had been drinking at work or on his way home, but I noticed it. He started going out with his friends more, and it didn't take long before he began coming home buzzed. I tried to ignore it at first, hoping it was just a phase, hoping that everything would go back to the way it was.

But I couldn't ignore it for long. Ryan breaking his promise to me, truthfully infuriated me. The anger bubbled up inside me, hot and tight, but I said nothing. What was I supposed to do? Tell everyone who was at our wedding only two months ago that I was leaving him for drinking with his friends? How would that even sound?

I would sound crazy, and I wasn't sure I'd want to do it anyway. Jenny was so happy, so content, and the last thing I wanted to do was mess her world up. She deserved stability, she deserved a family. Maybe, so long as Ryan never became violent again, I could just deal with it, pretend like everything was fine. I could tell myself that he'd get back on track. Maybe I could focus on keeping the peace for Jenny's sake.

But deep down, I knew that I was lying to myself. That this wasn't something I could just sweep under the rug, no matter how much I wanted to. The fear that the other shoe would drop, that the man I had promised to marry, the man who had pledged to change for us, would slip back into old habits... it kept me awake at night, twisting my stomach into knots.

Chapter 57

Around the time Ryan started drinking again, I got my first letter from Dad since he said he couldn't come to the wedding. I'd sent him a few pictures that my friends snapped, of me, Ryan, and Jenny. He told me he was happy for me and that Jenny and I looked pretty in our white dresses. He even said he thought it was nice that Mom had walked me down the aisle.

The letter was short, but it felt heavier than anything I'd held in a while. His handwriting, slanted and precise, still looked the same as it had on the notes he used to leave on the fridge when I was little—except maybe a little shakier now, as if time had added a tremor to his hand. I read it three times in a row, sitting at the edge of the couch while Jenny played nearby, and even though I smiled at his words, something tight wrapped itself around my chest. It was strange how something as simple as a few sentences in a familiar script could bring up a childhood's worth of longing.

Dad's next letter came in early December. He'd sent it a month earlier to make sure it came in time for Christmas. He wished my family a merry Christmas, and he told me he'd bought Jenny a present that he would mail in January.

It was a teddy bear. I didn't know that yet, but when it arrived later, the tag was still attached: "For Jenny – from Grandpa." Her eyes lit up when she saw it, and she held it like it had always belonged to her. I wanted to cry just watching her. It was the first time I'd seen something tangible from my dad become a part of her world.

While my relationship with Dad began to pick up, my marriage went stagnant. I wouldn't say it was exactly bad, but it certainly wasn't the fairytale I'd always wanted. Most of the time Ryan and I spent together was him pretending to be sober and me pretending not to notice that he wasn't.

There were nights I'd lie awake and listen to him breathe beside me, wondering if he was truly asleep or just too far gone to notice me crying. We'd stopped touching somewhere along the way, except in public, when we both seemed to remember we were married.

Jenny, on the other hand, was the light of my life. She turned two in October, and she amazed me every day. She was smart, silly, and sweet. Jenny was everything I could have asked for in a daughter, and she kept me pushing myself to be the best version of myself.

She was always singing little songs she made up, hopping from room to room like the floor was lava. Her giggle was sharp and high-pitched, like a hiccup that didn't know it wasn't welcome, and it always made me laugh no matter how tired I felt. Some mornings, when I felt too heavy to get out of bed, she'd peek her head in and say, "Mommy, it's morning time!" and somehow, that was enough to make me move.

One of Jenny's favorite things was playing in the snow. There was heavy snow one Friday night in January, so on Saturday, Ryan and I took her to the park to go sledding. Ryan pushed her around on the hills while I helped her build snowmen and throw snowballs at Ryan when he pretended he wasn't looking. It was the first time in a while that Ryan and I had genuine fun together.

For a few hours, it felt like we were a real family again. Like maybe we'd make it. Jenny's cheeks were flushed red with cold, and her mittens were soaked through, but she kept yelling, "Again! Again!" with such joy that neither of us had the heart to say no. When Ryan looked over at me, snow in his beard and a tired grin on his face, I saw a version of him I hadn't seen in months, maybe even years.

We went home around noon for lunch. Ryan took Jenny to her room to help her get changed while I started chopping vegetables. The phone rang, and Ryan shouted from upstairs, "Can you get that, Ness?"

I put down the knife and picked up the phone. "Hello?"

"Hi, *mi amor*."

It was Abuelito, sounding incredibly tired. "Hi, Abuelito," I said, trying to hide my concern. "What's going on?"

He got straight to the point. He was blunt and emotionless. I listened in silence, my heart thudding against my chest and my body growing cold and weak.

Once he said all he had to say, the call ended, just like that. I had so many questions. So many thoughts I couldn't process.

Ryan came downstairs with Jenny. When he saw me standing over the phone, he sent her to play in the living room.

"What's wrong?" he asked, walking over to me. "Who was that?"

"Jenny's grandpa." I looked at Ryan. "My dad's dead."

Ryan had no idea what to do for me. That was fair. I had no idea what I needed.

"Do you mind taking over the cooking?" I asked him, sounding like a robot. "So I can go and just...think?"

"Yeah, of course." He reached out as if to help me upstairs, but I shook my head and went up on my own.

I sat on the bed and slipped into thought. Abuelito left so many questions unanswered. The main one being how Dad even died. No amount of thinking would answer these questions, so I instead tried focusing on my feelings.

I'd spent years telling myself that I didn't care about Dad at all. Didn't care if I never talked to him again, didn't care if he died. If that were true, I wouldn't be shaking so hard or having to remind myself to breathe.

So I did care about him. Okay. He was my dad. But he wasn't a good one. But he was trying to become a good one. He was making an effort to create a relationship between us, as I'd secretly yearned for my whole life. But maybe it would have only lasted until he fell back into old habits and stopped sending me letters. I would never know because he was dead.

I decided in an instant that it didn't matter why I felt the way I did. Now wasn't the time to try and figure it out. Now was the time to just let myself feel whatever I was feeling.

And what I was feeling was sadness, so I buried my face in my pillow and cried.

The sobs came like a dam breaking. My body curled in on itself as though trying to protect the fragile heart inside it. I clutched at the blanket, wishing it were his letter, or even just something he'd touched. The pillowcase grew wet, and I didn't care. The room felt too big and too small at once, and I hated the way the world kept spinning as if nothing had changed.

I spent the next few days on an emotional rollercoaster that put my pregnancy hormones to shame. I would wake up, remember that Dad is dead, and just not care. I'd go about my day like nothing was different. Then, out of nowhere, I'd be hit with a wave of devastation and start to cry. I could be at home, at work, or at the grocery store. It didn't matter. I couldn't hold it in. And if someone asked why I was crying, I couldn't explain it. I felt sadness without understanding why I was sad.

I'd called Mom and told her about Dad the evening I found out. I declined when she offered to come over and be with me, saying that I was okay. She called a few times the next day to check up on me, and no matter what I said, her mother's intuition told her that I wasn't actually okay.

She took a few days off work and convinced me to do the same. She spent most of her time at my apartment, tending to Jenny and me. I found myself watching her like a hawk at all times. I wasn't sure why at first, until I realized it was because I didn't know how I was supposed to be feeling, and I was following my instincts to look to my mother to understand what to do.

It didn't help. Mom never hid the fact that she loathed Dad. She had been encouraging when I told her I was talking to him again, but she couldn't quite hold back the twitch of disgust on her face anytime I mentioned him.

Now, though, she was neutral. She acted happy around Jenny but not overly happy. She was sympathetic when she held me as I cried, but it was clear to me that the only sadness she felt about this all was overseeing me hurting. As well as I thought I knew Mom, I couldn't for the life of me decipher how she was actually feeling about this. It only made me more confused.

By the time Mom had gone back to work, Ryan had become tired of my weird emotions. "I don't understand," he said one night upon coming home to find me crying. There was an almost imperceptible slur to his words. "Remember, when you first told me about him, you said you hated him? He sends a few letters, and you suddenly love him?"

"I don't understand either," I told him. "I've been trying to figure it out."

Ryan just shrugged and left the room, saying, "It doesn't make sense. You hardly knew the guy."

He was right, but maybe that was part of the reason I was so affected. I *should* have known him. I should have memories of him to look back on, and future plans with him that I'd be missing out on now. I was losing the hope of having a dad rather than losing Dad himself.

That filled me with shame. Wouldn't he want me to miss him? When I died, even if it was after not having spoken to Jenny for seventeen years, I would still want her to miss me. But I would never leave Jenny in the first place, so I had no idea what Dad would want.

And I never would. What I knew about him now was all I'd ever have, no matter how badly I wished it could be different.

Chapter 58

The month after Dad's death consisted of me merely going through the motions of life. My performance at work didn't suffer, and I was still attentive to Jenny, but the spark that brought me joy in life was missing.

I did all the things I was supposed to do—made breakfast, bathed Jenny, clocked in and out of my job, folded laundry with methodical precision—but I felt like I was watching myself from outside my own body, like I was a character in a movie I didn't want to be in anymore. There were moments, usually when Jenny did something hilarious or sweet, when I'd laugh, and it would almost feel real, the laughter ended, and I remembered that it was just something I was borrowing for a second.

That all changed in February when I noticed my period was late. I took a pregnancy test, and lo and behold, it was positive. We were going to have another baby.

I didn't know what to think at first. Ryan and I were hardly ever intimate anymore. We certainly weren't trying to get pregnant. I was already so in love with this little baby, though, and that made me all the more nervous to give Ryan the news.

I stared at the test for a long time, sitting on the closed toilet seat in our tiny bathroom, knees drawn up, heart fluttering with both fear and wonder. I put my hand on my stomach, already imagining the new life growing inside of me. There was a quiet buzz of joy under my skin, and it scared me how badly I wanted this, how badly I wanted something pure and new to hold on to.

To my surprise, he was overjoyed. He kissed me and laughed, saying how excited he was to grow our family. Even more surprising was that he stopped hanging out with his friends after work and instead came straight home to wait on me hand and foot. This was the happiest our marriage had been since the wedding.

He'd rush to bring me tea in the morning, ask about my cravings, and rub my feet in the evenings. I wanted to believe in this version of him. I wanted to believe this baby had brought him back to life, that we'd turned a corner. We'd lie in bed at night and talk about names, and for the first time in a long time, I caught glimpses of the man I'd fallen in love with, the one who promised me the world, not the one who lost himself in a bottle.

Unfortunately, it didn't last. After a month or so, he grew absent again. He came home most nights with alcohol on his breath. I thanked God that I at least wasn't sick this time around. No way I could juggle my job and care for Jenny if I were sick again.

It was hard to be excited about this pregnancy when Ryan didn't seem to be. He went back to doting on me when we learned I was having a boy, but lost interest in me even quicker than before. I grew increasingly anxious to see the role he would play once our little boy was born.

He seemed to light up at the idea of a son, making vague promises about teaching him to play catch, how he'd build a crib himself, how he'd be different this time. But the promises always hung in the air like smoke—there for a moment, then gone.

When I was seven months pregnant, I got a phone call from Mia. She was letting me know that *she* was pregnant. She and Elijah had married two years ago when she graduated from college, and they were finally ready to start a family. I told her I was thrilled for her, and I really was. She and Elijah had a great marriage, and I knew they'd be great parents.

She was shocked when I mentioned that I, too, was pregnant. She asked why I hadn't told her, and I said it was just because I was so stressed lately and never got around to it.

Mia must have heard in my voice that that wasn't the full truth because she immediately asked when I was due. I told her in early November, and she said she was going to fly out to Stettler in October. She wanted to help me care for Jenny and prepare for the birth.

I was over the moon to have Mia come over, and Ryan didn't care either way when I brought it up to him later that day. Knowing Mia would be here with me made me so much more excited to have this baby.

That same night, I woke up after midnight to use the bathroom. I stared at Ryan as I tiptoed back in, making sure I wouldn't disturb him. I made it back to bed without stirring him, but I couldn't stop watching him.

Ryan and I had been together for nearly four years now and married for over one. We had a daughter together and a son on the way. And yet, as I looked at his face, peaceful in sleep, I felt no love for him.

My stomach rolled. How did I end up here? Having a second child with a man I had so many issues with? This was far from the life I'd dreamt of for myself.

I carefully opened the drawer of my nightstand and pulled out the notebook I used to keep track of my income and savings. The moonlight coming through the window lit up the paper enough for me to see all the numbers.

I'd been writing here weekly, out of habit at this point. But now, I really looked at those numbers and thought about what they meant for me.

The notebook suddenly felt like a map. Not a plan, exactly, but a way out. It reminded me that I wasn't trapped, not really. I was building something slowly, even if I didn't know what it was yet. The knowledge gave me a flicker of peace, and I held it close as I tucked the book back away.

I quickly put away the notebook and tucked myself into bed. I didn't think I was considering leaving Ryan or anything, but seeing those numbers comforted me all the same.

****

Mia arrived in Stettler on the last Sunday of October. Seeing her filled me with so much joy and relief that I could hardly stand it.

"I'll be able to stay for about a month," she told me as she drove us to my apartment in her rental car. "So, for the first couple of weeks of his life, at least."

"What about you?" I asked her. "When are you due?"

She smiled. "In April. I can't wait."

Mia told me how Elijah had a well-paying job, so she quit hers once she learned she was pregnant. They planned for her to stay home with their children until they were at least in school.

"I'm already so in love with being a mother," she told me as we got to my apartment. "You know how badly I've always wanted to be a mom. It was a big dream for both of us."

"It's so amazing," I told her. "Becoming a mom was truly the best thing I've ever done. I've never been happier."

Mia hesitated. "It's obvious how much you love your kids, but...Vanessa, you don't seem very happy."

My stomach dropped as she explained. "There was always this light in your eyes. To me, it looked like hope. You even had it when you left for Alberta. But it's gone now."

I looked at my lap, unsure what to say. Mia scooted close to me. "How are things with Ryan?" she asked gently.

I shrugged. "He's a good father to Jenny. I know he loves her. I know he loves me, too. He tells me every day." I swallowed. "He can get pretty distracted by work sometimes, but I think he really does try his best for us."

Mia sighed. "I won't pretend to know what your relationship with him is like behind closed doors. But Vanessa, love isn't always enough. Trying to be good isn't always enough. Does he respect you? Is he concerned about your happiness?"

I didn't want to admit it, but the answer to those questions was no. He broke his promise to stop drinking, and he spent more time with his friends than with me. Mia was right. Ryan saying he loved me was pointless if he didn't act like it.

When I didn't reply, she said, "I think you need to be selfish. Don't worry about what your family needs. Don't worry about what Ryan needs. Don't even worry about what your children need. Worry about yourself. If you do what's best for *you*, it'll naturally lead to what's best for your kids. I know you want to put your kids first, so maybe put yourself first for a little while so you can do that for them."

Mia gave me an encouraging smile. "You've toughed it out through *so many* tribulations, Vanessa. What's one more?"

Chapter 59

Five days after Jenny turned three, my water broke. I quickly called Mom and Ryan at work to let them know while Mia packed my hospital bag and put Jenny into her rental car. The moment my water broke, panic gripped me, though I knew it was time. The rush of reality that this was happening now left me dizzy and breathless. I grabbed the phone with shaky hands, hearing my voice trembling as I gave instructions, trying to remain calm for everyone else. I could feel the gentle kick of Adrian inside me, as though reminding me that, yes, this was the beginning of a new chapter.

Mom and Ryan made it to the hospital soon after I did. Mia stayed in the waiting room with Jenny while Mom and Ryan followed me into the delivery room. The sterile white lights of the hospital felt too bright, but the excitement I felt for meeting my son pushed me forward. Ryan held my hand, his face a mask of concern mixed with the faintest smile as he tried to keep it together. I could tell he was nervous, but we had been through this once before. We were going to make it through this again.

Unlike his sister, this baby was ready to come out. I was in labor for barely over an hour before my precious boy was born. The room was filled with the soft sounds of medical staff talking, the occasional beep from the machines, and my breathing, which felt so loud, so frantic. But then, there he was—a small, perfect human with his tiny fingers and the softest skin. The world seemed to pause, and in that moment, all of the fear and tension melted away.

"Well, Vanessa," Doctor Leonard said, "looks like you're two-for-two. You have another strong, healthy baby here. Congratulations."

His words rang in my ears, but I barely processed them. My arms instinctively reached for Adrian as the nurse gently placed him in my arms. I gazed down at my son, the rush of love overwhelming me in a way I never could've anticipated. How foolish I'd been to think I wouldn't love him as much as Jenny.

I had been admittedly worried throughout my pregnancy that I wouldn't love this baby as much as I loved Jenny. How could I love anyone as much as I loved her? As soon as the nurse placed my baby in my arms, I realized how foolish I was for thinking that. My heart flooded with love for my boy, just like it did for Jenny. There it was again—that magic, that deep connection that tied me to him, the same as it had with Jenny. The raw, unexplainable bond that only motherhood could bring.

Doctor Leonard checked me over and asked, "So. We have Jenny, and...?"

Mom brushed my hair away from my face, and I smiled at her, the kind of smile that spoke a thousand words. My mother, the woman who had seen me through every joy and pain of my life, was here, with me, at this moment.

"Adrian," I told Doctor Leonard. I looked at my son, whose name now sat so perfectly in my heart.

Ryan took his turn to hold Adrian, and Mom left to get Jenny. She brought her into the room, and Jenny looked around at all the people and equipment with wide eyes.

Her small, innocent face was full of wonder, and I could see that she was processing everything, unsure of what was happening but sensing the importance of the moment.

"It's okay, baby," I told her. I held my arms out to her, and Mom helped her onto my lap. "Are you ready to meet your little brother?" Jenny's eyes flickered between me and the tiny bundle in Ryan's arms, her curiosity winning out. I felt a wave of protectiveness wash over me, not just for Adrian but for Jenny, too. This moment was so significant for both of them.

She stared at the bundle in Ryan's arms with wonder. She nodded. I helped her adjust her arms, and Ryan placed Adrian in Jenny's lap.

The sight of her holding him so carefully, her little hands cradling him as though she had always known him, made my heart swell with pride. I could already see the deep love forming between them, even though they were just meeting.

"This is Adrian," I told her. "What do you think?"

"He's so small," she said, making the adults laugh. She bent over and gently kissed his nose. "I love you, Adrian."

The pure, unfiltered love in her voice had me holding back tears. I had never seen anything so simple and beautiful in my life. This was the first moment of sibling love between them, and it made everything, every struggle, every tear, every sleepless night, worth it.

My eyes filled with tears. Watching my daughter care for my son filled me with the purest love there could ever be. I thanked God for giving me such beautiful children.

At that moment, it didn't matter what else was happening in my life. I had these two, these beautiful souls who needed me, and that was enough.

Ryan was watching Jenny and Adrian with tears in his eyes, too, and a soft smile on his face. And yet, this didn't feel like a family to me. It felt like a mother and father who loved their children separately.
The tension I had been carrying for so long was still there, hanging between us like an invisible wall. There was love in this room, no doubt, but I couldn't shake the feeling that we were living parallel lives, not one shared life.

Please, God, I thought, *help us fix this.*

I had Mia to help me with my children for two weeks after Adrian's birth. When she had to go back to Québec, Mom took a week off work again to help me out.

Being around Mom and Mia kept my mind occupied, but once it was back to just Ryan and me, nothing could distract me from the sad state of our relationship. We hardly spoke to each other. He was wonderful to Jenny and Adrian when he was around, and for that, I was grateful.

But this was not how a family should be. This was a mother and father who happened to share children, not a marriage. Ryan had essentially tossed me aside, replacing me with the friends he still regularly drank with.

He obviously loved his children, so if he was spending time drinking when he could be with them, then this had to be an addiction. Maybe it wasn't completely his fault; life hadn't always been good to him. It wasn't my fault either, though, and it was unfair that I had to suffer because of it.

Chapter 60

Ryan found out that he would have to work late on New Year's Eve. His restaurant had a party planned, so he'd be there until midnight at the earliest.

It was an odd relief, honestly. I wasn't really in the mood for anything big, and with Adrian so young and Jenny so full of energy, I knew it would be a quiet night at home.

We weren't going to do anything anyway, so I wasn't too bothered. I invited Mom to come over since Lily was out with friends, and Aunt Nora tagged along, too. I put Jenny and Adrian to bed at their normal bedtime, then rang in the new year by having some champagne with Mom and Aunt Nora.

The evening passed like it always did when we gathered together—a little laughter, some quiet moments of reflection, and the comforting presence of family. It wasn't exactly festive, but it was warm and familiar, and I needed that warmth more than anything.

They left soon after midnight, so I went to bed. I awoke just after three to Ryan coming home.

I could hear him before I saw him, his footsteps heavy, uneven, like a boat rocking on rough waters. I couldn't help but feel a sense of dread wash over me. The hour was too late, and the smell of alcohol clung to him like a shadow.

I could tell by how heavy his footsteps were coming up the stairs that he was drunk. He came into the bedroom and turned the light on. I had to squeeze my eyes shut as he walked over and came into bed beside me.

The light burned my eyes, but I didn't want to start another fight. My heart felt heavy in my chest, my body tense with all the unspoken words we'd never addressed.

"I'm glad you're awake," he said, clearly wasted. "I was hoping we could spend time together."

The words stung, coming from him like that. Did he really think everything could be fixed in a single night? Did he think his drunken desire for intimacy could somehow erase everything else?

He grabbed my waist and pulled me into him. "Ryan, no," I said. "You're drunk, I'm tired, we're not having sex."

His grip tightened, but I pushed against him. The smell of alcohol on his breath was suffocating. I wanted to get away from it, from him.

"We haven't had sex in months," he said, his voice raising. "You won't even do it tonight to celebrate?"

It wasn't about sex. It never was. It was about power. And I refused to give him that control over me again.

I jerked away from him and stormed out of the room, asking, "Celebrate what? You being an alcoholic and a terrible husband?"

The words spilled out before I could stop them, sharp and raw. And Ryan—he wasn't going to let me walk away so easily.

Ryan immediately chased me down the stairs. "I'm a terrible husband?" he shouted. "That's what you think?"

His voice was a storm, and I couldn't breathe under the pressure of it. But I wouldn't back down. Not this time.

"Keep it down," I hissed. "You'll wake up the kids."

I had to protect them. I couldn't let them see this.

"Good," he yelled. "I want them to. I wanna tell them their mother is a whore who doesn't respect their father."

Every word he said felt like a punch. The fury in his eyes, so volatile, so desperate, scared me more than anything.

Hot tears stung my eyes. I tried to bite my tongue, but he had me so emotional that the words just spilled out of my mouth. "I want a divorce."

There, I said it. But saying it out loud didn't feel like a victory. It felt like I had just ripped apart the last bit of hope I had.

Ryan's eyes widened, and he rushed at me surprisingly quickly, considering his state. As soon as he grabbed my shoulders, I knew what was going to happen. He threw me to the ground, turned me so I was on my back, and hit me twice in the face.

It wasn't the first time. But this time, something broke inside me. I couldn't believe this was where we were. I couldn't believe I had allowed this to happen again.

I also knew that raising my hands to him in any way would only escalate the situation. I needed him to calm down before Jenny had a chance to wake up and see what was happening.

Every breath I took felt like it cut through my chest, my heart pounding in my ears as I tried to make myself invisible, to disappear into the floor. I couldn't let him hurt me like this again. I couldn't let him ruin everything.

Ryan stumbled backward, knocking over a floor lamp. It

crashed to the ground, and Adrian began to cry upstairs.

The sound of Adrian's cries sliced through the chaos, grounding me in the reality of the situation. My instincts screamed at me to go to him, to soothe him, but I couldn't leave Ryan behind. Not now. Not when he was in this state. I couldn't risk being vulnerable. Not while he was still unpredictable.

If I walked away from Ryan, he'd probably attack me again, so I racked my brain for an idea of how to get upstairs and keep Ryan away.

There had to be something. My mind was a storm of frantic thoughts, but nothing solid seemed to stick. Then, my eyes flicked to the pack of cigarettes poking out of Ryan's pocket. It was the only chance I had.

"We're not getting a divorce," he slurred. He clumsily unbuttoned his pants. "We're gonna go to bed and do what married couples do. You got it?"

His words twisted like poison, but I knew I couldn't fight him with force. I had to outsmart him, to make him think he was getting what he wanted while I figured out how to protect myself and the kids.

"Okay," I said, my voice shaking. "I got it. It'll be annoying to have sex while the baby is crying. Why don't you go out and have a cigarette, and I'll get him back to sleep?"

I made sure to keep my tone even, my voice laced with submission. I couldn't let him sense the fear coursing through me. If he thought I was complying, he might leave long enough for me to act.

Ryan pulled the pack from his pocket and went out the front door. Thank God. As soon as he shut it behind him, I ran over to watch him through the window. He'd walked to the far end of our carport, far enough away that he wouldn't hear the lock on the front door click.

I locked the door, confirmed he hadn't noticed, and then ran upstairs to our bedroom. I passed up Adrian's crib to grab the cordless phone.

The house felt so silent, too silent. Adrian's cries echoed in my mind, and I knew I couldn't wait much longer. My heart was racing, but I had one chance. I took the phone with me to the bathroom, where I could see the carport through the window.

I called the police, my voice trembling as I spoke. I told them that my husband was highly intoxicated and acting belligerent and aggressive, and said honestly that I was afraid for my and our children's safety.

The officer seemed to be taking this very seriously. He asked if I wanted to stay on the phone with him until the police arrived, and I said yes, not trusting myself to be alone in my own house for one more second.

Adrian's crying grew louder, but I couldn't go to him yet. I couldn't leave the bathroom and risk making any noise that might alert Ryan. I couldn't risk that.

I glanced at the mirror, and for a moment, it felt like I was looking at a stranger.

There was a face I didn't recognize, a face that looked like someone much older than me, someone who had been worn down by the weight of things I shouldn't have to carry. The bags under my eyes were dark, my face pale from the exhaustion and fear that had become my constant companions. I was twenty-four, too young to look like I'd aged a decade.

Red and blue lights bounced off the mirror. I spun around to see a police car pulling up. "They're here," I told the officer on the phone, relief flooding through me like a cool breeze after suffocating heat.

I watched as the officers got out of the car and approached Ryan. He immediately started to shout at them, eventually walking over to one of them like he was going to attack. That was all the officers needed to put him in handcuffs.

There was something so final about it. Seeing Ryan restrained, seeing him helpless in the face of something he couldn't fight against, felt like the end of a long and twisted road. But I knew it wasn't over. This wasn't a clean break. This was just the beginning of what I needed to face.

With Ryan gone, I could finally let my guard down. I went straight to Adrian. I rocked him and sang quiet songs until he drifted back to sleep.

The tears I had been holding back for so long spilled over. I wasn't sure if I was crying for the situation, for the pain, or for the loss of what could have been. I didn't want to think about it too much. I just wanted Adrian to feel safe, to know that I was there for him.

I crept into Jenny's room to make sure she was asleep. Thankfully, she was still a deep sleeper. She was lying in the exact same position she'd curled into when I first put her to bed.

The sight of her so peaceful, so innocent, was a balm for my bruised soul. I kissed her forehead, brushed her hair out of her face, and whispered a prayer that she would never have to experience the pain that had become my reality.

I was reminded of the night she was born when I visited her before bed and promised that I'd do everything I could to give her a great life.

Back then, I thought I knew what it meant to be a mother, to be the one who protected, guided, and shielded her from the world. But this was a different kind of protection, a protection from the man who was supposed to be her father. I had failed her in so many ways.

It was a promise I hadn't kept. Jenny was only three, but the peace she'd had on her face that first night was gone, replaced by the slightest puckering of her forehead.

She knew something wasn't right. She had seen the cracks in our family, the weight that Ryan's absence had left. She could feel it, even if she didn't understand it. And that hurt more than anything.

The pain from Ryan's blows hit me all at once, and I fell to the floor. I covered my mouth with my hands, trying to stay quiet as I sobbed over what Ryan and I had done to our daughter.

I had promised her so much, and now I was left with nothing but a broken promise and the hope that, somehow, I could fix it. I wasn't sure I could, but I knew I had to try. I had to keep fighting for her, for Adrian, and for myself.

Chapter 61

I called Mom as soon as I woke up the next morning. The morning light filtered weakly through the curtains, casting a dull gray hue across the apartment. My head throbbed, my body still exhausted from everything that had unfolded the night before. The silence in the apartment was suffocating, almost as if the walls were closing in on me. I needed her. I needed to talk, to hear her voice, to get through this.

I told her everything, from that first physical fight between Ryan and me to now, the weight of the truth spilling out in one long, unbroken sentence. As I spoke, I could feel the tears beginning to prick at the back of my eyes. It was all too much, too painful to recall, but I had to. Mom didn't interrupt, her voice steady on the other end, though I could hear the shock, the disbelief, the hurt she felt for me.

"I'll be over right away to help you pack up," she told me, her tone practical, focused. There was no question in her voice, no hesitation, just certainty. I could almost feel her moving already, the familiar sense of calm she always brought washing over me. She wasn't going to let me face this alone.

Before hanging up, she added, "I love you, Ness." And that was all I needed to hear.

There was no question I was leaving the apartment. Only Ryan's name was on the lease, and I knew that once I left, I was leaving for good. I couldn't stay here anymore. The apartment felt foreign, cold, like it had never truly been a home, not for me, not for the kids. It was a place full of broken promises and lost chances. I needed to leave behind the constant reminder of everything that had gone wrong.

I started by gathering up all my clothes, but even that felt like a monumental task. Every piece of fabric seemed to carry a memory, a whisper of the life I thought I would have. Once I was finished, Mom and Lily showed up. The three of us worked in quick, practiced silence as if moving in a quiet dance of survival, packing up everything I'd paid for, everything for the kids that we didn't have a duplicate of at Mom's house.

It was almost surreal, packing up life in boxes as if it hadn't been mine to begin with. Mom and Lily were organizing the packed car, making sure everything fit, when I was carrying out the last suitcase—heavy, full of everything I wanted to take and everything I was leaving behind—when Ryan pulled up in a taxi. My heart sank. I thought we'd be gone before he came back. I had hoped, prayed even that the timing would work out. But there he was, stepping out of the cab, eyes wide and disoriented.

Mom, Lily, and I went inside where the kids were. Ryan was right behind us, his eyes searching mine with a mix of confusion and dread. "What's going on?" he asked me, his voice small, as if he already knew but was hoping against hope it wasn't true.

I was surprised he couldn't see the swelling in my cheeks. The bruises were there, faint but undeniable. I had tried to hide them with makeup, but the physical pain was nothing compared to the weight of everything that had happened. I didn't answer his question right away. I just looked at him, feeling a thousand emotions bubbling up inside me.

"I'm leaving, Ryan," I said finally, my voice steadier than I felt.

His face crumpled, his eyes filling with tears. "You're *leaving*?" he whispered as though he couldn't fathom it. His voice was thick with disbelief, almost as though he was waiting for me to take it back, to tell him it was all a mistake.

I turned to Mom and Lily, my throat tight. "Can you take the kids outside to give us a minute?" I asked, needing a moment alone, needing to say what I had to say without the kids around, without their little faces watching us fall apart.

Mom and Lily took Jenny and Adrian outside, leaving us alone in the dim, quiet apartment. Once the door shut behind them, I turned back to Ryan. He stood there, frozen, looking completely sober and clueless, as if he had no idea what had happened the night before. I was still afraid, my heart beating a little too fast, but with Mom and Lily outside, with the kids safe, I had to believe he wouldn't react the way he had before. I had to believe I could do this.

"You started drinking again," I told him, the words coming out sharp, like they'd been waiting in the back of my throat. "You promised me you wouldn't drink ever again after getting drunk and attacking me."

His face fell, and for the first time in a long time, I saw something resembling remorse in his eyes. "You've been neglecting me for your friends," I continued, my voice growing firmer, more resolute. "You could be spending a lot more time with your kids than you are. And last night, you got wasted and attacked me, all while our baby was crying upstairs. I had to lock you outside and call the police."

Ryan covered his face with his hands, and for a moment, I didn't know if he was really processing it or if he was just putting on a show. Either way, it didn't matter. I had to say it.

"Vanessa," he whispered through his hands, his voice hoarse, thick with shame. "I'm so *sorry*."

I took a deep breath, holding back my tears. "So am I," I said, my voice barely above a whisper. "I'm sorry, this is how it ended. You knew what you had to do for your family, and you didn't do it."

I started to tear up, too, the weight of it all threatening to crush me. "I didn't hold up my end, either. I promised Jenny that I would do everything I could to take care of her, and I kept her in a strained environment for years. I had it all wrong, but I'm going to start working on myself for the kids. I'll pray that you do the same."

Ryan stepped toward me, his hands trembling as he reached for mine. "Give me another chance, then," he pleaded, his voice raw with desperation. "We'll work on ourselves together."

I shook my head, the words already coming, ready to fall from my lips. "We decided to do that when I was pregnant with Jenny, and here we are. There are no more chances, Ryan. I truly hope you get better, but I won't be around for it. I'm sorry."

I paused, taking a few deep breaths to steady myself. I had to stay calm for the kids. "We can't let Jenny and Adrian grow up and think this is how relationships should be," I said, my voice firm now. "They need to know it's not okay to be treated the way we treat each other, and it's not okay to treat anyone else like that. They need to learn that abuse doesn't deserve a second chance."

Ryan only stared at me, his face hollow, defeated. He didn't speak. There was nothing left to say.

"I won't ever try to keep you from the kids," I told him softly, my heart breaking for him even as I stood firm. "We'll agree on a fair custody schedule as we go through the divorce. But Ryan, you *have* to stop drinking. It's not safe for our kids to be in a home where the only adult there to care for them is drinking. I'd be happy to help you get into a rehab program, but that is the requirement for you to be able to care for them on your own."

I had said everything I needed to say. It was time to go.

I looked at Ryan one more time as he cried, and I realized that I did love him. I loved who he was before alcoholism took him. But this love wasn't enough to fix him, to fix us. This love wasn't enough to keep my children in a broken home.

With Jenny and Adrian in tow, I felt the same way I did when I left Montreal. Like I knew it was time to start over. But this time, there was so much more at stake. I wouldn't make the same mistakes again.

Chapter 62

As Mom, Lily, and I unloaded all our things at Mom's house, Jenny began to look anxious. Her little forehead was pinched up as she watched us move everything around, her wide eyes following every box, every suitcase, every motion. She had always been so perceptive, so attuned to the moods around her. I could see the worry building up inside her, just like it had in me when I was her age.

I walked over to comfort her, my heart aching at the sight of her unease. But before I could reach her, Lily was there, swooping in with her usual energy and optimism. Her face was happy and excited, her voice light and bright as she knelt down to Jenny's level. "I hear there's a lot of snow at the park. Want to go sledding with me?"

The mention of sledding perked Jenny right up, her face lighting up like a switch had been flipped. I bundled her up, wrapping her in layers of coats and scarves, and Lily took her by the hand, walking her to the hilly park down the street.

Mom sat me down on the couch, now that we were fully unpacked and Adrian was sleeping, blissfully unaware of the storm we'd just weathered. She settled next to me, her voice softer now. "Are you okay?" she asked me, her hand resting on mine.

"Yeah," I said, though my voice didn't feel as sure as I wanted it to. "I'm feeling hopeful about the future. I'll be back to work soon, so I'll be perfectly capable of getting an apartment for the three of us. I'd have to look into a babysitter for them, and I bet Christina would still do it."

I trailed off when I saw the look on Mom's face. Her brow was furrowed, her eyes full of something I couldn't quite place.

"What?" I asked, my heart sinking.

Mom shook her head slowly. "I just think you should...wait on all that. That's not what's important right now."

"How is that not important?" I asked, confused. Wasn't getting my life back on track the most important thing?

Mom put her hand on mine, her grip firm but gentle. "The mindset you have right now is the same one I had when I officially left your dad. I was so determined to build my life back up that I jumped right into a relationship with Oliver. We both know how *that* turned out. Before I knew it, I was right back in the situation I was trying so hard to leave."

Her eyes were sad, distant as she looked at me, and for a moment, I saw a flash of the pain she had hidden for so long. "I made that mistake, so now I can make sure you don't. You have family and friends from here to Montreal who will support you as you do whatever you need to heal and get your mind back on track."

This wasn't all that different from what Mia had told me before Adrian was born. If I'd heard it twice, maybe it was the best route to take. Maybe they were right.

I nodded slowly, feeling the weight of her words sink in. "I think the first thing I need to do is work on setting boundaries. I mean, it was my fault for letting Ryan get away with drinking again after we got married. All I did was convince him that I didn't stand by my word, and that he could get away with breaking his promises."

Mom's eyes watered, and before I could say anything, she was covering her face with her hands, the tears falling freely. "I'm sorry, Ness," she said between sobs. "I should've been able to see that Ryan was like this. After being with your dad and Oliver, I should've seen the signs. Instead, I told you how great of a person I thought he was."

I pulled her into a hug, my own heart breaking as she cried. I rested my head on her shoulder, whispering, "It wasn't obvious until now. I don't think anyone could've noticed how slowly and subtly things changed."

Mom nodded but didn't let go. She cried harder, and I held her tighter. It broke my heart to know that my choices had really hurt her after she did everything she could to help me.

Chapter 63

There came the big question: how did I start working on healing myself?

I considered therapy, but very briefly. I didn't have enough past success with it. The idea of sitting in a room with a stranger, talking about my feelings, felt like a dead end. So, then I had to try and come up with someone else who could counsel me emotionally and spiritually. I needed a guide, someone who could help me make sense of the mess I was in.

It hit me that evening as I sat with my thoughts. It was pretty obvious. I'd been faithful my whole life, so maybe it was time to actually start going to church.

I went to the nearest Catholic church that Sunday. The building was humble, its white walls offering a sense of peace that immediately washed over me. I liked the priest there right away; he was clearly very kind and caring, his presence calm and comforting. His sermons spoke to me in ways I hadn't expected. He offered messages of hope and strength that made me feel like maybe, just maybe, I could start healing.

After attending a couple of Father Tim's masses, I felt confident that he could help me. The next Monday, I decided to go back. I'd read in the church bulletin that they held confession at that time, and I figured I'd see if Father Tim would talk to me.

When I explained to him that I needed his guidance, he said, "Of course. What is it you need help with?"

I surprised myself by becoming overcome with emotion. The

weight of everything was too much to bear all at once, and it poured out of me in a torrent. "I need to heal," I whispered.

Father Tim nodded gently, his expression understanding. "You can't heal if you don't know what your wound is. Is that what you're trying to figure out?"

I shook my head. "No, I know what the wound is."

I told him everything: how Dad had treated Mom and me, how it led to me feeling rejected, and how I ended up seeking out similarly abusive men. I was honest, painfully so, and told him that I had abusive tendencies of my own. I needed to rid myself of these traits before I passed them on to my children. I couldn't let them grow up with the same patterns I had.

Father Tim listened patiently, allowing me to pour my heart out. When I finished, he spoke to me gently. "Have you ever spoken to your father about all this?"

I felt a knot form in my throat. "I was just starting to form a relationship with him for the first time when he died last year. I was hoping to eventually talk to him about it, but I hadn't been ready, so I'll never be able to now."

Father Tim held up his hands, palms out. "You know, Vanessa, the hardest thing to do in healing is to attack the root cause first. But it makes the rest of the process so much easier. You don't know why your dad did what he did, maybe, but we're not supposed to know everything. We're simply supposed to do our best to show grace whenever we can. Even to those we might not think deserve our grace. I think...perhaps in order to heal to the fullest extent, you try forgiving your father? If you ask God for His help in this matter, He'll deliver you through it."

I left the church that day feeling lighter but still uncertain. Forgiving Dad didn't feel fair, not when I wasn't even sure if he was sorry. But Father Tim's words had stuck with me. It was up to me to figure this out on my own, to learn to show him grace, even if I never got the answers I'd been searching for.

Christina agreed to watch Jenny and Adrian while Mom was at work and Lily was at school. In a few days, I would fly down to Miami to hopefully get answers to questions I'd had my whole life.

Chapter 64

I made it to Miami on Friday evening, my heart heavy with the anticipation of the week ahead. Abuelita and Abuelito were thrilled that I was visiting for a week. They showered me with hugs and warmth, their faces lighting up when they saw me. They were always such loving people, and I could tell they were excited, probably because I hadn't told them the main reason I was there yet.

I decided not to bring it up that first night. Instead, I spent the time catching Abuelita and Abuelito up on Jenny and Adrian. They were always so curious and eager to hear about them. When they asked me about Ryan, I lied, telling them everything was great with him and our family. The last thing I wanted was to add more stress to their already fragile hearts. They'd be stressed enough the next few days, so there was no need to lay that on them, too.

The next morning, Saturday came quickly. The sun was still low in the sky, and the air felt fresh, like the city was waking up with me. I decided to make a move first thing. I went out to the porch, where Abuelita and Abuelito were drinking their coffee in the cool morning breeze. The scent of dark roast filled the air as I joined them. I hesitated for a moment, wondering how to bring it up, but I knew I had to ask. "Do you have any of the contact information for Dad's old friends?"

They both immediately looked concerned, and I could feel the tension shift in the air. Abuelita's eyes widened, her face tightening as she put her coffee cup down. "Why?" she asked, her voice gentle but filled with worry.

"I wanted to talk to a few of them," I said, trying to keep my tone light, though I could feel the gravity of the conversation starting to settle in. "Hear what they have to say about Dad."

I paused for a second before continuing, trying to steady my voice. "That's the main reason I'm here. I want to learn more about him. I know next to nothing about him, and I really never have. I'm trying to work through the relationship I had with him over the years, and getting to know him more will help me a lot."

Abuelita and Abuelito exchanged a glance, their concern deepening. Abuelita's hand trembled slightly as she picked up her coffee again, but she didn't say anything for a long moment. Finally, she spoke, though I could tell it was hard for her. "You can talk to us about him, *mi amor*," she said, her voice soft but strained. "You don't need to talk to them."

"I want to know all sides of him," I said, my voice firmer than I expected it to be. I hoped they could hear the determination in my tone. "I'm doing this to become a better mother, so... I need to do this."

Their faces softened just a little, and they could see that I had made up my mind. Abuelita reluctantly reached for a small notepad from the table. It was filled with all the information they'd managed to gather about who Dad had spent his time with, each name and address written in a neat, familiar hand.

I thanked them both, and after a moment of hesitation, I slipped the notebook into my bag and left. My mind was already racing with what I might find.

The first bar they said Dad frequented the most was just around the corner from the house. Even this early in the morning, the place was already pretty full. There was a heavy buzz in the air, a mixture of voices and clinking glasses, and I felt the weight of it all settle on my shoulders. It was too early for this, but I had no choice. I had to keep going.

I flipped through the notebook they'd given me, scanning the descriptions of the people listed there. Some had tattoos, others were known for their distinctive clothing or hairstyles. One name stuck out: "Recon." His physical description matched a guy sitting at the far end of the bar, so I took a deep breath and walked toward him.

As I got closer, a wave of doubt hit me, crashing over me like an unexpected tide. Was it even safe for me to do this? I had no idea what kind of person this guy was. But there was no turning back now. I kept walking, and by the time I'd reached his side, he'd already noticed me.

"Hi," I said, trying to hide the discomfort in my voice. "Are you... Recon?"

"Yeah?" he answered, his voice sluggish, his pupils dilated, and his eyes bloodshot.

"I'm Vanessa," I said, trying to sound casual, though my heart was racing. "I'm Carlos's daughter?"

Recon squinted at me for a second, his gaze shifting slightly as if trying to place me. "Carlos Gallagher?" he asked.

I nodded, my nerves growing stronger with each passing second. He shook his head and took a long sip of his drink. "Yeah, I knew Carlos. I didn't even know he *had* a daughter, though."

The words hit me hard. It was like I wasn't even a part of his world, a realization that stung deep within me. My heart thudded painfully as I continued. "Well, I've always lived in Canada, so…"

I cleared my throat, trying to steady myself. "Anyway, now that he's gone, I'm trying to heal... over his death. I wasn't able to grieve properly, being so far away, and I think it would help me talk to the people who knew him best."

Recon held up his drink and gave me a nonchalant shrug. "All right. Ask what you want."

I let out a soft sigh of relief, though I still felt unsure about how much I'd actually learn from him. I sat on the stool next to him, feeling the cold wood against my legs. "I just wanted to know what you guys did together. What you liked about him.."

He shrugged again, his disinterest obvious. "We mostly just hung out here. Not much to it. We'd party together sometimes. Carlos was a cool guy. We'd have fun."

That was it. He wasn't offering anything else, and I realized that asking more wouldn't get me much further. "Thank you," I said, forcing a smile, though it felt more like a mask. "That helped a lot." I stood up and walked out, feeling more drained than before.

I visited another bar nearby, and the next friend I spoke to told me basically the same thing. I called another, but he was too hyped up on cocaine to give me a coherent answer. The only thing I got from him was that he'd spent time with Dad just a few days before he died. That was all I could handle for today. I decided I'd call one more person tomorrow morning and then just move on to my next step.

The person I found had the description of "went to rehab." His name was Wolf. I gave him a call, praying I'd get something more meaningful from him.

Right away, he sounded clearer than any of the others.

"Vanessa," Wolf said. "Carlos told me about you. Listen, maybe we can meet somewhere, and I can help you out?"

I was relieved. Finally, someone who might be able to tell me something useful. Excitedly, I agreed to meet with him at a coffee shop nearby. I borrowed Abuelito's car and went straight there, hoping he would have answers that would fill the gaps.

Wolf greeted me warmly, and the first thing he said was how nice it was to meet me. "The main reason I went to rehab was for my kids," he said, his voice calm and steady. "I'm a much better father to them now than I ever was. I was trying to convince Carlos to do the same. He'd mentioned a few times wanting to get better, and when I told him why I ended up going to rehab, he told me he was gonna try."

My heart leaped in my chest. "Did he?"

Wolf shrugged. "I don't know. He told me he wanted to try in November, and I never heard from him after that. The next thing I'm hearing is that he overdosed. I guess he never got around to it. I'm sorry about that."

So, he overdosed. Not surprising, but hearing it confirmed felt like a slap to the face. Now that I knew, I had to process it, even if I didn't feel ready. "Well, thank you," I told Wolf quietly. "That's good to know."

He walked me out to my car, his voice softening as he spoke. "I think Carlos was a good guy," he said. "Just had a lot of issues to work through. I wish I could've seen him get better."

The next day, I sat and had coffee with Abuelita and Abuelito. They were glad I was done reaching out to Dad's friends, and they seemed much more upbeat. There was a lighter atmosphere in the room, and for the first time in a while, I felt a little bit of peace.

As Abuelita poured the three of us a second cup, I knew it was time to start a new conversation. I saw my chance. "You said you'd talk to me about Dad?" I asked.

They were surprised, like they hadn't thought I'd bring it up. Abuelita raised her eyebrows, her face softening. "What do you want to know?" she asked, that uneasy look returning to her face.

"I just want to know what he was like," I told them, my voice barely above a whisper. "I don't know what he was like growing up or even after I was born. It's been twenty-four years. I need to know now."

They exchanged a glance before Abuelito sighed and leaned back in his chair. "He ran with bad crowds from the time he was a kid," he began. "He was always getting himself into trouble."

"We were hoping he'd straighten out once we left Cuba," Abuelita said, her voice full of regret, "but…" She shook her head, her eyes clouding with memories. "He only got worse. Soon after we moved up to Montreal, he started drinking a lot and taking drugs."

I listened intently as Abuelita continued, her words flowing from a place of deep pain. "It was this never-ending cycle of him getting really bad off on drugs, looking like he was quitting, and then falling right back into it. It took us a long time to accept that nothing would change, so we moved down here to see if a new environment would help. Well…" She shook her head again, the weight of it all visible in the curve of her shoulders. "That only made things worse."

"We wanted so badly to help him," Abuelito added, his voice

thick with sorrow. "But when he refused to get better, there was only so much we could do. We watched him bounce in and out of jail because of drugs and starting fights."

They both looked racked with guilt, the pain from their words raw. "We did everything we could think to do for him," Abuelita said, choking up. "We just couldn't figure out how to help him."

I watched Abuelita and Abuelito wipe away tears, and I realized that my own eyes were wet as well. "Is there anything else you'd like to know?" Abuelita soon asked, her voice tremulous.

I thought about it for a moment, then asked softly, "Yeah. I've been wondering why you two didn't keep in touch with me more. I can see why Dad didn't, but I never understood why I barely ever heard from you."

Abuelita and Abuelito shared a sad look, and I could see the depth of their regret in the way they looked at each other. "We were worried that talking to us would only remind you of your father more, *mi amor*," Abuelita said, her voice gentle but filled with sorrow. "We knew that not having a father was hard for you, and we didn't want to make things harder. We thought about you every day, Vanessa."

I looked down at my lap, trying not to cry harder. Abuelita's chair creaked as she leaned forward toward me. "I see now that we made the wrong choice," she said softly. "We did what we thought was best for you, Vanessa. I'm sorry."

I nodded, my throat tight. I opened my mouth to say it was okay but ended up saying, "I wish you had called."

"Oh, *mi amor*," Abuelita whispered, pulling me into a warm embrace.

She and Abuelito hugged me, apologizing for not staying in touch with me. I could see the sincerity in their words, and though the pain of the past was still there, I believed that they were doing what they thought was best. I forgave them. They promised that starting now, they would build back the relationship we had together before they left Montreal. And I believed them.

On Tuesday, my mission was to look through Dad's bedroom. He'd been living here for over a year when he died, so all of his things were still here.

Abuelita and Abuelito had most certainly cleaned the place up after he died, trying to erase any signs of his darker habits. There was nothing to hint at the man he had been – no empty bottles, no drug paraphernalia. The room felt sterile, almost as though it had been untouched for years. There was nothing very personal here, either, which made me feel like I wouldn't get much out of this.

I checked his closet before leaving, just to cover all my bases. And that's when I saw it. An unsealed box with my name and address written on it. My heart raced as I opened it, praying it was something significant.

Inside was a pair of light-up princess shoes for Jenny. I picked them up, noticing they were sized for a one-year-old, not the two-year-old Jenny was when he bought them for her. The gesture felt almost sweet in its misguided nature, a sign that he had tried but had still been so far off, so far removed from our lives.

And now, it could never change. The connection was gone, and the chances for reconciliation were forever lost. All I could do was hug the shoes to my chest and cry.

Chapter 65

I spent the next two days processing everything I'd learned since I arrived in Miami. The weight of it all was heavy on my shoulders, and I felt a constant churn in my chest as I tried to make sense of it. I prayed a lot, reaching out to God for guidance, for the clarity I so desperately needed. I knew I was standing at a crossroads, unsure of which path would lead to peace.

Every idea I had for my next step in forgiving Dad came up short. Nothing felt like it would work. I couldn't get past how much I wished I could just talk to him even one more time. Now that I knew more about him, there was so much more I wanted to say. There were so many things left unsaid, so many questions that would never be answered. The realization of that was suffocating, and I had no idea how to move forward.

Then, on Friday morning, an idea came to me, an idea so simple yet so profound. Dad and I had always communicated through letters. It was the one way we could share our thoughts and our lives without the noise of everything else in between. So, what if I wrote him one more? Maybe that would be a step toward letting go of the pain.

I grabbed a few sheets of paper and a pen, the familiar feel of the ink against paper bringing a slight sense of comfort. I closed myself in my bedroom, away from everyone else, away from the distractions. It was just me and the empty page in front of me. I stared at those blank sheets of paper, my mind racing, unsure where to start. This didn't have to be perfect; Dad would never read it. This was just for me. I could be honest, raw even, and write whatever came to mind.

I took a deep breath and began to write.

Dad,

My priest thinks that forgiving you will help me as I start my journey to heal. I still don't fully understand that, to be honest, but I need to heal for my children's sake. I'll do whatever it takes. I have to, for them. They deserve the best version of me, and I can't give them that if I'm still carrying around all this weight.

Maybe this is the wrong approach, but I want to start by airing out all my grievances. It would be insincere to pretend I don't harbor any resentment toward you. I've carried this resentment for so long, and it feels like it's been building since I was a little girl. I feel like now is the only time I'll ever have to speak my truth. So, here it is: the raw, honest truth. Here are all the things I used to not understand or just never had the ability or courage to say to you.

I do have resentment toward you. It's been growing since I was young, and I'm sure you could sense it, even if you didn't know why. I wanted so many things from you, things that every child deserves. I wanted you to play with me, to give me compliments, and to help me navigate the world as I grew up. I wanted the unconditional love of a father, the kind that gives you confidence and safety, the kind that shapes you into someone who believes they are worthy of love.

But instead, I felt like you abandoned me. I felt unloved, invisible, and unworthy of anyone's affection. I had to watch my mom, the only one who always stood by me, get attacked and bloodied because my ego was too big when all she ever deserved was respect. She was the one who single-handedly raised me, and you treated her like she wasn't worth anything. That was something

I'll never understand.

As a child, I felt like I didn't have a father, and so I tried to replace you with other men. I didn't know any better. As a little girl, I let myself be targeted by adults who could see my lack of self-esteem, even though I thought I had it all figured out. As an adult, I let men into my life who treated me just like you treated Mom. I didn't know any better. I thought that was love. That was how relationships worked. But you distorted that idea for me by replacing love with cruelty, rejection, carelessness, and violence.

But perhaps what hurts the most, what really crushed me, was how your actions became my example. You taught me that it was okay to be cruel, to lash out in anger. I said things I didn't mean. I hurt people just like you did. You're the reason I screamed at people and the reason my breath would catch in my chest when people screamed at me. You're the reason I hurt others and the reason I allowed others to hurt me.

But, for my children, I need to let all of this go. I need to forgive you. The longer I hold onto this negativity, the longer it weighs me down. I can't afford that. If I'm weighed down by all of this, how can I be the mother my children deserve? They shouldn't have to carry the burden of my pain.

I know it won't be easy because you're not around to right your wrongs. I can convince myself that you were sorry, though, since you reached out to me a few years ago. Why would you have done that if you didn't want some kind of relationship with me? You never got the chance to fix things, but I believe you would've if you had more time.

It took me a while, but I've come to understand the strange feelings I had when you died. I wasn't sad to have lost you. I was sad to have lost who you could've been and the relationship we could've had. We hardly had time to make up for everything we never had. The time we lost, the time you spent in your own pain instead of with us, will always hurt.

But you know something? Starting today, I'm going to be thankful for the life I had, for the lessons I've learned. I'll be thankful for the strength I've found in myself and for the wisdom I've gained from all the hardships. My children will never have to learn these lessons the way I did. I'll be wiser moving forward because I can promise you that I won't make the same mistakes again.

I'll also be the person I never had for myself. I'll be strong, and I'll be an advocate for anyone who isn't. I'll be kind, and I'll take myself and my kids away from anyone who isn't. I desperately needed someone to be this for me my whole life, but I see now that 24 is still young. It's not too late to make things right.

I'm going to start by forgiving myself. For hurting people who didn't deserve it. For not respecting myself enough to leave abusive relationships. For repeatedly stressing out the people who loved me with my bad decisions and wild behavior. I was who I am because of what you did to me, but I'm going to become the person I want to be because I choose to forgive you for it.

I'll have to learn to accept that I'll never know why you became who you were or why you did the things you did. I'll come to peace with it because I now know that my peace will have to come independently of that.

I hope you don't mind, but going forward, I'm going to make some assumptions about you. I'm going to assume you never meant to hurt me. I'm going to assume you never meant for your addiction to control your life the way it did. I'm going to assume you would've eventually told me you were sorry, and we would've had a real relationship. I'm going to assume you made it to Heaven and that you'll be able to hear me when I pray for you. I won't ever stop praying for you, Dad. I hope you can hear me now.

There will be no more abuse in my life. I won't hurt others, and I won't let anyone else hurt me. Closing this chapter allows me to let go of the bad you did and hold on to the good. I'll leave myself to remember that day at the beach when you held me in your arms, and I looked up at the sky, and we laughed together. I'll remember you as you were that day, and I'll believe that's who you always were deep down.

I hope you've found your peace. I think I've finally found mine.

-Vanessa

I put the pen down, the final words hanging in the air, suspended between me and a past I could never fully reclaim. I stretched out my right hand and wiped my tears away with my left, feeling a mix of relief and sorrow. I had no idea how this would turn out, but I never would've thought it would feel so... freeing. Weights I didn't know I was carrying were lifting off me. As I poured my heart into this letter, I was able to forgive Dad. For everything he did and for everything I thought he had done.

As I read over what I'd written, I stopped at the part about forgiving myself. More than ever, I knew what I wanted out of my life, and I knew what I would no longer tolerate. I would set boundaries and be relentless in making sure they were respected. I could feel it deep inside me, the clarity that was taking root.

For what might have been the first time in my life, the deep restlessness I didn't know I had inside me was gone. I was at peace with my past, ready to begin my future.

I went to my purse and took out my wallet, the photos of Jenny and Adrian staring back at me. I smiled to myself, feeling a renewed sense of purpose. Time to go home. Time to give them the life they deserve. The one I would work hard to build, one step at a time.

Epilogue

A love written in the stars as she stood on the edge of the cliff, the wind weaving through her hair like the whispered encouragement of the universe itself; Vanessa knew deep in her bones that she had finally come home. Not to a place but to a feeling. To the truth.

She had left behind comfort disguised as love, routine parading as devotion. She had walked through the fire of self-discovery, learning to trust the voice that had whispered all along: *There's something more.* And there was.

It wasn't just Alexander, with eyes that held galaxies, with a touch that sent electricity through her very soul; it was what they unlocked together. A knowing beyond words, a connection deeper than lifetimes.

They didn't need vows. The stars had written their promises long before their bodies had ever met. A dance of destiny, Vanessa laughed as the ocean kissed her toes, her arms stretched wide to the setting sun. He watched her from the shoreline, the warmth in his gaze feeling like home, not in a way that caged her, but in a way that set her free.

It hadn't been easy. Walking away from the life she had built, the security, the familiarity had felt like stepping into the unknown. But what she hadn't realized back then was that *her heart already knew the way.* It had led her here. To him.

With Alex, there was no questioning, no wondering if she was enough. They had met, and in an instant, they had remembered. The dance they had started lifetimes ago was merely continuing.

She turned back to him, smiling. "I finally understand," she whispered. "Why nothing ever felt quite right before." He took her hand, pressing a kiss to her palm. "Because you were waiting for me. And I for you."